T0040815

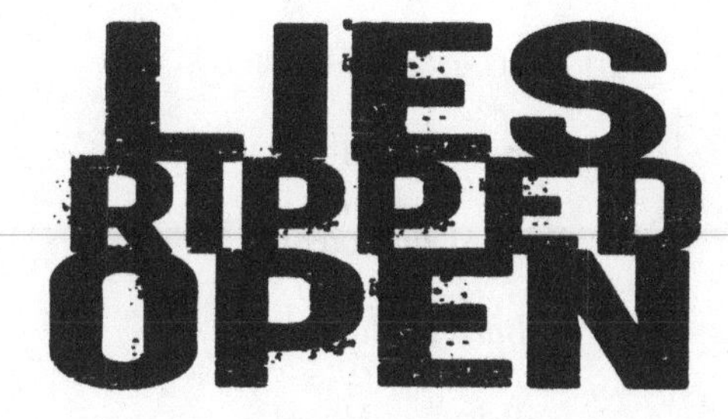
LIES
RIPPED
OPEN

By Steve McHugh

THE HELLEQUIN CHRONICLES

Crimes Against Magic

With Silent Screams

Born of Hatred

Prison of Hope

Infamous Reign

LIES RIPPED OPEN

STEVE McHUGH

47NORTH

This is a work of fiction. Names, characters, organizations, places, events, and incidents are either products of the author's imagination or are used fictitiously.

Published by 47North, Seattle

www.apub.com

ISBN-13: 978-1503946408
ISBN-10: 1503946401

Cover design by Eamon O'Donoghue

Printed in the United States of America

For my Dad.

Thank you.

LIST OF CHARACTERS

Flashback

Nathan (Nate) Garrett: Sorcerer. Once worked for Merlin as the shadowy figure Hellequin.

Diana: Half werebear. Roman goddess of the moon, the hunt, and birthing. Brutus's lieutenant.

Fiona: Conjurer. Undercover Avalon agent, answers only to Elaine.

Alan Daly: Summoner and thief.

Felix Novius: Sorcerer. Creator of the Reavers.

Elaine Garlot: Sorcerer. Mentor to Nate. Currently acting ruler of Avalon's council.

Enfield: Sorcerer. Reaver. Murderer.

Merlin: Sorcerer. Mentor to Nate. Supposed ruler of Avalon's council, but currently obsessed with keeping Arthur alive.

Gawain: Sorcerer. Head of Merlin's security force, the paladins.

Current Timeline

Nathan (Nate) Garrett: Sixteen-hundred-year-old sorcerer. Once worked for Merlin as the shadowy figure, Hellequin.

Erebus (Nightmare): The living embodiment of Nate's magic.

Thomas (Tommy) Carpenter: Six-hundred-year-old werewolf. Owner of a security company. Nate's best friend. Partner to Olivia. Father of Kasey.

Kasey (Kase) Carpenter: Fifteen-year-old daughter of Tommy and Olivia.

Avalon Members

Sir Kay: Director of SOA (Shield of Avalon). Brother to King Arthur.
Lucie Moser: Half-enchanter. Ex-employee of Hades. Current Assistant Director of the SOA (Shield of Avalon).
Olivia Green: Director of southern England branch of LOA (Law of Avalon). Water elemental. Partner to Tommy. Mother of Kasey.
Remy Roax: British son of a French aristocrat. Turned into a fox/human hybrid by a witch coven.
Fiona Daly: Conjurer, SOA agent. Married to Alan Daly.
Lir: Water elemental. Arranges transport from British mainland to Avalon Island. Father to Mac.
Manannán mac Lir (Mac): Water elemental. Arranges transport from British mainland to Avalon Island. Son of Lir.
Kelly Jensen: Fae. SOA agent.

Pack Members

Ellie O'Neil: Werewolf. Female alpha in the South of England werewolf pack.
Gordon Summers: Werewolf. Partner to Mathew Sheppard and aide to South of England werewolf pack.
Matthew Sheppard: Werewolf. Partner to Gordon Summers and male alpha in the South of England werewolf pack.

The Hole

Alan Daly: Summoner. Thief. Currently incarcerated. Married to Fiona Daly.
Warden Philips: Warden for The Hole prison complex.

Anthony Walker: Guard in The Hole.

Livius: Ogre. Guard in The Hole.

Helios: Dragon-kin. Brother to Selene and Eos. Son of the Titan Hyperion. Incarcerated.

Miscellaneous

Liz Williams: Psychic, ex-Avalon. Married to Edward.

Edward Williams: Enchanter, ex-Avalon. Married to Liz.

PROLOGUE

November 1888. London.

It's not every day you get to meet the Queen of England. It's even rarer when a human who rules a country gets a visit from someone in Avalon and the human ruler is *happy* to see us. But Victoria was a tough old lady, and someone I respected, if not liked. I've met her a few times since she took power, but only once since the death of her husband, Albert, some twenty-seven years ago. I found her to be a strong, honest woman, who said what she thought and rarely cared one way or the other about offending anyone. She was the queen; if you were offended it was your problem, not hers. But she wasn't exactly easy to get on with. She resented Avalon's influence in the world, and by extension resented the visits from Avalon's emissaries, such as myself.

But on this occasion I actually got a smile from her that didn't look like she was considering whether or not to attack me with a walking stick.

She'd thanked me, and then as she hurried away, clutching the small item I'd brought her, I'd been asked to leave so that she might have a moment alone. It was a fair request; I had returned something of her husband's, after all. Something that had been stolen by an annoying insect of a being by the name of Alan Daly.

I stepped out of Buckingham Palace and walked the few miles to where a carriage was waiting for me. It was outside of a house in Whitechapel that the SOA—the Shield of Avalon, Avalon's internal security force—used when spending time in London. The two horses were busy eating from their feedbags, although I didn't see either of the SOA agents that were supposed to be watching the prisoner. I reached the horses and patted one of them on the side of his neck. He flicked his ears in response, but was clearly more interested in his food than in me, so I left him be and checked the coach, but found it empty.

On the one hand, the locks were still in place and there was no blood inside the comfortable carriage, but on the other, Alan was a slippery little bastard. I entered the house and checked every room, but it was empty, too. One of the rooms had been changed to a prison cell, complete with rune-marked walls and floor, but it had been decided that we'd transport Alan the second I returned, so he'd been moved to the carriage.

His absence didn't raise any immediate level of concern. The likelihood was high the two SOA agents had taken him into the seclusion of nearby streets to give him a good kicking. They'd wanted to do it all day, and with Alan's almost continuous taunts about their wives, sisters, girlfriends, and in one particularly rage-inducing speech, their mothers, I figured he'd probably brought it on himself. Ordinarily I'd have left the agents to their fun, but they were liable to kill Alan, and for all of his irritating qualities, he didn't deserve to die.

I made my way back outside and walked off into the nearby gloomy streets in the hope that, just maybe, I'd find them before one of the many criminals in the city decided to find me.

Whitechapel, like a fair amount of East London, was riddled with crime and death, and large numbers of people doing incredibly unsavory things, a lot of whom lived in squalor. I'd questioned why they'd put a safe house in the middle of the area, but had been informed that it was the safest place to put anything. No one asked questions in Whitechapel, probably because they were afraid of the answers.

Even during the recent spate of horrific murders a few months earlier, no one had come forward to say they'd seen anything. And no one ever would. Either the police would resolve it, or the local people would get to the killer first, and then no one would ever find him. Those living in the East End of London trusted your average copper probably less than they did your average criminal, and people taking the law into their own hands was fairly common.

I had a pretty good idea where the SOA agents would have taken Alan. There was a small park down an alley a few hundred meters from the safe house. It was somewhere I'd heard that the police took suspects to *question* them when needed. It was dark, and from what I'd heard, it was a well-known area to stay away from, even in Whitechapel.

I reached the alley after being propositioned by half a dozen women, although I noticed that no one stood close to the mouth of the alley, as if it were creating its own barrier of fear.

I walked down the alley. The light from the street lamps appeared to be pushed back by the darkness, which was a stupid thought to have, but even so it still made me pause. Something about this place wasn't right. About half way down I heard grunts and groans.

"That's enough," I called out while using my fire magic to give me a semblance of night vision.

One of the SOA agents sat hunched over, leaning against the wooden panels that surrounded the park's long grass.

I walked over to the second agent, whose back was toward me as he stood a little further into the park, and placed my hand on his shoulder. "That's enough," I repeated, but he spun around and all of the breath left my body at once, followed immediately by pain as it exploded across my torso. I glanced down as a shimmering blade of ice was pulled free from my chest. It was covered in my blood. I dropped to my knees and watched as the magical weapon vanished from view. The pain forced me to abandon my night vision, and the darkness once again took control.

The overwhelming thought that bounced around my head was that neither of the SOA agents had been sorcerers.

My attacker crouched beside me. "They interrupted me and my prey got away," his accent was from East London, but sounded slightly different from many of those living in the city. As if he'd been away from here for a long time, and had not quite remembered how the accent was meant to sound.

I glanced up at him, still unable to breathe; the blade had punctured a lung. It wouldn't kill me, but it would be a few hours until I was back to normal, and without my night vision I could have been staring into Merlin's own face and I'd never have known.

The man got back to his feet and kicked me onto my back. "I should make sure you remember your time here, but I'm sure your comrades over there will be able to do that better than I could."

He sat on my chest—the weight of him making me gasp as the remaining air left my body—and placed his finger to my forehead. He moved his finger slowly, removing it every few seconds before returning it, newly wet against my flesh. "Don't go forgetting me now," he said, before almost jumping off of me and running down the alley.

"Anyone conscious?" I wheezed.

"Your agents are dead," Alan said. "I hope you weren't friends."

I closed my eyes and sighed, trying to control the anger that flared inside of me, while at the same time managing the pain that still coursed through my body.

I rolled onto my side. "What happened?"

"Your companions took me here to give me a good beating. But we found that man and a woman already here. She got free and ran for it, so he took it out on the agents. He had a knife."

"Not that blade of magical ice?"

"No, a real knife. He cut your boys to pieces." There was an unmistakable strike of match, and a sudden flare of light. Alan held the meager flame against a piece of paper he took from his pocket and soon there was enough light for me to see him.

"Holy shit," I whispered. "Did he cut you?"

Alan shook his head. He was drenched in blood; it covered every single part of him that I could see. "All of this blood belonged to your friends. He killed them while they were next to me." He raised his wrist, showing me the sorcerer's band—a small metal band that stopped him from using his powers. And would explode if he tried to remove it. "I couldn't do a damn thing."

"You could run now," I said. I coughed, which caused more pain, but once it had eased off I finally managed to sit up and use my own fire magic to illuminate the area. Night vision took too much control for me right now.

"Shit," I continued. One of the two bodies was in the deep grass, invisible to me as I'd entered the park. The side effect of my magical night vision was that everything was in shades of orange and yellow, so blood was harder to pick out.

"I'm not going to run," Alan told me, his tone hard and full of anger. "I used those agents to get me here so I could escape. I wasn't going to do this to them though. No, I'm going to help you find the man who did this. And then I'll escape."

I chuckled. "Deal. But first we need to get back to the safe house."

"Actually, first you need to know what that asshole wrote on your forehead," Alan told me.

"What?"

"It's in blood."

"What does it say, Alan?" I demanded, anger dripping into my words.

"It's just two words. It says *From Hell.*"

CHAPTER 1

New Forest, England. Now.

There are people out in the big wide world who don't believe in luck. They don't believe that luck plays any kind of part in our lives. These people are, if I'm brutally honest, fucking idiots.

The idea that luck plays no part in our day-to-day existence on this massive rock ignores the fact that it played a part in us being able to exist in the first place. Luck is evident in our lives wherever you look. Sure, ability, coincidence, and just downright hard work all play a massive role, but luck can sometimes mean the difference between being in the right place at the right time and, well, not.

Case in point, it was clearly a little bit of luck, whether good or bad, that saw me in the living room of my house, turning on the large HDTV and switching to one of the twenty-four-hour news channels at exactly the same moment as they cut to a clean-shaven, young man with short, dark hair, wearing a dark suit and talking in somber tones about a hostage situation that was taking place in the Southampton shopping center, West Quay.

I went to the kitchen to grab a bottle of water from the fridge and returned, taking a seat on my leather couch and increasing the volume of the TV.

"We're now entering hour four of the standoff," the man said.

Hour four? I'd been working out in the forest that surrounded my property, running and practicing various fighting and magical techniques, and had no idea of the crisis that had unfolded during that time.

"What, if anything, can you tell us about the situation?" asked a pretty blonde woman as the picture cut to include those sitting in a studio.

"We know that at approximately 10:30 this morning, an armed man entered Hopkins jewelers and proceeded to take the occupants hostage." The reporter turned aside to give a better view of the Southampton high street and the entrance to West Quay. Police vans littered the area, along with several ambulances. The police themselves were either shielded behind their wall of cars, or stood at the cordon not allowing anyone to get close to the situation.

"Has anyone been injured?" the news anchor asked.

The man nodded slowly, showing sadness, although I wasn't sure it managed to reach his eyes. This was clearly a big news story, and he was front and center. Still, it would have been nice if he wasn't quite so excited about the possibility of being part of such a big story. "It's believed that one man was shot as he fought back against the armed attacker. We haven't been updated as to his status since we learned that information."

"And is there anything else the police are saying?"

"Not at this time. As you can understand, it's an incredibly complex and fluid situation, where at least eighteen people's lives are at risk. The police are planning on giving a press conference in an hour, but it's believed that the information given out will be slight."

"Keep us informed," the anchor said as the camera cut back to her. She quickly started discussing the situation with an expert in the studio, and I switched the TV off. Studio experts being dragged in only meant one thing; they had nothing other than speculation and theory to fill the news with, but didn't want anyone to change the channel. Just in case something exciting happened.

I stood up and walked back to the kitchen to throw the now empty bottle of water into the recycling bin, before making my way upstairs and having a nice long shower in water that was hot enough to ease any tension from my shoulders.

Once out, and dry, I threw on a pair of dark blue jeans, and a black T-shirt with blue and red lightsabres crossed over the front and Darth Vader's head behind them. My best friend, Tommy, had picked it up for me a few months back, presumably in the hope that I'd join him in his love of *Star Wars*. It didn't work, but then his level of geekdom for those movies was something few people could possibly hope to match. I'm pretty sure he owns his own storm trooper costume. Which worries me greatly.

I sat back on my bed and breathed out slowly. A year previously I'd been involved in trying to stop Pandora from massacring everyone who'd ever pissed her off, including the woman I loved, Selene. We'd gone our separate ways after it ended—for various reasons—though I was hopeful that one day we'd be able to reconcile. But as Tommy's fifteen-year-old daughter, Kasey, explained, I couldn't sit around and mope about it.

Both Kasey and her mum, Olivia, had tried to set me up with various people over the last few months, but relationships should probably start off with the truth, and I don't think most people who've just met me want to know exactly the types of things I do.

As Tommy had helpfully pointed out, "trained killer" is probably not what most people want in answer to the question, "What do you do for a living?" In the last five months, I've been on several dates. So far, I've been "ex-military," "an Avalon specialist," and on one particularly boring date, "shark trainer," mostly just to see if she was listening to a word I was saying, or more interested in playing on her mobile.

Dating was a relatively new concept and one I don't think I was destined to master. I could be charming, I was in good shape, and was what most people would describe as ruggedly handsome, but apparently that didn't translate to "good at this dating thing."

So I'd thrown myself into my magic, trying new things and mastering those I could already do. I was able to merge two elements that I could wield—fire and air—into lightning, which now came easily to me.

Two of the six dark blood curse marks that sat on my chest had vanished, bestowing on me an increase in power, and my necromancy, in that order. No one knew what would happen when the remaining marks vanished, nor how long that might take, but I needed to be prepared for whatever their disappearance might bring. Be it good or bad.

I'd just decided that I hadn't bothered Tommy at work for several days and thought I'd take the drive to the massive building that housed his security firm, when I remembered that he was in Avalon with Olivia and Kasey. While trying to figure out who else I could contact, my mobile rang.

"Nathan Garrett?" a woman asked. Her voice sounded young, but the massive amount of stress in it could be clearly heard.

"That's me," I told her.

"My name is Kelly Jensen. I'm an agent with the SOA. Have you seen the news about the hostage situation in Southampton?"

"About twenty minutes ago," I told her.

"I'm liaising with the police in charge of what's happening. It's been escalated to a specialist branch of the armed response teams, Level 2 Cadre."

The Level 2 Cadre were the people who took over a firearms incident when the situation escalated and required a specialist approach. That's when a Regional Specialist Ops Unit moved in and took command. They have the authority to come in and take over the situation, no questions asked.

"Okay, what does that have to do with me?"

"Level 2 Cadre's entire staff are humans who have been placed there by Avalon."

"That still doesn't explain why you're calling me," I pointed out.

"Because the man who has taken the hostages wants to see you. In fact he's requested you by name."

I was a little surprised. It was certainly the first time anyone who'd taken hostages wanted to talk to me. Usually I was pretty far down on the list of people they'd be happy to see.

"What's his name?" I asked, hoping to jog something loose.

"He won't give it. He wants to be known as God."

"That's what he calls himself? God?" I asked, making sure I'd heard her right.

"Yep. He says seeing how he decides who lives and dies, it's a fitting name. I think he's seven kinds of crazy, but that won't help get those hostages free. We need you to come down here and see if you can help."

"You want me to go in?"

"Hell no," she said derisively. "Olivia told me all about you. I don't need a dead hostage taker, and with all the media and human police here, I also don't want the Cadre to be seen sending in a civilian. You come down, you talk to him, find out who he is and what he wants."

"Why is SOA involved?" The SOA, or Shield of Avalon, was Avalon's internal security force, sort of a combination of MI5 and the Secret Service. They were usually only involved in crimes that directly involved Avalon members, otherwise the LOA, or Law of Avalon, was involved. The LOA was a sort of cross between the FBI and Interpol. They investigated crimes against, or perpetrated by, members of the nonhuman community as a whole.

"There was a hostage injured when the shop was taken. We told the media that he was shot, but he was burned on the leg. The hostage taker is a fire elemental from the sounds of things, possibly a sorcerer. But the victim said the man's entire arm turned to flame, so I'm leaning toward the former."

It certainly sounded like an elemental, a being that was one with their element, able to control it with incredible ease and capable of immense power. But this sounded like something for LOA, so why were the human police involved at all?

"You haven't told me why the SOA are involved," I reminded her.

"We think the hostage taker might have been employed by Avalon."

"What makes you think that?"

"You know I can't share that kind of information with you. Will you come down here, or not?" she snapped, a little anger in her voice.

I really hated Avalon political bullshit, and I got the impression that Kelly didn't like me much. I've met several Avalon employees who see my leaving Avalon—and the manner in which I left—as a sort of betrayal of the principles they believe in. Personally, I didn't much care what she thought of me, so long as she could remain professional. "It's an hour's drive," I told her. "I'll be there as soon as possible."

My proximity alarm rang, signaling that someone was coming up the drive toward my house.

"Did you send people here?" I asked. "It seems I have visitors."

"Those would be the two LOA agents I sent to find you. They're going to escort you to Southampton."

"You don't trust me to turn up, Agent Jensen?" I asked.

"Actually I trust you to turn up fine. It's what you do when you get here that I want to control. See you in forty-five minutes."

She hung up and I opened the door to reveal two very large men with shaved heads, both wearing black suits. "Wow, you guys are very intimidating," I said with a smile. "What are you, half troll or something?"

The man-tower closest to me smiled. "You ready to go?"

"Let me get some shoes and a jacket," I said, grabbing both from beside me, and putting them on before pocketing my keys and wallet from the table next to the door.

"You're not going shopping," the second man said, his voice much deeper than his friend's, and his accent was South African, unlike his friend's English. There was some animosity in his voice. He was probably unhappy at having to give me a lift, which, considering the circumstances and that people's lives hung in the balance, was more than a little childish on his part.

"Just in case I see a bargain," I said. "Or, as is more likely, I have to make my own way back here when everyone is suddenly too busy to drive me home."

They moved aside and let me pass, walking with me to their black Mercedes SUV.

"Shotgun," I called.

"Fuck off," the South African said, and both men laughed as they got in the front of the car, leaving me to sit in the back. Couldn't blame them for having to babysit me on the way from my house to West Quay, but I could dislike them intensely for being dicks.

"The rules of the road clearly don't apply to you guys then," I said and lowered the electric windows, letting in a nice breeze as we sped off to deal with a probably very angry man and his scared hostages.

CHAPTER 2

The journey wasn't exactly one of fun and frivolity. I'd have asked for the radio to be put on, but I already knew the answer and didn't want to have to punch two agents the second we got out of the car.

I settled for dozing and trying to figure out why anyone would want to call me when they'd just taken a group of people hostage, managing to seriously hurt one of them in the process. The knowledge that Nathan Garrett and Hellequin were one and the same was now public. Although how far that information had traveled through to my old friends and enemies was unknown. The person calling himself God could easily be someone who took umbrage with something I'd done over the centuries—either as myself or Hellequin—and decided to get their revenge. I probably should have made a list of possible suspects. But it would have been a very long list of people, and I doubted I had time.

By the time we pulled up at the blockade, and one of my large escorts had raised the back window so none of the press could see me through the tinted glass—although I could still make out the flash of cameras—I'd come up with only one answer. The hostage taker was crazy.

The driver parked the SUV close to the entrance of West Quay, next to dozens of other vehicles. I got out and glanced at the massive entrance to the shopping center. West Quay claimed to be one of the biggest centers in Europe, and there was nothing about it that suggested that was an exaggeration. Three shopping levels and a food court, dozens of places to shop or eat, were contained in a mammoth structure of concrete, glass, and steel.

A tarpaulin had been placed beside two police vans, covering the makeshift command center that the Ops Unit was using.

"Nice to meet you," a young woman said as she walked over to me. She was about five-two and probably weighed the same as one of the legs belonging to my two massive babysitters. She was curvy and wore a blue skirt and white blouse that, while looking very businesslike, gave no illusions as to whether she was comfortable in her own body. Her confidence enhanced her natural beauty. She had a small nose and full lips, with dark green eyes that matched her hair in color, if not in tone. Her hair was the color of freshly mown lawn; dark and light greens crisscrossed through it as it spilled over her shoulders.

"Kelly, I assume."

"That's me," she said, with no hint of emotion. "Thanks for coming."

"You're fae."

There was an immediate flicker of anger, as if it were wiped onto her face in one smooth motion. "Is that a problem?"

I paused. People don't like the fae. They're not the cute little flying things at the bottom of the gardens, that's fairies, and *they're* mean little fuckers who eat people. The fae are creatures of magical energy, like sorcerers, but they're *also* mean little fuckers.

Ones that hold a grudge like it's a security blanket, and will do anything and everything to get revenge on people they believe have slighted them. The fact that they're able to use a person's blood to track them not only over thousands of miles, but also through realms, means once you've pissed one off, they can find you *anywhere*. The fae have small translucent wings, which they can turn invisible as they wish. Considering I couldn't see Agent Jensen's, it was precisely what she had done. The wings give fae the ability to hover. Fae can also control light or shadow magic, but like sorcerers, not everyone who uses shadow magic is evil and not everyone who uses light magic is nice. Also, for some reason their hair and eyes are always shades of the same color.

"I'm not aware of any problems," I told her.

Kelly's eyes narrowed for a moment, before the smile came back to life. "Good."

We left the two mountains standing beside their SUV; I almost waved, but thought better of it. I didn't want to piss everyone off after only being there for a few minutes; I normally leave that for ten, fifteen minutes at the least.

Kelly stopped beside a police van and turned toward me. "You're going to see the Ops leader; he's human but aware of things about you, although probably not everything."

"Not everything?"

"It hasn't quite spread to the humans that you're Hellequin. In fact it's only just started filtering through to Avalon."

I smiled. Over the last few years, I'd started using the Hellequin moniker again after burying it for three centuries. I wasn't hiding that we were one and the same, but from a small trickle of people who'd been made aware it was beginning to turn into an avalanche. I imagined it pissed Merlin off . . . so I guessed it wasn't all bad.

"I'll try not to bring it up," I said.

Kelly placed a hand on my chest; there was a surprising amount of strength in her slim arms. That summed up fae quite well . . . surprising. "Olivia tells me you have a natural disposition to piss people off. I'd rather you didn't do that today. Everyone is on edge and everyone is stressed. Don't start a dick measuring contest."

I took a step back, forcing Kelly to drop her hand or look pretty stupid, but even so, she only did it begrudgingly. "I'll try my best not to just whip it out and start flailing it around."

Kelly smiled and shook her head slightly.

"Can you tell me anything more about why I'm here?" I asked. "Other than because some asshole who wants us to call himself God asked for me."

"Nope. Maybe they can give you more info." She pulled back some gray tarpaulin, exposing the "they" in question, who turned out to be four men huddled around a computer monitor, while a fifth man spoke on the phone. Four of the men wore balaclavas and were of completely different heights and sizes. They each held Heckler and Koch MP5s. And all five of them had a confidence that showed that they were not to be screwed around with unless you liked a much shorter life expectancy.

The fifth man placed the phone on a table and turned toward me. He was over six feet tall, with a short, tidy haircut that was bordering on white, despite the fact that he'd probably not even hit his mid-forties. A dark moustache curled over his top lip, forming a horseshoe around his mouth. He looked hard and tough; a man who didn't find much funny and was even less inclined to let others joke around in his company.

"You're that Special Forces guy," he said to me, but didn't offer me his hand or even suggest he was impressed.

"Sure," I agreed. "Let's go with that."

"I spoke to Director Green . . . Olivia. She says you're a good guy. I heard you saved her kid, Kasey, that true?"

I nodded, and he offered me his hand, which I took. His grip was of a man perfectly confident of his abilities. "I like Kasey, Olivia too, you did good. The hostage taker wants to talk to you. Any idea why?"

I shook my head. "Been wondering that myself."

"This is very unusual. We don't normally let civilians talk to the person committing the crime; it can make things much worse. You know why, yes?"

I nodded. "They could hear something they don't like, or consider talking to the civilian their last act and just start shooting. I understand why you're cautious. I have no intention of making things worse; hell, I don't even know what 'worse' is."

"You can call me Mike," he said. "This guy in there wants to be called God."

"So I heard. You know anything else about him?"

"English accent, although we can't pinpoint where it's from, and from what our injured hostage told us, he's clearly not human. That's pretty much it. He's spoken to our hostage negotiator a few times, but he's not giving anything away and refused to talk more until you got here. The hostage taker fried the CCTV cameras inside, and the shop is at an awkward angle. Even with the footage we had before he broke it, we still can't get a look at him or the hostages."

"Anything else?"

"He hurt one hostage, but let him go in exchange for getting you here. I assume you've been told the hostage taker is an elemental."

"Yeah, it came up. Did you say he let the hostage go before I arrived?"

Mike shrugged. "He said he trusted us. And that he'd kill one hostage every sixty seconds after ninety minutes of waiting." He glanced at the watch on his wrist. "Which is in three minutes."

"Why ninety minutes?" I asked. "I could have been out of the country."

"He knew where you were," one of the balaclava-wearing men guessed.

"So, why not just go after you at home?" one of the other officers asked.

"Because my home has motion detectors. I'd have warning of his approach, and I'd be on my own ground. Here I'm not, I have no advantage."

"But so long as he has the hostages, he does," Mike said.

"You should have told me about the threats to the hostages," I said to Kelly.

"I didn't want you to be any more agitated than you needed to be. You didn't need to be worried about his threats; you just needed to get here."

"As a rule, threats don't make me agitated," I informed her. Kelly didn't trust me. That much was obvious, although why that was the case was something I didn't understand. Maybe it was purely that I'd quit Avalon and left Merlin, which some people found to be almost traitorous, or maybe it was just that she'd heard rumors about my past and wasn't sure how to be around me. Of course there was a third option. The head of the SOA, Sir Kay, wasn't exactly my biggest fan, and I thought he was a bully, thug, and about as much fun to be around as being bitten in the crotch by a honey badger. If Kelly and Kay worked closely together, then that would explain her keeping things from me.

"We're ready," Mike said and passed me a phone.

"Hello," said a voice on the other end.

"This is Nathan Garrett," I said. "And you are—"

"God," he said. He sounded like he was smirking when he spoke.

"Yeah, that's the name. You have all the power in the world."

"That's right, I do."

I heard screaming in the background, accompanied by whimpering.

"You don't need to hurt anyone else," I said.

"Don't tell me what I do or don't need to do," he snapped.

"Fair enough, so why did you want me here?"

"You're not here, you're out there. I want you in here with me. I want to talk to you face to face."

"That's never going to happen," I said.

"That's a shame, because I don't want to start killing these lovely people." His voice was completely calm, and I knew with certainty that he would carry out that threat without pause.

"Okay, let me talk to the guys here and see what we can come up with. You're going to have to give something though. You're going to have to give a hostage."

"You have five minutes. Then I start putting bullets in heads. You get in here, I send out one person." He ended the call, still sounding calm but certain of the power he held.

"I have to go in," I said.

"No fucking way," Mike replied.

"Do you have a better idea? Because in five minutes you're going to need a lot more body bags for when you finally do get in there."

Mike stared at me for a few seconds. "If you go in there, we have some rules. Don't antagonize him, don't let him rile you, and whatever you do, do not get into a physical confrontation. You get in, you keep your distance, and you get out."

"Unless he doesn't want me to get out," I said, and I noticed everyone pause what they were doing. "You've thought of that, I assume. That he wants me here to kill me."

Mike nodded slowly. "You still okay to go in?"

"Better him shoot me than shoot a bunch of people."

"Get him a vest," Mike told a nearby officer, and a few moments later I was passed a bulletproof vest.

"That's really not necessary," I explained.

"You know he could shoot you and then kill everyone else. I wasn't asking you to wear a vest. It's not open to discussion."

"Can you dodge bullets?" another of the agents asked. "Because if you can't you might need one."

"Point taken," I agreed.

"Hopefully you won't *need* it at all," Mike said. "This is just in case."

I put the vest on and glanced at my watch. "Sixty seconds left."

Mike walked with me toward a nearby barrier, which had two armed police using it as cover to keep their weapons aimed into the massive building.

"We sure he's alone?" I asked.

"No," Mike admitted. "Just another reason for you to be careful."

I turned and walked off toward the four sets of doors that made up the front entrance, pushing one of them open and stepping into the shopping center. I walked up the sloped entrance for about a hundred and fifty feet, passing half a dozen shop fronts, until I came to a temporary kiosk selling pretzels that had been left abandoned, the remains of the last purchases smushed into the tiled floor.

"That's enough," a voice called out from ahead. "Turn around, show me you aren't carrying."

"You're the man in charge," I said as I lifted my vest as best as possible and turned on the spot to show I was unarmed. From where I was, I still couldn't see whoever was talking, but at least I knew the rough direction he was in.

"Yes, I am," he shouted.

"Why pick these people? Why here?"

"I fucking hate malls, or shopping centers or whatever the fuck you want to call them. Mindless fucking drones all buying shit to make their miserable lives better for ten minutes."

"Well, there's a shop that sells ice cream. That's pretty good."

"Funny guy. Now walk toward me, slowly. Keep your hands up."

I did as he said, and after a few steps I saw the hostage taker for the first time, standing several meters away from the shop he'd taken control of. He was maybe six-two, with short hair, and was clean-shaven. He wore a long, black shirt, blue jeans, and white trainers. In one hand was a gun, which he held aimed at the head of a man kneeling beside him. The man on his knees was weeping softly; a gouge under his eye was fresh and blood was streaming down one side of his face.

In stark contrast the hostage taker appeared calm and relaxed. The splatter of blood on his shirt probably wasn't his, and his general demeanor suggested he was more than willing to kill someone.

"Stop walking," he demanded.

I did as I was told. "Where's the hostage?"

The hostage taker motioned for a girl of about thirteen who'd been standing just inside one of the shops to walk over.

"Go," the hostage taker demanded, and she glanced at me before sprinting off toward the entrance.

"Call me by my name," the hostage taker demanded when we were alone once more.

"I don't know your name," I explained.

"Yes, you do."

"You want me to call you God? Aren't you worried that's sort of begging for a lightning bolt to smite you? Does God throw lightning bolts? It's been a while since I read the Bible."

He raised his gun toward me. "I've got something better than a lightning bolt."

"So, God, how are things going?" I asked. "What do you want?"

The man laughed, the gun wavering for a moment, until he regained his composure. "I want to put a bullet between the eyes of everyone here," he shouted at the top of his voice, and there was a general cry from the crowd of people still inside the jewelry shop, although from where we were standing I couldn't see any of them. "But instead, you and me are going to take a walk."

He motioned for me to walk back the way I'd come and I complied. I hoped putting distance between him and the hostages would give them time to escape, or at the very least give one of the armed officers a clear shot.

We walked until we were about halfway between the front doors and Hopkins Jewelers—where the hostages were held—when he told me to stop. There was about ten feet between us; he'd certainly be able to get a shot off before I could turn around, and tackle him. But I could just blast him with a gust of air, throwing him into the nearest glass window. Hopefully hard enough to hurt. A lot. I went to use my magic and nothing happened.

The man behind me laughed. "How's that whole magic thing working out for you? I never said I was working alone. I have a void."

I cursed inwardly and turned back toward the hostage taker and to see that the man who'd been kneeling beside him was now on his feet, a look of concentration on his face. "I assume that's him."

"That's right. This means I could put a bullet in you right now and you'd be dead before you hit the ground. But that's not what this is about."

Voids are walking sorcerer's bands. Meaning I couldn't use any aspects of my magic or necromancy while in his proximity. There was a limit to the distance their power had an effect, but I had no way of knowing what that distance was, and without my magic, I was as helpless as a human. A less than pleasant sensation. "So what is this about?" I asked.

"I thought about telling you all about why you're here. About why you're going to die. But in the end, I think it's better that you go to your grave not knowing. I find that more entertaining."

"So, why haven't you killed me yet?"

"Because we're waiting for everyone to arrive."

There was a crack above me, and I glanced up as the dome imploded. Sharp pieces of glass rained down as I dove aside toward the shelter of the nearest shop front. The elemental tracked my movements, but gave no indication that he was going to fire. Then I saw why. A winged figure glided softly to the ground, its huge pawed feet barely even registering the broken glass beneath it. In one talon-tipped hand was a long, golden spear, several feet taller than the griffin that held it.

The bottom of the griffin was feline in nature, a deep mustard-colored fur covered it from the waist down, while the top half resembled a massive eagle, but with black and white feathers. It was a good foot taller than my own five-eight, and I doubted it was there to help me.

"Well, that's unexpected," I said, getting to my feet.

"Good-bye," the griffin said, and lunged forward with its spear. I pushed the weapon aside, and kicked out at the griffin, who staggered back, putting himself between the armed elemental and me. He swung his spear as I sprinted back into the nearest shop. I ran to the rear, past dozens of expensive suits, through some curtains and into the fitting rooms. They turned out to be a dead end, but I could hear people talking at the front of the shop.

"Why didn't you just kill him?" asked a man with an American accent. The void, I guessed.

"Because the griffin was meant to," the elemental I knew as God said.

I mentally reminded myself to ask, when I got the chance, why the griffin got that particular honor, and then searched the fitting area again. When it became apparent that there was no escape, I climbed up onto a small bench, moved a ceiling tile aside, and climbed into the roof space. Me against three killers, one of whom was a griffin, beings considered to be incredible warriors. This was going to be a very long day.

CHAPTER 

It didn't take me long to make it across the ceiling and drop down into a shop several spaces up from the suit store. The din the three attackers made as they tore apart the shop looking for me was easy to hear, but hopefully it would take them a few minutes at least before they figured out where I'd gone.

My main concern, apart from being hunted, was that they'd simply go back to the hostages and threaten them again. I needed to act before that could happen. I doubted any of the hostages would run, they'd very quickly be seen. And the shop the hostages were in had an open front, which meant that if they wanted to barricade themselves in, they'd have to use the shutters. Closing the shutters is a slow, loud process, and one that was liable to gain the attention of their captors very quickly.

The ceiling space actually ran for another few hundred feet, but that would have taken me opposite the hostages and I didn't want one of them to react to seeing me drop down, and give the whole thing away. Besides, I doubted the ceiling was built to support a person, and I didn't want it to give way while I was directly above them.

A year ago I'd been taught a rune that overrode magic-blocking security systems, allowing me to use my magic for a certain length of time. As a void was basically a walking, talking version of those systems, it made sense to think that it might work. But it didn't. I'd used some dust on my hand in the crawl spaces to try and get it to work, but it had no effect. Apparently the rune only worked to bypass nonorganic security systems, something that it would have been nice to know about before I'd needed it.

Fortunately, it appeared that while this particular void was strong enough to project a field that encompassed several dozen feet, he wasn't strong enough to pick out individual targets. That explained why the elemental didn't just throw fire at me. If the void wasn't skilled enough to pick out one target, he'd have to blanket the whole area, including his allies, which meant no fire ability for the elemental. That made me feel a little better, but not much, because at the end of the day they had guns. And griffins couldn't be killed, or even seriously hurt, by magic. My renewed optimism about my situation was rapidly dampening.

My magic returned after I managed to get myself a few feet away from my attackers. I used my air magic to project a thin cushion between the ceiling and me so I didn't accidentally put my arm through the thin tiles. The art of stealth does not normally include falling through ceilings and making shitloads of noise.

After looking around the stationery shop I found myself in, I discovered that I had a choice of truly dangerous weapons, such as felt-tips and Post-it notes. The pen might be mightier than the sword, but it's probably not going to end well for you if you bring one to a gunfight.

I had to get the three of them to separate. If I could nullify the void, I figured the elemental would be an easier target, with or without his weapons. The griffin, well, that was a whole different level of trouble. One I could hopefully leave for last.

The trick was figuring out what would split them up. Fortunately, a little bit of luck shone down on me when I heard the sound of footsteps coming my way. There was no way to quietly get back into the ceiling, so instead I crouched down behind a shelf of journals and notebooks, peering through the small slats in the shelving unit to see who was approaching.

It didn't take long before the elemental stepped into the mouth of the shop, gave the store a quick scan, and stepped back out again. "I've got this one," he shouted to his allies, and then walked cautiously into the store.

The shop itself was made up of several displays toward the front, along with a till and some glass cabinets to show off the more expensive objects. About a quarter of the way into the store, it changed into shelves stocked with all manner of writing aids and stationery. There were three paths he could take, the center one took him right past me, but he decided to pick the left-hand one, and quickly checked behind the till before making his way down the shop.

He didn't speak while he worked, his concentration was total. I created a small ball of air in my hand, and was immediately grateful I could still access my magic, although I wasn't going to count on it staying that way.

I crouched behind the shelves three rows back, giving me an excellent view of his approach. He'd be unable to see me until he reached my row. But on the downside, it gave the adrenaline longer to build up. I took some deep steadying breaths, making sure to stay quiet as I moved back from my hiding place until I was against the fourth set of shelves, the last in the store before the door to the staff rooms beyond. I just wanted to put a little more distance between him and the front of the shop before I did anything.

"Have you found anything?" the void shouted from the front of the shop.

I peered through the slats once more, although I couldn't see either of my attackers.

"Does it fucking look like it?" the elemental replied, sounding very close. "He's vanished. Where's our fearless griffin friend?"

"Down the other end, he's searching some massive clothes shop."

If it was a ploy to get me to reveal myself, it was a poor one. I wasn't about to risk fighting all three of them again, especially not in the stationery shop's close quarters.

"I'm going back to the hostages. I don't want anyone to think they can run off," the void told his friend, before turning and walking off. A few seconds later I heard him shouting at several of the hostages, followed by their cries.

"Fucking asshole," the elemental snapped and then breathed out.

I reached out with my air magic, using invisible tendrils of air to pinpoint the elemental's exact position; he was one step away from the third set of shelves. I considered using my magic in a subtle way, to drag the air out of his lungs or some such, but he'd likely recognize what was happening and start flailing about, making a big ruckus. Instead, it was going to be fast and nasty.

Once I knew exactly where he was, I slowly wrapped the tendrils around his body. It's harder than it sounds, making sure to wrap them around him, but not doing it so tightly that the air feels strange to him.

He took one more step, and the sound of his boot landing on the tiled floor was all I needed. I snapped the tendrils closed, throwing one of them down his open mouth to stop him from screaming as I tightened the air around him. I dragged him over toward me, his eyes wide and full of panic, any thoughts of using his own abilities lost in that moment of terror. I removed the gun from his hand and placed it on the shelf beside me as I squeezed the air tighter and tighter, until I heard bones break. He tried to scream once more, but I was stuffing more and more air down his throat into his lungs, until in one moment they reached their maximum capacity, I felt them burst like over-full balloons inside his chest.

After a few seconds, I released the air and he sagged forward, unconscious. I caught him and lowered him quietly to the ground. He probably wasn't dead, although he'd clearly stopped breathing. Elementals are tough to kill without removing their head or using silver, although I doubted removing the brain's oxygen supply did them a lot of favors. Hopefully he'd be able to heal any brain damage he might suffer so he could answer any police questions. I wanted to know who had sent them and why. The more of them I left alive to answer questions, the better.

But even so, I didn't want to make it easy for him, so I created a thin blade of air, and used it to cut into his spine, just above his pelvis, severing the bone and cartilage. Being unable to breath or walk would test even the most powerful elemental's ability to heal.

I searched the body, but found no ID or anything that might tell me exactly who he was. Instead, I found several magazines of silver bullets and a four-inch knife, both of which I took, along with the gun, a Sig 1911 Fastback. Not exactly my choice of weapon, but it would do in a pinch.

Something felt wrong. The elemental was far too easy to take out, even if I'd jumped him. Anyone actively going after me was either going to have a lot of power, or be completely crazy. Neither of those described the elemental. Of the three attackers, only the griffin was a serious concern. I searched through my mind to see if there was anything that might jog a memory of an elemental, griffin, and void working together, but I came up with nothing. There was more here than taking hostages just so they could get me here to kill me, I was certain of it.

Unfortunately, I now had a new problem. If I went after the griffin first—and I had no idea of his exact whereabouts—it would leave me vulnerable if the void decided to get involved. It would also leave the hostages vulnerable. But going after the void first would almost certainly draw the attention of the griffin. I couldn't walk in with magic, or guns, blazing; I doubted very much that the griffin cared even a small bit about collateral damage.

To be honest, it wasn't even a contest, and I was soon at the front of the shop searching the outside to make sure it was clear of griffins, before I figured out the best route to the hostages.

I took a step forward as an almighty crash sounded from inside the clothes shop, and a display stand flew out the front of the store, crashing into a kiosk. I ducked back into the stationery store, but no griffins surfaced, so I quickly ran the across the concourse and into a perfume shop. After trying not to cough from the almost visible fog of scents that still lingered, I climbed up onto a display case and back up into the ceiling.

As before, the space ran the length of several shops, with a small amount of light peeking up through the cracks in the ceiling tiles. Even so, I activated my night vision, making the spider-like walk I needed to perform a little more bearable.

After a few meters I heard muffled crying from beneath me. I used a cushion of air to ensure I didn't make any noise as I lay prone and slowly lifted one of the tiles an inch. The void was three feet to my left, with his back toward me. I could drop down and take him before he knew what hit him. But there were four people right below me who probably wouldn't appreciate me falling on top of them.

I lowered the tile and released my magic, creeping slowly another few feet, going through the whole rigmarole of lifting a different tile, and finding myself directly above the void.

The cushion of air that was holding me above the ceiling vanished. I fell only a few inches but it was enough to dislodge the tiles, and I crashed through the ceiling, landing with a resounding, and unpleasant, thud on the hard floor.

The void kicked me in the side of the head, and I rolled with the blow, trying to put distance between us, but the scared, huddled people got in the way. The void took full advantage and kicked me in the ribs, before trying to stomp on my head. I grabbed his leg just above the ankle and dragged him to one side, causing him to lose his balance and fall onto several people sitting beside us.

My magic remained switched off, which meant he was still capable of using his powers and fighting. That wasn't the best news I'd had. He shoved and flailed at the people, swearing at them as he got back to his feet, while I got back to mine. Once upright, he turned to face me and received a punch in the jaw that snapped his head aside with ferocity. He staggered back, but remained upright and put himself into a fighter's stance.

I didn't have time for a drawn-out fight; the griffin had probably already heard the commotion and would be on his way over to investigate, but from the look in the void's eyes, he wasn't going down easy.

He glanced to the side and I saw that when he'd fallen, his gun had come out of its holster. It was an identical piece to the Sig his friend carried, which he clearly recognized when he found me pointing it at him.

"Anyone who doesn't want to see this, turn away," I said.

"You're not going to kill me, not here."

I shot him in the shoulder, and he crashed back into a nearby display, bringing the glass cabinet and contents of jewels and watches down on top of his head, with more noise than I'd made when I'd come through the ceiling.

I walked over to the void and found that he was unconscious, but breathing. At least for the moment. Voids were basically humans who live twice as long. But despite the slightly longer lifespan, they could be hurt and killed as easily as any human. The fact that they're so rare, and capable of so much power, just made them more annoying.

"Is everyone okay?" I asked the hostages. I counted twenty-seven, and none of them appeared to have life-threatening injuries, although some of them looked like they'd been given a bit of a kicking at some point.

A few people nodded.

One, an elderly lady whose husband looked like he'd been punched in the face, walked over to the void and kicked him, causing the void to cry out.

She took my hand in hers. "My husband needs medical attention," she said.

"He'll get it," I explained.

She nodded thanks and then returned to her husband's side, although from the smile on his face, I assumed he'd have been quite happy if she'd wanted to keep kicking their attacker.

"How many were there?" I asked no one in particular.

"Just him and another bloke," another man said.

"Okay, well there's a third, so everyone stay here. I don't want to give him a chance to use you against me. You'll be home soon."

"Is he going to die?" a young woman asked, nodding at the void.

"If he sees a doctor soon, then no, probably not. If anyone wants to ensure he lives longer, put pressure on the wound to stop the bleeding. Personally, I'd let him bleed a little."

The young woman nodded and I looked over at where the spare gun had landed to see it in the hands of a big bloke who had military-looking tattoos on his arms. "You know how to use that?" I asked.

"Ten years in the army, so, yes. You want some backup?"

"You don't want to help out there, mate," I said, handing him one of the magazines in my pocket. "Just keep these people safe. If the guy who is currently bleeding out makes a move, or if his friend turns up, take them down. Don't hesitate. Because they won't."

He nodded once.

"I'll be back soon," I told everyone and strolled out of the shop, as the unmistakable battle cry of a griffin sounded out through West Quay.

The griffin was standing about fifty meters away from me, next to the kiosk he'd destroyed with his hissy fit in the shop earlier.

He immediately saw the gun as I got closer, and his forehead wrinkled in what passed for humor in a griffin.

"Do you really think that thing is going to hurt me?"

I shrugged. "I'm almost certain you're not bulletproof."

He banged his fist against his armor-plated chest. "Never going to get through here."

I ejected the magazine. Six bullets, and a full magazine in my pocket. I really shouldn't have given most of the bullets to the soldier, but the griffin was right, the gun wasn't going to get the job done. A kill shot would need to take his head or heart. And griffins were too fast and too dangerous for me to rely on bullets. Even so, it would be rude not to try. I fired five bullets in the griffin's direction, scoring two direct hits to his breastplate, while he used his spear to deflect the other three.

The griffin launched himself up into the air and then immediately dove down toward me, his deadly spear at the ready.

Griffins can't be hurt by magical attacks. It's one of the main reasons they're used as guards at Tartarus. If I wanted to even injure my attacker, I needed a bladed weapon, or an explosive device. Neither of which are exactly in abundance in British shopping centers. But that didn't mean I was helpless.

I created a column of air that slammed up into the griffin, driving him back with a shriek of rage. The magic couldn't hurt him, but it put him off balance for a moment until he threw a knife at me. I dodged aside, removing the column of air for an instant, giving him a chance to fly toward me once more. This time I stood my ground until the last moment, when I aimed the gun and fired the last bullet into the membrane of his wings.

The griffin dropped to the ground as blood poured from the injured wing. "You're going to hurt for that," he seethed.

I reloaded the gun. "Come show me how," I taunted.

He darted forward, dodging or deflecting the four shots I fired in his direction. The loss of his wings did little to slow his speed. He jabbed up at my throat with his spear, which glistened in the sunlight coming in from the glass dome overhead. It appeared to be covered in something. I dodged the attack, and knocked him back with a blast of air.

I waited for the griffin's next move, but all he did was smile again and look past me. I immediately risked a look, moving just in time to avoid the jet of flame from the hands of the elemental crawling on the ground toward us.

I fired twice at his head, stopping him and removing a sizeable portion of his skull. I spun back to the griffin, and used a blast of air to stagger him as he lunged forward with his spear. I barely managed to blast the spear tip aside, moving its trajectory from my heart to my shoulder.

The griffin pushed until the blade of the spear reappeared out my back, tearing muscle apart. He pushed down harder, forcing me to my knees, while blood poured freely down my chest and back. Only then did he tear the spear free, and I collapsed, the warm blood a stark contrast to the cold tiled floor.

"Why you? Why did *you* have to be the one to kill me?"

"I was given the honor. And what an honor it is, to kill the famed Hellequin."

Since the return of Hellequin, I'd expected people to come after me, to gain revenge, but the fact that a griffin wanted to kill me was a bit of a shock. I couldn't think of a single thing I'd ever done to a griffin that would lead them to go to this much trouble to try and kill me. "You're a disgrace to your people."

Anger lit up in his eyes. "My *people* are nothing more than slaves to Hades and his allies. They know nothing of freedom and are not worth the blood that runs in their coddled veins."

The griffin glared down at me. "Any last words?"

"Fuck you very much," I said and shot him in the head.

The griffin managed to dodge in time to avoid a kill shot, but the bullet still smashed into its skull, just above its eye, before ricocheting off and hitting a nearby wall. I held the gun in the hand of my ruined arm—that one shot had been more than I'd hoped for—but the pain wracked my body, and there was no way I was going to get a second.

I used my good arm to pull myself to a sitting position as the griffin screamed in pain and anger, the blood pouring over its face pretty much blinding it in one eye. I forced myself to stand and picked up the gun, being careful to avoid the spear that the griffin was swinging around like a mobster using a baseball bat. The second bullet took it in the throat, causing it to stagger back as the sound of shouting echoed around me.

The griffin crashed to its knees, its one good eye zeroed in on me with all the hatred it could muster. I remained upright as the armed police unit shouted orders and ran up. I'd dropped the gun by that point, and Mike came over and helped steady me.

"And you didn't come in earlier because?" I asked.

"It was my decision," Kelly explained, as she appeared beside Mike, her tone suggesting that she had made the right decision and wasn't about to apologize for it. "I knew you'd be able to deal with them. And the hostages were the main concern."

She showed zero concern for my current state of injury. I got the impression that so long as the hostages were alive, it didn't really matter what happened to me. That knowledge, along with the considerable pain wracking my body, didn't exactly elevate my mood.

"Yeah, that worked out well for everyone, didn't it? You fucking idiot," I said to her and then threw up blood all over the floor. I glanced down at the mess I'd made and turned to Mike. "Get me to an Avalon hospital. Now."

CHAPTER 4

I don't really remember too much about what happened after that. I had a vague recollection of me talking to a paramedic, or doctor, but it could have been a big, fluffy pink bunny for all I knew.

I opened my eyes and stared at a ceiling for a few moments before I realized I was on a bed. I glanced around as much as possible, a difficult feat when your body is telling you that sitting up is not in your immediate future. I was on a hospital bed. I appeared to have my own room, complete with small TV mounted on the wall, and an uncomfortable chair the color of puce, for visitors. The walls were green. I was pretty certain that detail didn't matter in the long run, but for some reason I found myself staring at a spot of it that was a slightly different green from the rest.

"Feeling better?" someone asked as they walked through the door.

I was still a little groggy from whatever the hell had happened to me, so my response wasn't up to its usual wit. "Eh?"

"Your monitor said you were no longer asleep, how are you feeling?" The woman who spoke wore a white lab coat over a navy blouse. Her dark hair was put back into a bun so tight you could probably lose a finger if you decided to touch it. She held a chart in her hands.

"Where am I?" I finally managed to ask.

"You're in an Avalon hospital. You were admitted just over twenty-four hours ago."

"What happened to me?" I glanced down at my arms and found that my glyphs were lit up, only faintly, but enough. I was using air magic, but certainly not consciously.

"Ah, yes, the magic. Unfortunately, we had to place runes in the room to force you to use your magic on a constant basis. Only a small measure, enough to ensure the venom inside your body doesn't gain hold. Jorōgumo venom is incredibly potent stuff. The only way to ensure it doesn't take hold is to—"

"Continuously use magic," I finished for her. "Yeah, I know." I'd been bitten by a jorōgumo several centuries earlier when I was in Japan. It was not a fun experience, and I'd almost died before realizing that the permanent use of my magic was the only thing that could save me.

"You've taken a large amount of the venom, I'm afraid, certainly enough to kill you."

"The spear the griffin was using. It was covered in the stuff."

The doctor nodded.

"You can remove the runes now; I'll sort it out from here."

"I'm afraid not. You're going to stay here for the next five days and have a very small amount of magic in use the whole time. Any more than that and we risk bringing out your nightmare, but we have ways to ensure that doesn't happen."

Magic is a living thing that yearns to be used; any sorcerer who used too much, too quickly, risked having their magic take control of them. The magic would tell the sorcerer that it would make them stronger, better, someone who would be feared and respected. Whatever worked for the sorcerer to give control over to the magic inside of them. At some point in time it had been called a nightmare and the name caught on. Although my own appeared to behave in ways I had never expected. Like giving my subconscious mind cups of tea. However strange that sounded, it was weirder to live through it.

"I'm not staying here for five days," I said with all the categorical certainty of someone explaining that water was, in fact, wet. "Someone tried to kill me."

The doctor shrugged. I imagined a lot of her patients were here *because* someone had tried to kill them, one more stubborn bastard wasn't going to change her mind. "And then here is the safest place for you. We have LOA agents in the building. No one will hurt you while you're here."

"What is this air magic doing?" I asked. "I can't feel anything different after using it."

"Nothing," the doctor explained. "The runes in the room just force the magic out of your body. It doesn't actually *do* anything."

"Do you know what happened to the hostages or the people I fought?"

"Ah yes, apparently the hostages were taken to the closest human hospital. They're all doing well. And as for their assailants, I can't say."

"You mean, you don't know, or you can't tell me."

"One of those," she said with a slight smile.

"So, Doc, you got a name?"

"Heather."

"Well, Heather, it's nice to meet you. Can I get my phone and stuff back?"

"It's in the drawer beside your bed. Although I advise against doing anything that will rile you up. You need rest and calm if this venom is to be treated in anything close to a successful manner."

"And my shoulder?"

"Almost completely healed. It's quite the marvel. The rest of your body healed very quickly. In fact if it weren't for the venom coursing through your blood, I'd say you were the picture of health."

"I ache like crazy, but I'm glad to amaze and astound." I forced myself up to a sitting position and took a deep breath. "So, you're not going to let me leave."

"The aches are probably a mixture of the damage you sustained and the venom. It should hopefully pass. As for the possibility of allowing you to leave?" She raised an eyebrow in question. "No one is forcing you to stay here. This isn't a prison. You're here because if you weren't you'd be dead. And you're staying here because I don't like it when patients I've spent time and effort keeping alive decide to go die on me due to their own stubbornness."

I smiled. "Okay, Heather."

The door opened and a short, bald man walked in. The white-haired goatee that he'd worn the last time I'd seen him had extended to an entire beard. He carried a plastic shopping bag in one hand. "Doctor, can I have a moment?" he asked.

"Of course, Doctor Grayson, but please don't over excite him."

"Yeah, Doc, please don't over excite me," I said.

Grayson smiled and Heather shook her head and left us alone.

"I haven't seen you since you were in *my* medical care a few years ago," Grayson said. "I heard about your injury and thought I'd pay you a visit."

"Thanks, Doc." I shook his hand, and he held onto it so he could test my pulse.

"Jorōgumo venom, eh?" he eventually said.

"Apparently so."

"It's deadly stuff. I hope you're taking it seriously."

"As seriously as the time I was bitten by one of the bastards a few centuries ago."

"Good, I'd rather not have to perform your autopsy; I haven't done one in the few years since joining Tommy's organization."

"I'll try not to die on you, Doc."

Grayson smiled. "Good, now for the bad news. I spoke to some friends of mine in Avalon about what happened. It appears the griffin has vanished along with the body of the elemental you killed."

"The attackers were working with someone."

"That's my assessment too. Any idea who?"

I shook my head. "People have always wanted me dead, but those guys knew I'm Hellequin. Apparently it's beginning to get around."

"That's a lot of trouble just to get you though, don't you think?"

I nodded. "I thought that myself. Why take the hostages? Even if they wanted me dead, why open themselves to so much trouble. If they went with a long-range sniper rifle instead, I wouldn't even know about it until it was too late." My memories flicked back to a New York morning when I was looking down the barrel of my own sniper rifle, killing the evil piece of shit known as Mordred once and for all.

"You think they were after something else?"

"I can't begin to think that the void or elemental were particularly highly trained. It felt like they were the kind of people you'd send on an easy errand. And killing me is probably not on that list." I paused for a moment, before continuing. "Can you look into the hostages? I'm sure the human police took details of everyone."

"I can, but shouldn't you be asking someone who still works within Avalon's immediate structure?"

"You mean Agent Kelly Jensen? I find it odd that the SOA were there in the first place. She mentioned that one of the hostage takers had ties to Avalon. Something feels off here. There's too much we don't know about the hostage takers and why they decided to go to West Quay, of all places, to get to me. And I think the SOA know more than Agent Jensen is letting on."

"I can ask around. There are a few people I trust who work for Olivia in Winchester. Who, by the way, should probably be informed of this—she is still the director of the LOA in the South of England."

"She's in Avalon with Tommy and Kasey. I'd rather not bother her unless we need to."

Grayson looked as if he were about to say no and leave, but he nodded instead. "I'll get something for you in a day or so. Just stay here until then." He upended the contents of the bag onto my bed. Clean clothes, jeans, a blue T-shirt, boxers, and socks all stared back at me. They were a beautiful sight.

"I grabbed some stuff from Tommy's office for when he changes," Grayson explained. "I figured he'd be okay with you having them when you're ready to leave."

"Thanks for all of this," I said. "But hurry back. I don't think whoever these guys are, that they're anywhere near done."

It took a total of four hours before my plan of staying in place and waiting for Grayson to return was blown all to hell. To be fair, I really did plan on staying in the hospital until I'd gotten what I needed, and then I was going to leave whether they liked it or not. For the first hour I watched TV. The news was on a constant repeat of the day's events, with little, if any new information actually being explained to the viewers. I flicked through a few channels and found some Wile-E-Coyote cartoons, which served me well as a diversion.

I'd always liked Wile-E-Coyote. He was persistent, inventive, and interesting. Okay, he was as dumb as a bag of hammers, but you couldn't blame the guy for really wanting to eat that Roadrunner, who was, from my point of view, a colossal fucking asshole. Wile should have just blown its head off with a Mossberg and called it a day. To be fair, he probably tried that and hurt himself.

The cartoon finished and was replaced by one starring Tweety Bird, who was probably the single most annoying character ever created that didn't have the words Jar-Jar in his name. Tommy might have been trying to get me to love *Star Wars* as much as he did, but there was pretty much no chance in hell that even Tommy loved that stupid fucker. He should have been shot into the nearest sun at the first available opportunity.

Eventually I gave up watching TV as apparently cartoon characters made me angrier than was probably normal, so I settled for playing on my phone while it charged. Due to the tiny amount of magic I was using to keep the venom at bay, I was fairly groggy, and so didn't see the door open, nor anyone step inside until they walked toward me.

I placed my phone back on the bedside cabinet, and eyed the emergency button.

The void stood at the foot of my bed, pointing the tip of a dagger at me. "If you press it, I'll be forced to kill whoever comes in here. I already had to kill the two guards to get to you; I'd rather not kill innocent doctors and nurses unless I have no choice."

I gave the void my full attention. "How's the wound?"

He raised his hand to his shoulder. "They brought me here after I was arrested, but they say they can't use magic on me to heal me too quickly. My power rejects it. They've done enough so that I can use my arm, but the pain will be there for a long time to come."

"Good. Let me know how that goes. You should write a blog about it, I'm sure it'll be riveting."

"I had to kill the two guards who were watching me upstairs too; they were both LOA, I believe. They didn't believe I was a threat. I guess they were wrong, although I don't think I'll have long before more agents are sent here. I have just enough time to slit your throat with this silver dagger."

A moment later and my magic simply stopped working. Panic settled inside of me. I didn't have long before the effects of the venom would once again take control.

"I want you to feel some pain first," he said and sat beside me.

My head spun, and heat began creeping up my chest and neck. It suddenly felt as if my muscles were on fire.

"I've heard it hurts," the void said. "I've heard it's agonizing."

"Go. Fuck. You—" I managed before the pain wracked me once again. I swung my legs over the bed and tried to stand up, but my body had other ideas and I crashed back to the bed as the void laughed from behind me.

"I could watch this all night," he told me, and got to his feet, wandering around the bed toward me. "But it's time to die now."

He bent down, the knife only inches away from me, when I grabbed the remote control from beside me and smashed it into the side of his head. It knocked his head aside and he dropped his knife, but his power didn't waver, and he dragged me from the bed, throwing me to the floor. He punched me in the side of the mouth, busting my lip open.

Any strength in my body left as the pain of the venom made my vision darken. I tried to push myself up, but the void kicked out at my elbow and I fell, face first, back to the tiled floor. The void kicked me in the ribs, forcing me to roll onto my back. I raised my hand in a weak attempt to fend off further attacks, but he grabbed my arm, locking it, and pressed his knee down across my throat.

I fought for breath, but the void's weight made it impossible. Clawing at his leg did nothing but gain me another punch to the mouth. I was going to die in a hospital room by someone who had no right to last ten seconds in a fight with me. Rage filled me and I opened my eyes wide, staring up at the void, while I struggled beneath his grip. I punched up with everything I had, hoping to connect with his gut. Fortunately, I hit something a bit lower.

It wasn't exactly a killing blow, but it was enough to ensure he dropped his concentration for a moment as he roared out in pain and released my arm. My glyphs instantly flared to life. I drove a blade of fire through his knee, immediately extinguishing it as the use of magic once again overwhelmed my exhausted body. The void, now unbalanced, crashed to the floor at the foot of the bed, screaming obscenities at me as he held his bloody limb.

I took a few moments to stop the room from spinning and then gingerly got to my feet. I'd reapplied the air magic, and was using it to increase my speed and agility, as opposed to just having the magic evaporate into nothing as the runes in the room had done. I was soon beginning to feel more like my old self.

I saw that the knife the void had been using had skittered under the bed, but I didn't really have time to fish it out as he dragged himself toward the door, leaving a bloody smear in his wake.

"Who do you work for?" I asked, and took a step toward the void, who ignored me and continued to crawl away.

I grabbed him by his shirt and dragged him upright, slamming him up against the nearest wall, and then head-butting him to ensure his concentration didn't return anytime soon. He slid down the wall with more blood running down his face.

"Don't make me ask again," I snapped.

"We're all coming for you," he said, a hideous grin on his face. "You can't beat us all."

I grabbed him by his ears and lifted him off the ground, much to his obvious discomfort.

"Last chance."

He spat blood onto the light blue hospital bed shirt I wore, getting it right on my chest. I punched him in the kidney and he spat up more blood, although this time it was onto the floor between us.

Holding him by the back of his collar, I dragged him over to the hospital room's door, pushing him roughly against it. There was a bag on the floor beside it, which I hadn't noticed before. I held the void upright with one hand and picked up the bag, which was unzipped. The gleaming metal of a gun shone through the darkness of the bag. I picked the gun out and upended the bag onto the floor. It contained a mixture of drugs and magazines of bullets.

I removed my hand, letting him fall as I stepped back, and checked the gun, which was loaded. "No, not this way," I said, more to myself than to him and drove a wall of air into his chest. He crashed through the door and into the hallway outside.

Pieces of wood and plastic littered the ground as I stepped through the ruined door. The corridor was silent, I saw a body lying further up it, but kept my gaze firmly on the man before me. The void was barely moving, but his eyes were still open, still locked on me with a stare of hatred.

"What did I do to you?" I asked.

"You should have never interfered in our plans. In our *quest*. We will have our revenge."

"You want to tell me who *you* are?" I raised the gun. "Who sent you here? Why were you in West Quay? What were you looking for? You got me to West Quay to kill me. It's a lot of trouble."

"No trouble at all. Your death, in full public, was to be a message to our enemies. We are coming for all of them. And there's nowhere you can hide, even in full view with the world watching."

"If you wanted me dead, why coat the blade with a slow-acting poison?"

"We were prepared in case you fought back. To weaken you and then kill you, it would have been glorious."

"Your elemental friend is dead; your griffin friend is missing. It's just you. How do you want this to end?"

"I told you before that you wouldn't kill me, and you didn't. You need answers, and I can't give them to you if I'm dead." He raised the sleeve of his shirt, showing a dark mark. "It scrambles our spirit's memories upon death. There's no way you can kill me and get what you desire most. The knowledge of who we are."

I stared at the mark for a heartbeat. I'd seen it before, on several people over the centuries. The last time had been on someone evil, a man consumed with his own need to destroy and kill for pleasure.

"Show me your full arm," I demanded.

The void smirked, but did as he was asked, unbuttoning his shirt and dragging his arm free, showing me the mark I'd dreaded to see on his shoulder. The black-bladed scythe in front of an eye with a blood-red iris.

"You know who we are," he said with just a little joy in his voice. "If you want more, you'll have to take me alive."

I heard footsteps from my side and turned slightly, to watch Heather run around the nearest corner, flanked by two large guards. She immediately crouched by the man the void had killed on his way to get me.

I glanced back at the void, who hadn't moved.

"Put the gun down," Heather shouted at me. "This is a hospital."

I ignored her. "I don't need you for anything," I told him and shot him three times in the head.

I immediately dropped the gun and walked back into my room, pulling off my bloody hospital shirt and putting on the clean clothes that Grayson had brought for me.

Heather stormed into the room as I finished pulling my T-shirt over my head. "This is a hospital," she screamed at me. "A place of healing."

"And a place of death," I pointed out, feeling slightly lightheaded after the revelation I'd discovered. "I just saved him the time of having to live through the healing part of his stay."

I put my phone and wallet into my jeans pockets and strolled out past her. The Reavers were back. And that meant all kinds of trouble for me.

CHAPTER 5

November 1888. London.

After what had happened in the alley, Alan and I left the bodies of the two SOA agents where they lay and went back to the safe house. London was ruled over by Brutus, who considered himself the king of the city. When he'd first arrived in England after the fall of Troy, he'd spent some time killing all of the giants who'd lived here at the time, and then getting into a confrontation with Merlin. It had resulted in Merlin allowing Brutus to stay in the country, but only in London.

Brutus had a network of runners who gave messages to him for a fee. I managed to find one of the Whitechapel runners and told him about the two agents. Brutus would arrange for them to be taken care of, at least until they could be collected by others within Avalon.

"Is it wise involving Brutus?" Alan asked, as he washed the blood off his body in the back garden of the house. Luckily it was still dark, so there would be very few people around to complain about the naked, blood-covered man washing himself.

"It's not like we had too many options," I pointed out. "We couldn't leave the bodies there indefinitely, and besides, Avalon isn't allowed to have people in the city without Brutus's permission."

"Yeah, but he's going to know everything now."

"Well, I'm sure he'll want to discuss it all. But we probably have a while before that, so we'd best get on and find out who that man was, and why he attacked us. Also, why didn't he kill us?"

"And why did he write *From Hell* on your forehead in your comrade's blood. Don't want to miss that bit," Alan said and tipped the metal bowl full of now red water onto the grass.

"Thanks for the reminder," I said with as much sarcasm as I could muster. Scrubbing off the bloody writing was the first thing I'd done when returning to the house. "Do you remember anything else about what happened?"

Alan thought for a moment. "He had a mark on his forearm, a tattoo."

"Of what?"

"I only glimpsed it in the light of the torch one of those SOA agents was carrying. An eye of some sort, but there was something in front of it. Sorry, that's all I got. Does that mean anything to you?"

I shook my head. "Not that I can recall. Lots of tattoos have eyes in them. Lots of organizations tattoo their members. It's basically a needle in a haystack. How'd you see it anyway? He was wearing a long coat."

"Not when we arrived he wasn't. He only put that on after killing the agents. He was wearing a dress shirt, but the sleeves were rolled up. Who wears an expensive shirt to go murdering?"

"Someone who thinks it'll be easier to get victims from around here if he looks the part of a wealthy john."

"You think the woman was a prostitute?"

I nodded. "That would be my guess."

"Why do you want to help?" I asked after a few moments of silence. "I know you said you were never going to kill the agents, but why help me? What do you honestly get from it?"

Alan was quiet, and for a second I didn't think he would answer, or that he would lie and tell me some frivolous tale about being chivalrous or wanting to be the better man.

"I saw the look on his face while I lay in the dirt and watched him butcher two people. I saw the joy and excitement it brought him. I was scared. I was helpless and scared, and I thought I was going to die in this shithole of a city lying in the dirt and blood and semen of however many others frequented that alley. I want to pay him back for that. I want to show him what I can do when I'm not helpless. But more than anything, I want to make sure no one else sees those eyes before he carves them up."

Alan wiped his face with the palm of his hand and walked off into the house, leaving me to sit on the makeshift wooden bench and stare up at the fading moonlight.

Alan returned a few seconds later. "There's someone here for you. She's pretty, but I already know she despises me, so I'll wait out here. If this is the caliber of visitors we're going to get in the middle of the night, I may have to stick around after we've caught these bastards. She's in the . . . whatever passes for a drawing room in this place."

I moved past him without comment; there was really little point in replying to him, it would only create the impression that I wished for him to continue discussing the matter. I walked through the house to the front room, opening the door to be greeted by a woman of staggering beauty.

"Diana," I said with a smile just before being enveloped in a hug.

"It's good to see you, Nathan," she said, her Italian accent just creeping into the words.

Diana, the Roman goddess of the moon and hunting, and probably other things I couldn't recall, was one of the most beautiful women on the planet. Her long, dark hair was loose over her shoulders. She wore a simple blue top with dark trousers, which wouldn't have looked as good on anyone else.

"I assume this isn't a social call," I said and offered her a seat on one of the two leather chairs in the room.

She nodded a thank you and sat down. I removed a bottle of red wine and two glasses from a cupboard next to an old fireplace that would probably turn into a death trap should it ever be lit, and passed a half full glass to Diana, before pouring my own.

"The wine was unnecessary," she said as she savored the smell. "But thank you."

"I remember you like your red wine, and if you're bringing bad news, I figured it might be pleasant to have something nice to go along with the unpleasant."

We toasted and both drank a measure. I wasn't a wine connoisseur. To me, if the wine tasted like wine and didn't make me want to vomit, it was good enough to drink. But Diana preferred wine over almost any other alcoholic drink, and, as she smiled, I knew she appreciated the bottle I'd uncorked for us.

"You sent me two bodies tonight," Diana said.

"That I did. Although I assumed they were going to be Brutus's problem, not yours."

"Brutus very kindly gave the problem to me to sort out. In fact, I believe his exact words were 'Sort this shit out before we get more Avalon bastards running around.' He was quite animated in his speech."

"He's not happy with me."

"Actually, no, not at all. As you know, he likes you very much, but he does not like your employer. You sending him bodies is barely thought about. But these are Avalon bodies. And we both know that once Avalon gets wind of what happened here tonight, they're going to send more people to investigate."

"I'll be doing the investigating," I said. "Whoever killed them attacked me and Alan. We're going to figure out who did it and then deal with him."

Diana laughed. It was a beautiful sound. "You and I have history. Good history." The word history was accompanied with a smirk. "*Alan* and I have the kind of history where he stole something he shouldn't have, and I'd like to tear out his lungs for it."

"What did he steal?" I said with an audible sigh.

"One of my arrows. Caught the bastard red-handed and he tried to use his manly charms on me. So I kicked him in the cock, but he got away before I could cut it off and stuff it in his mouth. I did get the arrow back though."

Diana was an incredible hunter, but part of her ability to hunt was her arrows. Legend had it they were blessed by the ancient Norse dwarves themselves, using runes to ensure that they always killed what they hit. Those arrows were one of the things she cherished the most, considering it an utmost honor to use them when she hunted. The dwarves were no longer around, having vanished many centuries previously, and her arrows were one of the few weapons made by them that still existed in the world.

"I'm not going to say that he's even close to being trustworthy," I explained. "But I saw what he went through tonight. He'll be with us until he gets his revenge. Once that's over, all bets are off and he'll run like a spooked gazelle."

"Good enough for me, but if he steps out of line, I will hurt him."

"You make it sound like you're joining us."

"I am. This is Brutus's city and someone has spent the last few months murdering women in this area. And now *also* in Whitechapel someone kills two SOA agents. I'd like to believe they're not connected."

I told her about the *From Hell* that the murderer had written on my forehead.

"You know that was written in a letter to the police by the man they believe to be Jack the Ripper," she said softly.

I nodded. "I think it's the same man, or at least someone who wanted to copy those murders. I think his kill was disturbed and he took his anger out on those who'd disturbed him."

"We've had nearly a month with no murders. If this Jack the Ripper has resumed his crimes, and that's a pretty big if, we can expect more. And soon."

"We need to find him. Alan saw a tattoo on his arm."

"Lots of people have tattoos."

"This one was of an eye."

"Again, not narrowing it down much."

"That was my sentiment too. But it's what we have to go on."

"There was a scythe," Alan said as he opened the door and waved at Diana. "It was over the eye. I've just remembered it."

Diana had an expression that suggested she might hit Alan with the glass she held in her hand, but decided to place it on the floor beside her feet instead. "An eye with a scythe? Still doesn't mean anything to me."

"It does to me," I said, and really wished it didn't. "If it's who I think they are, then that's the tattoo of the Reavers."

"Umm," Alan said after Diana and I had been silent for about half a minute. "Any chance you could expand on who the Reavers are?"

"The Reavers work for Avalon," Diana told him without taking her gaze off me. "You think they could be involved in this? You know what that would mean."

"I don't," Alan interjected. "I'd quite like it if someone fucking well told me though."

"Have you ever heard of the Harbingers?" I asked him.

"Sure, they're the best of the best. The toughest, brightest, most dangerous agents in Avalon are given special training and turned into an elite fighting force. They're not exactly people I'd like to bump into."

"They're sent to situations that Avalon considers to be out of control. They stop uprisings, or go in and deal with problems that other branches of Avalon have failed at. Usually when Avalon casualties are involved. The Harbingers go into other realms too. They help the leaders keep control of any problems they might have. To say that they work in the shadows is an understatement. Normally they hit without warning, leave no witnesses or targets alive, and then vanish again." .

"What's this special training they undergo?" Diana asked, clearly very curious about the subject.

"No one really knows," I told her. "I've been told it's some sort of mental conditioning. A psychic puts them into an unconscious state and then they live out their lives in that dream world, while learning new skills at an astonishing rate. How true that is, I don't know. Apparently during the day they live in the dream world, and when they're sleeping, their bodies are put through conditioning in our world. Like I said, how much is truth and how much is fairy tale, I couldn't tell you. Whatever they go through, though, it's so classified that not even I'm allowed to see it. Nor are the knights of the realm."

"What do the Harbingers have to do with the Reavers?" Alan asked.

"Not everyone passes the Harbinger trials," I explained. "And once you've failed, that's it, you can never try again. Some simply go back to whatever they were doing before. But others banded together, and formed the Reavers. Originally they did it off their own back, but it didn't take long for them to get Avalon backing. I have no idea what they do, or who they report to, but they work for Avalon and they're meant to be fiercely loyal."

"So, why are they killing SOA agents in some dark little patch of grass?" Diana asked.

I didn't really know the answer to that. "It's perfectly possible it's not the Reavers who are involved. But they're the only ones that I know of with that tattoo. It could be an ex-member, or someone who tried out for them and got rejected. Decided to muddy their name."

Diana stood. "Wait here."

She left the room and a short time later the front door opened. Alan remained standing, but leaned up against the wall.

"Why would one Avalon group kill members of another?" he asked, mostly it seemed to himself. "It explains why he let you live though. If he recognized you as Merlin's errand boy, I mean."

"Alan, is now really the time to start trying to piss me off?" I asked.

Alan raised his hands in mock surrender. "You're right, sorry. Force of habit."

The shutting of the front door signified Diana's return. She reappeared in the drawing room's doorway holding a box, which she passed to me before retaking her seat.

"And this is?" I asked as I opened it and saw a lot of pieces of paper.

"Those are copies of Brutus's case file for the Jack the Ripper murders. They have things in them that aren't in the file held by the police. He wanted the murders looked into, he felt something was off about them."

I removed a handful of documents and passed the box to Alan, who did the same. It didn't take long for both of us to come across crime scene photos of the victims, and the horrific way in which they had been killed. Detailed information on their wounds came with them and I was suddenly very grateful that I hadn't been one of those first police officers who'd found the bodies. There's a big difference between finding a normal dead body and discovering one mutilated by someone for their own amusement or perverse satisfaction. Both leave memories of the event, but the latter is liable to leave a mark on your soul, and years after you think you've moved on, something will flash into your head and it's like reliving it all over again.

About halfway through the stack that I'd taken I came across something that wasn't macabre or full of details of the murder of young women. It was a drawing of a rune. One I'd never seen before. It was a wash of dark lines that started with very little space between them as they crossed over at the bottom of the rune, but ended with much thinner lines at the top. It was an odd, and very complex, pattern. Not the type of things drawn in a hurry by someone who didn't know what they were doing.

"What does this mean?" I asked, gaining the immediate attention of Alan as he found two more drawings in the pile he was checking through.

"Each of these was drawn at a different murder scene," Diana told us. "There are eight in all, going back six months."

"There are only five Ripper killings," Alan stated.

"Officially, yes. But our people inside the investigation believe there were several more. And now two SOA agents." Diana removed a folded piece of paper from her pocket and passed it to me. I opened it to see a drawing of an identical rune. "It was found drawn on the alley wall near where you were attacked."

"It's identical to the others," I said, mostly to myself. "What the hell is this rune?"

Diana glanced at Alan. "Can you give us a second?"

"You don't trust me?"

Diana shook her head. "Not even slightly."

Alan laughed, but didn't complain and dumped the files back into the box, dropping it to the floor with exaggerated finesse, before leaving Diana and me alone.

"You might want to work with him, but I don't trust him," Diana said when she saw the expression on my face.

"I don't trust him, but I also don't want to alienate him. If it comes down to needing his help, I don't want to wonder if he's going to put a knife in my back so he can make his escape."

"Well, he doesn't need to know this, anyway. In fact, I'm not sure if Brutus would be happy with you knowing."

"Spit it out, Diana."

"That rune is dwarven. One of the original twenty-one that they created."

I absorbed the information as if swirling an aged Scotch slowly around my mouth, assimilating every aspect of it before digesting it. The original dwarven runes were thought long lost in the annals of time, something I was fully aware that Merlin wanted to ensure. They were powerful in a way that made normal runes, even those created by an exceptionally powerful enchanter or sorcerer, look like something used by children. I'd met very few people who knew any of the dwarven runes, and even fewer who thought that using them was remotely close to a good idea.

"What does it do?" I asked, hoping for, but knowing I wasn't going to get, good news.

"It takes someone's soul and captures it, placing it inside an item of the rune wielder's choosing."

"That sounds complicated. Why not just use a necromancer? He could have torn the soul out and put it in something. I've seen Hades do it."

"Yes, but there are two problems with that. Firstly, they would need a very powerful necromancer, and secondly, the condition of the soul in question. This rune will ensure that the soul is always put inside the vessel in an undamaged condition. It's painted near the body, but not on it. The rune draws the soul from the body and then it's absorbed by the vessel. No matter how badly damaged the body is, the soul always remains intact. That doesn't happen with necromancy."

She had a valid point. A necromancer could remove a soul and place it in a container, but any damage done to the victim would be reflected in damage to the soul in a serious way. The soul would be tainted. Being able to ensure the soul was in one piece meant they were taking the souls to use in some way.

"So they're killing these people in such a horrific manner, knowing their souls will still be usable. That means they're hurting them for fun. It also means someone is using these souls for something." Even I had to admit my theory was vague.

Diana nodded. "You can see why Brutus wants it kept quiet that someone is running around the city butchering women and using an old dwarven rune to capture their souls. People are scared. There are more murders than this Jack the Ripper; bodies found in the Thames with pieces missing, people bludgeoned to death for no apparent motive. We don't need to create more fear."

"But we need to find out who's killing these people, why, and what they're doing with the souls they take."

"There's more. Brutus's investigation has shown that at least three people are carrying out these murders. One calls himself Jack, we've had several letters from him, taunting the police. None have been released. He mentioned that he and his *lads* will continue to do their work."

"Could just be bluster." Even as I said it, I doubted very much that the man who'd written *From Hell* on my forehead did anything for *bluster*.

"Possibly, but then there's one of the bodies." Diana got up and flicked through the pile of paper in the box on the floor, passing me a document.

As I read it, my head began to hurt and I wished I'd never come to London in the first place. It stated that while several of the marks on the victim—a twenty-two-year-old woman, who hadn't been linked to the Ripper killings—were clearly from a small-bladed knife, there was one mark that appeared to be similar to the bite of a lion. It had been delivered after the death of the victim. The coroner had served overseas in Africa and had seen several people inflicted with such bites.

"Werelion," I said after finishing the document and passing it back to Diana. "So we have a sorcerer and a werelion. And the third killer would be?"

"We don't know. One of the three could well be Jack himself. But one witness, a policeman out on his beat, said he saw a hooded man attacking a young prostitute. When confronted, the man turned to the policeman and hit him in the chest with a blast of water. Possibly an elemental or another sorcerer. The rune was drawn on the wall behind the victim's head. They'd gone down a nearby alley to, we assume, carry out a transaction."

"At least three then," Alan said as he re-entered the room. "Probably."

Diana opened her mouth to speak.

"Don't look so shocked and angry; listening in on other people's conversations is part of my job." Alan turned to me. "Three vicious murderers who are killing in a horrific way for fun, and then tearing the souls away from the dead and placing them in some sort of container. That about sum it up?"

I nodded.

"Well, that's just a massive kick to the bollocks. So, any idea where we go to first?"

I nodded again. "I might know someone in the city who could help us."

"How?" Diana asked.

"He's got knowledge of the Reavers, he might be able to point us in the right direction, or at the very least tell us why some of these people are doing this."

"There's a downside, isn't there?" Alan asked. "There's always a downside."

"Yeah, the downside is he isn't the most friendly of people and he's a little paranoid about members of Avalon trying to kill him."

"Why?" Diana asked, probably already knowing the answer.

"Because members of Avalon regularly try to kill him. He's a wanted man. He tried to kill some people he shouldn't have, an act that Avalon declared treasonous."

"So, how is he going to be of help to us?" Diana asked.

"Because he was one of the founding members of the Reavers. And he owes me a favor or two."

"Why?" Diana and Alan asked together.

"Well, when I say someone went to kill him, I meant me. I was the one sent to kill him."

CHAPTER 6

November 1888. London.

"This doesn't strike me as being the best idea anyone has ever had," Diana mentioned as our carriage pulled up outside the gates of an old mansion that from the outside appeared to have had better times. Diana had contacted someone, who supplied a driver.

The ride to our destination in South London had taken just over an hour to complete, and as the sun had begun to rise, more and more people either left home to go to work, or arrived at home after being out all night.

"This park is called The Grove," I told Diana and Alan, motioning to our surroundings.

"I've been here before," Diana said. "I don't know anyone who goes here willingly though."

"I thought Brutus ruled London," Alan said with just enough condescension to annoy, but not enough to be turned to paste as he sat beside Diana.

"Brutus does," Diana snapped. "But he's named this off limits to pretty much everyone. He says it's because he's made a deal with the people who live here that they can keep the place to themselves."

Alan looked out of the dark windows, as rain began to beat against the roof of the carriage. "And your friend lives here?" he asked me.

"I wouldn't call him a friend," I admitted. "He's more of a. . . ." I paused. I wasn't exactly sure how to categorize him. "He used to be my trainer when I first started working for Avalon. He's an old soldier who deserved better than the bullshit Merlin allowed Avalon to pile onto him."

"So he's not a traitor?" Alan asked.

"If he's a traitor then something bad must have happened."

"But Avalon sent you to kill him," Diana pointed out.

"That they did. It's why he lives in London now, under Brutus's protection. Officially I was unable to complete my task. Merlin wasn't best pleased."

"There are things out there in the trees," Alan said, finally looking back from the window. "What the hell is running around this park?"

"There's a clan of wood trolls who live in the park. Felix Novius is someone who inspired a lot of loyalty in a lot of people. Even after his exile from Avalon."

I pushed open the carriage door and stepped out into the rain, pulling the collar of my long coat up to stay as dry as possible, as the rain fell at unrelenting speed.

"Wait in the carriage," I told Diana and Alan, neither of whom seemed inclined to argue that they wanted to come out and get drenched.

I felt a twinge of guilt for the carriage driver sitting in the pouring rain and scanned the surroundings, my gaze flicking back and forth every few seconds when something else caught my eye in the woodland not too far from where I stood. The driver glanced down at me, although I could barely see his face due to the shadows that covered it. He dropped to the increasingly soggy ground and gave some food to the two horses.

"I won't be long," I told him, but he didn't appear to care one way or the other.

I walked up to the massive iron gates, which barred the entrance to the property. They were attached to a ten-foot-high stone wall. It was all very imposing and certainly gave the impression that whoever was behind it didn't wish to be bothered in any way.

I pushed open the gate, which made a noise that made the inside of my brain hurt, accompanied by the exact same noise when the gate sprung closed after I'd taken a few steps.

The garden was overgrown, but the grass and plant life didn't impede anyone walking toward the house. The vines that ran up over the front wall of the house moved in such a way as to suggest they were meant to go there; they gave the appearance of being messy and uncared for while being the exact opposite.

I reached the large oak door and used the brass knocker to announce my presence. After a few seconds, I found that the door was unlocked and pushed it open, stepping into the dark mansion. The foyer was lit by only a few gas lanterns that sat on either side of an ornate staircase that ascended up to a small platform before splitting off to go in two different directions to the floor above.

"Why are you here?" a voice boomed from the darkness beyond.

"Felix, it's Nathan Garrett. Cut the theatrical bullshit. If we were a threat your troll friends would already have torn us to pieces."

There was a moment of quiet, followed by the sound of footsteps making their way toward me. It didn't take long for Felix to come into view, walking down the stairs as the lights flickered to life.

The entire mansion would have made most museum curators blush with envy—it was full of old paintings, ancient pieces of art, and furniture that actually seemed to look better as it got older. There was no dust, or anything to suggest that the interior wasn't kept as immaculate as the exterior. It would have taken a lot of effort. Sometimes giving the impression that you want to be left alone is more work than actually *making* people leave you alone.

"You promised you'd never be back," Felix said as he strolled toward me.

"Sorry, needs must," I explained.

Felix Novius was old enough that he saw the Romans move from small beginnings all the way to controlling a large portion of Europe, Asia, and Africa. And then watched it all crumble down to nothing not that long after. He had long white hair, but was clean-shaven. He wore a dark suit more appropriate for fine dining than sitting all alone in an empty house. He'd long ago lost his Roman accent and had replaced it with a nondescript English one.

"They'd better be some damn good needs, boy," he snapped. "Last I heard you still work for Merlin, and he still wants me dead."

I bristled at the use of the word *boy*. Felix was fully aware of how the word annoyed me, but never did seem to care enough to not use it. "We've got a lot of dead bodies in the city with ties to the Reavers."

"You mean the Reavers are murdering citizens of this city? This is the first I've heard of it."

"You've heard of Jack the Ripper, I assume."

The shock on Felix's face was easy to see. "You'd best tell your friends to come in then."

"Are you sure you trust him?" Alan asked as we followed Felix through his mansion to the rear of the property.

"More than you," I pointed out.

"You still don't trust me, Nathan?" Alan asked with a grin. "I'm hurt. Wounded. My heart cleaved from my chest and tossed aside like—"

"Do you ever shut the hell up?" Felix snapped without turning back to us.

"Old man, I've had a shit few days," Alan said, an edge of anger in his voice. "I might take shit from Nathan here, because I actually understand why he doesn't like me. And I may take a whole lot of things from the very beautiful Diana, but I'm damned if I'll have some old fossil tell me what to do."

Felix stopped and turned back to us. Alan tensed for a fight and I could see Diana getting ready to break them up. Felix walked toward Alan until they were only a few feet away from one another. "I like you," he said and laughed as he resumed walking.

"Is he touched in the head?" Alan whispered.

I shrugged. To be honest I wasn't entirely sure anymore.

Eventually we made it to a large library, the shelves completely overfilled with books. A desk and a red leather armchair sat in one corner, piles of paper and books atop the desk.

"You're probably wanting to know who the Reavers are?"

"Already know that," Alan pointed out. "Nathan here gave us the information. People who didn't pass the Harbinger tests and all that."

"I bet you don't know what they were formed to do," Felix said, and all three of us shook our heads. Felix pointed to an old couch, which had clearly seen better days. "Sit, I'll explain."

We all sat while Felix uncorked a bottle of Scotch and removed four glasses from one of the drawers on his desk, passing each of us a drink.

"Not for me," Alan said. "Don't touch the stuff."

"Then hold the glass and at least try to look like a man with his own set of balls," Felix said, much to Diana's amusement.

Alan knocked back the drink on one go. "I don't like the stuff, didn't say I can't drink it."

Felix laughed and poured Alan a much larger, second drink.

"You both done?" I asked.

Felix knocked back his own drink before turning to me. "You of all people should be in no hurry to find out more about the Reavers."

"Why?" I asked, genuinely confused.

"I'll explain in a minute. First, you need to know that the Reavers' sole mission is to keep Arthur alive."

"Wait," Alan said. "How do you know these people? I mean, this could all just be some made-up fantasy you've been living in your head."

"I was one of the founding members," Felix told us all and promptly knocked back a second Scotch.

"Please go on," Diana told him, glaring slightly at Alan.

Felix nodded graciously. "As Nathan will tell you, I used to work for Merlin. What he doesn't know is that I was responsible for the Harbinger training program. It was my job to ensure that everyone who came into the program made it to the end. That was through either passing or failing the experience, and in some cases, not living through it."

It was common knowledge that anyone who decided to try and become a Harbinger didn't take the decision lightly. I'd known several people who hadn't passed its difficult tests and more than one of them who hadn't come back at all.

"As you probably know," Felix continued, "the Reavers were created to allow those who failed the tests to still be of great use to Avalon. They were still highly trained and, for the most part, a group of people who wished to do good. They had one job. To harvest souls for Merlin to feed to Arthur."

Diana and Alan glanced at me. I could feel both of them wanting to ask if I knew.

"No," I said softly. "I had no idea."

"Nor should you have," Felix said. "Merlin wasn't exactly thrilled that the souls of the slain were helping to keep Arthur alive, and that they were much more effective than his own magic."

"How did it work?" Diana asked, as I sat dumbstruck.

I'd been in the room with Arthur a hundred times, seen him floating in that *glass coffin*, his body encased in magically enhanced water. I'd seen Merlin feeding his own magic into the coffin, giving Arthur his power to sustain him. I'd helped Merlin break away, weak and exhausted from continuous magic use. My anger boiled over and I stood, kicking a book across the room and into a pile, which spilled over the floor.

"Feel better?" Felix asked.

"How did it work?" I asked, repeating Diana's words. "How do the souls help Arthur? I saw Merlin use his own energy to sustain him."

"The souls only ensure that Arthur's body remains alive. Merlin's magic is what keeps him active. Without Merlin's magic, he'd go insane."

I almost crashed back to the ground. "Arthur is conscious?"

Felix shook his head. "He's in a state of deep sleep. From what Merlin told me, Arthur's brain is unable to wake him. He can't communicate with anyone. One day in every seven, Merlin must spend at his side. Any more than that and it would burn him out. That's where the paladins come into it."

The paladins were people who surrounded Arthur day and night. Twelve heavily armed men and women who stood guard over their fallen king, waiting for the day he awakes.

"Originally the paladins fed him too," Felix said. "Each of them was linked to Arthur every day. It's why there are over a hundred of them. They had to rotate every week so they didn't all burn out and die."

"And the souls?" Diana asked.

"A few hundred years ago, Merlin discovered that the soul of a being was much more powerful than having the paladins constantly feeding Arthur. A soul would sustain Arthur for years, with minimal input from the paladins. So Merlin changed things. He fed the soul of the deceased to Arthur and had the paladins help feed the magic inside his coffin instead. It meant that Arthur had more people giving him stimulation and hopefully a larger chance to wake up.

"Souls were easy to come by. There are no shortages of enemies of Avalon, and mostly the Reavers just waited about until those enemies came to them. There's always someone in Avalon who has a price on his, or her, head. They'd take the souls and Merlin would ensure that they were fed to Arthur."

"Does it work?" Alan asked.

"Arthur's vitals appear to be stronger, but there's no change in anything you can see. Merlin seems certain that what they're doing is working."

"And at what point did they go from taking the souls of enemies to murdering women in the street?" I asked.

"Merlin. Merlin's what changed things."

"In what way?" I asked, already dreading the answer.

"It was his plan to have the Reavers take souls in the first place. His plan to feed them to Arthur. And now it's his plan to take the souls of *innocent people* and feed them to Arthur. Merlin's the one who sent the Reavers to London."

CHAPTER 7

Winchester, England. Now.

I left the hospital and made my way toward my home in the New Forest. The journey was an unpleasant one, as my magic had to be used constantly to ensure I didn't pass out from the jorōgumo venom, which still coursed through my body. I'd settled for using my air magic—just a tiny amount to make me slightly faster and more agile than normal—but wasn't entirely sure how much the small amount of magic used would hold back the venom. Hopefully long enough. I needed to find out why the Reavers had returned. I couldn't do that from a hospital bed.

I got out of the cab I'd taken home and took tentative steps toward my house. When there were no obvious attacks, and my house was still in one piece, I opened the door, disarming the security system before enough toxins were pumped into the hallway to knock out a charging rhino. Sometimes it pays to be overly careful.

I needed to figure out my next move. Tommy, Olivia, and Kasey were in Camelot, so calling them was out of the question. If I wanted to contact them, I'd have to contact the island of Avalon and have them relay the message through the realm gate to someone who could find Tommy and company in Camelot.

I'd gone upstairs and had a shower, trying to get my brain to work out what my next step would be, when someone knocked on the front door. It was a polite knock, the knock of someone who probably wasn't going to bust the door down or try to shoot me. Those people don't normally knock first anyway.

I used my fire magic to instantly dry me, and then quickly pulled on some jeans and a T-shirt, before answering the door and finding Doctor Grayson standing in what was quickly becoming a rainy day.

"Doc," I said and held the door open. "Want to come in?"

"No, I'd rather talk out here," he told me.

I stepped barefoot onto my porch, the rain beginning to make the roof above my head sound like I was walking into a hurricane. "Why are we out here?"

"Safer," he told me. "Avalon likes to bug people's homes."

"Avalon hasn't bugged mine," I assured him. It was true too; I had it checked every few months by some of Tommy's employees.

"Just humor me," he said with a slight smile.

"Okay, Doc, the floor is all yours."

"I contacted Olivia and informed her of what's happened here." He raised his hand to stop me arguing. "Yes, I'm aware you asked me not to. But Tommy would yell for a very long time if he'd not been told. He asked if you needed help and I said you'd let him know. I think while he'd drop everything to come back here, it would be a strain on Kasey. She's there for her naming ceremony after all. Not every day you get one of those."

While I could use Tommy and Olivia's help, Kasey was down there for a reason. Besides, they were safer away from me if people were trying to kill me.

"Anything else?" I asked.

Grayson placed his leather briefcase onto a nearby black metal flowerpot stand, and opened it with a loud click. He removed a piece of paper and passed it to me. "The information on the hostages."

I read through the list of names and their details—dates of birth, addresses, and a smattering of personal information—but nothing jumped out at me. "Okay, I don't get it," I said after reading it again just to make sure I wasn't missing something. "I was certain the Reavers were there for more than me. It was such a huge risk to take otherwise."

Grayson reached into his briefcase once again and passed me another piece of paper. This one contained only two names. The first was a seventy-six-year-old woman by the name of Liz Williams, and the second was for an eighty-two-year-old man by the name of Edward Williams. I compared the lists and the names appeared on both. "I don't get this either."

"The first list was the names of everyone there, compiled by the human police. I had someone run all of the names through a human database and that's the information we got. The second list was compiled by a friend of mine in the SOA."

"These two are Avalon?" I asked.

Grayson nodded. "Their files are sealed though."

That was interesting. I didn't know many people who had sealed files; normally that was reserved for people deep undercover, exceptionally powerful individuals, or those who had left Avalon.

"I assume you'll want to visit them," Grayson mentioned when I hadn't said anything for a while.

"I think that's probably a good idea." I pocketed the paper and re-entered my house to grab a set of car keys, and put some more clothes on.

"You know, you pissed off a lot of people by killing a man in the hospital," Grayson called from the doorway.

"I thought you were worried about bugs," I shouted back, as I picked up some shoes and socks and finished getting dressed.

"They already know you killed someone. Probably a lot of people by now."

"I haven't killed a lot of people since this morning," I said as I made my way back toward him.

"I meant, a lot of people know about you killing the Reaver."

"I know what you meant," I told him. "He came to kill me in a hospital. And he was a Reaver. I really don't have a problem with killing him."

"Me neither, but I wanted to let you know it annoyed Heather and some people who work at the hospital."

I glanced past Grayson at the orange and black Fiat Panda on my drive. It was the newer version of the car, so it no longer looked like the world's ugliest box. Instead it appeared like someone had taken a bigger car and squashed it. Then added chrome in an effort to make people forget about the rest of it. In short, it wasn't what I'd have called a looker. "Is that yours?"

"It's my work car. You'd be surprised how easy it is to damage your car, working with injured werewolves and the like."

"You want to follow me, so I can pretend I don't know you? Or do you just want to take my car? I'll drop you back here after."

"It's a very good car."

"Okay, but it's also a Fiat Panda."

Grayson held my gaze for a short time. "You're a bit of a car snob, aren't you?"

I nodded and clicked the button on the garage door opener. One of the three doors slowly moved up, revealing a Jaguar F-Type R, in British racing green. Otherwise known as dark green. It looked how a sports car should look: sleek, sophisticated, and sexy. Everything about it was as close to perfection as a car could be. It helped that it drove like a dream, as if the wide grille on the front of the car ate the road as it went.

I turned to Grayson as we reached the garage and he saw the Jaguar in all its glory. "Yes, I'm a bit of a car snob when given the option. You want to go out in your Panda, or in this?"

Grayson glanced over at his small car, and then back to the Jag. "Is it fast?"

I unlocked the car and we both got in, where I turned the engine on and allowed the sound of the V8 to wash over us. "Is it fast?" I asked. "A bit."

There are few cars that sound or look as good as the Jaguar, and from the smile on Grayson's face as we made our way toward the elderly couple on the list he'd given me, he agreed with me.

The constant use of my air magic while driving was an odd experience. I had to keep it activated until I was certain the venom had left my body, which would take several days. I was very aware that just one slip in concentration meant the venom would once again attack my body, and that would be very bad when driving at seventy miles per hour. It was a concern that I was sure Grayson shared as I felt him glancing my way every few minutes, and I was happy to leave the motorway and get back to city speed limits.

It didn't take long for us to reach the outskirts of the village that the Williamses lived in. Netley Abbey is a village that starts from the water's edge of the River Itchen and slowly rises up to a peak a mile away. It's full of old postwar housing, and new identi-kit flats, with a smattering of ancient buildings, such as the abbey the village was named after.

We drove past the abbey—an old, crumbling building, which is rumored to be haunted—and down the main road that crosses through the village. At the far end, we took the car toward Victoria Country Park, a massive place that used to house a hospital until the 1960s, when most of it was finally demolished, leaving only the hospital chapel to tower over the rest of the park.

I followed the Sat Nav and took a small road up away from the seafront and toward a gated community of several large houses, most of which had been converted into flats many years previously. I stopped at the gate and pressed the intercom button.

"Can I ask whom you're here to visit?" a man asked, his voice crackly with static through the small speaker.

"The Williams," Grayson called out. "It's a police matter."

There was a pause. "Do all police drive fancy cars?" the man replied.

"Open the gate and I'll show you my ID if you'd like," Grayson snapped.

There was no immediate reply, but soon after a heavyset man, wearing a dark blue uniform, appeared out of one of the building's front doors and almost swaggered over toward us.

"Don't you wish you were more of a punch people person?" I asked with a smile as Grayson ignored me and exited the car.

He removed his ID from his trouser pocket and passed it to the guard once he was close enough. The guard made a big deal out of looking at it, turning it over and over in his hands, as if somehow it would change from turn to turn. He grudgingly passed it back to Grayson and activated the nearby gate controls.

He watched intently as Grayson climbed back into the Jag and we drove onto the most exclusive patch of the small village, parking between a white and black BMW i8 and a blue Bentley Continental GT. Even my Jag felt out of place.

"Do you know where you're going?" the guard asked in the tone of someone who has just discovered that the people in front of him have more power than he does.

Grayson pointed to the building furthest from us. "Flat four," he said.

"Well, if you need anything," the guard told us cheerfully.

"We won't," I called back, which made Grayson grin as we reached the massive building's front door and entered into a lobby.

To suggest the interior of the building was every bit as grandiose as the stunning white exterior, would be a little like suggesting the sun was a bit warm. The lobby had a marble floor, intricate carvings on the wooden banister, and ornate mirrors all over the place. That and some artwork that didn't look like a five-year-old had done it on MS Paint. In short, it was the exact kind of lobby designed to take your breath away and get your wallets out.

"Wow," Grayson said as we walked past the spiral staircase, and stopped outside a lift whose golden-colored doors wore a mirror shine.

"It's pretty impressive, isn't it?"

The doors opened and the classical music inside settled over us.

"I have no idea who the Williams are," I said as the doors closed once Grayson pressed the number four button. "But doesn't this all seem a bit much to you? Marble floors and the like. I'd be scared to break something."

"That's because you're an uncouth ruffian," Grayson said with a laugh. "The more refined among us need not worry about breaking things; they merely glide through life, never really touching anything."

I paused and stared at Grayson as the doors opened. "That might be the single most depressing thing I've ever heard."

"I know," he said with a sigh.

A moment later he stopped walking and turned back to me. "We'll take this slow. We don't want to go spooking anyone."

As the Williamses' home was the only one on the whole floor, it wasn't exactly difficult to find. I knocked twice and waited for a few moments until the door was unlocked and pulled open slightly. The woman in the doorway was the same elderly woman from the hostage situation.

"Remember me?" I asked.

Liz Williams nodded.

"You feel like telling me why the Reavers want you or your husband dead?" I turned to Grayson, who appeared as though he'd like to find a big hole to climb into. "Slow enough for you?"

CHAPTER 

Liz Williams invited us both into her home, which turned out to be a tasteful and exquisitely furnished flat. She took Grayson and me through the massive, open-planned entrance and front room, to a small breakfast nook with a balcony that overlooked the wooded area of the park behind the house. Her husband, Edward, was already there, a pot of tea and four cups sitting on the table beside him.

"Waiting for us?" I asked.

"I'm a psychic," Liz told us. "I knew you'd be here today. Timing was a bit off though, I thought you'd be ten minutes ago."

"So, what are *you*, Mister Williams?" I asked.

"I'm an old man," he said with a smile. "And an enchanter. Mostly the former these days."

Grayson was staring at Liz. "I've never met a psychic who lived past forty. I've only heard of a few who made it to fifty."

"You can thank my husband for that," she said with a smile, and patted Edward's hand as she took a seat next to him. She lifted the sleeve of her blue blouse and showed us a black rune tattooed there. "It means I only use my ability when I want to. I can switch it off most of the time. It's a lifesaver. Literally." She poured four cups of tea. "You going to sit, or stand and make the place look untidy?"

Grayson and I did as we were told and sat down, taking the cups in front of us and adding milk and sugar as taste dictated; which for me consisted of just milk.

"The Reavers in West Quay. Were they after you both?" Grayson said.

"Just me," Liz said. "I did some work for a Reaver many years ago. Helped him root out some very bad people in his midst."

"You worked for Avalon?" I asked.

"We both did," Edward answered. "I was in the BOA."

The BOA, or Blade of Avalon, were Avalon's army. A group of highly trained warriors who defended Avalon from external threats.

"And you?" I asked Liz.

"LOA," she told us.

"How'd you end up working for the Reavers?" Grayson asked.

"I didn't work for them; I worked for a friend of mine, who happened to be working undercover as a member. He had been getting some notions that a few of the members of Avalon were no longer in it for the best of Avalon. Turns out those responsible were members of the Reavers. He went undercover to figure out who was involved, and I was going to help him, but he got killed before I could start. Avalon did nothing to help find his murderers, so I left Avalon and wanted nothing to do with them."

"The Reavers weren't meant to exist after the twentieth century," I pointed out.

"You're not meant to exist either, Hellequin," Liz said with a smile. "Yet here you are right before me."

I couldn't help but smile. "You got that from touching my hand back at West Quay. You must have some serious power."

"That's what everyone told me. As for your point, you're right; the Reavers were officially no longer an entity. Unofficially, well, you know how Avalon works."

Unfortunately, I did.

"And they want you to go back and do some more work for them?" Grayson asked.

"They came here a week ago," Liz said. "They wanted me to find someone for them."

"Who?" I asked.

Liz and Edward shared a glance.

"Who did they ask you to find, Mrs. Williams?" I repeated.

"Felix Novius," she said.

I paused and let the name wash over me. "Why would they want to find Felix?" I asked, keeping my voice steady.

Liz shrugged. "They weren't exactly forthcoming with information."

"Wait," I said, annoyed at myself for not realizing it earlier. "You need to be able to touch Felix to get a reading."

"Psychics do need contact to do a reading on someone," Liz agreed. "But they can also use something that a person has had contact with to be able to track them. Not all psychics can do it, but the more powerful of my kind certainly can."

"Did they have things with them that were from me and Felix?"

"I only saw one thing, although they took it with them when I refused to help."

A terrible feeling sat in my stomach. "What was it?"

Liz nodded. "A piece of shrapnel; it was a torn and twisted piece of metal. It was covered in dried blood, so I couldn't see what it would have looked like clean."

"It was about this big?" I asked, moving my fingers a few inches apart.

"Yes, that's right."

"How do you know that?" Grayson asked me.

"Because the blood on it is Felix's. He saved my life and took the blast from a bomb."

"Who planted the bomb?" Grayson asked.

"Jack the Ripper."

Everyone stared at me for a few seconds. "So the blood on the shrapnel was over a hundred years old?" Grayson asked.

I nodded. "Must have been."

"So, who was the evil bastard?" Edward asked. "Jack I mean."

"That's complicated," I said, unwilling to elaborate further. "But I don't understand how anyone could keep the shrapnel safe for all these years. It would be a hell of a feat."

"Magically, one assumes," Liz said.

Edward nodded. "Runes could do it. Stick it in a box and leave it there. That would work. The question is, why bother?"

"And why come after him now?" I asked. "If the Reavers had the shrapnel, why wait? And if they didn't, then who did?"

"I don't know," Liz said, "but they were very insistent when they first arrived here."

"You refused?" Grayson asked.

"Of course," Edward said. "But they're not exactly good at taking no for an answer. The runes on this place make it impossible for anyone to get in here without us wanting them. But they followed us to West Quay. They cornered us in that jewelers and demanded that we help them. The griffin wasn't there then, just the other two. One of the other customers saw a gun and raised the alarm. The next thing we know everyone's a hostage and they start hitting me until Liz talks."

"You agreed to help?" I asked, without judgment.

Liz nodded. "Didn't have much of a choice. They told me that once they were finished, they'd take Edward and me away to help them."

"One of the three Reavers told me that they wanted me to die in public," I told them. "I was to be an execution to show their enemies that they were powerful."

"I touched the hand of one of those men," Liz told me. "He wanted you dead, Nathan. I saw the burning hatred in his soul for you."

"When they first took the hostages there were only two of them," Edward said. "Then they made a phone call and told whoever was on the other end to check on their next target, I assume that was you, Nathan. They wanted to check you were in."

"So they know where I live. Well, that's not reassuring. Although if they wanted to attack me there, they already would have, maybe this morning's incident has given them a reason to pause and be concerned about attacking me again."

"They're not going to stop," Liz said. "They're fanatical."

"It's a concern to think how many more are out there," Grayson said.

"Two of them won't be a concern to anyone ever again." I drank the remainder of my tea.

After I'd been silent for a while, Grayson asked, "You okay?"

I nodded. "Publicly executing me was never the original plan. Not in West Quay anyway; they had to improvise when it all kicked off. They were watching me already, probably planning an attack at my property." I paused. "You know, I came here to get answers, but have ended up telling you both more than I probably should have. Why is that?"

"There are runes in the flat," Grayson said. "They get people to be open and honest. It's impressive work."

Liz smiled. "How'd you know? You're not an enchanter."

"I'm not easy to deceive."

I glanced at Grayson. I had no idea what he actually *was*, but I was certainly intrigued.

"Okay, honesty time," I told Edward and Liz. "Why did they come to you? I'm sure they know other psychics."

"That's a long story," Liz said.

"We have time," I told her. My words were slightly harder than I'd planned. I was annoyed at the revelation of the runes making me talkative, although whether I was more annoyed at them or at me for not noticing it, it was hard to tell.

"Like I told you, my friend, who I worked for, was killed a few days after he asked for my help. I was the first to his house after his death, and I took a lot of the information he'd been gathering about those he thought were his comrades in arms. I took it all to my superiors in the SOA. That was forty years ago. I quit Avalon soon after and, with a little help, went into hiding with Edward."

"Who were the people in the files?" I asked.

"I didn't look. I knew if I did that someone would kill me for it. My supervisor at the time was a psychic, he'd have known if I was lying. Like I said, they didn't do a thing to help find my friend's murderer; I didn't trust them to keep me alive if they thought I was a threat."

"So how did anyone find you?" I asked.

Liz shrugged. "I don't know. But I'm not moving. I'm not running. If they want to come for me, they're more than welcome to. They know where we are."

I was impressed with Liz's determination to not be scared or bullied into leaving the place she called home. I glanced across the thick treetops that littered the view for several miles behind the house. I probably wouldn't want to leave here either.

"It can't just be the three of them," I said. "Let's say the griffin was at my house, someone had to decide he needed to leave. It certainly wasn't those two incompetent idiots I killed. That means there are more involved. The last time I dealt with the Reavers, their organization wasn't massive, but it was full of devoted individuals."

"I'd put money that nothing has changed," Edward said.

I glanced down at the car park beneath us, and noticed that the guard who'd let us through the gates was searching through the boot of his car; his back was toward us and he didn't appear to be overly concerned about anyone watching him.

"His name is Mortimer," Liz told me. "He's worked here for years. While he's a bit of a stickler for the rules, he's a nice enough man."

"Does he know that you're not human?" Grayson asked.

Both of them shook their heads. "This is a mostly human community," Edward said. "No one here knows who, or what, we really are."

I glanced back down at the car park, but it was now empty. A few seconds later the intercom buzzed and Edward got up to answer it.

Liz reached out and grabbed her husband, bringing his head in for a kiss on the cheek. "I love you, you crazy old bastard," she whispered.

He held her gaze for a heartbeat. "Right back at you, beautiful."

Liz released Edward and he walked off to answer the door.

"Thanks for your help," I told Liz, while she looked away toward where Edward had walked.

She smiled. "You're welcome. If the Reavers have targeted you, they won't stop, and if they can't get to you directly—"

"They'll find other means, I know," I finished for her. "I'm hoping to cut that idea off at the pass. Do you have any idea where those in charge will be?"

"Avalon," Liz said without hesitation. "The most powerful of them will be in Avalon. I don't know what game they're playing, I don't think anyone outside of their organization does, but when I investigated them it involved high-ranking Avalon members."

"Did you ID them?" Grayson asked.

Liz shook her head. "I'd be wary of Avalon if I were you. You don't know who's a friend. And it sounds like the Reavers have a plan in motion."

"Pretty much par for course with Avalon," I said with a slight sigh. "I'll look into the Reavers. If their plan is to see me dead, I'd really rather they didn't get the opportunity to complete it."

Liz sighed and took my hands in hers. "This is where it all begins for you, Nathan."

"Where what begins?"

"Eventually you'll discover the truth, eventually you'll learn exactly who you are. But there's going to be an awful lot of pain and death between now and then."

"You're a lot more powerful than you let on, aren't you?" I asked.

Liz nodded. “I wish I knew who was behind everything, but I can’t see them, only you. Everyone’s face is a blur except yours. All I know is that you need to go to Avalon for answers. Can I give you some advice?”

It was my turn to nod.

“Sometimes you have to trust those who have never given you reason to do so. Sometimes you have to be the bigger man and accept the past for what it was, if you have any hope of moving forward. And sometimes you have to bury everyone who dares oppose you. You’ll have to do all three at some point. I just hope you can figure out what goes where.”

“And if I can’t?” I asked.

She held my gaze like she was made of granite. “Then we’re all fucked.”

I opened my mouth to speak but a doorbell rang and Edward called out a few seconds later, “Just Mortimer, he’s got a parcel for you.”

“I guess that’s our cue to leave,” Grayson said.

We got up from the table and Liz offered both of us her hand. “Remember what I said, Nathan,” she told me. “I wish you luck in your investigation.”

“I’ll find out who did this. I’ll stop them before they come after you.”

“I know you’ll try,” she said with a smile, and led us both into the front room, where Edward was talking to Mortimer about the weather.

Edward motioned for Mortimer to wait for a second and came over to shake hands with Grayson and me. “It was a pleasure,” he said with a genuine smile.

"Thanks for your time," I told him and Liz opened the front door and we stepped through into the hallway.

The unmistakable sound of a gun being fired echoed out of the front door almost the second the door was shut behind us. I spun and kicked the door as hard as possible, but it didn't budge.

"Damn runes," I snapped.

"Let me try," Grayson said as a second shot rang out. He kicked the door just under the lock and the entire side of the doorframe disintegrated from the power behind it.

We were both through the ruined door before I'd had time to consider what Grayson had done. Edward was on the floor, blood staining the carpet beneath him. "Go," Grayson shouted. "I'll check if he's alive."

A third shot sounded out from the kitchen, and I vaulted over the nearby couch and ran toward the noise. I entered the room and saw Mortimer, his expression fixed on Liz as she stood up. He turned slightly and fired the gun at me, tearing through the plaster near where my head would have been if I hadn't dived aside, over the kitchen table.

I stood in time to see the first bullet take Liz in the jaw, almost completely removing it, and spinning her aside. The second slammed into the back of her head, pushing her onto the floor. I was already back on my feet and moving toward the shooter, when he put his foot on the nape of her neck, holding her steady so that a third crashed into the back of her head.

Mortimer spun toward me; but rage and power fueled my run and I collided with him, forcing him back over the breakfast table and through the balcony doors with a crash. He slammed the gun into the side of my head and tried to push me away, but I wasn't about to be denied. I blasted him in the chest with a torrent of air.

Mortimer was thrown back at the balcony, which tore like paper from the force of the magic I'd used. A second later Mortimer impacted with the roof of whoever's car was under him. He wasn't going to be getting back up anytime soon. Except he then rolled off the car roof onto the ground and stuck one finger up at me.

I didn't think twice and jumped from the balcony, using my air magic to slow myself before I hit the ground. The amount of magic I expelled to make the considerable fall doable without injury caused the ground beneath my feet to crack as I impacted.

Mortimer ran toward his car, and his head whipped around to see me stalking toward him. He raised his gun in my direction, but a ball of flame struck the weapon before he could fire, and he dropped it.

I walked toward him without pause. He reached inside the car boot and I sprinted the remaining few feet, my fist connecting with the side of his jaw, snapping him around and dumping him on the ground. I kicked him in the ribs as hard as my magically enhanced strength allowed and felt one of them buckle from the blow.

He rolled aside from a second kick and drew a small silver dagger, waving it toward me as he got back to his feet.

Any questions I might have asked about why he was suddenly trying to kill me would have resulted in him telling me to go fuck myself with various implements. I knew the type, I'd spent several hours cutting pieces off the type, and it normally takes a lot of effort for a small benefit. People like him, sent in to kill in such a brazen manner, aren't meant to be able to tell anyone anything, because they don't know anything.

He came at me with the knife, which I pushed aside with a blast of air and drove my fist into his stomach, before unleashing a second blast, which threw him back over his car's bonnet and to the ground beside his vehicle.

Mortimer quickly ran to the rear of his car and drew a silver machete out of the still-open boot. He waved it around wildly, before running at me. He screamed like a madman the entire time he came at me, a lunatic given form. I wasn't about to take chances.

I slammed a blast of air into his chest, probably breaking a few more ribs in the process, knocking his weapon aside, and throwing him back up against his car's rear windscreen, which shattered from the impact.

"They deserved it," he said as he got back to his feet.

"I don't care," I told him and wrapped coils of air around his arm, increasing the pressure, wrapping it tighter and tighter like an anaconda until Mortimer screamed out in pain when the bone snapped like a brittle twig.

"The Reavers should have stayed dead," I said.

The shadow that was suddenly cast over me was the first clue I had, allowing me to move in time to dodge the griffin's attack, and put a little distance between us.

"You're not dead. I'm sort of impressed," the griffin told me.

I released the air magic around Mortimer and threw it at the griffin's wings, which couldn't handle the newly twisting and turning current. It blew him back several feet. After putting some space between me and the greatest threat, I sprinted toward

Mortimer, grabbing the silver machete without pause, and driving it into his stomach.

"Stay put," I told him, punching him in the face, knocking him out, before I pulled the machete out.

I turned back to the griffin, who had recovered from his momentary lack of equilibrium and held a sword in one hand. "I'm going to cut your head off for what you've done," he seethed.

"Anything in particular?" I asked as I shrugged off my jacket, tossing it onto the top of a nearby car. "I mean, there's probably a long list of things I've done to piss people off."

"I've changed my mind. First of all I'm going to cut out your damn tongue."

"Good luck with that."

The griffin's massive wings beat once and then he swooped toward me, the sword gleaming in his hand. I readied myself for a fight. And then he stopped. Not slowed to stop, just ceased to move toward me. His head snapped up toward the building. I followed his gaze and found Grayson standing on the ruined balcony of the Williamses' home. He was just standing there, staring at the griffin without anger or concern. I couldn't have told you what he was thinking if someone had offered me a million pounds to do so.

The griffin screamed. Not from pain, but out of pure fear. He saw Grayson standing motionless and wanted to be as far away from him as possible. He flew back several feet and then dove toward Mortimer, grabbing him before I could get to them and flying off above the trees.

I glanced up at Grayson. What the hell had happened here?

CHAPTER 9

Grayson contacted the LOA and they arrived about five minutes after the griffin flew away, leaving me twiddling my thumbs. They asked over and over again why we were visiting the Williamses, presumably hoping that we were going to break under their incredible interrogation techniques, while they checked out who we were.

Once they finally got the information about who I was, and that Grayson was an ex-LOA doctor, they backed off and gave us some space.

"So what the hell happened?" I whispered to Grayson. "That griffin was terrified of you."

"He was a little bit, wasn't he? Presumably he knew he couldn't take on two of us and the reality of the situation hit him. It happens."

"No, it doesn't," I argued. "But I assume you're not going to tell me what you are."

Grayson looked me in the eyes. "That's a pretty good bet."

"Well, that's a fucking surprise," Agent Kelly Jensen shouted as she made her way through the throng of people who had come to clean up the mess that Grayson and I had been involved in.

"Yes, yes, I'm involved in something bad again," I said with just enough annoyance in my voice to make it known that taunting me was probably a bad idea.

"Actually I'm surprised you're still alive. Everyone seems to want you dead."

"Apparently I'm really popular with a certain demographic of psychopath. Makes me feel all warm inside."

"Still no ideas *why* everyone wants you dead though?"

"They're Reavers," I told her. "They hold a grudge."

Agent Jensen appeared shocked for a second before regaining her composure. "You sure about that, that it was the Reavers, I mean?"

I nodded. "The void in the hospital, he showed me their mark. They're Reavers. Back from the dead, which is where their entire fucking group should have stayed."

Anger flashed across Agent Jensen's face; apparently she wasn't a big fan of the Reavers either. "Damn it," she snapped, before taking her phone out of her pocket and walking off.

"She's not very happy," Grayson said. "I assume you're planning on visiting Avalon."

I was loath to return to Avalon, especially considering it might put people I cared about in danger, but hopefully I could get in, get what I needed, and leave before anyone tried to kill me. "According to Liz, that's where the person in charge is, and she told me I'd find answers to the Reavers there."

"You know that if she's right, then you arriving there is going to cause all kinds of problems the second you step foot in the place. You need to take someone with you that you can trust."

"You offering your services, Doc?"

Grayson shook his head. "Avalon isn't very welcoming to me. I don't think my presence would help matters."

"Wait, you worked for the LOA. For Olivia. And Avalon doesn't like you?"

"I doubt Olivia made it well known that I was helping her. I'm sorry, Nathan, I can't accompany you."

I was about to say more when Agent Jensen reappeared. "Do you know anything else about the murderer?"

"His name was Mortimer," I said. "He was a guard of some sort. Is there anything in Avalon's records about him?"

Jensen shook her head. "Not a damn thing. We'll find him though. And that griffin. Just try to stay out of trouble for a while. Are you going to be staying at your house?"

"I'll be around," I said, not wanting to tell her about Avalon. "You've got my number if you need me."

Jensen didn't appear to like my answer, but accepted it without comment and walked off again.

When she was out of earshot, I turned to Grayson and said, "After that, I'm even more convinced that something is off here."

"You think she was lying?"

"I think the SOA aren't above keeping information to themselves if they think it'll benefit them long term. Something isn't right, and I can't quite put my finger on it."

"Even more off than Reavers wanting you dead?"

"People want me dead quite often, it's an occupational hazard for living the life I do. But there's more to this than revenge on Liz and me. The Reavers stayed quiet for a long time. Liz's friend investigated them when they first reappeared, but that was forty years ago, and he was murdered for his trouble. What have they been doing between then and now? They've reappeared now for a very good reason, and that reason has to do with Felix Novius."

I paused for a moment while I tried to figure out what I was missing. "I'm sure the SOA know more than they're willing to share. The question is why? Unless they're investigating the Reavers themselves. That could be it; maybe the SOA were looking into the Reavers, but they couldn't shut them down before they did all of this."

"You think they're keeping it quiet so as not to cause any political problems for themselves?" Grayson asked.

"It's certainly in keeping with Kay. He wouldn't want to be embarrassed by the knowledge that his people were investigating something that blew up in his face. Kay was angry enough about the Vanguard attacks that took place at Hades's compound last year. If it got out that two threats attacked Avalon personnel in the space of twelve months, people might start asking about his suitability, and the professionalism of his people."

"You need to talk to Kay?"

"No, Lucie Moser. Kay will lie, and lie well. Lucie isn't stupid, she's his deputy, so she knows what's going on. I can't imagine her allowing anyone under her command to fuck up an investigation and then hide it. Looks like I have more reasons to go to Avalon."

"Anything you want me to check while you're gone?"

"Can you keep an eye on things around here? If the Reavers have gone after me, they might go after others. Contact the LOA too, see if they know anything. That okay with you?"

Grayson nodded. "Of course. I'm happy to help. These people need stopping, and I doubt they're going to be satisfied with the murders of the Williamses."

"You're not wrong," I said with a heavy heart. I hadn't been quick enough to save Liz or Edward. I wouldn't make that mistake again. Their murderers would be brought to justice.

"Nathan Garrett," one of the SOA agents called out.

"Yeah, what's up?" I shouted back.

A young man walked over to me, a clipboard in one hand and pen in the other. "You're Nathan Garrett?"

"I hope so; I'd hate to have spent all my life pissing people off only to find I have the wrong name."

The agent didn't smile.

"You're free to go." He turned to Grayson. "You too, Doc. If we need anything more, we'll let you know."

"Make sure Liz and Edward get Avalon funerals," I said.

"They're not Avalon. They both quit."

I grabbed the agent by his shirt and dragged him over to me. "They both get treated like damn heroes, or I come back, find you, and stuff this clipboard up your ass. I've had a shit day; people I liked have been killed in front of me. They worked for Avalon, they deserve an Avalon funeral."

"We'll arrange it," Agent Jensen said, as she arrived next to me. "They'll be taken care of, I promise."

I released the agent. "Sorry," I said softly. "Long day."

He smoothed down his shirt, his eyes always on me, as if challenging me to continue my manhandling of him. He wanted a fight right there and then, and that was all because I'd let the day's events make me angry and it had spilled out onto someone who was undeserving of it.

"Sorry," I repeated and then walked off back to my car with Grayson.

"Are you okay?" he asked as we climbed back into the Jag.

"No," I admitted. "But when I find more of those Reavers, and wring their murdering necks, I will be."

I dropped Grayson off outside Tommy's main office in Basingstoke, and made a call, which got picked up on the third ring.

"Hello," a man asked.

"Gordon, is that you?"

"Nathaniel, what a pleasure, it's been too long. How are you?"

Gordon Summers was the pack aide to Matthew Sheppard, who just happened to be the male alpha for the largest werewolf pack in England, and one of the largest in all of Europe. He was also one of the twelve members of the werewolf contingent to Avalon. Basically, Matthew was a very big deal, and a very powerful man.

"I'd love to chat," I said. "But I need your help. Are you around?"

"Come over, we'll be here," Gordon said, his voice immediately serious.

I thanked him and hung up. I hadn't seen Gordon or Matthew for a few years, but I'd heard that Matthew had finally appointed a female alpha, something the pack had been sorely missing, as it had allowed Matthew's enemies to try and lay claim to his pack, resulting in the deaths of innocent people.

I stopped my car at the entrance to what, the last time I was here, had been a large field. It had been changed into a car park, albeit a nice one with lots of flowers and trees around. There was a hut at the far end, and I noticed another two guards standing outside it. One of the two men standing at the gate walked over to me, sniffing the air as I lowered the car's window. I didn't recognize either of them. Matthew had eliminated any trace of the taint that his enemies had put in his pack, and it had grown in stature and power as a result.

He signaled to his friend, who pulled the gate aside and motioned for me to drive through. I did as asked and parked before getting out into what was now drizzle. I was grateful the field had gone; otherwise, I doubted I would have been able to get my car out without a tow truck.

The walk from the parking area to the pack's main living area was a few minutes, giving me time to notice the snipers who were still placed in the trees above me. Matthew was even more careful than before about his and his pack's safety.

I entered a massive clearing where the pack met once a month. Several children were running around the place; the weather not really an issue to them. I walked past one of three huge fire-pits, when I heard someone call my name.

Gordon, umbrella in tow so that his expensive suit didn't get wet, limped toward me, a smile on his face. He embraced me with one arm, keeping the umbrella above us both at all times. "It really is good to see you," he said.

"I keep meaning to come over and say hi, but the last time I was here—" The last time I was there I took the pack to war. Not all of them had made it back. "I need someone I can trust."

"You want me or Matthew?"

I shook my head. "Matthew's too important. And you're too—"

"Injured?" Gordon asked.

I stopped walking a few feet from Matthew and Gordon's house. "Really? You don't think I'd ask you because of your limp? I saw you fight; I'd ask you in a heartbeat. But without you, Matthew would be intolerable."

A recognizable laugh came from the front door of the house. I hadn't heard Matthew open it, but he stood on top of the steps leading up to the beautiful home, wearing only a pair of jeans. He jumped down the stairs and ran over to me, grabbing me in a massive hug.

"Do you think me so awful that I could not cope without my man, here?" Matthew released me, and leaned over, kissing Gordon. "You're free to go with him, but why don't we discuss this inside, where it isn't raining."

"Why don't you wear a coat?" I asked. "Or a shirt or hell, a towel would be good."

Matthew flexed his considerable muscle and laughed. "If you had this upper body, you wouldn't wear a shirt either."

"If I had your upper body, I'd shave some stuff," I said, making Gordon laugh and pretend to cough into his hand.

"My hair is manly," Matthew retorted, in a mock indignant tone.

"I have a hairy chest," I said. "Yours looks like you might have animals hiding in it."

Gordon gave up on the pretext of pretending not to laugh and hurriedly made his way into the house.

"I believe my better half enjoys your mocking of me," Matthew said with a gleam in his eye, as he looked over at the front door.

"I believe your better half went inside where it's warm and dry."

Matthew glanced back at me. “Point taken, let’s go.”

I followed Matthew and couldn’t help but smile. Matthew and Gordon’s relationship had been one that was responsible for certain people in his pack going against him. Matthew had seen the appointment of a female alpha, not as a necessary part of a strong pack, but as a lie to his relationship. I was glad to see that since accepting what he needed to do, he was also more open with Gordon.

The change was evident inside the house, too. While Matthew had told me that he hadn’t kept his relationship a secret, there had been nothing to suggest that they were together. Now, pictures of them both adorned the walls of the house; it felt different, more comfortable.

Matthew led me into the front room. Gordon followed a few moments later with a pot of tea, a jug of milk, and some cups on a tray.

I sat down in a very comfortable leather armchair and waited for Gordon to finish pouring drinks and giving them out. As Matthew’s pack aide, it was his job to keep things running smoothly, to deal with problems before Matthew had to get involved.

“I can pour the tea,” Matthew commented.

“I love you dearly, Matthew, but we both know that what you call tea, I would affectionately call cups of warm watery milk.”

Matthew sat down opposite me. “And they’re the best damn cups of warm watery milk you’ll ever drink.”

“That they are,” Gordon said with a chuckle.

“Enough frivolity,” Matthew declared. “You came seeking our help. What do you need?”

I told them both about everything that had happened from the hostage situation to having called Gordon. They both listened intently, neither asking questions until I'd finished.

Matthew placed his cup back on the saucer. "You sure they're Reavers?"

I nodded. "You've had dealings with them?"

"Once back in 1532, or was it 1535? I forget. Either way, I was less than impressed with our time together. They say they're working for Avalon, but on the evidence I saw, they work only for themselves or whoever gives them the most money. They're a corrupt organization that gets away with more than most on the basis of some kind of tenuous link to Avalon. No one outside of the group knows who's in charge; it's all far too much cloak and dagger for my liking. But what does it have to do with you being here?"

"I need to go to Avalon," I said. "I need someone to watch my back. Someone I can trust not to be involved with the Reavers, and someone I know can handle themselves if anything happens."

"We'd be happy to help," Matthew said. "My pack members will be happy to help too."

"I didn't want to involve your pack. I don't want to bring more pain to your people, but I'm short on time. I'm sorry for that."

"Nonsense," Matthew exclaimed. "My pack thinks highly of you. The children here are regaled with tales of how we fought alongside you, killing something evil. You never, ever have to feel guilty about people who died helping you. You can go out there and talk to their children and they will look you in the eyes and tell you how proud they are of the people they lost. How proud they are that their names will go down in pack history as warriors of virtue. If I went out there right now and told them that Hellequin needed their help, I'd have more people here than I knew what to do with."

I smiled. "Thank you."

"Is that why we haven't seen you? You're concerned about dragging us into your life once more?"

Matthew stood and strode over to me, lifting me onto my feet. "You are welcome here any time." He hugged me. "But on this occasion, I don't think I'll need to get a volunteer. I know someone who's already going to Avalon. She'll join you. She's on her way there for Kasey's naming ceremony."

"Ellie?" I asked. I knew that Kasey and she had grown close over the years.

"She's going down there for Kasey's naming ceremony as one of her sentinels," Gordon said. "She couldn't get away from pack duty until now, so she's been here. I called her while I was making tea, she'll be here shortly."

Matthew slapped me on the back, and my lungs protested that they weren't meant to try and come out of my chest.

The three of us sat and drank tea, talking about various topics to catch up until Ellie arrived twenty minutes later. She walked into the room wearing a pair of dark green combats, an orange T-shirt, and with her dark blue hair pulled back into a ponytail. She saw me and smiled.

It didn't take long before Matthew had explained everything to Ellie, who looked over at me when they'd finished and smiled. "Road trip," she said.

"Looks that way, you sure you're okay with me tagging along?"

"Do you have a change of clothes?"

To be honest, I hadn't thought about it. "I guess we'll need to swing by my place."

"Good, you can drive. Saves me taking my car too. If needs be I can always get a lift back with Tommy and Olivia."

"What am I going to do without my alpha?" Matthew asked.

"Hopefully nothing stupid," Ellie replied with a smirk.

"I'll keep him out of trouble," Gordon assured everyone.

"You do all realize I'm right here, yes?" Matthew asked which got a laugh from everyone in the room.

Once Ellie and I had left Matthew's house, with both of us promising to keep safe, we went back to my car and then took the hour or so drive back to my house. Ellie waited in the car while I grabbed some clothes from my bedroom and threw them in my bag, along with my jian and a silver dagger. If the griffin reappeared, I was going to be prepared.

I climbed back into the car and we set off on the four-hour journey.

CHAPTER 10

"So, it appears that congratulations are in order," I said to Ellie as I drove onto the A31 dual carriageway.

"Thanks. Being an alpha is a lot of responsibility, but I'm enjoying it. It's been over a year now, and no one has challenged me for the position, so I guess I'm doing something right."

"I'm glad to hear it."

We were both quiet for a moment. "You can say it, you know," Ellie eventually said.

"What?" I asked.

"That I've only been a werewolf for eighteen years, that's very young to be an alpha."

"I didn't want to bring up any unpleasant discussions."

"I was twenty-six when that bastard turned me," she said softly. "In eighteen years, it doesn't look like I've aged a day. I hate him for what he did to me, but if I can be strong, then others like me, those who weren't born a werewolf, those who were turned by a maniac, maybe they'll gain something from that."

"I'm happy for you. It takes a lot to put what you went through behind you."

"Yeah, well, it helped that someone tore his head off. Saved me the job."

The man who'd changed her was a nasty piece of shit by the name of Neil Hatchell. He'd been a werewolf who'd raped and bitten a number of women, the latter act turning each of them into werewolves. Without the aid of a pack when they had their first change, most of the women died or were mentally broken. Eventually, something even more evil than Neil decided he was better without his head. Precisely zero people mourned his passing.

For several miles we listened to the various local radio stations, none of which played anything I was a huge fan of, until Ellie said, "You know, you're a real idiot sometimes."

I wanted to slam on the brakes and ask where the hell that had come from; instead I waited for her to continue.

"You know why I'm going to Avalon, yes?" she asked.

"Kasey's naming ceremony. Gordon told me."

"You know that Kasey wanted to ask you to be her second sentinel."

"What, why?" I asked, taken aback by the news, and I decided it best to leave the road and park the car outside a small pub.

Naming ceremonies were carried out for all of those who wished to take part in Avalon life, and had started to show their powers. The person being named was then granted the full privileges of anyone of Avalon, including being able to work for them and use those appointed for their species, such as Matthew for the werewolves, to push forward a vote that they wanted. Kasey, at fifteen, was still considered a child, and would be until she turned eighteen, but it was a big step toward her life in Avalon.

Each named person got to pick up to two people to be their sentinels. They couldn't be family, and had to be people who would take responsibility to help show the named how to use their abilities, and live within the world they were accepting. It was an honor to be asked.

"I don't understand. Kasey never asked me, not once," I explained.

"She knows that you and Avalon aren't exactly best friends. She didn't want you to feel like you had to go, like you had no choice. She didn't want you to feel uncomfortable. So she simply didn't ask you. I'm surprised you didn't think it might be worth talking to her about, didn't you realize she might ask you?"

I sighed and shook my head. "She should have said something."

"She might have done if she hadn't heard you say that you wouldn't go back there if you could manage it."

"I was talking to Tommy. I didn't mean to . . . hell, if she'd have asked me I'd have gone back there like a shot."

"Tommy and Olivia told her that, but she didn't want to risk it. She looks up to you like an uncle. I think if you'd have said no to her, it would have hurt more than she wanted to admit."

"I don't even know what I can offer." During the ceremony sentinels state what they would bring to the table.

"Are you serious? Hellequin doesn't know what he can give her?"

"Ah, yes I think the ability to murder people, might not be the way she wants to go. These things are logged forever. Kasey gets paperwork with what the sentinels say on it."

"You can protect her, you can always be there for her, and you can help her. You cannot be so damn blind not to realize she needs you."

"Who did she get to do it?"

"She hasn't decided yet. There are some people in Avalon she wants to ask. But if you get there first, she'd love it to be you."

I sighed. "I've never done this before."

"This is my first time too. I had two friends be my sentinels. We were all terrified together." Anyone not born into their abilities can also undertake the naming ceremony; it's exactly the same process.

"I mean I never had a naming ceremony," I corrected. "I got all of the paperwork and the like, but never had a ceremony."

"How the hell does that happen?"

"It wasn't high on anyone's list at the time. I was twelve, nearly thirteen, when I started to show my magic. I wasn't given the chance to do anything else before Merlin told everyone we were off to China." The memory brought with it fresh anger. For centuries, I'd believed I was in China with Merlin, I'd remembered the journey, learning the language. It was all a lie.

"I think you must be the only person I've met who never had one."

"It was less popular back when I was young, certainly less of a big deal than it is now. People want the ceremony and all that goes with it; it's a sort of rite of passage. But back then, we were all too busy, and it wasn't seen as an important thing to do."

"I feel bad for calling you an idiot now."

"Don't. Why didn't Tommy or Olivia mention it to me?"

"It's her decision at the end of the day. Both of them knew she wanted to ask you, but she'd decided not to, so that was that. She made them promise not to tell you. She didn't make me promise, though."

"When we get to Avalon, I'll go find her. I'll tell her I'll do whatever she likes. My dislike of Avalon has nothing to do with not wanting to be there for something that's important for her."

I put my foot down and we soon returned to the dual carriageway, although this time I was driving a bit quicker than I had been a few minutes earlier.

The remaining two and a half hours of driving were done in relative quiet, as Ellie took the time to get some sleep. She woke as we reached the outskirts of Tintagel village in Cornwall.

"We there yet?" she asked.

I told her exactly where we were.

"Tintagel, eh? How long has it been since you were last here?"

"Over a century," I admitted. Things had certainly changed since I was last in the area. There were more houses and shops, and at some point in the 1990s people had come to excavate the nearby castle—Tintagel Castle—as it was believed incorrectly to be the birthplace of King Arthur. Olivia had informed me a while back that the number of tourists was negligible; the village kept the number of accommodations low as a way to control the number of outside visitors.

"Damn Monmouth," I said as I drove past several obvious tourists, taking photos of everything and everyone in sight.

"What?" Ellie asked.

"Geoffrey of Monmouth. He was the guy who wrote the *History of the Kings of Britain*. In it, he wrote about Arthur. It took a long time for Avalon to get people to believe it was all myth, and even then, centuries later, people still want to believe that his words were the truth."

"Everything he wrote was true?"

I shook my head. "Most of it was half-truths, rumors he'd heard from working with Avalon, that sort of thing. But in amongst it all were kernels of truth; such as Arthur being born in this area. At some point that became the idea that he was born in Tintagel Castle, despite it not having been built when Arthur was born. Oh, and he wrote a lot about Merlin, who I can tell you was less than pleased to play a starring role in someone's story. After that, it was made known that anyone publicizing his or her knowledge about us will be killed."

The practice had lessened somewhat over the years, and now anyone trying to reveal information about Avalon and its allies are only discredited and vilified. It's still a crime to publicize our existence, but actually discovering it isn't even frowned upon. I have no idea how it's enforced, what with the increasing use of the Internet, but as we haven't been on the front page of every newspaper in the world, I guess it's working.

I drove through the small village and parked outside an ancient building. The old dark stones that had been used to build the property had vines that ran up the side of them, presumably to help keep the building upright.

"Who lives here?" Ellie asked.

"Nathaniel Garrett," a voice boomed from the newly opened front door.

"Lir," I said with a smile.

Lir enveloped me in his gigantic arms, but I never felt crushed. He was well aware of his own strength. Eventually he released me and held out his hand for Ellie to shake.

"I assume this isn't a personal visit?" he asked in his thick Irish accent as he rubbed his beard. "You want to go to Avalon?"

I nodded and he beckoned both Ellie and me into his home.

Lir's home was barren, and the little furniture he had—which amounted to a small coffee table, a unit with a TV which had probably been purchased twenty years ago, and a bookcase overflowing with miscellaneous crap—was all handmade, and so held the same rugged look that Lir himself had.

The couch was a collection of large beanbags, which threatened to envelope me as I sat down. The entire room smelled like cannabis, and I suspected that no amount of window opening or scented candles was going to change that. The smell was part of the building now.

"I've always liked a spliff," he said as if aware of my thoughts. "It calms me."

"Probably for the best then," I said, which got a laugh from him. A calm Lir was unpredictable at best, but one who's lost to his emotions was downright deadly.

"You want a drink?" he asked Ellie and me.

"What have you got?" Ellie asked.

"Tea, ale, vodka, water, and coffee. I've discovered in my travels that a man needs very little else."

"Water, please."

"Same for you, Nathaniel?"

"Yes, and you can call me Nate."

"Nate, what kind of name is that?" Lir asked with a shake of his head.

"What kind of name is Lir?" I asked before I could stop myself.

Lir's smile dropped. "It's the one me dad gave me," he said sternly.

"I was jesting," I quickly told him. "Meant nothing by it."

Lir smiled again. "I know, just pissing about. Back in a second."

"Who is this guy?" Ellie asked when we were alone. "And is he high right now?"

"Probably, yes. He usually is. As for who he is, Lir is a water elemental. People used to think of him as the god of the sea, or at least the Irish did. That was before his son took over, and Lir settled for living in a small house and smoking pot."

"And he can get us to Avalon?"

Apart from being an organization that existed throughout the world, it was also an island about ten miles off the Cornish coast of England. The only way to get to the island is to use a ferry crossing. There are three. One of which goes from a private harbor just outside of Tintagel, one from the western coast of Wales, and one from Ireland. The ships that go have a water elemental of exceptional power on board, making the normally incredibly dangerous crossing a much safer prospect. At a certain level of power, elementals can fuse themselves with their elements, allowing them a much easier time of controlling them. They have to be careful not to lose their mind within the element, however, as their body can become broken up over a vast distance, especially with water elementals. But it does mean that they can control large amounts of their element at once.

"He'll talk to the harbor master for us," I explained. "I might not be well thought of in Avalon; the island or the organization. They may refuse to take me, or tell me I have to wait until they clear it with Avalon themselves. Neither of which are good. I'm hoping Lir can smooth things over."

"And how is he going to do that?"

"My natural fucking charm," Lir stated and placed the tray containing a jug of water with slices of lemon in it, and three glasses. He poured the water in the glasses, passing one each to Ellie and me, before he took his own and almost flopped back into a beanbag, which appeared to groan under the strain.

"So, will you do it?" I asked.

"Why didn't you go see my boy and ask him?"

Lir's son, Manannán mac Lir, or Mac for short, had taken over the calming of the seas between the mainland and Avalon several hundred years previously. He was easier to talk to, less combative, and didn't smell of drugs.

"I'd have owed him a favor. And I don't want to owe Mac a favor."

"Because you don't trust him," Lir said.

"Not this again. Look, he was friends with Mordred. So was I. He never got on with Arthur, and, yes, after Arthur was attacked there was suspicion his way. But that was thirteen hundred years ago. We're not friends simply because after what happened to Arthur, Mordred's friends scattered."

"Because of the witch hunt," Lir said, his voice low with tinges of menace.

"It wasn't a damn witch hunt," I snapped. "In fact I was the one who stood up for Mac when people like Kay were clamoring for his head as some sort of traitor. You want to know why we're not friends anymore? Because he believed that Mordred could be saved and I didn't. And now Mordred is dead, and when I see Mac that's going to bring up some very awkward questions. Questions

I really don't have time to discuss. I came to you because it's quicker and time is of the essence here."

Lir drank his water. "I've always thought you honest. Why didn't you tell me all this years ago?"

"Did Mac?"

Lir shook his head.

"It wasn't my tale to tell. Mac wanted nothing to do with Avalon for centuries after Mordred's attack on Arthur. He's only been back doing the job for a few hundred years; whatever his reasons for leaving or returning are his to tell."

"He set out for Avalon a few months ago," Lir said, almost absentmindedly. "He's been in Camelot since then. He's helping someone there, didn't say what or who. He's not exactly the open type."

I smiled. "No, he's not."

Lir finished his drink and put his glass back on the tray. "Drink up," he said to Ellie, who'd remained quiet throughout the exchange. "Why are you with him? Why don't you go on ahead? No one's going to stop you taking the crossing."

"I agreed to keep him company and watch his back. He tends to get in trouble when people aren't around to watch him."

Lir laughed, a great big laugh that came from his stomach. "Do you remember that time Mac and Mordred stole a sword from the local blacksmith?"

I laughed as the memory came forward in my mind. "They were idiots." I turned to Ellie. "I'd just passed some sword training, I can't even remember it, but they were going to get me the finest sword their minds could find. They stole a ceremonial sword, which was about as much use in battle as a tree branch.

The thing would have killed its owner quicker than anyone on the pointy end."

"What happened?" Ellie asked.

"Merlin found out. Discovered that Galahad had helped too, and punished all three of them to work in the blacksmith's for a month. At the end of it, the blacksmith had thrown away more than he'd made, but he presented each of them with a small dagger. The three of them were allowed to work after hours and they made me a sword. It was a knife really, but well made considering their total lack of talent. We were all ten or eleven."

"Mordred was a good boy."

"And an evil man," I reminded him.

"I know, I know. I just wonder what happened to him. What made him so twisted and malevolent? I don't think Mac ever got over his betrayal."

The mood had turned somber in an instant, so I finished my water and placed my glass next to Lir's.

"I'll help you," he said. "Give me an hour or so and then come to the harbor. Don't drive that car, you can leave it here. I can't guarantee it'd still be there if you left it at the harbor. Nathaniel Garrett, the man who walked out on working with Merlin. The man who attacked Merlin for that matter."

"Do you know why I did it?"

Lir shook his head. "Merlin's an asshole. He's deserved being thumped more than once. Just surprised it was you. I'll tell you something for free though: Merlin doesn't let his guard down twice. If you see him, I doubt you're going to get a warm reception."

"If I see him, you'll be able to hear the argument from here."

CHAPTER 11

We gave Lir an hour before setting off across the expansive fields toward the nearby cliffs, which overlooked the often rough waters of the Celtic Sea—the part of the sea where the Irish Sea and Atlantic Ocean meet.

A fence had been built around part of the cliff, littered with lots of signs showing the area to be dangerous. A large metal gate, with dozens of steps just beyond—all of which were built into the side of the cliff—led down to the bay below.

"We have to go down there?" Ellie asked, peering over the cliff edge at the stairs. "That handrail doesn't look very sturdy."

"It's fine. Alchemists remake them every few years. It's perfectly safe." I pushed open the gate and began taking the steps down to the soft sand a hundred feet below. I'm not a big fan of heights, and being able to see the earth through the metal, lattice-like steps made me uncomfortable.

"See, it's not just me who doesn't like them," Ellie called from behind me.

I picked a point on the cliff wall in front of me and dared not look down. "Less talking, more walking."

Ellie laughed for a moment and then we both continued our descent in silence. I almost jumped the last half dozen steps, but managed to contain myself enough that I stepped onto the sand with a slight sigh.

"They need a lift," Ellie said, pointing to the stairs. "Or a slide. Anything but those."

"They're meant to be a deterrent, I assume. Like the fence and gate. I thought you'd been to Avalon before."

"I went from Wales. They don't make you scale a cliff face."

We were silent for a few seconds until Ellie shivered slightly. "So, where to now? This is just an empty bit of beach."

I looked around, and to anyone unaware of where they were, she was right. The beach consisted of a nice bit of sandbank, some large rocks and a few even larger ones. The sea beat a rhythm against the two cliffs that enclosed the bay, the acoustics making it sound much louder than it might otherwise.

I walked over to one of the large rocks—one that looked like slightly awkward stairs—and climbed up onto the almost flat top. "You coming?" I asked Ellie, who obviously wanted to ask me what I was talking about, but instead just followed without complaint.

"Now what?" Ellie asked.

I pushed my hand to the cliff face beside me and it went right through the pale rock.

"What the hell?" Ellie exclaimed.

"It's an illusion," I said, grabbing an unseen handle and pulling it up with an audible crunch. I removed my hand from the illusion and took a few steps to my right before doing the same thing with a second unseen handle.

"That's some powerful magic," Ellie almost shouted over the sound of the hidden door sliding open.

"Ta da," I said with a smile.

"How does it work?" she asked as we stepped through the illusion and arrived in a brightly lit corridor.

"I honestly don't know. Runes maybe, or some sort of illusion magic. It's not something that's ever come up before."

We followed the corridor down, the sounds of our shoes echoing off the metal floor until they were replaced with the voices of people talking somewhere in the distance. The voices got louder and louder until we exited the corridor into a massive cavern that sat inside the cliff itself.

The cliff had been hollowed out centuries previously to create a small harbor capable of holding three ships, all of which were lit up by the powerful lights that sat high above us. The closest ship was a Sunseeker yacht, although I wasn't familiar enough with either the make or model of any yachts. As we took the steps down to the harbor itself, the second yacht—another Sunseeker of identical model—and the third, some sort of speedboat, were easier to see as they bobbed gently in the dark water.

The two men we'd heard talking stopped as Ellie and I approached them. Both of them were thin, although one had a bushy beard while his companion was clean-shaven. They didn't give off any indication that they were unhappy to see us, but by the same token they didn't rush over to greet us.

"You're that Nathan fellow?" the clean-shaven of the pair asked, although he made it more of a statement of fact that anything else.

I nodded. "You know where Lir is?"

"I'm here," he bellowed as he left a small nearby office. "I've arranged for a boat to take you both."

"Thanks," I said and shook his hand.

"Yes, thank you," Ellie said. "That's really helpful."

"Not a problem. You're going in the one on the far end."

I followed Lir's point toward the predator speedboat. "Nice."

"Actually, it's because they want you gone as quickly as possible. There's some concern that if you manage to piss people off, some of that is going to splash on the people who took you across. The less time they have to spend with you, the more they can deny they had any idea who you were."

"Sounds fair," I agreed. "Thanks for all this."

"I don't care what you say, you and Mac are still friends. Any friend of my boy's is a friend to me. Be safe." He glanced at Ellie. "Both of you."

Then he turned and walked away, disappearing in the corridor that led to the hidden entrance.

A middle-aged woman left the office and walked over to me. "You must be Nathan; we leave in ten minutes. Get on board and get below deck. I'll get the crew ready. I hope you haven't forgotten anything."

"Too late if I have," I said.

"Yes, yes it is," she agreed and walked off a few steps before pausing. "And it's a conjurer who made that entrance."

Ellie looked surprised. "How did you—?"

"It's bugged," the lady explained. "Just in case we get some unsavory types we need to prepare for."

"Do you mean me?" I asked, a little anger creeping into my voice.

"Actually, no. I think, as per usual, Lir has exaggerated just how well known what you did to Merlin is. You'll have some issues with his inner circle, but the majority of people there won't even know who you are, let alone care enough to find out.

I wouldn't hang around though. Merlin's inner circle are a pretty fanatical group."

"They always were," I agreed.

"Yeah, well, I also heard that Hellequin has a price on his head," she said with a knowing glance. "You might want to warn that fellow if you see him."

"You mean the Reav—?" I started to ask.

"You don't need to tell me who they are. I don't *want* to know. I'm just giving you a friendly warning from one person to another." Having obviously finished what she set out to say, she walked off.

The island of Avalon was about thirty nautical miles off the coast. We set out, the front of the cliff opening to allow the ship to pass into the choppy open waters beyond. After a few seconds though, the water calmed considerably and we set off at speed.

The whole journey took over an hour, but it allowed me to grab some sleep and I woke up just as the boat pulled into the island of Avalon's port.

Avalon wasn't a very big island, you could probably walk from one end to the other in a few hours, and the only things on it were the port, a few large buildings, and a perimeter of trees. It's not on any maps, nor anywhere near flight paths or shipping lanes.

The boat slowed to a crawl and then stopped altogether as someone above shouted that we had arrived. Ellie and I left the cabin and thanked the ship's crew, although all of them appeared to want to depart as quickly as possible.

We got off the boat and walked the considerable length of the harbor, the roar of the boat behind us as it pulled back out into the open sea.

"How long has it been since you were last here?" Ellie asked as we approached the guard station that allowed visitors onto the island itself.

"Over a century," I said. "I guess I'm about to find out what's changed."

The guard station, and the dozen heavily armed guards who manned it, were accompanied by an anti-aircraft gun and a large tank.

"What the hell do you need a tank for?" I asked the first guard who wanted to know my name. His armor was jet black with a large red symbol on both arms depicting a stone with a sword in it. They were Avalon elite guards. Used only for working within Avalon itself. A nametag on his chest said "Hendricks."

"Name, sir?" Hendricks repeated.

"Nathan Garrett."

Hendricks tapped a few things on his electronic tablet and then paused for a second before looking up. "You taking the piss?"

I shook my head. "Nope. Nathan Garrett is my name."

"Are you armed, sir?"

I shook my head. "No, not armed. Not planning to do anything that needs being armed."

Ellie was taken away into a nearby hut by a second guard, a small woman with a round face and a nose that had been broken badly at some point and never properly reset.

"Your name has been flagged, sir," Hendricks said to me, bringing my attention back to him.

"Flagged for what reason?"

"Because we've been asked to notify our supervisor when you arrive on the island, before you're allowed to go through the realm gate to Camelot."

"How long will that take?"

"That depends, sir, could be a few minutes or hours."

"Am I to be under surveillance?"

Hendricks shook his head. "Not at all, there are no restrictions on you visiting or leaving either the realm or the city of Camelot. But before your initial visit, you must wait for our supervisor."

"Why?"

"Can't say, sir."

"Can't, or won't?"

"Both."

I admired him for his honesty if nothing else. "Fair enough, where do I go to wait?"

"You can stay in one of the guest houses up by the hill; myself and some other guards will escort you there."

"You gonna tell me why you need a tank?" I asked. It was obvious that arguing how much I needed to be allowed into Avalon would change exactly zero things about how quickly their supervisor appeared. In fact being a smart ass might make them take more time.

"Precautionary measure," he assured me. "Not everything can be stopped with our abilities, or bullets. Sometimes you need to make a bigger statement."

"And a tank does that?"

"It's one of half a dozen on the island. All packed with the latest in ordnance. All are just there to ensure that people know we're not to be taken lightly."

"It's very imposing." I agreed.

Hendricks glanced behind me at the massive vehicle, its green paint job allowing it a measure of camouflage amongst the trees. "Sir Kay is always thinking of the safety of Camelot and its people."

"I'm sure he is," I said, trying not to put any sarcasm into the words. Kay was an asshole, but he was also a powerful one. Pissing off those who worked for him was unlikely to end well for me.

"Wait just a moment, please," Hendricks said and then walked off past the checkpoint barrier and into a building behind it.

I took the time to look around. There were two guard towers farther down the tree line, both with snipers in them. I waved to one and he waved back, which was nice. Apart from them, I counted another eight guards, half of whom carried what appeared to be Heckler and Koch MP5's, and the other half held swords, or axes. A fence ran from either side of the barrier all the way to the end of the harbor. It was chain link and about ten feet tall. A notice on it warned that it could be electrified. Kay had clearly been busy. The last time I'd been on Avalon the guards had been much fewer in number this far from the realm gate. I hated to think just how much extra security he'd placed up there. Maybe there was an entire army waiting, or Apache helicopters. I wouldn't put it past him to have a submarine patrolling the waters, either. I had the sudden urge to glance around the ocean to see if I could tell if one was there.

Ellie returned from out of the hut and smiled. "They say we have to wait for someone. Well, I don't have to, I can go right in, but I said I'd wait with you."

"Thanks, but you really don't have to. They're worried about me for some reason."

"Actually, I don't think they are. Someone clearly wants to talk to you; I think they're just keeping you here so they can. The guard I spoke to didn't even seem to know anything about you. I'm usually pretty good at spotting liars, I can smell the sweat. Nothing told me she was lying though. They are worried about something though. I got the impression that something has happened. They're a little on edge."

I was about to say more when the guard who'd been speaking to me returned. "If you both can follow me, please."

Ellie and I did as he asked, following him through the raised barrier, and on past the checkpoint. We stopped by a jeep, and the three of us piled in, finding two more guards, including the woman who'd talked to Ellie, sitting in the front.

"Well, this is cozy," I said as the jeep started up and we drove through the break in the trees, and then up the road to one of several large buildings that serve guests who were about to enter, or leave, the realm.

The jeep pulled up outside the building and we all got out, with the guards taking Ellie and me inside. The whole place reminded me of an expensive hotel, with beautiful furnishings and pleasant music playing in the foyer. The armed guards were somewhat of an oddity amongst all of the beauty, but at least none of them were pointing weapons our way. The guards led us up a set of stairs, and down a corridor, stopping outside a room that sat opposite a massive bay window, overlooking the courtyard below.

"If you would go inside, someone will be with you shortly," Hendricks said.

"Thanks," Ellie and I said in unison.

"Hope I didn't cause you any trouble," I said.

Hendricks shook his head. "No trouble, sir, I hope you have a pleasant visit in Camelot." He paused for a moment, allowing his comrades to walk away slightly. "I've heard of you," he whispered. "I wanted to say thank you."

"What for?"

"You used to work for Merlin. I've heard some of the tales from older members of the SOA. You did a lot of good. I just felt I should say thanks."

I stared at him for a moment, unsure whether he was being serious or not. "I was happy to," I said eventually.

He nodded once and then walked off to join his comrades.

"Well, if the rest of the day is as nice as that, then this might turn into a pleasant visit," Ellie commented.

"If the rest of the day is as nice as that, I'll eat my hat."

CHAPTER 12

The room Ellie and I had been placed in was very nice. There was a TV, a computer with Internet access, and a very comfortable couch. The windows overlooked the rear of the property, which consisted of a well-maintained lawn and some colorful flowers of unknown species. I hated it. I hated the waiting, no matter how nice the surroundings, I hated not knowing what was going on, and most of all I hated that there was nothing I could do about it.

Ellie fared considerably better than I, and found that one of the TV channels was showing *Ghostbusters*, and sat down to enjoy. Normally I'd have joined her, and I still managed a smile every now and then, but I wasn't in the mood to be made to laugh.

"You know, there's nothing we can do," Ellie said, without looking up at me, just as Bill Murray proclaimed that the man beside him had no dick.

I sighed. "I know. But I also don't know why Avalon has decided that I need to speak to someone if I'm not on any kind of restrictions list."

"We'll find out soon enough. Just sit down; your constant pacing is beginning to make me nervous."

I did as was asked and sat beside her, forcing myself to watch the remainder of the film. Fortunately, it ensured that I wasn't checking my watch every few seconds, and the time became more manageable.

As the credits rolled, Ellie checked what was next. "*Mannequin*!" she shouted with delight.

"What?" I asked.

"Oh, it's eighties-tastic, but it's got James Spader and Andrew McCarthy in it. You'll love it."

I didn't really get a chance to find out my opinion on the film as there was a knock on the door only a few minutes after it started.

"Damn it," Ellie proclaimed, as I opened the door and found a young woman standing in the corridor. She wore a dark blue suit, which couldn't cover the bandages that were wrapped around her hands. Her brown hair was pulled up into a bun and stuck in place with a chopstick. She wore no obvious jewelry and smiled briefly as she saw me.

"Lucie," I said, and offered her my hand, which she took.

"Nate," she said, releasing my hand as I moved aside to let her into the room.

"You're the Avalon person we're waiting for?" I asked.

Lucie nodded. She was the deputy director of the SOA, directly under Kay. Our relationship was an awkward one. We trusted one another, but weren't exactly friends. I'd spent a large portion of the first decade that we'd known each other lying to her about the circumstances surrounding her family's murder. When I'd finally been allowed to tell her the truth, our relationship had improved, but it was too late for us to ever become firm friends.

I introduced Ellie and Lucie, and Lucie caught the slightly strange look that she got from Ellie as she paused before shaking Lucie's hand.

"It's the bandages, yes?" Lucie asked.

"Sorry, I didn't mean to stare. I just wondered why you have your hands bandaged. I don't want to hurt you if you're injured."

"I'm an enchanter," Lucie told her. "I've placed runes all over my body. But they have to be constantly covered, otherwise I'd keep activating them by accident. I find the bandages to be easier to wear than gloves."

"Wow, that must be some serious body art."

Lucie smiled. "That's one way of looking at it." She turned to me. "We need to talk."

"I'll go for a walk if you like," Ellie offered, getting to her feet.

"That's okay," I said. "I trust her, Lucie. She came here with me; she might as well know why you needed to talk to me."

Lucie nodded. "You might want to sit down."

I did as she advised and waited for her to continue.

"I heard about Liz and Edward Williams," Lucie started. "And the attack on West Quay. An agent informed Kay, and I happened to overhear the conversation. I doubted he'd have told me otherwise. He seems to want to keep knowledge of those behind it a secret."

"The Reavers," I said.

"That would be the group. I can understand Kay's reluctance to let everyone know that a group of highly trained psychopaths are running around killing people. But I disagree with him. Seventy-two hours ago one of my agents was contacted by Liz Williams with information that she had been threatened by the

Reavers, who wanted her to help them find Felix. A man I'm sure you know, Nate."

"We go way back, yeah," I admitted.

"Forty-eight hours later, that same agent was attacked in her own home. She's currently in intensive care after being stabbed with a silver blade, which was coated with jorōgumo venom."

"I have the same stuff going through me," I said.

"So I hear. My agent is a conjurer and should be able to fight it off, but she's in a coma."

A dark cloud settled in my mind. "Oh, no," I whispered.

"You know her?" Ellie asked.

"It's Fiona?" I asked Lucie. "Isn't it?"

Lucie nodded solemnly. "I didn't realize you knew her."

It felt like I'd been punched in the gut. "We worked together in the past. Does her husband know?"

Lucie shook her head. "Someone is killing people who have either gone against, or are looking into, the Reavers and their return. The stab wound on Fiona was on her back." Lucie turned and pointed to a spot just above her kidney. "She let them into her house, which means she knew them, and they stabbed her. Then they ransacked the place, looking for something, and left. We decided it best to not tell her husband anything for the moment. He's due out of prison in six months. Right now, Fiona is stable. Telling her husband about the attack is more likely to make him angry enough to do something stupid. I'd rather we know exactly what was happening before we do that."

"He deserves to know," I said.

"And he will. But I don't want to have to put The Hole on lockdown after we tell him. We both know he'll attempt to escape if he finds out."

It wasn't like I was best friends with Fiona's husband, but I liked the guy and still felt that he should be told. I know I'd want to be.

"So you're here to warn us?" Ellie asked.

"Yes," Lucie explained. "I knew that Nate was looking for the Reavers. I knew that without ever being told. As soon as I'd heard you were there when the Williamses were murdered, I knew you'd make your way down here. There are people in Avalon who support the Reavers, Fiona told me that much, but she didn't have the names. If they thought she'd figured out who they were, or even knew that she was investigating them, then there's no doubt they'd try to kill her for it. They'll try to kill you too."

"Best of luck with that," I said, and let the heat of my anger into my tone.

"I don't want you turning Camelot into a war zone, Nate," Lucie said. "I don't mind you looking around, or even talking to people. Hell, you probably know more dirty little secrets than I do, but this is an SOA case. If you discover anything, you bring it to me. And only me."

"You don't trust your own people?" I asked.

"Fiona's supervisor is missing. There aren't enough agents I trust, so I trust no one. I only trust you because I know for a fact that you're not a Reaver." She turned to Ellie. "I assume you're not."

"I doubt it," Ellie said. "I only heard about them for the first time a few hours ago."

"I want to see Fiona," I said.

"You sure?" Lucie asked me.

I nodded. "I want to see her house too."

"We can arrange that."

I stood up. "Let's get going then."

It didn't take long to make it out of the building and across the island to an identical building, which housed SOA agents and the realm gate.

The guardians opened the realm gate and the giant circular device, made of wood and rock, shimmered slightly before the empty center filled with the image of the realm on the other side of the gate.

The realm itself was called Albion, an entire world linked to our own by a gate controlled by the forces of Avalon. The largest city in Albion was Camelot, which housed upwards of two and a half million people. A few million more lived in the dozen or so smaller towns and villages that had been created away from the large population of Camelot.

"You ready for this?" Lucie asked.

I wasn't, but I stepped through the realm gate anyway and instantly found myself on Albion ground. An SOA guard, one of the same elite as those who controlled the island I'd just left, ran up ready to catch me should I pitch forward. Some people's first trip was a little on the discombobulating side.

"I'm good," I told him, and he stepped back as Lucie and then Ellie came through the gate.

"Ma'am," the guard said and snapped to attention.

"We're going to need transportation," Lucie said to the guard, who ran off, I assumed to arrange something.

"What are we taking to get around?" I asked.

Avalon had its own power source, and had long since joined the technology age that the realm of Earth took for granted. Anyone wanting to get messages from Albion to Earth would have to travel to Earth to do so, but while in Avalon they had mobile reception, something approximating Wi-Fi, and even an underground tube system that made regular stops in all parts of the city, as well as those places outside of its limits. There's a reason humans tend to get the best technology a few years, or decades, after Avalon; and it was mostly so Avalon could keep it for themselves.

The Albion realm gate sat inside a massive hall that was a few miles away from Camelot. A mansion had been built beside it at some point, and housed several dozen SOA agents, along with some BOA. Everyone coming and going was checked before being allowed anywhere.

A half dozen guards stood inside the room, their weapons—a mixture of bladed instruments—hanging loosely from their sides.

We made our way through the mansion and out into the rain that was pouring outside. Avalon rain is clean enough that you can drink it if you so wish, although it has a slightly odd, almost sweet, taste to it.

The guard whom Lucie had sent to find us transport was waiting diligently, the rain slowly soaking him more and more. A car sat behind him, although it looked like something out of a science fiction film. It was sleek and black, with pulsing yellow lines down one side.

"What the hell is that?" I asked.

"Ah, you've not seen these before," Lucie commented. "About ten years ago Camelot put together a system that allowed cars to be automated. You program in a destination and the car takes you there. There are sensors all around the car that feed back to similar ones under the ground. They measure speed and distance, and things like that. It was a nightmare to come here for a few years while they were digging everything up, and they're limited to only certain routes, but they've been incredibly useful."

The guard opened the door, changing the pulsing color to red, and Lucie, Ellie, and I stepped inside. The interior was dark, with lights in the roof providing all the light you needed, considering the windows were blacked out.

I took a seat opposite Lucie and found it to be incredibly comfortable. "Are these always blacked out?" I asked.

Lucie nodded and tapped the side panel. "The windows don't move, and they're always blacked out. No one uses these for more than short journeys. They basically go between the main buildings in Camelot, or to the realm gate. There's no deviation from that."

"It's certainly impressive," I said, although I found the idea of automated cars a little creepy, but that was probably due to the need for me to retain some control over my destination.

"Hospital," Lucie said, and after a few seconds the car lurched forward and then set off as some classical music came through speakers on the roof.

"Is there anywhere you want to be dropped off?" Lucie asked Ellie.

Ellie turned to me. "You going to be okay without me for a while?"

"I think I can manage."

Ellie smiled. "The hospital is fine. I can grab the tube from there to where Olivia and her family are staying."

"Where is that?" I asked.

She fished out a piece of paper and pen and wrote down the address, which I instantly recognized.

"Thanks, I'll make my way there once I'm done."

"I'll tell them you're coming. Hopefully Kasey hasn't asked anyone else to be her sentinel."

"You're going to be a sentinel?" Lucie asked. "Is that Thomas Carpenter's daughter?"

I nodded.

"I heard he was in the city. I was going to take time to say hi, but things have sort of gotten away from me. The SOA lost a good man when he left."

"The SOA seems to be taking a very active role in security," I pointed out, wondering about why there were so many on Avalon Island.

"That was Kay's doing before I took the post," Lucie explained. "He wants to make sure that Avalon is safe."

"And tanks do that?" Ellie asked.

A thin smile crossed Lucie's lips. "After what happened at Tartarus last year, there was some concern that people might try to attack Camelot in the same fashion. Kay took it upon himself to . . . protect the people here."

A group of insane idiots who'd claimed to be from the Vanguard, a paramilitary-style pro-Camelot organization, attacked Tartarus with the aim of releasing Cronus. They succeeded, but were all killed by their own allies to keep them from talking. Those same allies—a coven of witches—ended up putting a number of children in harm's way, just so they could continue Hera's insane plan to free Cronus.

"You know they wouldn't," I said. "You're still watching those witches, I assume."

"Indeed we are. Officially we're still concerned that their exposure to Cronus must have had a serious impact on their psyche. How's the girl doing?"

Chloe Range was the daughter of the coven's leader, Mara. Mara used Chloe to help her carry out her plan, passing the young teenager over to a monster so that her coven could distract everyone enough to get Cronus free. The monster was dead, I'd killed it myself. But Mara was a whole different kind of monster, one I really hoped slipped up so that her poisonous self could be removed from her daughter's life. So far, Mara had been the picture of a well-behaved witch.

"Chloe is okay, I think. Kasey told me that she spends a lot of time at friends' houses so she doesn't have to go home. Can't say I blame her."

The car stopped and a blue light flashed across the roof before an audible click could be heard.

"Doors are unlocked," Lucie told us, before she pushed open the door beside us and stepped out into the steadily increasing rain.

"I'll see you later at the address," Ellie told me, before saying goodbye to Lucie and making her way toward the nearby tube station.

The hospital consisted of dozens of large buildings put together to form one gargantuan structure that loomed over everything around it. The different colors of brick and paint, and the different sizes of the various buildings, gave it a Frankenstein's monster-like appearance.

A large garden sat at one side of the building, with several people in gowns ignoring the weather to walk around there. At the opposite side of the hospital sat a large sign declaring it to be the entrance to the emergency wing of the building. We entered at the front of the main building and I waited while Lucie walked off to talk to the receptionist, who, after a brief conversation and a glance at Lucie's identification, waved us through.

It took a walk to the rear of the hospital, a lift ride up several floors, and then a walk through three separate—and heavily armed—guard posts, to get to the high-security section of the hospital.

For as long as I could remember the top floor of the main hospital building had been reserved purely for high-security cases. For instances when an agent of Avalon—or even one of the high-ranking lords or ladies—needed medical care they were always taken to this secure part of the hospital. It was better safe than sorry.

We walked past a dozen identical doors, each with its own room number on the wall beside it, until we turned a corner and encountered a half dozen guards outside one of the rooms. A closer look told me they were SOA agents, and none of them appeared pleased to see me, until they noticed Lucie standing beside me.

"Kay's in there," one of the agents, a woman with bright pink hair, said.

Lucie paused for a second and then opened the door to the hospital room, stepping inside, with me following a few steps behind.

The room itself was large and bright, the windows stretching from floor to ceiling, allowing in a huge amount of light. Fiona was lying in the bed; her almost black hair was cut much shorter than when I'd last seen her. Her face was ashen, pale, and motionless. Her normally green eyes closed to the world.

Like me, Fiona accessed magic to use her abilities; hopefully that same magic could be used to keep her alive, to keep the venom inside her from killing her. Conjurers share a lot of similarities with sorcerers; they age slowly and heal quicker than humans, but their power centers on manipulation and illusion. Conjurers are normally quite secretive people, but Fiona wasn't like that.

A doctor was examining Fiona's vitals, checking the various readings on the beeping machines around her, without acknowledging our presence. Kay sat on a chair beside the bed, an expression of concern etched on his face. Behind Kay stood his Faceless.

The Faceless were officially described as bodyguards to the more prominent or powerful members of Avalon society. I knew that many of them did a lot more than just protect their master. Many were used as assassins or thieves, blackmailers or thugs, depending on their master's needs.

The Faceless wear a mask that covers their face. Only their master knows their true identity. Every member's mask is different, their masters deciding how they should look. The only similarity was that they cover the entire head, fastening around the neck so as to be impossible to remove. A dark, mesh-like material was set in the eyeholes.

The Faceless that belonged to Kay wore a mask that was all black, with a red swirl around the right eye. The nose was protruded slightly, with two holes for the wearer to breath normally. The mouth was a smooth piece of polished metal with two rows of three holes each punched into it. The mask was also raised in certain parts around the eyes, giving it a menacing appearance.

I didn't trust the Faceless at the best of times. But while I didn't like Kay, I trusted him to have the best interests of Avalon at heart. He was always loyal to his brother. Even as Arthur lay in an unconscious state, Kay still believed in Arthur's dream of a powerful and united Avalon.

"This is awful," Kay said and stood to shake my hand. His Faceless didn't move any part except for his head, which turned slightly toward me. A shiver ran up my back. He was one creepy bastard.

"Did you know Fiona?" Kay asked me.

"We're friends," I said and glanced from her still form to the doctor. "How is she?"

"Dying," he said, his word filled with anger. "Jorōgumo venom is more potent than that of most other creatures. We're using runes to keep her magic in use, but it may not be enough. She wasn't found for almost six hours. Long enough for the venom to do a lot of damage."

I pointed to a gash on the side of Fiona's head, near the temple. "What happened?"

"She was attacked after the stab," the doctor said. "Hit with something multiple times, our guess is a knuckleduster of some kind. Her body is too far damaged to heal it until the venom is out of her system."

I turned to Lucie. "You didn't mention that."

"Sorry. When I found out you were friends, I didn't want to make you angrier than you already were."

I was *plenty* angry.

"Who found her?" I asked.

"Remy," Lucie said. "He lives nearby."

"How is he?"

"Raging. He wants revenge for this. Fiona and he were close. I imagine you'll be seeing him at some point, if you stick around."

"You're staying in Camelot?" Kay asked.

"I don't know yet," I told him, honestly. "I didn't know Fiona had been hurt. I'm going to find out who did it."

"We have people for that," Kay assured me. "We don't need you rushing around attacking people."

"Sure," I said, ignoring his words and just wanting him to shut up.

"Her supervisor is missing," Kay continued. "We're looking into his disappearance." He turned to his Faceless. "How's that going?"

"He vanished," the Faceless said, his voice slightly muffled from behind the mask. "We'll find him, though. Vengeance will be served."

"You're sure he did this?" Lucie asked. "I've had no confirmation of her attacker."

"Who else, Lucie?" Kay asked. "Fiona is attacked in her own home, and her supervisor is missing. Clearly he did it. Maybe they were lovers and she called it off. We're looking into the possibility."

"You think Fiona was cheating on her husband?" I asked, trying very hard to keep the anger and sarcasm from my voice. "She wasn't that kind of person."

Kay stood and walked over to me, patting me on my shoulder. "In the right circumstances, people are capable of things you'd never expect. Her husband is in jail. Has been for years. After all that time, her needs must be great. A forbidden love, a regretted moment of passion. It doesn't take much to take things from friendly flirting to a more physical relationship. If she'd have only picked someone else, someone only interested in the physical. Maybe she wouldn't be in hospital. It's so sad."

Kay and his Faceless left the room before I could reply, which was probably for the best.

"Keep her safe, Doctor," I said after a few moments of calming myself down.

"She's in the best hands, I promise," Lucie told me. "You look angry."

"Do you think she was having an affair?"

Lucie shook her head. "She wasn't the type. Kay just wants to believe whatever idea gives him the most ease."

"I need to see her house. I want to see where she was attacked. And I want to speak to Remy."

"I'm sure he'll enjoy that a great deal. I can't officially sanction his help in the investigation. Kay has already told him to stay away from it. He thinks Remy is too close to Fiona. That his judgment is impaired."

"Is it?"

"I'll let you decide that for yourself. All I know is that Remy would very much like to get his claws on those responsible and tear them apart. Kay doesn't like him, doesn't trust him either, which is precisely why I do."

I glanced at Fiona again and mentally promised to find those who'd attacked her. "Let's go say hello to our little friend then."

CHAPTER 13

November 1888. London.

I'd been silent for an unknown amount of time since Felix had told Diana, Alan, and me that Merlin was the one who'd sent the Reavers to London. That he'd been the one behind them murdering and stealing the souls of innocent people, all to feed to Arthur in some attempt to make him stronger.

I hadn't wanted to speak because if I had, then my incandescent fury would have boiled over and I'd have done something stupid. Instead I sat and listened, all the while fully aware of the growing tension in the room.

"Can you give us a moment, please?" Felix asked.

The other two agreed and left the drawing room, although both glanced back at me before doing so.

"You got something to say to me?" Felix asked.

"How long have you known?" I asked, every word taut. My anger was a fragile beast willing to explode with the slightest pressure.

"That Merlin was having innocent people slaughtered and their souls fed to Arthur? It's been about a century. It was why they sent you to kill me. No one was meant to find out. Only the

Reavers and Merlin know, and I haven't been a Reaver for the better part of four hundred years."

"I can't believe that Merlin . . ." I stopped. I could believe that Merlin would arrange something as horrific as the murder of people just to get what he wanted; he'd been using me to do it for centuries. "Why prostitutes? Why London?"

"London is a city of crime and poverty. People will look the other way for very little, and others can vanish without trouble. Most of the previous victims simply disappeared to the wind. Prostitutes are easier to make vanish than most. But this is different. Whoever these Reavers calling themselves Jack the Ripper are, it's clear that they're more interested in the murder than the reasons behind it."

"They leave the body in full view of everyone. I think it's safe to say they're enjoying themselves. They won't stop, not unless they're caught. And there's no chance of the humans doing that."

"There's a man in London, he runs a shop just outside of Covent Garden. I've heard he works for anyone with money, but I know he's supplied the Reavers in the past. Although I wouldn't mention them to him at first, just ask about anyone wanting knowledge about Whitechapel. That's where the killings have been, and they'll have needed information on the best places to strike. They'll have come to him. He'll get anything for anyone. For the right price. He might be able to point you in the direction of the killers. It'll take some persuading though. Or money. And he's not above waiting until you've gone and then telling people that they're being hunted."

"He sounds delightful. What's his name?"

"Mister Baker. No idea of his first, I've heard about six different ones. He can't be trusted, even by the normally dreadful standard of people in his job."

We were both silent for a few seconds.

"You're going to confront Merlin, aren't you?" Felix asked.

"Someone has to. He's murdering people to keep Arthur alive. Taking the souls of your enemies in battle is one thing, but having prostitutes butchered in the streets by a gang of lunatics is going so far over the line, it's now a distant blur."

"He won't see it like that. He'll see it as doing what needs to be done."

"Merlin is not the man he once was," I admitted. It had been bubbling inside of me for years, centuries probably, but I'd avoided the issue by just staying away from Camelot, by not being given missions directly anymore.

"None of us are," Felix said, his tone soft and full of regret. He glanced down and then back up at me. "There are some things you need to know. About Merlin. About you."

"Like what?"

"He's not always been honest with you."

I laughed, I couldn't help it. "I think I came to grips with that a very long time ago. What Merlin says and what actually happens are usually widely different. There's very little you could say to surprise me about his lies."

"When this is all done, I'll tell you about them," Felix said. "Promise me you won't go to Merlin before you know everything."

I stared at him for a heartbeat. "I promise. I'll come to you first." I walked to the drawing room door and opened it, expecting to find Alan listening in. Instead I found Alan face down on the floor with Diana standing above him, her foot on the small of his back. "Trouble?"

Diana shook her head. "He was unflattering. I corrected him."

"I only grabbed her behind. It was very friendly," Alan pleaded.

"Did I ask you to grab my bottom?" Diana asked.

"A gentleman knows when a woman wants her bottom grabbed," Alan said.

Diana looked down at Alan with disgust. "Can I tear his arms off?"

"Later," I said. "Alan, at what point in your life were you led to believe that grabbing the behind of any woman who has stated her desire to tear you apart was a good idea?"

"I thought it would break the ice a little," Alan explained. "You know, I grab her, she laughs, and I make a funny joke."

"And that works?" Diana asked.

Alan remained quiet for a second. "There's always a first time."

"You're an idiot," I told him and motioned for Diana to let him up.

She did as I asked and then punched him in the jaw the second he was upright. The blow lifted him off his feet and dumped him some distance back, where he tried to get back to his feet and thought better of it.

"Now I'm good," Diana said with a smirk.

"I've got the name of someone who might be able to help," I told Diana and a newly upright Alan. I turned to Felix. "We'll be a few hours. Are you going to run for it if I go?"

Felix shook his head. "They won't come for me. Trolls are outside, and I'm not exactly a slouch. I'll be fine."

I walked toward Alan, as he held his bleeding nose. "You going to behave?"

"You keep asking me that as if I haven't been so far."

"Alan, if you think pissing off Diana is behaving, I think your life expectancy is going to be very low."

"This is a lot of effort just to go to jail at the end anyway," he bemoaned.

"Keep on behaving like a lout around Diana then. I'm sure she'll endeavor to arrange for you to take a much quicker, albeit longer term, punishment."

Alan glanced at Diana and then back at me. "I promise I'll behave myself."

"Excellent," Diana said with a smile. "But if you ever grab me again, I won't hesitate to launch you off the tallest building I can find."

The carriage ride through London was an uncomfortable one, and not because of the uneven roads. Diana and Alan sat opposite one another, barely registering the other's existence, let alone actually communicating with each other.

I was beginning to wish I'd left one of them with Felix when Alan opened his mouth. "I'm sorry," he said looking at Diana. "I did not behave in a gentlemanly manner and for that I offer my humble apologies. You may not like me. You may loathe me. But we have to work together for a common cause. After this is over, you can go back to hating me again."

Diana stared at Alan. "Okay, but if you touch me—"

"Yes, I know, launching, high buildings. Probably some face punching. None of it sounds like something I wish to visit anytime soon."

After that the atmosphere wasn't quite so inhospitable, despite the continued silence.

Diana's carriage driver stopped outside the address Felix had given me for Mister Baker, and I looked out into the morning light.

"It's quiet here," Alan said. "I was expecting it to be busier."

"Covent Garden doesn't get really busy for a few hours," Diana explained. "It would be best for us to conduct our business before the local residents begin setting up their wares for the day."

The three of us left the coach and walked down a nearby alley, stopping outside of a large wooden door.

"Go find somewhere safe," Diana told the driver. "Be back in an hour."

The driver nodded, and I watched him drive the carriage off.

Alan glanced around. "You sure this is right?"

"Did you expect a shop with a big sign that says 'criminals welcome'?" I asked.

"I just expected guards or something more foreboding than a door in an alley."

Diana knocked on the door once, and when the reply wasn't immediate, she turned the handle, which moved freely, opening the door.

"Mister Baker?" Diana called out to the rooms beyond.

"Come in," a voice shouted back.

I didn't need to tell Alan or Diana to be careful as we stepped into the building, closing the door behind us. The room we found ourselves in was bright, and devoid of anything but a green and red rug covering wooden floorboards, and a coat stand, which held an umbrella but no garments of any kind.

There was only one exit—an archway—that led to a short, thin corridor, at the end of which was another door, which was ajar.

Diana, being in front, pushed the door open, which flooded the dark, windowless corridor with light. The three of us walked into the large room, only to be confronted by a wood troll. At ten feet in height, and almost as wide, it was an imposing sight. Of the four different races of troll, wood trolls tended to be the most receptive to other species, although the one before us certainly didn't seem happy to see us.

"Tarin, move," someone commanded.

The large Tarin did as it was told and stepped aside, walking over toward one side of the expansive room and taking a deep breath, as if the mere act of allowing us to retain all of our limbs was too much for it.

Now that the troll didn't obstruct my view, I noticed the man before me for the first time. He stood behind a wooden counter, which ran almost the length of the room. He wore a suit of red and black, and a lengthy moustache adorned a chubby face. He wasn't large himself, although the suit did appear to be a little too big for his frame.

"He's a grumpy bastard," he said.

"Mister Baker?" I asked, walking up to the counter and offering my hand.

Mister Baker glanced down at my hand. "Depends who's asking," he replied, giving a nervous glance over to his friend.

Two doors were on the wall behind Mister Baker, both of which were closed, and I wondered if he thought he'd be able to dart through one of them before I could grab hold of him.

"My name is Nathan Garrett," I told him, lowering my hand. "My associates and I wish to speak to you about a matter of great importance. We require information." I removed a small gold bar from my inside jacket pocket, and placed it on the counter between us.

Mister Baker's eyes slowly moved down to the bar and then slowly rose back toward me. This time there was a beaming smile on his face. He grasped my hand as if I'd never lowered it, shaking it vigorously.

"Of course, of course, come with me," he announced and turned to one of the doors, pushing it open slightly. "Fiona, fetch some tea, we have guests." He didn't wait for a reply, merely flicked a hinge beneath the counter, pulling part of it up and then ushering Diana, Alan, and me through the second door and into a drawing room.

A lit fireplace warmed the entire room, which was a good size, even with the half dozen comfortable looking chairs, a table, and several cupboards.

All four of us sat on the chairs, with Mister Baker taking up residence in front of the large window; the yellow curtains closed, ensuring the room remained free from external prying eyes.

"So, what do you want to know?"

"Several people might have come through here recently asking for information about Whitechapel, maybe requesting soul jars," Alan said. "We wish to find them."

"Whitechapel you say?" Mister Baker asked in a tone that suggested he bloody well knew all about the people we were asking about but was going to find himself suddenly unable to remember.

The door to the room opened and a young woman walked in with a tray containing several cups, saucers, a pot of milk, and a teapot. She placed the tray between us and glanced over to Mister Baker. "Anything else, sir?" she asked. Her accent was Scottish, although it wasn't thick; I imagined she'd spent a lot of time away from her native country.

"No, Fiona. Once you've poured the tea, you may leave."

Fiona brushed her long dark hair over one ear and nodded. She poured four cups, placing milk in each, and passed each of us a cup and saucer. As she turned to leave, I noticed that Alan was watching her intently. Before she left, she glanced back over at the four of us, and allowed her gaze to take in each of us in question. She noticed me watching and quickly left the room.

"She's a good maid," Mister Baker said. "She makes a good cup of tea and knows how to clean. Both helpful traits in a woman."

Diana tensed and pretended she hadn't heard him.

"We need your help," I said, moving the conversation away from something that was liable to make Diana tear his head off.

"Yes, I remember." Mister Baker took a sip of his tea. "Why do you want to find them?"

"They happened to cross Brutus," Diana said.

Mister Baker turned to stare at Diana. "Brutus sent you? Well, that changes a lot, doesn't it? I can't say no to our illustrious king. The price is one hundred pounds and a meeting with Brutus to discuss an expansion of my operation."

"We can discuss that," Diana said immediately.

"Do you mind awfully if I go talk to Fiona?" Alan asked. "She was quite lovely."

Mister Baker waved his arm in the direction of the door. "Don't distract her for too long from her duties, but be my guest."

When Alan stood up and walked past me, my hand shot out and grabbed his arm. "What are you doing?" I whispered as Mister Baker and Diana hashed out terms in more detail.

"Trust me," Alan whispered back.

I thought about it for a moment. Trusting Alan wasn't exactly something I was used to. But he'd given his word that he would help, so I released his arm. He nodded thanks and then left to find Fiona.

"So, it's settled then," Mister Baker said. "One hundred pounds and an hour of Brutus's time." He shook hands with Diana, who appeared to want to wash the moment he turned back to me.

"So, you'll help?" I asked.

"Money up front."

I removed two more gold bars and placed them on the table next to the tea tray. "This should satisfy you."

Mister Baker nodded, and then snatched the thin bars from the table. "Three men turned up here a few weeks ago. They asked for some information on the seedier parts of the city, but they didn't need any soul jars. They did, however, ask for a collection of urns to be dropped off at an address. I didn't ask questions and they didn't seem the type to give answers."

"Where was the address?" I asked.

"Whitechapel. I'll go get it." Mister Baker got up and left the room.

"Looks like they made the soul jars themselves. You think he's lying?" Diana asked.

"I doubt it."

"Where the hell is Alan?"

"I don't know," I admitted.

After a short time the door opened and Fiona walked back in. She moved over to the tray and began placing the various cups and saucers on it. "Your friend came and found me," she whispered. "You're being set up."

"Alan set us up?" Diana demanded to know.

Fiona shook her head. "I'm SOA, Alan recognized me from a few years ago. Baker is out there right now, contacting the Reavers. I assume that's who you're after."

"How do you know?" I asked. "And where is Alan?"

"Alan is creating a distraction. He'll be along shortly. The rest I'll explain later. We need to get you out of here before Baker's friends show up."

"Friends?" I asked.

"Reavers. He's one of them."

"Shit!" Diana said and stood, readying herself for a fight.

"Give it a few seconds."

The explosion sounded like it had torn the house in two. The entire building moved as if someone had picked it up and shaken it. I fell back onto the chair, while Fiona and Diana steadied themselves against the nearest wall.

The window behind Diana shattered. "We have our exit," I said. "Everyone out. That includes you, Fiona, I think your cover is officially blown."

"What about Alan?" Fiona asked.

"I'll grab him," Diana said and ran through the doorway. A short time later, she flew back through the wall, pieces of brick and plaster covering the room. The wood troll stood in the gaping hole that was left in the wall and glared at the three of us.

"You okay?" Fiona asked.

Diana didn't answer. She just got back to her feet and moved her neck from side to side. It audibly cracked. She ran at the wood troll, grabbed the larger creature around the waist, and lifted it from the ground, before continuing to run through the wall behind it.

"She'll be fine," I said. "Where's Alan?"

"I'm here," Alan said from outside the window. "You planning on leaving, or do you want to stay and watch Diana kill that troll?"

Fiona was the first out of the window, helped by Alan. I looked back at Diana and the wood troll as their fight raged on. Diana had transformed into her werebear form and was tearing large chunks off the wood troll, which was doing its best to not die. Wood trolls are strong and resilient, but even they can only take so much damage. I jumped out of the window, and looked around. Alan and Fiona were sitting on the ground nearby.

"What the hell did you do?" I asked him.

"It's surprising how explosive things you can find in a pantry are," he explained.

"We shouldn't stay long. Baker and his friends will be back soon," Fiona said.

"Not leaving Diana," I explained. "She'll be done shortly."

"How do you know she'll win?" Fiona asked.

"I know Diana, she'll win. She doesn't know how to do anything else."

"How long has Avalon been investigating the Reavers?" I asked Fiona.

"I don't know who you are. I'm not about to give away Avalon secrets, primarily because you turning up has blown our whole operation."

"My name is Nathan Garrett," I explained. "I think I have clearance to know."

Fiona stood to attention. "I'm sorry, sir."

"Don't do that," I told her. "I'm not your commander. I just want to know what's going on."

Another explosion of noise sounded from behind me as the troll came through the front of the house that used to be Mister Baker's workplace. It impacted with the stone-laced ground, and bounced a few times. It didn't move again.

Diana stepped out of the rubble. No longer in her were-bear form, she was completely naked, and covered in blood. Wounds littered her body, several of which were closing as she walked toward us. She carried a pair of trousers and a shirt with her, which she proceeded to put on once she'd kicked the troll in the head one last time.

"I lost my shoes," she said as she fastened her trousers. "I liked those shoes."

"Is it dead?" Alan asked.

"Broke its neck," Diana confirmed. "It's as dead as can be. Anyone see Baker?"

"He scarpered," Alan said.

"Thanks for the warning," Diana told Fiona, before looking down at a still-seated Alan. "Looks like you were useful after all."

"So, you feel like answering my question?" I asked Fiona.

"Several members of Avalon no longer believe that the Reavers are doing what's best for the organization. There are rumors that they've killed people who have investigated them. Merlin has a lot of influence within the group, and still uses them for many of the shadier ventures, but a few of us have been tasked with looking into them."

"Who tasked you?" I asked.

"Elaine," Fiona answered immediately. "I answer only to her."

I was about to say more when Mister Baker staggered around the corner, his chest covered in blood. He saw us, paused, and then fell face first on the ground.

I walked over to him; a blade of fire already formed in my hand, and kicked him onto his back. Someone had cut his throat in one neat, but deep, slash. I cursed loudly. Without Baker we had no idea where the Reavers were hiding. We were back to square one. I glanced around the gloomy morning, and for the briefest of moments, I could have sworn I'd heard someone laugh.

CHAPTER 14

November 1888. London.

"We need to speak to Felix," Diana said as the four of us reached our destination outside of the SOA house in Whitechapel.

"Baker knew you were coming," Fiona told us. "He had some of his friends in waiting just outside. Four men, all in fancy suits, I didn't see any of their faces; I was banished from the room while they spoke."

"Reavers," I suggested.

"That was my guess, yes," Fiona confirmed. "Someone told Baker about your arrival. He was told to keep you all in the building, make his excuses to leave and then they'd come in and kill you all."

"Didn't work out too well for them, did it?" Alan said, his voice angry and low.

I glanced at him as Diana and Fiona left the carriage. "You okay?" I asked.

"Felix set us up. I don't like being set up."

I had to admit, I'd come to the same conclusion. "We'll get to Felix. But first, we need something else."

"What? What's more important than finding that old bastard and making him tell us where these psychopaths are?"

"You'll see."

I exited the carriage and entered the house, finding Diana and Fiona in the living room. "Diana, can I have a word with Fiona, please?"

Diana looked between us before she nodded and left the room.

"I know what you want," Fiona said. "You want to talk to Elaine."

"How long will it take to prepare?"

"I haven't said I'll let you."

"I'm not asking, Fiona. How long will it take?"

Anger shone in her eyes, but it vanished as quickly as it had arrived. "About an hour, although I don't understand what good it will do."

"I have questions that she can answer. If I go to Merlin with this, he'll deny everything. I want to talk to someone I can trust will be honest with me."

Fiona stood up and stretched. "I'll be back shortly." She left the room, and a moment later Diana and Alan appeared.

"She didn't look very happy," Alan said.

"I've asked to speak to Elaine."

Diana nodded. "Probably for the best."

Alan looked between us. "Who?"

"Elaine Garlot."

"Mordred's aunt?" Alan asked, surprised. "She doesn't want you dead, then?"

"Elaine's family and I have a complicated relationship," I admitted.

To be fair, complicated was probably underselling it. Elaine was the sister to Morgan Le Fay, a woman I'd loved who'd betrayed me to help Mordred try and kill Arthur. I hadn't seen Morgan since that day so very long ago, although rumor had it Elaine was still in contact with her.

Over the years and the many arguments that Elaine and I had been a part of, there was one constant. I trusted her. Yes, Morgan and her other sister Morgause—Mordred's mother—had both betrayed Avalon, but Elaine had always been a steadfast supporter of the organization, if not of Merlin, nor his actions in running it.

I left Alan and Diana to their own devices and went to my bedroom, taking some time to lie down and rest until someone knocked on the door, and almost immediately opened it.

"It's ready," Fiona told me.

I got to my feet and thanked her, before following her toward the bedroom at the rear of the building.

"You know how these work, yes?" she asked as we stopped outside the room.

"I've used it more than once to contact Merlin."

"Well, once you activate the rune, it'll connect with Elaine. Or at least let her know you're trying to connect. Whether she'll answer or not, I don't know."

"I'll take what I can get," I said.

Fiona pushed the door open and we both stepped inside. She closed the door behind us as I took in the room's contents. There was a bare bed at the far end of the room, with a small chair next to it. The rug that usually covered the floor had been rolled up and placed in the corner, exposing the floorboards beneath. A large circle had been drawn on the boards in what appeared to be chalk. A rune had been drawn on north, south, east, and west points; the same rune each time. The word Elaine had been written at the top of the circle, near the opposite wall. The same circle and runes had been drawn on the wall at about the height of a person's head if you were sitting on the ground looking at it.

It didn't really have a name, or at least not the same one that everyone used. Some called it a vision circle, others a summoning circle, but either way it did the exact same thing. Someone draws the circle on the floor with the correct runes, and then copies that in a smaller scale on a flat surface in front of them. You write the name of the person you wish to communicate with at the top of the circle, and then sit inside. Once comfortable, you concentrate on seeing them inside your head. So long as they agree to talk to you, their face appears in the circle on the wall. It takes a little getting used to.

The whole method was devised by the Norse dwarves thousands of years ago. The runes you have to use are one of the twenty-one main runes that they created. One of only a few I'm aware of that still exists in any kind of regular use, as the dwarves took that knowledge with them when they vanished centuries ago.

Not just anyone can use the circle. You have to know the name of the person you're after, and you have to have some sort of connection with them; a friendship, rivalry, something that links you both. Having never contacted Elaine this way before, she would have no way of knowing it was me, therefore I needed Fiona to clear it with her before I could attempt it.

I sat cross-legged in the circle and took the piece of white chalk from the floor, using it to write Elaine's name in front of me inside the circle. I closed my eyes and took a deep breath as I concentrated on picturing her face in my mind.

After a few seconds, I began to feel as if I were no longer able to open my eyes, as if my entire world was now one of darkness, one of sleep. It's a terrifying experience, and something that only lasts for a microsecond, but it feels as if for that moment all of time has stopped. Some people let the fear creep up inside them, consuming them, and there have been tales of people becoming changed once they finally wake up. Or never waking up at all.

My body began to relax once more and Elaine's face remained in my mind. I kept it there until it spoke to me. "Nathan," she said, softly.

I opened my eyes and saw Elaine's face inside the circle on the wall, while all around me was darkness, with occasional flickers of light. Time had paused for Elaine and me while we spoke. Conversations held in the circle had to be brief, and to the point. Taking too long was dangerous.

"Elaine," I said with a smile. "It's good to see you." Elaine had long, dark brown hair, which was plaited around her ears, the plaits a mixture of her hair and colored fabric of reds and oranges. Her face was kind and approachable, and her smile was something that could cause even the stoniest of hearts to soften. She appeared to be in her late thirties, although in reality she was somewhere around the two and a half thousand mark. Elaine was widely considered to be one of the most powerful sorcerers on the planet. Even Merlin would think twice about going up against her.

"It's been too long," Elaine said. "I'm surprised it's you here. Fiona told me you needed to talk. She was most apologetic for disturbing me."

"Reavers. Merlin. How long have you known what he has them doing?"

"A long time. There's no proof that Merlin is doing anything. Everything is rumor and hearsay. But we're not trying to find anything on Merlin, that's a waste of time. But if we can find that the Reavers are abusing their power, and their position in Avalon, we can have the organization excommunicated."

"I want them dead. Finished. The Reavers *will* be done."

Elaine paused. "Not possible. We don't even know who the leader is. Fiona told me what is happening with the prostitutes in London. You need to concentrate on stopping them there. Send a message that they can't do what they like without consequence. Stopping the Reavers as a whole would involve Merlin, or enough evidence that the council can't ignore it. Without it, he's unlikely to help."

"I need to talk to him."

"Merlin? When was the last time you were in Albion? Hell, when was the last time you spoke to him?"

It had been too long. "I need help, Elaine. I need to find these people, I need to stop them. I've stayed away from Camelot, I've buried my head in the sand, not dealing with Merlin's changes over the centuries for fear of what might follow. I'm done. When this is over, I'm done."

"What does that mean?"

"I . . . I don't know yet. But it can't go on like this. I can't keep pretending I'm doing good when I'm ignoring what's happening in Avalon. Does Merlin even attend the council meetings anymore?"

Elaine shook her head. "I've taken control of them. Merlin is so consumed with Arthur." She paused. "But you didn't contact me for that."

"I know," I said with a sigh. "We went to see Felix. It's likely that he's betrayed us. The others want to go visit him again, but if he did betray us, we'd be walking into a trap. I need to know if the Reavers have any property they use in London. I need to know where to go next. The last murder was horrific, even more so than what came before; the next one will be too. They're going to try and constantly better themselves. This is a game to them."

"Felix would never betray you unless forced to."

"I'm not so sure about that. Avalon isn't exactly his biggest love."

"You don't understand. Felix would never betray *you* without a good reason."

I opened my mouth to speak and then closed it again. "Why me?" I asked eventually.

"That's something you need to talk to him about. I'm sorry, Nate, but I can't answer that. My advice is to find him."

"And if he didn't betray us?"

"Then he might have more information on his former comrades. He might know who leads them."

"Once this is done, I'm coming to talk to Merlin."

"Can I change your mind?"

"No," I almost whispered.

"He'll not take kindly to your interference."

"I don't care, Elaine. He needs to be told, he needs to stop turning a blind eye. He's slipped into darkness. There's still time to stop him from submerging in it."

My hours immediately following the time talking to Elaine were spent sleeping. Time in the circle for those unused to it was always exhausting. Once I was up, I gathered everyone in the living room downstairs.

"I'm going to see Felix," I said.

"Not alone you're not," Diana said. "We'll all go."

I shook my head. "If he betrayed us, he'll try to kill you."

"But not you?" Alan asked.

"Apparently not, no."

"So what are we meant to be doing?" Fiona asked.

"Felix said the Reavers were in Whitechapel. I don't think that's a lie. I think the murders are taking place there because it's where they're staying. I need you to search the place."

"Search Whitechapel?" Alan asked with a laugh.

"If you come with me to Felix, he *could* kill you," I snapped. "Otherwise you're just going to stay here and wait. You can either go out there and try to find something, anything, which might help. Or sit on your arse and twiddle your thumbs. Which one do you think is more likely to stop the tally of dead from growing again?"

"Fine, we'll look around," Alan grudgingly agreed. "Maybe we'll get lucky."

"Take the carriage," Diana said and passed me a silver knife. "This might be helpful."

I lifted my jacket and showed her the row of six silver blades that sat on the small of my back. "I'm good. I'll be back here in a few hours."

I left the house, pulling the collar of my jacket up to stop the rain, and told the driver, who was sitting inside the carriage, to take me to Felix's house. He agreed and after one sizeable bump as we set off, we were soon on our way.

If I was honest, I didn't know what to expect when I arrived at Felix's. The possibility that he'd betrayed us stung. I'd been told to kill him and I'd let him live, surely that meant something. But then Elaine said he'd never betray me. Was that because I'd let him live? Felix had said that we needed to talk; maybe he wanted to confess that he was involved with the murders. Maybe Felix was still in charge of the Reavers. There was a whole lot of maybe, and not a lot of definitive answers.

The carriage stopped and I got out, telling the driver to wait for me. He nodded once, and I wondered exactly what he was. He hadn't spoken the entire time he'd been driving the coach, and didn't appear at all concerned about the trolls in the grounds. I made a mental note to ask Diana when everything was done, and walked up to Felix's house.

I'd considered how I was going to get inside. Knocking on the door was the most logical, but if he was working with the Reavers, then it was also a good way to give him the advantage. I shrugged and knocked on the door; I was in no mood for games. If he wanted a fight, I'd give him one the likes of which he'd never forget.

I knocked a second and third time, before getting fed up and placing my hand against the door, using fire magic to burn a hole through it, melting the metal lock. The door swung open with a small push and I stepped inside the dark and quiet house, closing the door behind me.

"Felix, I don't have the temperament to fuck around today," I called out.

There was no reply.

I took a few steps further into the house and the door swung open. I readied a ball of flame, until I saw that it was Fiona, looking very wet as she entered the house.

"What the hell?" I asked.

"I thought you might have noticed the bump on the carriage when I grabbed hold of it."

"That was you? Why are you even here?"

"To help. I'm a conjurer; I might be able to see if anyone starts throwing illusions around the place."

"Felix isn't a conjurer," I explained.

"Well then, in that case I'm here because Elaine told me to go with you whether you liked it or not." Fiona smiled, although it was more of a challenge than an expression of happiness. "Apparently she's worried you'll get yourself killed."

I considered arguing, but what was the point? Fiona was here now. "We need to search the house."

"I'll take upstairs, you down here," she said and ran off before I could reply, leaving me alone in the foyer of a cold, dark house.

I ignited my magic, giving me some semblance of night vision, and began searching through the numerous large rooms that made up the ground floor of the house. After half an hour of meticulous searching, I'd found neither Felix nor anything that might suggest where he'd gone. There were no signs of a struggle, no notes or messages that could indicate anything. In fact everything looked much tidier than when I'd last been here.

Eventually I'd made a full circuit of the floor and found myself back in the foyer, next to the grand staircase. There was a door on one side of the staircase, which stuck slightly as I opened it. More stairs led down into the darkness beyond. I remained cautious as I descended them, not because I was concerned about who, or what, might be lurking at the bottom, but because the stairs were steep and I didn't want to slip and embarrass myself as I flew down and landed in a heap.

The basement contained half a dozen tall, wooden cabinets, all of which were locked, and none of which could be distinguished one from the other. I considered just breaking the locks, but if Felix had any kind of security measure, not using the key was likely to end in a very bad way for me. I left them alone and went back up the stairs, hoping that Fiona might have had more luck.

I found her sitting on the bottom step of the staircase.

"Any luck?" I asked.

She shook her head. "I found these in a drawer." She threw me a large keychain, with several different keys on it. "Couldn't find anything to use them on though, but I assume they unlock something."

"I found a bunch of cabinets in the basement. These might work."

Together, we made our way back downstairs and used the keys on the cabinets, unlocking all six of them, before opening them in turn. The first three contained files, hundreds of files about past operations, notes about people and who they worked for. It appeared as if Felix had documented everything he'd ever done or been aware of.

We spent a good half hour picking files at random and reading through them.

"Some of these files describe criminal acts that Avalon was involved in," Fiona said. "There's a whole section here about some assassinations that Avalon authorized and the Reavers carried out. On other Avalon personnel. Did Merlin authorize them?"

I grabbed the file from her hands and apologized before reading through it.

"This here is the mark of the Reavers," I said, pointing to a red seal mark. "And this one is just some depressed wax, there's no mark or anything. They clearly didn't want to be discovered."

"You think Merlin did this?"

I honestly didn't know. I flicked back through the file. "The Reavers were tasked with killing a family in France. I'd like to think Merlin would draw the line at the murder of children, but I can't say that for sure."

"This is the evidence that Elaine needs."

I passed Fiona the file. "Take that one. It should be enough to help Elaine. We don't have time to grab all of these."

I opened the fourth cupboard and found weaponry hanging inside it; swords, knives, axes, even a crossbow. All neatly arranged. The fifth cupboard contained more files, but after grabbing one and reading through it, they appeared to be files of those people whom Felix had put through the Harbinger trials.

Fiona grabbed a file and started reading too. "These trials aren't for the fainthearted, are they?"

"Apparently not, no. The subjects believed that they were living their lives off somewhere for ten to fifty years. The loves, the sights, sounds, everything they experienced was all a construct inside their head. Fifty years of near daily mental programming just to make a soldier as good as the Harbingers. I wonder if it's worth all that effort?"

Fiona grabbed a second file and a large number of them teetered toward us. We tried to stop the pile from falling, but it was too late, they spilled out of the cabinet, all over the floor.

"Shit," Fiona snapped and started grabbing files from the floor, stuffing them back into the cabinet. "You take a look in that one."

I did as she asked and moved to the final cabinet, opening it up and finding it empty except for a note of paper stuck to the rear of it and a file on the bottom. I removed it from the cabinet and began reading. *Nathan, they're coming for me. They're going to find me and they're going to kill me. They took someone dear to me; I had to inform them that you were going to Mister Baker's. I'm so sorry for never telling you the truth. If you find me before I die, I hope I can apologize for what I did. For everything I did.*

I placed the note on a nearby table and picked up the file, opening it to the first page and reading it with almost immediate horror.

SUBJECT: *Nathaniel Garrett*

AGE: *Approximately 13*

HARBINGER TEST TIME: *Approximately 15 years*

CARRIED OUT BY: *Merlin and Felix Novius*

OBJECTION: *Harbinger testing to commence in earnest at the request of Merlin. Let it be known that I, Felix Novius, am against this procedure being conducted on a thirteen-year-old, no matter his supposed potential. May whatever gods exist have mercy on our souls for what we are about to do.*

CHAPTER 15

Camelot, Albion. Now.

Lucie and I left the hospital, and caught the subway to the third stop in the residential district. It was a fairly short walk through crowded streets to reach the row of three-story houses that Fiona had lived in. It was a fairly quiet neighborhood, with each house having a small lawn with a brick wall and gate.

"Every house here is owned by an Avalon employee," Lucie told me as we reached the gate for Fiona's house. "And yet no one heard anything, no one saw anything."

"You think some people in Camelot are helping the Reavers?"

"Some probably are, some are probably scared it'll happen to them. Whether they mean to help the Reavers or not, they still are by staying quiet."

I pushed open the gate, which squeaked slightly, and took the steps to Fiona's front door.

Lucie arrived beside me and removed a key from her pocket, using it to unlock the door and push it open. We both stood there for a heartbeat. I didn't want to go in, I didn't want to think about Fiona being attacked in her own home, a place of safety. The thought made me angry, and I was already plenty angry.

I took a deep breath and stepped into the house. Pictures adorned the wall of the corridor I found myself in. I walked over to one, a painting of a large green dragon, and saw that her husband had signed it.

"Alan painted them for her while he was in prison," Lucie said. "He appears to have a talent for it."

Indeed he did, the paintings were lovely. I'd have never guessed that Alan, a man whom just over a century ago I couldn't have trusted with a pack of oranges, would end up married to Fiona.

"Where was she found?" I asked.

Lucie pointed to a door at the end of the corridor. "The door was open, she was half in the corridor and half in the room beyond. Her hands and feet were tied together with cable ties."

I walked to the end of the corridor, past a set of stairs and two more doors, and opened the door, discovering that the room beyond was a massive kitchen. "They just left her here?" I asked.

Lucie nodded. "It looks like they went through to the study. It was torn apart."

"Fiona is a conjurer, any illusions she's placed are going to stay there until either she removes them or she dies. She could have put anything about the Reavers anywhere."

"That's why we've got so many agents at the hospital. I think someone will try again once they learn that they didn't get the job done the first time."

"Okay, so let's say she found out something about the Reavers. She'll have hidden it behind a veil. We've got no chance of finding it until she wakes up. Anyone checked her computer?"

Lucie nodded. "First thing we did. It's passworded like you wouldn't believe. She's got some sort of software on it that fucks the entire hard drive should anyone try to crack it. She mentioned it to me a few months ago. Whatever is on there isn't coming off anytime soon."

"Her attacker didn't take the computer?"

She shook her head. "It was scribed in runes. Picking it up would have caused a bit of a mess."

"She really was paranoid."

"The Reavers make you that way. She'd spent a long time looking into them before you arrived back in the late nineteenth century. And with their re-emergence she jumped back in with both feet. I should have done more to keep her safe."

"Like what? Post permanent guards? Then you'd just have an even bigger body count." I walked over to the next door on the corridor and opened it. The mess of paper all over the floor led me to believe it was the study.

"We didn't try to tidy it. No telling with a conjurer what's to be moved and what's a nasty illusion just waiting to do something to some unlucky bastard. Let me ask you something, Nate, would you attack a conjurer in their own home?"

"Not even if you paid me all the money in the world," I said, meaning every word of it. Conjurers weren't as outwardly flashy as sorcerers, but they were just as powerful. Illusions, veils, tricks, and traps; most of which contained the types of things that you really didn't want to stumble across. The problem was they had to keep in proximity to their illusions. The few miles from the hospital to her home was certainly enough for Fiona to keep her secrets, but if she went through the realm gate, or even left Camelot, those illusions would probably crumble.

"Several of the rooms appear to have been searched. I think they were in a hurry. Beds flipped over, that sort of thing. If they had more time they'd have been more meticulous."

"What if they were just making it look like something was searched for? That way they can trash the house and leave. Maybe they assume that whoever Fiona is working with will lead them to the information she had on the Reavers. If she gets hurt, those she's working with will panic and reveal themselves to her attackers. Or maybe it was a threat to someone else. A case of, if we can get to Fiona, we can get to anyone. They stab her, she crashes forward, but isn't instantly dead. They didn't expect her to be, that's why they coated the blade with jorōgumo venom, so they tie her up to keep her in one place. But then why attack her after then? She was of no threat, so why assault her? If you want her dead, why not just stab her again? Why let the venom on the blade do its job, and risk her being found?"

"Two people?"

"One stabs her, goes off to make it look like her attacker wanted something, the other decides to attack her while she's vulnerable. The first was quick, clean, and professional. One stab, ties her up, goes off to do his work. But whoever attacked her while she was tied up, that's either personal or because they enjoy it."

"Someone who knows her? I can check on anyone with a grudge."

"But then if one of them is trying to kill her, why stop and leave? Her attackers took a big risk coming here, and an even bigger one not killing her. But they had to know they'd never find anything. All this mess is to make it look like something it isn't. No, this is about the attack, not the ransacking."

"Maybe they really did mean to kill her. Do you think her attackers were interrupted?"

"If someone knocked on the door, they'd see them. The door has a glass window in it; anyone standing in the corridor is exposed to the person at the door. And they'd just kill them so they weren't exposed. What else would disturb two killers from actually killing someone?"

"Another question. There are a lot of them."

"I don't like questions with no answers." I leaned up against the wall and closed my eyes. "The knife guy hears the commotion downstairs and comes to find his partner is attacking Fiona, and then stops him or her. The knife guy wants her to die of the venom, slowly. Maybe that's personal too. A slow, painful death, especially as no one found Fiona for six hours, so it wasn't anyone coming to the house that stopped them. What scares trained killers off?"

"You?" Lucie guessed.

"I wasn't here though. Otherwise you'd have two very dead assassins scattered throughout the house."

"Someone contacted them, told them to stop the attack and leave. No idea what else could have spooked them into leaving before finishing the job. Maybe they weren't scared off at all. Maybe the one who stabbed her came back downstairs, found their partner kicking the shit out of an unconscious Fiona, and dragged them away."

"It's possible. Okay, we'll put that to one side."

"I wondered when you'd get here," a male voice said, in a slight posh English accent.

I turned to see Remy step through the newly opened front door and into the house. A few centuries ago, Remy had been known as Remy Roax, the English son of a French aristocrat. Remy had moved to England to spend his time avoiding having his head removed by the rest of his countrymen, while drinking himself into a steady oblivion. Unfortunately, he'd met a lovely young lady whom he proceeded to cheat on. She caught him and punished him.

Witches have funny ideas when it comes to punishment. They tend to be creative. Her coven decided that if Remy was going to behave like an animal, they'd turn him into one. The idea was, according to Remy, they were going to turn him into a red fox, hand him over to a huntsman so he could be torn apart by their hounds at some point in the near future. The spell didn't exactly work. The twelve members of the coven were using magic well beyond their capabilities and it ended up killing all of them and feeding their souls into Remy. Remy kept his intellect, his human nature and personality, while adding the life force of twelve young women to his newly changed body.

Remy was now part man, part red fox. He was about three and a half feet tall, and covered in the fur of a red fox, from his fox muzzle to the tip of his bushy tail. He walked upright on legs that were more human in shape than animal, and had fingers, although each of them was tipped with a sharp claw. And he could talk, which allowed him to express his pissed-off-with-the-world nature on a regular basis.

"They hurt my friend," he said as he walked into the house. He carried a basket-hilted sword that was specially designed for him, strapped across his back, and a belt of small knives around his hips.

"I know, we'll find them, Remy," Lucie said.

"I know we will. And then I'm going to tear their fucking throats out," Remy said with a smile, showing his sharp teeth.

Lucie left a short time later after getting a phone call from someone at her office, and because neither Remy nor I wanted to spend more time in Fiona's house than necessary, and as it had stopped raining and was now quite sunny, we took a stroll to a nearby park.

"I want to help you," Remy said as we passed a few people walking dogs, one of which became quite enthusiastic at Remy's presence.

Its owner pulled the dog, a large mastiff, away.

Remy sighed. "Every year more people get dogs here. They either see me as potential food, or a potential threat."

I doubted that Remy was overly concerned about a dog attack. For a start he was an expert swordsman, but the side effect of having the souls of twelve witches dumped into his body not only gave him the ability to resurrect himself twelve times, but also strength several times that of a normal fox.

"You found Fiona, I hear," I said.

Remy stopped walking and nodded. "I smelled the blood as I reached the front door. She'd left me a key a few years back, so I opened it and went in. I hear the knife she was stabbed with was coated in jorōgumo venom. Nasty stuff. Someone wanted her to suffer. I don't think she was meant to die quickly. She was meant to be a warning to others. You look into the Reavers and this is what happens. We all knew she was looking into them, she wasn't frightened about telling people."

"She must have found something."

"She wanted to talk to you."

"What?" I almost snapped. "Since when and why is this the first I've heard of it?"

"About a month ago she told me she'd found something that you needed to see, but she didn't want to inform you until she could verify it. As far as I know, I'm the only one she spoke to about it."

"Reaver related?"

"No idea. I assume so, but it could have just as easily been about her husband."

"Why would Fiona want to talk to me about Alan?"

"Don't know that either, just offering possibilities."

We stood in silence for a moment, then I said, "If some people in Avalon are involved, your life is in danger. You were Fiona's friend; you're looking into her attack. Past actions lead me to believe that you're likely to be on their hit list."

"They're welcome to try. I've still got more than enough souls left to spare a few on those murderous bastards." Remy looked away across the park. "Do you think she's going to make it?"

"I don't know. I hope so. She's strong; she'll fight as much as she can."

"She's one of the few people who treated me like a person, not a sideshow."

"I didn't know anyone treated you like that."

"I'm not like a kitsuni; they can change from fox to human, to mist. I'm somewhere between a were in their beast form and a human. And do you know how many people witches have changed into something like me? Three. In a thousand years, witches turned three people into an animal-human hybrid. Three that we know of, anyway. I'm rare enough to be a curiosity. I guess that means I won't be having any little fox . . . cubs, I guess, to carry on the family name. I'm a rare fox-human, with the souls of witches inside me. Can you imagine what a certain mindset would like to do with me? I'll give you a clue; it's not to re-create a cherished Roald Dahl novel."

I could imagine. It wasn't a pleasant thought.

"And to make matters worse, there was a movie with a talking fucking raccoon in it. Did you know that Camelot has a cinema? That they import movies from Earth? Well, they fucking well do. For months all I heard was how maybe for the sequel they could have me be his stunt double, or that they should paint me brown and make me a star. I began to get angry with the rabid little fucker. And he's not even real! I was angry at a fucking comic book character."

I didn't really know what else to say. "Good film though."

Remy stared at me. "You're sort of missing the point of my anger, here."

"No, I get it. You know, even for my life it's a little weird that I'm talking to a fox about how unhappy he is that people compared him to a raccoon in a science fiction film about a bunch of comic book characters saving the galaxy."

"When you put it like that, I sound downright silly."

"Yeah, *wording*, that's the issue here."

Remy chuckled for a moment, before becoming serious once again. "You know I'm coming with you to find those who attacked Fiona?"

Talking to Remy was hard work sometimes. He had this tendency to switch topics at the drop of a hat. "Wouldn't have it any other way."

We left the park and caught the tube to the residential area at the far edge of the city. It was dusk by the time we arrived. It was quieter here, more open spaces and fewer buildings. Most of the people who lived here were high-ranking officials, and the increase in guards was evident for anyone to see.

Visiting dignitaries, which is what Olivia as a director of the LOA was, were all placed in one of two huge hotels next to a sizeable park. Before Remy and I entered the hotel complex, I spotted Tommy and Kasey running in the park.

We were maybe a hundred feet away when Remy and I entered the park, but Tommy stood up, sniffed the air, and looked back at me. I waved and he began jogging over, Kasey just behind him.

"What are you doing here?" Tommy asked, after giving me a hug.

I explained about what was happening with the Reavers, the hostage situation, the murders of the Williamses, and Fiona's attack. Despite Kasey standing by Tommy's side, I left nothing out. She was fifteen and about to have her own naming ceremony, she was old enough to hear the truth in this matter. Tommy had told me long ago to continue being honest to her, to never sugar coat anything just because she was his daughter.

"We should talk to Olivia," Tommy said when I'd finished. "She might be able to help."

"I was going to go to Merlin or Elaine," I said. "But Olivia sounds like a better idea."

"You came all this way to talk to Merlin?" Remy asked with a slight laugh. "And they say I'm crazy."

"I never said he would be happy to see me," I pointed out. "Hence my reason for also saying 'or Elaine.'"

Tommy opened his mouth to say something, but all that escaped was a low growl. I turned my head and saw the half dozen men walking toward us.

"Kasey, go over to the trees with Remy," Tommy told her.

"Dad . . ."

"Please."

With that one word, Kasey nodded and rushed over to the nearby trees, only to be confronted by another half dozen men leaving their shelter. Remy and Kasey immediately ran back over to us.

"How can we help you?" Tommy asked.

"You and the girl can leave," a short, thin man with a bushy beard, said. "We just want the freak and the sorcerer."

"Did he just call me a freak?" Remy asked. "That's uncalled for."

"You do realize they're probably going to try to kill us," I said.

"Of course, but they could at least be polite about it." He drew his sword. "I guess they need to be taught manners."

The four of us backed away from the two approaching crowds. This had the unfortunate side effect of them merging into one larger, more dangerous crowd.

"I've changed my mind," Bushy Beard said. "Take the girl and her dad too. They had their chance."

There are probably a lot of things in life to ensure you remain part of the living. Threatening the child of a werewolf is not one of those things. Threatening the daughter of Thomas Carpenter is akin to walking into a pub in Liverpool and saying that Manchester United is great. There's a chance you're going to make it out alive, but it's remote, and if you do, you're going to forever remember the time you had your head inserted up your own ass.

Tommy's growls became more pronounced and it wasn't long before the ripping of fabric signified his change from human to werebeast. He howled and the hairs on the back of my neck stood to attention.

"You know, I wondered how long it would be before you got into trouble."

The crowd almost as one turned to find Lucie standing behind them. She wore only a blue sports bra and some green Lycra shorts. Her tattooed runes were available for all to see.

"My name is Lucie Moser. I am the deputy director of the SOA. You gentlemen have two choices. Surrender, or die. Pick quickly, my werewolf friend over there is impatient."

Several of the twelve had turned into werebeasts of their own. I spotted four wolves and a lion, the latter of which had its gaze firmly set on Tommy. Werewolves and werelions had been at war for centuries, before they signed an uneasy peace between the races. Some of them still held grudges.

"Kill them all," Bushy Beard demanded. "But leave Hellequin alive long enough to tell us what we want to know."

"Keep Kasey safe," Tommy shouted just before the werelion charged into him, lifting him from his feet. They both tumbled down the nearby steep bank, the splash signaling that they'd found the stream that ran through the center of the park.

Two of the werewolves ran toward me, both gaining blasts of air for their eagerness, which sent them spilling back into the rest of the group like big, hairy bowling balls.

"You okay?" I asked Remy and Kasey.

"Go," Remy replied. "Kasey is safe with me. We'll get her back to the hotel."

I sprinted toward the group and drove a blade of fire into the nearest werewolf, who howled with pain. I dodged a swipe from a silver blade from another attacker, pushing the wounded werewolf into my path, so that it got sliced across the belly. The werewolf dropped to its knees as the silver burned its flesh, and I threw a ball of air into the face of the knife welder, knocking him back several meters.

Lucie was taking on a brute of a being without breaking a sweat. Every blow it threw at her was countered or dodged. She was fast, and her punches and kicks were doing serious damage to her attacker.

I glanced over at Kasey and Remy and saw that Remy was using his sword against one of the werewolves, while Kasey kept behind him. Another werewolf stalked toward the pair and I ran toward it, wrapped air around its body and squeezed tight, until I felt its bones break.

I removed the magic, and struck it in the back of the neck with a blade of fire. It probably wouldn't kill the werewolf, but having some of his vertebrae severed would hopefully put him out of the fight long enough to deal with his friends.

"Are you o—" I began to ask Kasey, but was grabbed around my waist and tackled to the ground.

A werelion, this one much darker in color than the one Tommy fought, was kneeling on my chest, raining down blows, which I avoided as best as I could, until I heard a low growl and something slammed into the werelion with incredible speed, taking it off me.

I rolled to my feet to see a werebeast Kasey, her tattered clothing clinging to the muscles and fur that had torn through it, trying to disembowel the werelion.

The werelion took a moment and then caught one of Kasey's hands in his, lifting her up off the ground as she snarled and tried to bite him.

I created a sphere of air in my palm, slowly rotating the magic until it was a blur. "Release her, or die," I said.

"I'm going to tear her arm off," the werelion said, as Kasey continued to thrash in his grip.

The werelion laughed, and I took a step forward. I needed to be able to get to the werelion without Kasey getting hurt. The sounds of the fight around me faded as everything in my world became the werelion and Kasey. The werelion's smile faded as water exploded from behind him, swirling over his head and arms, before freezing solid into hundreds of spikes, which punctured his chest and head.

The werelion released Kasey and pitched forward onto the ground. Olivia stepped over the body and took her daughter's hand in hers, speaking softly to the obviously scared Kasey.

I turned back to the melee and found Tommy, covered in blood and wounds, barreling into the fray, tearing chunks out of anyone in his path. One of Lucie's arms was limp, hanging uselessly by her side, but two werewolves lay unmoving at her feet.

Whips of fire trailed from the ends of my hands. One cleaved through the nearest werewolf, decapitating it, while a second removed a chunk of flesh from the chest of another.

I turned as a wood troll strolled toward me, murder in his eyes. At ten feet tall and probably weighing the same as two of me, he didn't need to hurry. Wood trolls are usually quite pleasant and shy away from violence unless forced into it. From the expression on this one's face, that wasn't going to be an option.

I removed the whips and created another sphere of air in my palm, allowing my fire and air magics to merge until the normal white and orange glyphs that adorn my arms and chest when I use magic intertwined. The sphere of air crackled as it changed into one of pure lightning.

I ran toward the troll and plunged the sphere into the creature's stomach, which caused it to scream out as its body was torn in two. Then I released the magic. It cleaved into the troll as if it were shot from a tank cannon, ripping the troll apart as the magical maelstrom consumed it, before throwing it back toward the tree line with incredible force.

The battle stopped around me. Lucie and Tommy stared at me, while our enemies moved aside. I'd just used the kind of magic that makes people take notice. A huge amount of magic that turned a troll into several hundred pounds of bloody goo. It might still be alive, but it certainly wasn't going to be feeling good about itself.

There were four attackers still standing, and several still moaning on the floor. Those capable of verticality charged at me, but the fight was short-lived. Tommy, Lucie, Remy, and I ensured that each of them would never be an issue again.

I glanced at my bloody and battered friends, and then over at Olivia and Kasey, who was now lying on the ground.

"She passed out," Tommy said. "She's not gone through enough changes to be able to cope with the strain."

"Grab those still alive," I told everyone, feeling the anger settle inside me like a cold stone. "I've got some questions they're going to answer."

CHAPTER 16

As it turned out, very few of the attackers had actually been killed. Of the initial twelve, three had died at the scene, including the werelion that had attacked Tommy and the one who'd grabbed Kasey.

Of the remaining nine, five were too seriously injured to do very much other than be arrested and transported to an LOA lock-up. The last four, who included the person I assumed had been in charge, Bushy Beard, were all taken to a building just outside the city limits. The building was well known throughout the various Avalon agencies as a place to take people you wished to interrogate. Whether that meant physically or conversationally was entirely up to those who brought them.

I'd left the interrogation to Olivia's people, who after an hour had confirmed that they weren't saying much.

Lucie had joined us and spent most of her time on the phone to various people yelling at them. She wandered off after a particularly intense conversation and only returned after half an hour.

"We have a problem," she told me.

"And that would be?"

"The five who were being taken for medical treatment never made it. The transport was found abandoned about ten minutes north of the city."

"Any of the SOA agents hurt?"

Lucie shook her head. "They're all gone too."

A horrible feeling bubbled up inside me. "Is there a security detail on Tommy and his family?"

"Olivia arranged it before she went with Tommy to get Kasey checked over. They're LOA, she wouldn't let me put SOA agents in her detail. Elaine has put Olivia in charge of the investigation. Apparently it pissed off some of Olivia's bosses, but no one is going to question it. Besides, if Olivia hadn't been put in charge, she'd have only done her own investigation. I think Elaine would rather have her doing it officially than busting heads trying to find everyone who helped attack her family."

"Probably for the best," I said, knowing full well what a pissed off Olivia is capable of. Better to have her on your side, than doing it herself. "It looks like you have some bad elements among your people."

"It does appear that way, doesn't it?" She sat beside me.

"Check your people for the Reavers tattoo. All of them have it. Like some weird badge of honor."

"Slight problem with that, the ones we took in today don't have one."

That was a bit of a surprise. "So, these won't be the original Reavers. Felix once told me that all of them had to get the tattoo. These are new, and by the way they fought today I'd say they hadn't gone through the Harbinger trials. On the one hand that makes them easier to fight when they present themselves, but it also makes them harder to identify. I don't envy your job."

"Have you heard from Olivia or Tommy?"

"Not yet. I'm going to go over to the hospital once I'm done here."

"We could be here a while longer, yet. It doesn't sound like the prisoners are very chatty."

I paused for a moment. "Let me talk to one of them."

"Not unless I have no other choices. You interrogated a man at Hades's compound a year ago. I heard what you did to him. I can't have dead prisoners here; we have to be better than that."

"I didn't kill him," I objected, remembering the murderous bastard who'd tried to kill Hades before he'd been caught. Unfortunately we hadn't stopped him from killing his own wife and children.

"You took his hands. You know he killed himself in our jail?"

"Yeah, well, I'm not going to kill anyone. Just talk. They wanted to kill me back in Southampton, now they want to take me to talk. I'd like to know why. And I heard your prisoner died by getting into a fight with another prisoner."

"He walked up to a cave troll and kicked him. The troll tore his head off and threw it fifty feet away. What would you call that?"

"Suicide by troll. That's new."

Remy came out of the building and walked over to us. "They're not talking at all. We had to restrain one before he bit his own tongue off. There's a possibility they're a little fanatical."

"Only a possibility?" Lucie asked.

"They could be clinically fucking insane," Remy said with a slight shrug. "Possibly both."

"Do we know any of their names?" I asked.

Remy shook his head. "They haven't been forthcoming, and as you know Avalon doesn't keep fingerprint or DNA records, much to my annoyance." He turned to Lucie. "Look, boss, I know you don't approve of violence against prisoners, but on this occasion I can't see how else we're going to get anywhere. These guys aren't talking, and everyone is getting fed up with going through the same spiel. It's getting us nowhere."

"I don't want my agents committing violence against them," Lucie said.

"Is it my turn now?" I asked.

"You okay doing this?" Remy asked.

I shrugged. "It's something I'm good at."

"And that is why I'm grateful we're on the same side," Remy said with a chuckle.

"Nate," Lucie said, taking hold of my arm. "It looks like I don't have a lot of choice in this, does it? No deaths, no missing parts. I'm asking you to go in there as Hellequin and get answers."

"You're Hellequin?" Remy asked.

"You'd not heard?"

"I'd heard rumors about his re-appearance, but didn't know it was you. You're a celebrity. So long as you call someone who a bunch of people actively want to kill a celebrity."

"No killing," I said to Lucie, ignoring Remy. "Promise."

I entered the building and was taken by one of four guards to a corridor containing the first set of interrogation rooms on the floor above.

"Which one is Bushy Beard in?" I asked as I glanced around the four identical doors, arranged as two opposite one another.

The guard pointed to the room closest to the end of the corridor. "Best of luck," she said and walked off.

I opened the door to the room and found Bushy Beard sitting on a chair with a table between us. I grabbed a second chair, which was closest to the door, and sat down. There were no two-way mirrors or hidden cameras in the room. There was one quite visible camera above the door and another at the rear of the room. They recorded on a continuous loop when someone was inside the room. The feed was displayed on a monitor on the ground floor, which I was sure was currently the most popular monitor in the building.

Bushy wore a sorcerer's band. It's a small metal bracelet with runes carved into it, which negates the magical abilities of whoever wears it. I hate the things, but I had to admit I didn't mind Bushy wearing one.

"Do you know who I am?" I asked.

"Hellequin, of course I know. I've been waiting for you."

"You have? That's nice, why's that?"

"You are one of those we will slaughter for past transgressions against the Reavers. You thought us dead, we will never die."

It didn't surprise me that he knew I was Hellequin. Those in West Quay had known who I was, so I assumed it was common knowledge throughout the Reavers. "You attacked me and my friends. I wondered why there were no magic users or elementals in your group."

"Too flashy. We were meant to overpower you. But Lucie and Olivia arrived. We hadn't expected them. Nor that werewolf and his young bitch."

I fought the urge to dent the table with his face. "I wonder, why not just wait until I was alone?"

"I was impatient. I thought you'd be an easy target with so many of us."

"That's not working out so well for you. First West Quay, now Camelot. Two public venues, precisely zero me deaths."

"West Quay was a mistake. They should have waited. They did the best they could."

"So, who's feeding you information about what happened in West Quay?"

Bushy paused. "We are a large organization. With many willing members. The information will always get to those who need to know it."

"Why did you want to talk to me? You wanted to kill me back in Southampton."

"Things have changed."

"What things?"

"You know where Felix Novius is. You will tell us."

"Who told you I know that?" I wondered.

"That's not important. You will tell us where he is or we will exact pain upon those you care about. After that you will die, and die soon. At the hands of the newly reborn Reavers. Once our enemies are out of the way, we will ensure that Avalon becomes the force it needs to be. A force of power and strength."

"Tonight, twelve of you got your asses kicked by two werewolves, a fox-man, an enchanter, an elemental, and a sorcerer. And one of those werewolves is a fifteen-year-old girl. That doesn't strike me as an overly strong group. You're not even the original Reavers. You haven't gone through the Harbinger trials, you haven't got tattoos. You're a pale imitation of those I helped destroy. Lucie is going to make it her mission in life to root out any and all Reavers within the SOA and purge you from existence."

"We may not have the knowledge of our predecessors, but we have the numbers and the will to do what must be done. As for Lucie, she'll be dead long before that happens."

"You're going to kill Lucie?" I laughed. "I've seen her go toe-to-toe with Helios. You think a few assholes with delusions of grandeur are going to stop her?"

"I'll see your head on a pike beside hers, before our mission is done."

"Does Merlin know you're back? I'm betting not. I doubt Elaine allows him the sort of freedom he used to have."

"Elaine is a traitor. She will be purged too."

"You're going to kill Elaine, now? Wow, you really are fighting above your weight class. Even Merlin wouldn't start that fight, and from the last time I spoke to him, I didn't think there was much he wouldn't do anymore."

Bushy launched himself up, his face a mass of redness. "Merlin is not aware of our existence. We do these things to make us strong. Not to make him strong."

He immediately realized his error in having told me anything, and lunged at me. I grabbed his hand and twisted, forcing him face first onto the cold metal table. I punched him in the kidney, and the air rushed out of him.

"That was rude. We were having a nice chat and you had to go and ruin it by being rude." I held his arm steady; if I'd decided to I could have broken it in half a dozen places. "Now, if I let you go, what are you going to do?"

"Kill you," he seethed through gritted teeth.

I punched him in the kidney again. "Either you be nice, or I'll stop pretending I don't want to hurt you."

I applied a little more pressure on his arm.

"Fine," he snapped and I released him, pushing him back onto his chair, while he rubbed his elbow.

"Who's in charge of this new movement? Please remember, I'm being very nice. If you'd like I could just as easily stop."

"I don't know. We get our orders from an agent who works in Avalon."

"And that agent's name?"

"We called him Daniels. He was in charge of taking those injured prisoners to the hospital. I assume none of them made it." He finished his sentence with a smirk.

"Okay, so who attacked Fiona?"

"I don't—" he began.

"Let me finish. If you say you don't know, I'm going to hurt you."

"I can't tell you the answer to something I don't know. You might as well hurt me."

I sat back on my chair. "I have a better idea. You're going to tell me about the Reavers, about their command structure, about why you've suddenly started killing people, and why you're interested in finding Felix Novius."

"Are you going to beat me if I don't talk?"

"Actually, I'm going to go into those other three rooms and tell your friends that you told us everything. And then I'm going to make sure that it gets out that you're cooperating with me, personally. Then we're going to take you and your friends to a holding facility, where you can all bond together and discuss how much you betrayed them. Or we can let you all go, and see how long it takes for your old friends to find you. I wonder how they'd punish a traitor to their cause."

For the first time since I'd arrived in the room, Bushy looked genuinely scared. "You can't do that."

"Can. And will. I don't give two shits about your piss-awful excuse for a life. So, wanna help and have it be kept secret, or wanna keep schtum and be a traitor to your precious Reavers?"

"Schtum?"

"Means keep quiet. So which one is it?"

Bushy bowed his head slightly. "They use these on traitors," he said quietly and lifted his hand. "Sorcerer's bands. Then they force the wearer to remove it without the key."

Apparently Bushy feared his allies and what they'd do to him a lot more than anything I could do.

Anyone trying to remove a sorcerer's band without the key activates another rune inside the metal, which turns the band into a magical napalm bomb, killing its wearer in as horrific and painful a way as possible.

"If no one has ever mentioned it before, the Reavers are one classy group."

He ignored my taunt. "What do you want to know?"

"Everything you do."

"You swear whatever I say is between us?"

"Not quite ready to die for the cause?"

Bushy looked at the floor.

"You tell me what I want to know and we'll keep it between us. If you decide to mess me about, I promise to turn and look the other way while your friends tear you apart."

Bushy nodded and looked up at me. "The Reavers are set into different groups; each one is given a different task. No one knows the current command structure. That way if any of us get caught, we can't give the game away. My group was tasked with your questioning and murder. We were also tasked with killing Remy, he's become too vocal an opponent of ours to be allowed to live. His friendship with Fiona sealed that deal."

"Who attacked Fiona?"

"I've already told you, I don't know. I can't tell you how many Reaver groups there are in Camelot, but it wasn't done through mine."

"How many more members of your group are there?"

"Those of us who attacked you. Then there's Daniels, three other SOA agents, and a few others who have probably gone to ground by now. Twenty in all."

"I want the SOA agents' names." I removed a piece of paper and pen from my pocket, and passed them to Bushy.

He wrote down four names, including Daniels, although I didn't recognize any of them.

"Why now?" I asked.

"I don't know the answer to that. We've been Reavers for years, waiting in the shadows for a chance to strike."

"Waiting in the shadows? Seriously?"

"What would you call it? We've lived our lives as good Avalon subjects, and now we're joined as one to remove those who once tried to destroy us. Why now, I have no idea. But I'm glad to be a part of it."

He was beginning to sound like the same idiot I'd met when I'd first arrived. Apparently just telling me their plans raised his confidence.

"Why Felix?"

"He betrayed us. He needs to die. After Liz Williams, we couldn't risk trying another psychic and having them alert the wrong person, or not being powerful enough to track him. However, we will find him, no matter how long it takes, or how many bodies have to be piled up. We will find Felix and we will extract our vengeance for his betrayal."

"What happens once all of your enemies are dead? What's the plan once you kill Felix?"

"Felix's death will usher in a new era for the Reavers. He was the one who helped create us, and from his blood and knowledge we will be reborn."

It sounded like the ranting of someone who'd listened to the spiel so many times he believed it. But then one of his words stuck in my mind. *Knowledge*. "He knows too much, doesn't he? That's the problem here. You're scared that Felix knows who you are. He once had the greatest catalog of Reaver activity; he monitored all of you, and you're scared he's still doing it. You're scared he has this massive file of Reavers and he's going to expose those of you in charge."

"You don't know anything," he stammered far too quickly, the confidence evaporating once again.

"That's really it, isn't it? You need Felix dead because if he's still alive, he could give away who's in charge of your little group before you reveal yourself. But you don't know where he is, and once you killed the Williamses, you somehow got it into your head that maybe I knew where Felix was."

Bushy turned away from me. "We will be victorious."

"The Reavers are an antiquated idea, a group whose very existence is an affront to everything Avalon is meant to hold dear. You can throw as many people at me as you like, I'm happy to keep killing you until you finally get the message. Your kind isn't wanted."

Before he could say more, I turned and left him alone in his small room.

"He's still alive," I told Lucie and Remy, who'd waited outside.

"We found the escaped Reavers and SOA agents," Lucie said. "All dead."

"Bushy said that there were a few who didn't take part, I'd keep an eye out for them." I passed her the paper with the names. "All of these SOA agents are working for the Reavers."

Lucie scanned the list. "Two of these are dead, including this Daniels person. The other two will be taken before the morning. Anything else?"

"Whoever killed those injured Reavers will come for your guests."

"I know. That's the plan," Lucie told me. "They come for these men and we grab them."

I should have expected Lucie to have already come up with the idea to use the prisoners as bait. "I'm going to the hospital to see everyone. If you need me . . ." I patted my pocket. "I didn't bring a phone, I'm sure Olivia has one."

"I've got her number. Be careful, Nate, these guys aren't the type to stop after only one try."

"I'm coming with you," Remy said. "They want me dead too. I'd like to give them a harder time of accomplishing that plan."

"Like I said before, happy to have you on board," I said.

"You need anything else?" Lucie asked.

"They won't know who attacked Fiona. There's at least one other group of Reavers in Camelot. I'd guess more SOA are involved. I'm going to be leaving the realm soon, take care of yourself."

"You're leaving the realm?" Lucie asked, slightly surprised. "You just arrived."

"These people are after Felix. They thought I might know where he is, but there's only one person on Earth who knows where Felix is. I think Felix has been looking into the Reavers again. The Reavers certainly believe he has, and from knowing the man, it's not exactly a difficult leap to assume. At some point, the Reavers are going to go after the man who knows where Felix is. I plan on getting there first. That is if they haven't already gone after him."

"And who might that be?" Lucie asked.

I considered not telling her. For a brief moment I wondered, what if she's involved, what if Lucie has betrayed us all? I immediately felt foolish for thinking it. Lucie was, while not my friend, someone I knew I could trust. "Fiona's husband, Alan."

Remy gasped, which is an odd thing to hear from a fox. "She never told me that Alan knew where Felix was."

"She probably didn't know. No one does. Not unless Alan's started opening his big mouth again."

"If you're off to see Alan Daly, you're going to need Olivia's help," Lucie pointed out. "And I spoke to the warden there a few hours ago. Alan is fine."

"You trust this warden?"

Lucie shook her head. "Elaine does though. She gave him the job."

That would have to do for now. Even so, Alan was in danger, if not immediately then in due time. The Reavers might not control the prison, but that didn't mean they couldn't get to Alan.

Alan Daly, Fiona's husband of over seventy years, was being held in The Hole. It was one of several high-security prisons dotted around the globe. The Hole was on an island in the North Atlantic, with a permanent no-fly zone above it for anyone who wasn't pre-cleared by Avalon. The building on top of the island was unofficially a research station, and anyone actually landing there required a helicopter, so for the most part the island was ignored by the masses.

Beneath the exterior buildings lay several miles of underground prison, making a total of ten floors; the higher the number, the deeper underground, and the more dangerous the prisoners. Floors eight to ten don't even have any guards; they're ruled by the prisoners themselves. These floors are a bad place, full of bad people. Alan was on the first floor, where most of the prisoners are political in nature, or are there to serve years or decades rather than centuries. They're still pretty dangerous people, but not so dangerous that you might not make it out before someone tried to eat your face.

Lucie got another call before I could say anything else and waved as she walked off to answer it.

"You know, I might have some issues leaving this realm," Remy said as one of the cars pulled up and we climbed inside.

"I know," I said. "You may have to stay here."

"I want to help, Nate," Remy said. "If I stay here, what am I going to do? I'm a target; whoever is around me is going to be a target too."

"We'll figure something out."

Remy didn't speak again for a few minutes. "This is going to get worse isn't it?"

"Someone is behind the resurgence of the Reavers. Someone has placed people inside the SOA, and who knows how many other organizations. Right now, I'm not in the mind to trust anyone I don't already know. But someone has to be in charge. Until we figure out who it is, yeah, it could get worse."

I got the impression that was what Remy had expected me to say, but that it definitely wasn't what he wanted to hear. Him and me both.

CHAPTER 17

The hospital was teeming with LOA agents; trying to kill one of their families tended to have a pretty immediate response, and trying to kill the family of a director of the LOA was normally a reason to increase the DEFCON level of everyone.

Remy and I were let into the hospital foyer, mostly because people recognized Remy. One of them told him that Olivia was up on the sixth floor, so we walked through the hallways until we reached the lifts, where I spotted Tommy at the far end of the hall. He was standing up against a door, looking through the glass to the gardens at the rear of the hospital.

"I'll catch you up," I told Remy, who noticed Tommy and nodded.

"Tommy," I called out as I walked toward him.

He turned back to me and waved. He looked tired.

"You okay?" I asked.

Tommy nodded. "We're all good."

"Hey, I'm sorry I got you involved in this. Those Reavers were after me. I'd hoped that by coming here, I could warn you in case they tried to get to me through you. Turns out you were only in danger when I turned up."

"Knock it off, I'm glad you came. You'd be dead if you hadn't. I'm not worried about people getting to you through my family and me, and neither is Olivia. In case you hadn't noticed, we're quite capable of taking care of ourselves. You should speak to Elaine; she might be able to help. You know I can't go with you if you leave Camelot, though. I can't leave my family."

I knew. "I'd never ask."

Tommy patted me on the shoulder. "How are you? I heard from Ellie about the venom. Has your nightmare come calling yet? I imagine your constant use of magic to keep the venom away will make it easier for it to say hi."

A year ago, my nightmare—the living embodiment of magic that's inside every sorcerer, one that wants to be freed to take over the body of its host—decided to help me fight a man who was making me relive the worst moments of my life. My nightmare had decided to call itself Erebus, but since then it had been mostly quiet. I hadn't told Tommy about what happened, nor anyone else for that matter, because allowing the nightmare to take over your body was a death sentence for the host. Even if you survived the transformation, Avalon hunted down sorcerers who had allowed it to happen. So I kept it to myself. I didn't want to have to explain that I was in control. They wouldn't have believed me.

I looked outside and saw Kasey, her back toward us, sitting on a bench. I spotted four agents all watching her in the least discreet way possible. "Why are you watching Kasey as if she's about to burst into flame?"

"She changed today. Went full werebeast, I'm worried about her."

"Was that her first time?"

"Fourth. Two in the space of a week though. That's a lot of strain on her body."

"So, you're standing here so you can give her space, but be close enough if she wants to chat?"

"I've already spoken to her, she's scared. Her werebeast just took over. Emotions are high in young people as it is; those emotions make it easier for the beast to take over. The other changes were calm, controlled. This one wasn't. She doesn't know how to handle it. I told her it's fine, told her not to worry. I'm just giving her some space to work it through. The agents were always there. Apparently an attack involving Olivia has sparked the LOA's parental side."

"Can I go talk to her?"

"Sure, you're not a wolf though. Not sure how much good you'll be."

"I'm going to offer to be her sentinel."

Tommy stared at me, and then enveloped me in a hug that was pretty close to breaking bones.

"Thanks for that," I wheezed when he finally released me.

"Kasey will be over the moon. Hell, I'm over the moon. She didn't want to ask you because . . ."

"Yeah, Ellie told me. Sorry for not even considering she might want me there. Where is Ellie anyway?"

"She's with Olivia. She's pretty angry she wasn't there earlier. I don't think she'll be letting us out of her sight for the rest of the time we're here. You really think they'll try again?"

"I don't know. I doubt it, not now that the LOA are out in force. Unless the LOA are involved."

"Olivia and I thought that too. We don't think they are though. No LOA agents have been involved up to now, and Olivia knows the main members in Camelot pretty well. Even so, they have psychics and sorcerers with mind magic going around checking things out. If anyone in the LOA is involved, we'll know. At least anyone in Camelot."

That was probably the most reassuring thing I'd been told since this whole thing started. "They seem to want to attack weaker targets; people alone or out of their element. Going after someone who has an army of heavily armed agents is probably not on their to-do list. Even so, you're best to keep an eye out. There are members of the SOA involved in this. I can't say that the disease of the Reavers hasn't spread to other groups within Avalon."

"Olivia isn't exactly the most trusting person on the planet when it comes to other Avalon agencies, so I can't say that knowing the SOA are compromised will change her perception."

I pushed open the door. "I'll be back in a few," I told Tommy and walked out into the splendid garden.

The flowers, the names of which escaped me, were stunning. It was a cascade of color that swept across the garden, and probably took longer to maintain than I'd have thought possible.

"Hi," I said as I sat beside Kasey on the wooden bench.

She turned to look at me. "Hi. I guess you're here to tell me everything is okay. That I shouldn't worry about the werebeast. Dad already tried that. It didn't make me feel better."

"Oh, you should totally be concerned about the werebeast form. It's dangerous. You lose control and you could kill someone."

Kasey's jaw dropped open. "Seriously? How the hell is that comforting?"

"I'm not trying to comfort you. My job is to be honest; I thought we'd agreed on that several years back."

"You can be a little comforting."

"Oh okay. Let's try this. The werebeast isn't anything to be scared of; it's really just a big teddy bear that needs a hug. Or teddy wolf as it were. Feel better?"

"Not even slightly."

"Sucks to be you then."

Kasey glared at me and then laughed. "You know fifteen-year-old girls are full of hormones, you say the wrong thing and we just go up like kindling."

"Not literally I hope. I'd like to think spontaneous combustion is outside the realm of abilities for most teenagers."

"Did you just come here to mock me?"

"Well, I'd mock your dad, but he's tired and liable to punch me. I've had enough people try to punch me for one day."

"I could punch you."

"True, but you're smaller than him. I'll take the risk."

Kasey laughed again and glanced behind us. "Those agents will not go away. I tried."

"They're here to keep everyone safe. There's some weird shit going on in Avalon. Your mum's people are probably best placed to make sure it doesn't get worse."

"I'm really sorry about losing control." Kasey's voice was soft, barely above a whisper. She turned away, ashamed at what she'd done.

I placed a hand on her shoulder and she looked back at me. "Don't be daft. Do you know what happened the first time I met your dad and he turned?"

"He ate a boar."

"He did. But a few times after that, he lost his cool and changed into his werebeast form to attack a nightmare. Almost got killed for his trouble. He let his emotions get the better of him, as everyone does on occasion. You're no different. You lost your cool and tried to disembowel a werelion. You probably stopped me from taking any more hits, and you certainly stopped me from having to turn him into werelion jerky."

"But I've known for years not to lose my cool when I finally change. And I ignored all of that."

"In the heat of battle, emotions aren't so easy to control. Even those of us used to fighting, used to that feeling of life or death, we can still lose it, still snap as the red mist descends across our vision. The trick isn't stopping it from happening, it's recognizing when it happens so you can control it. You're not exactly trained in combat, Kase."

"I need to be. I'm a werewolf, at some point I'll have to fight. I need to be ready for that."

"And that's why Ellie is going to be one of your sentinels."

"You know about that?"

I nodded. "She told me. She also told me that you want me to be your second sentinel. That true?"

Kasey nodded. "But I understand if you don't want to. Dad says your history with Avalon is complicated. Actually he used more swear words than that, but I'm cleaning it up."

I laughed. "Complicated is a good way to describe it. The problem is between me and Merlin, and a few others. Not Avalon as a whole. If you want me to be your sentinel, I'd be honored. I'll need to figure out what the hell I'm meant to say though. I think Ellie has the wolf part of your life well and truly covered."

"I don't mind what you say. I just want the people I love to be at the ceremony."

"That's a good trick," I said with a smile.

"What?"

"Saying the exact right thing at the exact right moment. You didn't get that from your dad."

Kasey laughed, glanced over at Tommy, and waved. Tommy smiled and waved back. "He's worried about me."

"You're his daughter. He has every right to. In fact I'm pretty sure it's almost his entire job when it comes to a teenage daughter."

"I went on a date the other day. With a boy. Dad wanted to greet the door in wolfbeast form. He was going to threaten to eat him."

An image rushed to the front of my head and made me laugh. "You'll have to give your dad some leeway on boys. He doesn't trust them. He was one, so he knows the mindset."

"We just went to the cinema. Nothing scandalous occurred. Chloe took her boyfriend too. We've been hanging out a lot since what happened in Tartarus. I don't even think her mum notices."

"She's lucky to have a friend like you. And you like her. It's good to see."

"Will dad ever be okay with me and boys?"

"He'll get used to the idea. Or your mum will make him live in the shed. Either way, you win."

We sat next to one another in silence for a while, listening to the wind as it rustled the leaves on the nearby trees.

Eventually, Kasey broke the silence, "Can you teach me?"

I was confused for a moment. "About boys? Yeah, sure, they're all idiots. If you use that as a baseline, you can't go far wrong."

Kasey laughed again. "I meant about how to fight. Can you teach me how to fight?"

"Don't you want your mum, or dad, to teach you that? Or Ellie for that matter?"

"You were Hellequin. I've seen you fight, I want to be able to do that."

I shook my head. "You really don't. No one should want to be able to do what I do. I go to a dark place where I don't care about what I have to do to win. I can switch off that place in my head that makes me feel anything for removing someone in my way. You don't want that."

"No, you're right, but I do want to be trained by the best. That's you. Dad and Mum both said in a straight fight, you're probably better than them. Having werewolf strength is great, but if someone can use that against me, what's the point?"

I stared at her for what felt like hours. "I'm really sorry, but I don't think that's a good idea."

She looked deflated, but not hugely upset; she'd probably already figured out what my answer was going to be. "Sorry, but I had to ask. Even if you say no, at least I know I've asked."

I stood up and stretched my back. "I need to go talk to your mum."

"Thanks, Nate. I'm glad you're here. I hope you find these Reavers before they hurt anyone else."

"So do I, Kase, so do I."

Olivia and Ellie were both in an office on the fourth floor. As I walked in, alongside Kasey and Tommy, and gaining glances from the agents posted outside, Ellie rushed over to hug me, while Olivia was on the phone. Remy was sitting in the corner; he nodded in my direction when I saw him, and I returned the gesture.

"You okay?" Ellie asked.

I nodded. "All good. You missed all the fun."

She rolled her eyes. "You say it's fun now, but I doubt it was much fun at the time."

She had a good point. "I've arranged with Kasey to become her second sentinel," I said.

Ellie hugged me and kissed me on the cheek. "I told you she'd be happy."

"That you did." I looked over at Olivia as she hung up the phone. "It's one of the things I need to talk to you about, Olivia."

Tommy entered the room, walking over to Olivia and giving her a kiss.

"Talk away," Olivia said to me.

"How long before the naming ceremony takes place?"

"A few days," Olivia said. "With all of this, I want to be assured that we're safe before we go ahead. Thanks for deciding to be involved, by the way; I'm sure Kasey is thrilled."

"Well, all of this happiness is about to take a nose dive," I said. "I need access to The Hole. To Alan Daly in particular."

"First, tell me everything that happened in the interrogation."

I explained what Bushy had said, leaving nothing out, no matter how small. "He said that they were going to kill their enemies and make Avalon stronger," I finished.

"Take over," Olivia said. "They want to make Avalon strong by taking power. The SOA is already corrupted."

"That's my interpretation too," I said. "But what about the rest of Avalon? What about the LOA? Lucie said you've got people working on it, but what if they're involved?"

I'd expected some argument from Olivia for my suggesting her own organization could be involved but she just sighed.

"Lucie said not everyone has a tattoo, that makes things more difficult, but we are working on it. Trust *me*, Nate. As of thirty minutes ago, Lucie and I agreed to remove the SOA from all positions and have them under house arrest. Over five thousand people in Camelot are now being relieved from their roles and replaced with LOA personnel. If I don't know who I can trust, I don't trust anyone."

"And then what?" Remy asked. "You're just going to throw dissent in among the SOA."

"Better than leaving them in positions of power. Officially, it's a screening check of their personnel. They've had people turn against them; they need to know who *they* can trust."

"Unofficially?" I asked.

"We're dredging their lives. Friends, family, anyone they work with, we're checking all of it."

"How did Kay take it?" I asked.

"Surprisingly well. He agreed with the plan, he wants to interview the prisoners himself. He's certainly very angry that his people have betrayed us. It's personal for him."

"Be careful he doesn't try to take control," I said. "He's good at that."

"You don't need to worry about that," Olivia explained. "Elaine is in charge of it. She has me and three other directors organizing the whole thing. She wants to see you before you leave, by the way. I got the feeling it wasn't a request."

"Yeah, she was on my list," I admitted. "So about my access to Alan?"

"Tommy told me that the Reavers wanted you alive to find Felix. That's who I was on the phone with. You should be able to access the prison in about twelve hours. Plenty of time to leave

Albion and get over there. You have clearance to remove Alan from The Hole if need be. But he's then your responsibility and you have to put him back where you found him."

"I'll make sure not to damage the prisoner," I promised with a smile.

"I'm coming with you," Ellie said. "Frankly, Olivia and Tommy are safe here. You . . . well, I need to make sure *you* come back in one piece. I can't very well give Matthew an assurance that I'll watch after you, and then abandon you."

"What about you, Remy?" I asked. "You still on board? Olivia's arranged a helicopter to take us from Avalon Island to The Hole. That limits the number of people who might be surprised to see a talking fox. I owe it to Fiona to tell Alan what's happened. And even more to help find her attackers."

"As if there was any doubt that I'd join you," Remy said.

"You really think Felix knows who's behind the Reavers' resurgence?" Olivia asked.

The more I thought about it, the more it made sense to me. Felix wasn't exactly the type of person to just give up. Especially not on his need to expose the people he thought were destroying everything he'd worked to establish. And that's not including the fact that they ousted him as the leader of the Reavers all those years ago. I imagined that still stung.

I nodded. "I think they want to find him because he can expose them. Wherever he is, he clearly can't contact anyone. I'm certain he'd have tried to contact myself, or even Fiona."

"Maybe he did contact Fiona?" Tommy suggested. "Maybe that's what got her attacked."

"It's possible," I admitted. "But then why not contact me? There are too many questions, and the Reavers want Felix, so that means I want him too. None of the Reavers know that Alan is aware of Felix's whereabouts. They can't know, otherwise why bother going to Liz Williams, except to kill her. They needed her help, she refused, so they killed her. They were always going to kill her; as a psychic, Liz knew that."

"Why not hurt her husband to force Liz to tell them?" Tommy asked.

"I don't think Liz would have broken that easily, even doing that. I think timewise, it was easier to threaten their lives or kill them to ensure silence. I have this awful feeling that they decided to kill them the moment I turned up."

"If that's even true, you can't blame yourself," Ellie said.

"I don't, I blame them. I intend to ensure they understand that when I find those responsible for all of this. The Reavers killed the Williamses, tried to kill me, Remy, and Fiona. So far they haven't exactly put a lot in the win column, I'd like to ensure it stays that way."

"Maybe they weren't trying to kill Fiona," Olivia said.

Everyone looked at her.

"Well, what if her attack was a message? They turn over her house, attack her, but make sure not to kill her. They use venom that is slow acting, and only stab her once. Lucie told me your idea about two attackers. It makes sense, one goes off to make it look like they were searching, the second decided to take it further. First comes back, stops his partner from killing Fiona and they both leave. I think that has merit."

"Who is it a message for?" Tommy asked.

"No idea. Maybe Lucie, maybe Alan. Just because he's in prison doesn't mean no one can get to him. But if they kill him then all hell will break loose and the Reavers would be exposed too early. So they keep him quiet and well behaved by telling him what happened to his wife. If he says anything they kill her. Six weeks until he's out. Plenty of time for whatever plan the Reavers have to be unstoppable. Lucie says you trust the warden, Olivia."

"Very much so. He was an excellent agent. And that's coming from someone with trust issues."

"What about the people who work for him?"

"You think there's a guard there working for the Reavers?" Tommy asked.

"They got into the SOA, but not the LOA or any other part of Avalon. At least none that we know of. I think they would have sent someone to keep an eye on Alan."

"Get Alan out and get Felix," Olivia said. "If he does know who those in charge are, then we'll use that name to burn the Reavers to the ground."

I turned to Ellie and Remy. "You both have four hours to get ready. Meet me at the realm gate. I'll be there as soon as I'm done at the palace."

CHAPTER 18

The palace in Camelot was once a sizeable castle in the center of the city. Over the years the castle had been built up, with new parts added time and time again. It was now several times larger than it had first been.

The city had spilled out from the palace at an astonishing rate, moving from small village size to the sprawling metropolis that currently made up the city. Over the centuries, smaller towns and villages that had once been numerous across the realm had been folded into the city as well.

With the increase in members of Avalon, came an increase in those governing them. There are several groups who all hold a piece of Avalon's power. The lords and ladies of Avalon—each among the highest ranked members within their races—made up a substantial portion of the council of Avalon. The more powerful groups had broken off into their own sects; the werewolves, vampires, Hera and her group, along with several others—including Hades—all had their own personal stake.

Above it all had once sat Merlin and his knights. The knights were a separate group, capable of wielding their own power, although their ranks were barely recognizable compared to those who'd been considered knights when Arthur had first taken the throne. Merlin still considered himself the leader of Avalon, keeping the spot warm for Arthur's eventual return. But he barely took part in the day-to-day running, only appearing for the more important votes, much like Hera and Hades.

For the most part, Elaine and those she trusted ruled Avalon, but it was an uneasy rule. She rarely did anything that might gain the attention of Merlin, lest he decide to start interjecting once again, and so she'd kept everything in a state of status quo. A fact that most of the larger powers within Avalon actively encouraged; they didn't want anyone upsetting the apple cart, so to speak. All the while Elaine grew more and more annoyed with how things were done.

I walked up the steps to the grand palace, which loomed over me and the gardens that separated the rest of the city from the palace.

"Can I help you?" a rotund guard asked as I reached one of several palace entrances.

"Here to see Elaine," I told him and he tapped the side of his head, his eyes going pure white for a moment. He was a telepath; a rare and powerful being, often used by Avalon to do non-invasive interrogation.

"She's in the council room. She'll meet you there."

"Thank you," I said and entered the palace.

The old brick of the original castle had been removed and replaced with more modern steel and concrete well before I'd last visited the realm, but the interior reception area held the same art that would have been found inside the old castle. I paused for a second, noticing the paintings which hung around me. They were mostly of Arthur, or Camelot, but a few were of the kings from long ago. There was even one of Galahad, something I found strange as he'd left Avalon to join—and eventually become the ruler of—Shadow Falls, another realm completely separate from Avalon's influence. Merlin would never have allowed the painting to be on display. He didn't take rejection very well.

I walked past dozens of people, most of whom were working, or visiting the palace, and tried not to stop and stare at every new thing I saw. It was a lengthy walk to the council chambers, which sat at the left wing of the palace, and I had to go through three different checkpoints—each time answering the same questions—before I reached the massive wooden doors, each with intricate carvings adorning them. Two guards pulled the doors open, and I stepped into the council chamber.

The room had a raised platform on one side, beneath a massive screen. A simple throne sat on the platform, behind two smaller chairs. The throne hadn't been used since Arthur had been attacked. Set out in a horseshoe formation before the platform were a dozen rows of tables and chairs. Each was divided into several sections, depending on their species and ranking within Avalon. When it was full, there were close to three hundred people in the room. It was currently empty except for one woman who sat on a table usually reserved for Hera. I chuckled to myself; Hera would be so mad if she knew Elaine was sitting on it.

"You should do that when Hera's here," I told her, my voice echoing around the chamber.

Elaine wore an elegant red and black kimono, her hair tied up in a bun, and her face lit up as she smiled. She pushed herself off the table, her heels clicking against the polished marble floor as she walked toward me.

"You look good," she said and hugged me.

"You too, but then you always do," I told her as she released me.

"I feel tired and old," she told me. "It's been a long century. Running this place, but not really being able to run it. It's fairly exhausting."

"I can imagine."

"Are you still mad at me?"

I shook my head. "You knew what Felix and Merlin did. You knew and never told me. I was mad as all hell, but even if you had told me I probably wouldn't have believed you without proof."

"Can I ask you a question?"

I was about to say yes, when Elaine interrupted. "Before you agree, know this. I want the truth. Anything less than that and I don't know what will happen."

"At no point have I ever lied to you, Elaine. Not once. I may have avoided the truth, I may have not wanted to talk about something, but I've never lied. Ask me."

"There's more. Someone else here wants to know the answer to this question. With your permission I'll let them hear it."

I nodded.

Elaine raised her hand and a spark of flame leapt from one finger. Somewhere in the dark edges of the room a door opened and closed. A moment later Lir's son, Mac, came into view. Facially, Mac was the spitting image of his father, but he was considerably more muscular, and his red hair was tied back in a plait.

"You still want to answer this?" Mac asked.

Part of me was annoyed that Elaine and Mac had colluded to ensure I had to tell both of them the answer to the question I knew was coming. But another, larger part, was just grateful I could get it over and done with.

"Just ask the damn question," I said, surprised at the annoyance in my voice.

"Did you kill Mordred?"

And there it was. The question I'd hoped she wouldn't ask. In fact it was the entire reason I had hoped to leave Avalon without her notice, although being attacked in the middle of it had put paid to that idea. "Yes."

Elaine swallowed, and took a deep breath. Mac's hands balled into muscular fists.

"I went to New York, acquired a rifle, and waited for him," I told them. "Three shots later, he was dead."

"Are you sure?" Elaine asked.

"I put one through his eye. I don't know of anything that can get up from that. I think even Merlin would die from a silver rifle round to the eye."

"Did you have any other options?"

"Mordred was involved in turning children into weapons. He was helping someone, who I later found out to be Ares, to create their own Harbinger project, as well as try to create his very own set of Fates. People died, Elaine. A lot of them, most of them kids. I couldn't let him get away with that."

"He was so full of rage," Elaine said with a sigh. "He never saw a line to cross in his need to get revenge on Merlin."

"Why? Why would he hate Merlin so much? We were friends for a long time, then I went away and when I returned he was . . . evil. What happened to him during that time?"

"I wish I knew. He never spoke of it. I know that Merlin sent him away for a few years, but other than that neither Mordred nor Merlin spoke of it. And now we'll never know. I'd always hoped that my nephew could be saved from his darkness. I'm sorry for everything he put you through."

I'd always known that Elaine had found it very difficult to reconcile Mordred's insanity with the boy she'd watched grow up. The fact that we'd been such good friends, to have it turn so quickly to something full of rage and hatred was never easy for her to accept.

I turned to Mac, who'd been quiet since my revelation. "You want to kill me?"

Mac took several steps toward me. In a fight, I was pretty certain he'd beat me. He was certainly stronger than me, and with his elemental powers my winning would take a considerable amount of luck. He stopped a step away from me, and stood there, staring down.

I looked up into his eyes, and readied myself for what I was sure was coming.

"I once told you that if you ever killed Mordred that you'd have me to deal with. I told you that he was sick. That he could get better. Whether or not I agree with what he'd done, I still need to follow through on that promise." He raised one hand and tapped me slightly across the chin.

I blinked.

"I was wrong, Nathan. The Mordred we knew had vanished a long time ago. He had to be stopped. And I don't think I could have done what you did."

Mac offered me his hand, which I took. He pulled me toward him. "Forgive me for my foolishness," he whispered.

"There was never anything to forgive," I said honestly.

Mac nodded a thanks, released my hand and turned to Elaine. "I'm going back to the Island. If you need anything let me know. Nathan, when you arrive, I'm coming with you. I owe you a debt and I plan to repay it by helping you find these Reaver bastards."

There was no point in arguing with him. "I'd be grateful of the help."

Elaine and I waited for Mac to leave the chambers before either of us spoke again.

"Thank you for being honest," she said.

"Are any of his allies going to seek retribution for what happened?"

"I don't know. My sister, his mother, might send people after you. Very few know it was you who killed him. Even Mac and I had only guessed before you admitted to it. My sister might just assume you were involved, or she might stay in her little realm. If I knew where she was, I might be able to have a better idea of what she wanted to do. But I haven't seen her in a long time. I haven't seen either of my sisters."

Elaine's sister Morgause had long since fled to a realm known only to a few. She'd once tried to use the rumor that Mordred had been exiled from Avalon because his father was Arthur, her half-brother. It was a lie. No one knew who Mordred's father had been, but considering Arthur and Mordred had only a few years between them, Morgause's lies were easily discredited.

Elaine's other sister was Morgan. As in Morgan Le Fay, a woman I'd once loved dearly, despite her exile from Avalon for speaking out against Arthur and Guinevere. Eventually she'd betrayed both Avalon and me, when she'd sided with Mordred. I hadn't seen her since she'd left me for dead next to Arthur. Any feeling I'd had for her had long since faded, but occasionally

I'd catch myself thinking of her, wondering where she might be. Thoughts I brushed aside as quickly as possible.

"I need to go," I told Elaine.

"I miss you being here," she said. "Even before what happened between you and Merlin, you were rarely here. I miss being able to talk to you about anything. I miss Avalon feeling like my home."

"It is your home."

Elaine shook her head. "There's so much going on here, so many people who want something, who need to be watched to ensure they don't overstep their boundaries. So many relationships that need to be juggled. It's exhausting. So much has changed, and sometimes it would be nice to go back to those simpler days, when you'd come to me for advice and I could be honest and open. It's too rare these days."

I looked at Elaine for a few moments. "Once I'm done, I'll return here. We can talk like old times about anything you wish." I wondered whether to stop, but the realization that I may not get another chance for a long time spurred me to continue. "I wish things could be different. I wish I hadn't blinded myself to what was happening with Merlin for so long. But it's all too late now. Everything has changed, but that doesn't mean things are worse. It just means that we all have to figure out where we stand in this new world that we helped create. I can't come back here on a regular basis, Merlin and his allies would never allow it."

"Do you ever wish you could have just stayed as things were? Stayed in Avalon?"

"Not for one second. Leaving here, leaving Merlin, was the healthiest thing I ever did. The thought that he might still be involved in the Reavers burns at my soul. He's a cancer in this realm. One that needs to step aside before he's forced out."

"That's pretty close to treason."

I shrugged. "It's also pretty close to accurate. And everyone with an ounce of objectivity can see it."

"I agree with you, Nathan. But there's nothing that can be done without it coming off like a coup. And I won't be part of that."

"I know. Hopefully, one day, he'll either heal Arthur and this whole thing can go away, or he'll fuck up so badly that he'll have no choice but to leave."

"You really think he can revive Arthur?"

"Not for a second. Which leaves him fucking up. And when he does that, when he's finally forced from his cozy little space of helping exactly no one, I'll be the first person in line to clap my hands as he's ceremoniously told to go fuck himself."

I was leaving the palace when someone shouted my name. I turned and found Kay walking toward me, his Faceless a few steps back like a good little doggy.

"I hear you're leaving already," Kay said, the smile on his face never reaching his voice. "I hope the attack that took place the other day wasn't responsible."

I didn't like Kay. He was always looking for the angle that would best suit his purposes—whatever they might be—and I didn't like the idea that he knew more about what had happened than I was comfortable with. "Lucie and Olivia have things in hand here. I have a few ideas I'm following up. I'll be back soon enough. I want to be there when Fiona wakes up."

"So she can identify her attacker, I presume."

"No, so I can make sure she's okay. We'll find out who attacked her, we'll make sure that justice is done."

"Oh, you can be assured that those responsible *will* be shown to the world."

"Is there any change in Fiona's condition?"

Kay shook his head. "Sadly, no. How is your condition? I hear you're infected with the same venom."

I glanced down at the faded white glyphs on the backs of my hands. It had gotten to the point where I'd almost forgotten all about them. I hoped that there would be very few more occasions to use too much magic, lest the nightmare inside of me—Erebus—try to gain some measure of control over me. I hadn't thought much about Erebus in some time. All nightmares communicated with their sorcerer hosts, it was how they corrupted the sorcerer to allow them to take control, but I'd never heard of a nightmare actually helping their host beyond simple survival. I meant to look into it, meant to discuss it with people who might have answers, but I never did. I was afraid of what I'd find.

I guessed if I kept using magic, I'd soon get to speak to Erebus again. Maybe he'd have answers, or maybe everything he said was a lie. I didn't know. It didn't feel like lies or deception, but then the very best deceivers are those who get you to think that the deception was always the best idea.

"I'm okay," I told Kay. "The venom will be gone in a few days, I hope. After that I'll probably sleep for a few months."

Kay laughed. "Did I ever tell you the time I was bitten by a jorōgumo? I can't begin to tell you the pain it causes. Well, clearly you know. You're very lucky that someone knew that the use of magic counteracts the venom. Very lucky indeed."

"I already knew," I said. "No luck involved. I got bit by one back in Japan a long time ago."

"Ha!" Kay laughed. "Just think if your attackers had known that, they might have used a different venom. That right there is some luck after all."

"I guess so," I agreed. "Now, if you'll excuse me, I have to leave."

"Of course," Kay said. "Just do me one thing. If you find out any information, contact me with it. I want the names of those who have betrayed the SOA, I want to be there when you bring them down."

"I will," I lied. There was no way in hell I was going to willingly give Kay the chance to jump up and down and tell everyone how he'd saved Avalon single-handedly. He already had enough power and influence; adding to that total was unlikely to end well for those who had to work with him.

"Good trip, my friend," Kay said and walked off. His Faceless stopped before me and stared, his mask giving away nothing of the emotions he might be feeling.

Kay stopped and turned back to us. "Oh, that's right, my Faceless has something he wishes to say to you. You may talk."

"You killed one of ours," the Faceless said, his voice muffled by the mask.

"I did," I said. "He called himself Reid, and he deserved a lot more than what I did to him." He'd betrayed Olivia, her LOA agents, and people who trusted him. He'd given Tommy and Kasey over to an inhuman monster. All on the say-so of his master in Avalon. A master I never found. Eventually, Reid had confronted me in an act of supreme arrogance. He hadn't fared well in the encounter.

"Killing one of us does not sit well with the rest of our order. There are those out there who may try to gain retribution for your act."

"Well, the Reavers appear to be first in line for retribution, but if the Faceless want to queue up behind them, I'm sure to get to you eventually."

"You mock, but I don't think you understand the danger you'd be in if any of the Faceless decided to come for you."

"I've killed Faceless before. Did you think Reid was my first? I'm sure if anyone wants to try me he won't be the last either. You're more than welcome to let your friends know that."

"I shall."

"Who did he belong to?"

"I am not at liberty to say."

"Not at liberty or don't want to?"

"Both. If his master wished to send Reid to kill you, I'm sure he'll want to try again at some point. It is not my place to reveal a master to the victim of a Faceless. I'm just giving you a warning. The Faceless don't like to lose members, we take it very personally."

"I take people trying to kill me personally," I explained. "Trust me when I tell you that if your friends come for me, I'm going to start sending them back on a more regular basis."

"The mighty Hellequin can't have eyes and ears everywhere."

"You'll be surprised what I can and can't do."

"I shall endeavor to pass along your sentiments to those who seek retribution."

He walked off with Kay. I knew the Faceless would probably come after me for killing one of their own. I'd killed members as Hellequin, but done so in the shadows. Reid had confronted me at home, and that was always going to go down badly. Kay and his Faceless merged with the crowds at the bottom of the palace steps. I trusted both of them about as much as I did a rattlesnake not to bite me. Kay was a self-serving asshole, and his Faceless was quite possibly going to try to kill me. They say you can't ever go home, and my visit back to Camelot was a pretty good testament to that fact.

CHAPTER 19

I found Ellie and Remy sitting by the realm gate, while the Avalon guards tried very hard not to stare at them every few seconds. They weren't exactly used to people just hanging around the realm gate for several hours.

"You ready?" I asked them both.

"I'm leaving Avalon for the first time in over a century," Remy said. "Frankly, I know we're going to stop a bunch of murderous bastards, but I can't wait."

"Who was that big guy who came through about an hour ago? He announced he was helping you, and went through the realm gate."

"That would be Mac."

"He's helping us?" she asked with a touch of interest in her voice.

"That's the plan," I told her.

"Yeah, he'll be a big asset," she said with a sly smile.

A few minutes later the realm gate was open and we stepped back through to Avalon Island, where an impatient Mac greeted us.

"You took your time," he said as he unfolded his arms.

"Is the helicopter ready?" I asked the guard, Hendricks, whom we'd met when we first arrived on the island.

"Yes, sir, if you can follow me, we'll get you airborne."

We did as he asked and followed Hendricks out of the building and into a jeep. He drove to the far edge of the island, where a green Chinook sat idle.

"It's a modified Chinook HC8," Hendricks told us. "It's a couple of years in advance of what's currently out there. It'll get you to The Hole without a need for refueling."

There was a time when flying of any kind terrified me. And while I still wasn't fond of the whole process, I no longer needed a large amount of alcohol to get me through the trips. A year ago I'd parachuted out of a helicopter flying over Stonehenge. It was not one of my fondest memories, and the idea of doing anything similar ever again was simply not on my to-do list.

"Where did this thing come from?" Ellie asked as we entered the helicopter.

"There's an underground helicopter garage," Mac explained when he sat opposite her. "They can raise a helicopter from the garage whenever they like. It's actually quite interesting."

"Why don't they use them to get to the island then?" Ellie asked.

"Ah, well, they can only have one operational at a time. So they're used for emergencies and high-ranking dignitaries. It's just easier to have everyone else arrive by boat."

I sat next to Ellie, while Remy almost ran to the nearest window and stared out of it while the engines roared to life.

"Are you all ready?" Hendricks asked.

We all assured him we were and he wished us a good flight, closing the door behind him as he left the fuselage.

A guard appeared from the cabin and ensured the door was locked. "This is going to take a few hours, you might want to get comfortable." With that he vanished back into the cockpit.

Soon after, there was a slight jolt and we lifted from the ground.

Ellie pointed to the headphones above our heads, and I put mine on, canceling much of the noise from the nearby, powerful engines. Ellie put hers on and pressed the communication button. "So what happens when we get there?"

"I'm going to go speak to the warden and ask to have Alan removed. It'll probably mean having to go down to get him, but it shouldn't take long. Then we go find Felix, and figure out exactly what he knows about the Reavers."

"And if you're wrong? If he doesn't know anything?"

"Then at the very least we've kept someone from their grasp. We'll figure out things from there."

Ellie glanced over at Mac, whose eyes were closed.

"He's quite . . . strapping, isn't he?"

"Yes, if there's one thing that accurately describes Mac, it's that he's strapping."

"Is there a Mrs. Mac?"

"I have no idea. Ask him."

"I might just do that."

Mac opened his eyes, retrieved his headphones and put them on. "Female wolf, I understand your need to mate with me. It's only natural. I am, after all, exceptionally desirable. But maybe it should wait until we've finished our current assignment. Then I will show you pleasures you've only dreamed of." Mac's smile was broad enough to have been seen from space.

"You arrogant little . . ." Ellie paused. "You're taking the piss, aren't you?"

Mac laughed. "You should know, I can hear you just fine even without these headphones. And yes, I am jesting. Although if you still wish to discover if there's a Mrs. Mac, I'll be more than happy to educate you once we're done."

I leaned over to Mac. "It's the accent isn't it? The Irish thing always seems to do well."

Mac laughed. It was a deep belly laugh, and he pushed his fingers through his long red hair.

"Bloody hell," Ellie whispered and then immediately removed her headphones and walked off toward Remy, who'd didn't even turn to acknowledge her presence as he watched the ground fly past far below us.

"Was I cruel to mock her?" Mac asked.

I moved the tips of my thumb and index finger a small measure apart.

"I shall make it up to her. I was only having fun. I did not mean to offend." He removed his headphones and walked over to Ellie.

Remy finally took notice and ran over to sit beside me. I gave him some headphones. "How do your kind not fly *all the time*?"

"You're enjoying yourself?"

"I've heard about these machines, I've even seen pictures and footage, but this is incredible."

"I'm glad you're having fun."

Remy's smile faded. "I'm sorry, I didn't mean to imply that this wasn't serious."

"Mate, be my guest to enjoy the flight. I doubt there's going to be a lot of room for fun once we reach The Hole. You might as well get it in while you can."

Remy tore his headphones off and dropped them at his feet, before running off to find another window to look out of. I glanced over at Ellie and Mac, who were deep in conversation. Ellie giggled at something, caught herself, and then nodded sternly to whatever Mac was saying. A few hours left of flying. I shut my eyes and decided to get some sleep. It took a while to realize I couldn't go to sleep and keep my magic active. I was clearly tired, so I kept myself busy with thoughts of Liz Williams telling me that Avalon would give me answers as to who was behind the Reavers. In reality there had been few answers, but certainly more questions.

Eventually we reached our destination with a jolt when the helicopter landed. The pilot re-entered the fuselage from the cockpit and opened the door.

"We need to refuel," he told me once everyone else had thanked him and left the Chinook. "Be a few hours."

"That's fine, this might take a while anyway," I admitted. "Avalon bureaucracy isn't exactly speedy."

I stepped out of the vehicle and immediately wished I'd brought more than a thick hoodie to wear. With no barriers around the edge of the island, the wind tore through the heliport with a fierce determination to make anything there regret its decision to come.

We made our way toward the entrance to the prison, while my paranoia about someone in the prison working against us ran rampant. Despite Olivia's assurances that she trusted the warden, I wasn't going to let my guard down until I'd reached Alan and we were safely away. Hopefully my thoughts were baseless, but considering people had been trying to kill or capture me for the last few days, I was rightly concerned about where the next attack was coming from.

The building was one story high and sat in front of two taller buildings, one of which contained offices, and the second living accommodations for the staff. Another building sitting behind those contained supplies.

The automatic door opened for us and we soon found ourselves in a warm reception area. Two guards stood at opposite ends of a lengthy desk, watching us intently. A door sat at either side of the room, each with a red and white sign. One said staff only, and the other said visitors. The actual prisoner entrance to the island was a building identical to this one, but on the opposite side of the island, next to its own helipad. The last time I'd been to The Hole, it had been crawling with guards. They took security at The Hole very, very seriously.

"And you are?" a man asked from behind the desk. He wore an immaculate gray suit, the jacket of which almost entirely covered the bulge of his holster and gun.

"Nathan Garrett," I said. "This is Remy Roax, Mac, and Ellie Ryan."

"Mac?" the man asked.

"Is there a problem with my name?" Mac asked. "If you'd prefer you can call me Manannán mac Lir."

The man raised an eyebrow. "I was not made aware that someone of your . . . stature would be arriving." He glanced at Remy.

"Well, let's forgo the pomp and ceremony," Mac said. "Just open the door and let us go find Alan. Then we can go."

"The warden wants to speak to you first."

"Okay, and where is he?"

The printer next to the man began to hum, and soon after he passed us each our own IDs. "Through the Staff Only door, to the left, follow the signs. Do not deviate from that path. Those passes are not an all access tour."

One of the guards walked over to the door, and swiped his card though the reader beside it. The door opened, and we all walked through, then followed the directions until we found ourselves outside a door marked "Warden." An intercom sat beside the door, and I pushed the button; a woman's voice came through. "Yes?"

"Nathan Garrett and company to see the warden."

A second later the sound of a lock disengaging rang out, before the door slowly opened, revealing a small room beyond. A woman of about forty sat behind a mahogany desk and looked up from her computer screen.

"Only one of you need visit the warden—Nathan Garrett himself—the rest can wait just there," she told us.

Everyone turned to look at the couch and table that had been hidden from view by the door. Magazines were scattered across the table.

"Be back soon," I said and walked across to the room to the only other door I could see.

The woman pressed a button on her desk and another lock disengaged. "You may go in," she told me, so I turned the handle and pushed the door open, stepping inside.

The first thing I noticed upon stepping into the room was the fish tank that encompassed the entire wall on one side of the office. It must have been twenty feet long and eight or nine feet high. There were dozens of species of fish in the tank, and it was easily wide enough to fit a fully grown person in it, although not wide enough for them to be able to turn around once they were inside.

"Impressive, isn't it?" a man asked in an accent that reminded me of my time in the Southern states of America. He offered me his hand, which I shook.

"It's quite the talking piece," I agreed.

"I'm Warden Philips. Been in charge of this place for nearly twenty years now. First time I've ever had a request to let someone go into the custody of a non-Avalon agent." Warden Philips was a lanky man, with a few days worth of dark beard, although his head was totally bald. He smelled of tobacco, the cause of which was probably the pipe that sat on his exceptionally neat desk.

"This is sort of an unusual case," I explained.

"That it is. Some of my guards aren't happy you're here. Vocally so."

"We all have to put up with things we don't like," I said. "Has Alan been told?"

The warden shook his head. "We thought it best not to tell him. He can be quite . . . difficult if given news he doesn't wish to hear."

"Has he had any other visitors?"

He shook his head. "Not for the last few months. His wife was the last person who visited him. I heard about what happened to her. I hope she pulls through."

"Does Alan know about Fiona?"

"If he knew about Fiona, we wouldn't be here talking about him, we'd be out there trying to find him."

I couldn't argue with that summation.

"I want you to know something, Mister Garrett. Alan is almost a free man. He came here of his own choosing, and we've tried to ensure he stays as far away from trouble as possible. I like the man—I'm not ashamed to admit it—anyone who married someone and then agrees to go to jail so that they can start fresh is someone with conviction. If you'll pardon my pun. Ten years he's been here. A model prisoner in every regard. I do not wish to see him tarnish his reputation by an explosive outburst. Do you get what I mean?"

"Don't tell him anything until we're off the island."

"Exactly. I'm glad you see things my way. I'd hate for Alan to serve more time because he decided to lose his temper. You should know we're having a few technical problems today, radios have been shutting off and the like. There's no problem with safety, but you do what you're told, when you're told, am I making myself clear?"

My paranoia alarm went off again, but outwardly I remained calm. "Of course. So what's the plan?"

"One of our guards will escort Alan to you and your friends. You'll pick him up and return here. The guard's name is Walker. He's been here for many years. In fact I believe he and Alan have created a good friendship over the years. Not normally something I encourage, but it can't be helped when you see someone every single day for years and years at a time. Obviously, on the lower levels it would be a lot more than just discouraged, but we rotate the guards every few days there anyway."

"I want to be taken to Alan," I told him to his obvious surprise.

"That's an unusual request. We don't normally allow civilians onto the prison floors. Can I ask why?"

"I want to be there when he's taken from the prison. I know that Olivia trusts you, and I have no reason to believe you're anything other than you appear to be. But I've had people who are meant to be Avalon employees try to kill me. And they will try to kill Alan too if they think he's no longer of use. I want to escort him out of the prison to ensure his safety."

"You don't trust my people?" he asked, anger creeping into his voice.

"Right now, I don't trust anyone who I haven't known for a long time. It's nothing personal, although I'm sure it feels it. And for that I am sorry. But the request stands. I want to be there to escort Alan from his cell."

The warden stared at me for what felt like minutes. "I'll arrange it. But only because Olivia trusts you, and therefore so do I."

His comment stung a little. Maybe I should trust him to have good people, just like I trust Olivia, but I couldn't. "Thank you for this."

"Don't thank me. Olivia called and asked for this favor. She's a formidable woman, and one I owe a lot to. I wasn't about to turn down her request. Have you ever been here before?"

"Not for a long time, but yes."

"Were you a prisoner here?"

"No, just dropping off some deliveries. I visited a few inmates."

"Of those you dropped off. Any still here?"

"I imagine so."

"Be careful then. Some of these people hold grudges. And level one or level ten, it doesn't matter if you cross the wrong person and they stick a knife in your spine."

CHAPTER 20

We had to go through a lot of security before we were even allowed on the lift to take us down to Alan's level. All weapons were passed over to a quartermaster, who issued each of us a little sticker, something Remy was the least happy to comply with.

Each floor of the prison was set out in a similar way. There were two sections of cells, each facing away from the other. Each section was four cells high and twenty-five cells long, meaning a hundred prisoners could be housed here at any time. There was a sizeable empty gap between the two sections, an area where prisoners could congregate. A set of double doors at the far end of the main hall led to various other rooms such as showers, recreation rooms, and the hall where prisoners ate. The higher floors were allowed excursions to the island itself once a week in a purpose-built area behind the prison entrance. I'd asked why Alan couldn't be brought to us there, and was told that the second floor was using it and it would be unwise to change their routine.

The lift doors opened, and I for one was grateful that I no longer had to listen to the guard's incessant humming of a butchered tune. I glanced up at the lights on the ceiling—massive black disks that absorbed and poured natural light into the floor, and on occasion the guards even made it rain for the prisoners.

"Prisoners, back to your cells, please," a guard said over the intercom.

I watched as the prisoners in the center of the floor made their way back to their cells.

"While I'll open Alan's cell, do not touch the bars on any other cell doors," the guard told us.

"Why?" asked Mac.

"We have a security measure that only guards and the prisoner inside can touch the bars once the cell is in use. Anyone else touching the cell will receive a rather unpleasant shock. Just so you're aware, this high up, males and females are integrated. We stop that on floor four. It used to be true of all floors, but a number of males were being killed and we decided it safer to separate them. Most of the very dangerous female prisoners are housed elsewhere."

"Most?" Ellie questioned.

"A few on the lower levels refused to leave. We don't send guards down there. They tend to . . . umm . . ."

"Never return?" Mac offered.

"Yes. Or when they do come back, they're very much not the same. It's just safer to avoid the whole bottom floors altogether. They rule themselves for the most part."

"Why hasn't anyone ever tried to claim it back?" I asked. "Starve them out, or gas them, something?"

"A previous warden tried several of the methods, but some of the people down there are immune to various gases, even without their abilities. As for starving them out . . . it ended badly."

"Some of them ate the others, didn't they?" Mac said.

Walker nodded. "There are people down there in charge who made a deal with the current warden. They gain a measure of autonomy and they give us no reasons to go back down there except to deliver supplies as needed. It's worked for over a decade now."

Thoughts of who might be in charge down there swirled around my mind. I probably helped put some of them there.

The prisoners had all returned to their cells, and Walker led us up three sets of stairs to the top row of cells. "Alan's is the fifth down here." He turned to a keypad on the wall and inserted a card before putting in several numbers that he hid from view.

There was a slight buzzing noise and then silence.

"Alan's cell is open," Walker told everyone. "Before you go there are other things you should be aware of. Each prisoner on the sixth floor and above wears a sorcerer's band, so they are unable to access their abilities, but that doesn't mean these people aren't dangerous given the right set of circumstances."

"You think some of these might attack Nate?" Ellie asked.

"Oh, no, not at all," the guard quickly clarified. "But it's something you should be aware of. It would also be best if only one of you went down to the cell. Other inmates may not like seeing large numbers of strangers."

"I'll go," I said and walked down to the fifth cell. I stopped outside and took in what had been Alan's home for ten years. It was ten by ten, with a single bed, a toilet and sink, and a small desk and chair. Photos adorned the walls.

Alan was lying on his bed, looking up at the wall. He wore the regulation green uniform for prisoners at The Hole, and appeared to have not shaved for several weeks.

He looked over at me and sighed. "Oh great, why did I think it wouldn't be long before you showed up? Fuck off; I've only got a few weeks left."

"Yeah, well, you get to come play outside today."

"Every time you get me involved in something, I end up having bad things happen to me. Can't you just piss off and leave me be? Seriously, you're a walking curse."

"I wish I could, Alan. Can I come in?"

"It's a prison cell not a fucking show room. I'm a prisoner. You can do whatever the fuck you like."

"I see being here hasn't improved your personality much."

"Oh, I'm sorry, should I be all smiles and sparkles? Should I jump up out of bed and sing a musical number? The guards brought in *Wicked* for us to listen to the other week; I think I do a rousing version of 'Defying Gravity.'" He leapt off the bed and looked about to sing.

"Fine. You don't have to be happy to see me. But I need your help."

Alan sat back down. "Look, Nathan, I'd like to. I really would. But I can't. I don't even know if I'm meant to be talking to you, that was never one of the rules, but I sure as hell can't leave this fucking shit heap."

"Call me Nate," I said. "And why not?"

"Nate? You've gone all modern."

"You never answered my question."

"I've been told to keep my mouth shut, Nate." There was some fear in his voice. It wasn't something I heard a lot from him.

"What's happening, Alan?" I asked slowly, not wanting to say something that might set Alan off. If he was afraid of something, I was certain it was something I needed to be wary of.

"About two months ago, Fiona comes here telling me that she's discovered something about the Reavers. I tell her to drop it, that it's not worth looking into. She told me that she'd heard rumors that I knew where Felix was, that the Reavers had started searching for him. I told her I had no idea what the hell she was talking about, but she still made me promise never to reveal his location." The fear was back, but it was joined with a lot of anger. Whether that anger was directed just at those who had blackmailed him, or also at me for turning up, I wasn't sure.

"About six weeks later," he continued after a slight pause, "a guard told me that he was a Reaver and that I either stopped my wife from searching into the group, or something bad would happen. Apparently she really struck a nerve, so I told him to go fuck himself. A few days ago he comes to me with photos of my wife's body lying in our house. He told me that she's still alive, but if I wanted her to stay that way I was to ensure I didn't help anyone coming here to ask for it." Alan stood and punched the wall and faced away from me. "They hurt her, Nate. They hurt Fiona." His voice was almost breaking.

"I'm sorry," I said.

"Fuck your sorry," he snapped, and turned back to me, rage filling his face. He rubbed his eyes and spat into the toilet. "If they've gone after Fiona again because you turned up—"

"Lucie is guarding her," I interrupted.

Alan paused. "I liked Lucie. Okay, so Fiona is safe." The relief in his voice was palpable.

Alan splashed water on his face and returned to sitting on his bed.

"They don't know that you're aware of Felix's location?" I asked.

"Putting myself in here made me somewhat bulletproof. They can't kill me, it would bring a lot of awkward questions their way, but they can hurt the people I love. I always figured they assumed that I knew who might know Felix's location, but they've never actually asked me. That was until two days ago, when they came to me to ask who knew where he was. I gave them your name. Figured you could take care of yourself, sorry about that."

"That explains why they switched from wanting me dead to believing I knew where Felix was. They attacked a bunch of us in Camelot. Thanks for that."

"You're welcome."

"Do you know the name of the corrupt guard?"

"Livius. I assume by now he already knows you're here."

"One guard? I think we're okay then. It's why I had the warden let me come to you instead of you coming to me. I wanted to make sure you were safe."

"Livius is still going to do something."

"Whatever he does, we'll handle it."

"Who is 'we'?"

I told him about the people I'd brought with me.

"You always had the habit of picking good allies, Nate."

"Present company excluded, I assume."

Alan laughed and the tension melted from his shoulders. "The Reavers don't want us getting to Felix, but they really want to know where he is."

"Because they know he's keeping tabs on them?"

"How'd you know that? Yes, he's been using his mind magic to observe the Reavers. He's been doing it for . . . well, since before I got myself locked up. No idea why they suddenly want to find him though."

"Why hasn't he told anyone?"

"Haven't spoken to him in over a decade. He was still searching for those in charge at the time. He made it sound like a bit of a maze, and didn't want to go after them prematurely. Also, Avalon still wants him dead, so he's unlikely to want to let them know where he is."

The fact that Felix had been searching for them for so long meant that the Reavers had been planning something for a long time. I was angry that I had assumed they'd gone, angry that they'd been allowed to continue unabated. But more than anything, I should have gotten Alan to tell me where Felix was. Someone should have known all of this was going to happen. "So, are you coming with me then? I'd like to find Felix and then go kick the shit out of the Reavers."

"That I can do. What guard is with you?"

I shrugged. "Walker, I don't know his first name."

"Seriously?" Alan pushed me aside slightly and glanced down toward the guard.

I thought I detected a slight sigh of relief from Alan. "Anthony. He's a nice guy."

Alan walked off toward the guard, while I walked behind him. He shook Anthony's hand and then said hello to Remy, Ellie, and Mac. He stared at Remy for a few seconds.

"Yes?" Remy snapped.

"You work with my wife, don't you? She's mentioned you before. I always wondered, how long ago did you piss the witch off?"

"Few centuries now, why?"

"I was always curious about what you'd done to piss off a witch so much."

"They were going for full-blown fox, they just weren't very good."

"Thank heavens for incompetent villains. May they always fuck up in the simplest of ways."

"Amen to that," I said as I rejoined everyone.

"Are you ready to leave?" Anthony asked Alan.

"I'll decide when we get topside."

Anthony glanced at me, but didn't say anything else; instead he took us back to the lift and once we were all inside, the lift ascended. And then it stopped almost immediately.

"What's going on?" Ellie asked.

"I don't know," Anthony admitted. He opened a panel near the doors, which contained a small monitor with a keypad beneath it. He tapped a few of the keys and the monitor flickered to life, showing another guard.

"Hello, Anthony," the guard said. "Need help, do we?"

"Don't be an ass. Just figure out what's happened and get us out of here."

"I know what's happened. I switched off the elevator."

"Why would you do that?" Anthony demanded.

"Livius," Alan said through gritted teeth. "I wondered how long it would be before you showed up."

"Alan, do you remember what I told you? I said you kept your mouth shut and you'd be allowed to see your wife again. Guess you just don't love her enough. I didn't expect to have so many people to get rid of, but the more the merrier."

"She's safer than we are. When I get out of here, I'm going to tear you in half," Alan said.

"Best of luck with that," Livius said, and the screen went blank.

"So, Livius, he's one of the Reavers, I assume," Mac asked.

Alan nodded. "He arrived a few years after I did. Never spoke to me until a few weeks ago."

The lift began to move down. I glanced over at the numbered buttons on the door panel as each number lit up briefly in turn.

"We're going to level ten," Anthony said. "This is very bad."

"We'll still have our abilities though, right?" Ellie said. "We're not wearing sorcerer's bands, so we'll be fine. The prisoners still have the bands on, yes?"

Anthony shook his head. "We blanket the whole lower floors with runes. The second those doors open, you're going to be no better than any other human."

I glanced down at my glyphs as they flickered on my arms. The lift stopped and my magic vanished. I expected the effects of the venom to rush back into me, making me drop to the ground, but instead it started with a dull ache.

"Oh, I have more information for you," Livius's voice sounded from the small speaker. "By now you're probably aware that this lift is going to the tenth floor. When you get there, you have ten seconds to get off the lift or the explosives I've placed under the floor will detonate. Also, the internal cameras and systems are offline; it's been glitching all day. I'm sure the warden told you."

"How many guards have you hurt to do this?" Anthony demanded.

"No one important. I imagine it won't take long for someone to notice what's happened, but I'll be gone by then, can't really keep this job after this. Bet you wish you'd gone to the armory to get a weapon, eh, Anthony? Too late now. Bye." He signed off and the lift began moving again.

"I'm really beginning to hate that bastard," Mac said.

"Why are the guards unarmed in this place?" Remy asked.

"Because if an inmate got hold of a weapon . . . ," Anthony said, leaving how bad it would be unsaid.

After what felt like a lifetime, the lift came to a halt and the doors opened. All six of us rushed out of the lift as soon as possible, the doors closing behind us. Immediately outside of the lift on all but the top three floors was a security checkpoint. It consisted of a bulletproof glass window that allowed the guards to watch the prisoners, along with a locked armory and three-foot-thick steel door that led to the prison floor.

Once past the door, the stairs led down into a holding area that was separated off from the rest of the prison floor by several feet of concrete walls. The guards might not stay down here, but they still needed to be able to access the floor on occasion; to bring food or aid as required.

The tenth floor was set up slightly differently, with each of the sets of cells looking across at one another. In between them were dozens of prisoners, who all turned toward us at the sound of the lift arriving.

"Ah, look, my friends," a man's voice boomed around us. "We have guests."

The voice was familiar and I stepped out on to the secure gangway and searched for owner. He was a tall, muscular man with a patch over one eye. He didn't seem keen to see me.

"Nathan Garrett, how I've longed for this day."

I looked down and my blood froze as the one-eyed man beamed. Helios would finally have a chance to get his revenge.

"Oh, bollocks," I whispered as the rest of the lift's occupants joined me on the gangway.

"I assume you and Helios know one another," Mac suggested.

"You see that eye patch?"

"Oh for fuck's sake, Nate, did you take his eye?" Remy asked.

"Pretty much."

"Weren't you shagging his sister too?" Alan piped in.

"How the hell does that help?" I snapped.

"Never said it did, just pointing out he might want to kill you for that too. I didn't realize we were trying to be useful. We're stuck on the lowest floor of The Hole with the worst criminals that Avalon's ever had. Unless you have a mini-nuke in your pocket, I think usefulness is something we're going to be in short supply of."

"How many inmates are here?" Mac asked.

"Two hundred and seventeen at last count. That was three years ago. Some of those could have been killed."

"I doubt very much that by some, you mean all?" Mac said. "I guess we should be grateful for the box we find ourselves in."

"So we're safe so long as we stay in here, yes?" Remy asked as he opened the armory and found it empty. "This isn't looking great. How long before someone figures out we're not where we're supposed to be and comes looking?"

Anthony didn't answer, he was too busy watching the prisoners below as they filed out into the large area between the sets of cells. "We're going to be killed, aren't we?"

I glanced out of the window as a loud thud sounded out. "Can you get the lift back down here?" I asked Anthony.

He shook his head. "There's a service hatch, but it's quite the climb and there's no way I could manage it all the way back to the surface. It's a long climb in almost complete darkness."

Everyone turned to Remy. "You can see in the dark, yes? Fancy a climb?"

"Sure, why not. It's not like I like having clean fur anyway."

"Can you get Remy to that service hatch? Make sure he gets to the top and sees the warden."

"How certain are you that the warden isn't involved?" Ellie asked.

"Fair point. Anyone you trust, Anthony?"

"The warden is a good man. I can't see why he'd be against us. He certainly has no love for Livius."

"Okay, we'll go for the warden then. Remy, if you get a hint he's against us, you do what you need to, to get that lift back down here."

"And what are you lot going to do?" he asked.

"Stay here and wait," I told him. "If we go out there, we're all dead. And I'm not entirely sure how long I have before the venom inside me really kicks in."

"Right, come on Anthony, you can show me exactly where I can start the really shitty climb."

I turned back to the glass and was surprised to see that all of the prisoners were standing motionless, staring up at us, while Helios climbed the staircases attached to one set of cells, until he was on the fourth level. There were murmurs below him, although they sounded more like laughter.

"It appears that our new guests don't wish to come out and see us," Helios shouted.

"How is he doing that with his voice?" Ellie asked.

I watched Helios as he touched his lapel before he spoke. "Maybe we should bring out our old guests to show how well we play with others."

"He's got some sort of amplifier on him."

"They're used throughout the prison," Anthony said as he returned. "They're small devices, all he'd need was to wear one and he could use all of the speakers on the floor to make it sound like he was everywhere at once." Anthony walked over to the door and opened a panel, picking out one of the small amplifiers.

"What older guests?" Mac asked.

His question was answered quickly as the crowd parted and two guards were pushed through. They were kicked and spat on by various prisoners until someone forced them both to their knees, and made them look up at us. Two men, both beaten and bloody. Even with the distance between us, I could tell that both looked terrified.

"A lovely guard brought them both to us a few hours ago. We've had such fun."

"Livius," Anthony whispered. "They were meant to be with him today. Their names are Willis and James."

"Oh, Nathan," Helios said. "Have you decided on whether you'd like to come down here and talk to us? It's been such a long time since we last saw one another. Obviously I don't *see* you as well as I used to." There was enough hatred in that last sentence to fund a war.

I took a step toward Anthony and collapsed to my knees as the venom inside me decided to start its relentless attack on my body. "Damn it," I snapped.

Ellie was by my side, putting my arm over her shoulder and lifting me to my feet.

"Nathan, I'll make it easy for you. You come out here and talk to me, and your friends get to live. As do these two guards."

"Give me the amplifier," I asked, and Anthony attached it to my lapel.

"Just touch the amplifier when you speak."

I did as was told. "Give me a minute, Helios."

"You have sixty seconds. Then someone here will tear off one guard's head and see how far it can be thrown."

I removed my hand from my lapel. "I need to go out there."

"You'll die," Mac said.

I coughed up bright blood onto the floor. "If I don't, they're going to kill those two guards. Besides, in case you didn't notice, without my magic I'm already dying."

"Doesn't mean you should hurry that along," Alan pointed out.

"Tick tock, Nathan," Helios said. The background laughter of a few hundred prisoners, all seemingly eager for my blood, was an unnerving thing to hear.

"Gotta go," I said. "I'm not planning on killing myself. But I need to do this." I glanced around the room. "Anyone got a pen?" A year previously I'd learned how to use one of the original twenty-one runes created by the Norse dwarfs before they vanished. Once the rune was drawn onto me, it allowed me to bypass any security stopping my magic. It used a large amount of energy to keep it activated, but I thought that being surrounded by dangerous prisoners was probably as good a time to use it as any.

Everyone looked confused. "No," they all said almost in unison.

"Well there's that plan ballsed up then," I said and then coughed again.

"What are you going to do?" Anthony asked. "None of you can you use your powers."

"I just need to get down there like this," I said. "I need for them to see me weak and incapable."

"And then?" Mac asked.

"Then I thought I'd kill a large chunk of them."

Alan and Mac laughed.

"Mate, I don't think killing is on the list of things you'll be doing today," Alan told me.

"You look like shite," Mac followed up with.

"Trust me," I asked.

Ellie held my gaze and then nodded. She walked over to the door and pulled it open.

"Thank you," I said and stood up, but staggered forward and was caught by Ellie once again.

"Looks like I'm going with you," she told me as she helped me walk.

"Noooo," I said, but didn't have the strength to fight.

"If Ellie is going, so am I," Mac said and lifted my other arm up and over his neck.

"You're all fucking nuts," Alan said. My vision was beginning to darken, my original plan lost to the pain that wracked my body. "But if you're going, then I can hardly stay here and play the big hero while everyone else dies. Besides, if I stay and Remy gets back, I get the feeling he won't be happy with me. I can't go back to Fiona and tell her that I let you die."

So as my body decided it no longer liked being alive, three people I was trying to protect marched me down toward a person who really wanted me dead. I was in no position to argue, I just hoped I could keep conscious long enough to try and stop three hundred prisoners from tearing us limb from limb.

CHAPTER 21

Anthony had used his key on the massive security door below the glass box, allowing us to enter the prison floor. We were immediately catcalled and threatened by everyone until it was a constant din of noise.

"So we get four for the price of one," Helios shouted as Mac and Ellie carried me further into the throng of prisoners. Alan was somewhere behind us, although I wasn't able to tell how far behind that might be.

"Let them go," I called out, motioning toward the two guards.

"We are people of our word, Nathan," Helios said. "Let the guards go. No one will harm them, or they'll face me."

The guards were roughly dragged to their feet and then shoved forward. They both quickly thanked us as they moved as fast as they were able back to Anthony. I glanced over and he nodded toward me before closing the door. I couldn't exactly blame him for being afraid, and if I was honest I didn't want him to come with us. He would have broken quickly, and been forced to either hurt us or someone else in return for his life. He'd have regretted his actions afterwards, but he'd have still carried it out. He was an added complication I didn't need to worry about.

"See, we are not the cruel beasts that those above assume we are," Helios said. "We have feelings. We're not uncaring."

The crowd around us laughed, although it was not full of joy and fun. At least not the type of joy and fun I'd actually want to be a part of.

"Let me go," I whispered, and both Ellie and Mac did as they were asked. I wobbled slightly, but remained upright. I placed my hands together and without taking my eyes off Helios, I traced the rune on the back of my hand, using the blood on my fingers that I'd acquired thorough my earlier coughing. But there wasn't enough to even manage a faint outline.

"Shit," I whispered. I needed a new plan and fast.

"Helios, why don't you come down here and speak to me?" I demanded.

Helios's gaze remained transfixed upon me for a moment before he walked off and made his way down the stairs.

It didn't take long before he stood before me. "You're sick," he said. "Your skin is pale and you look like you can barely stand. What's wrong with you?"

"Jorōgumo venom," I told him. "Probably not got long left before my body starts to permanently shut down."

Helios grabbed me by the scruff of my T-shirt and brought me within an inch of his face. "This won't do," he whispered. He tore the amplifier from my lapel and then shoved me to the floor.

"That's enough," Mac said, stepping toward Helios.

Helios stared at Mac for a second before a broad smile lit up his face. "My fellow prisoners, this is a rare treat. Here, before us, we have a celebrity. The great and wonderful Manannán mac Lir has graced us with his presence."

"What do you actually want, Helios?" Alan asked.

"Shut up, little man," Helios snapped. "I'd momentarily forgotten about you when I saw Nathan up there. Good thing you joined him—saved us the trouble of going up there to get you. You'll get your turn soon enough. I made a deal with that lovely guard fellow to ensure *you* don't leave here. If I were you, I'd try and make myself as inconspicuous as possible and drag a few more minutes of life out of your worthless body."

Alan bowed and took a step back.

"You said you'd let them all go," I said. "It's me you hate. These people have done nothing to you."

"I lied. I agreed to kill Alan. You are just a garnish on the top. But Mac and this woman, they entered here of their own free will. It's just their tough luck really. None of you are leaving."

I got back to my feet, ignoring the fact that my guts felt like they were on fire.

"Going to die on your feet?" Helios asked with a laugh. "Don't worry about that, you'll soon be back on your knees, begging for death. I'm going to take special care of you myself. The venom will hurry my timetable, but there's still enough time for me to enjoy myself."

"Let them go, or I'll kill you," I said.

Helios stared at me and then burst into laughter, along with most of the prisoners around us. "You can barely stand; you look like if I hit you, I'd break you in two. Exactly what do you think is going to happen that makes you believe you can win?"

"Because I kicked your ass last time, I'm happy to do it again."

Helios punched me full in the mouth, sending me sprawling back to the ground. Mac stepped in front of me, only inches away from Helios.

"You want to have a go, Irish boy?" Helios asked.

Mac moved much quicker than I could follow, and Helios was knocked down. "Sure, why the hell not?" Mac snarled.

Helios shook his head and returned to a standing position. "You always were more brawn than brains. Someone kill him."

Mac spun to fight whoever wanted a piece of him, but he couldn't be everywhere at once. Alan and Ellie were too far away to help, and I was never going to get to my feet in time to stop the prisoner stepping toward Mac, taking his attention as another stepped behind him. The attack was fast, but as the prisoner moved away from Mac, I saw the blood that covered his lower back. He'd been stabbed repeatedly. He dropped to his knees as Helios stood above him.

Ellie darted forward, but someone caught her in the jaw with a punch that sent her back into Alan, and they both tumbled to the ground.

"Bye, Mac. You always were an annoying little prick." A prisoner passed Helios a blade and with one quick slice, he cut through Mac's throat, and then kicked him back to the ground.

Roars of cheers erupted from the prison floor, many people stamping on the ground and banging against the metal bars. I moved over to Mac and he blinked, while blood continued to flow out of the wound in his throat. I tore off my T-shirt and pressed it to his neck. "It's okay, we'll get you out of here, and we'll get you help. You'll be fine."

Ellie was by my side a second later, her jaw already red from the blow she'd received.

"Keep pressure," I told her. "Don't let go, no matter what happens." I coughed, as the fire inside me moved up to my chest.

Alan was being held by two prisoners, who'd forced him to his knees, holding his arms behind him.

"Just you left, Nathan," Helios said.

I dipped my fingers into Mac's blood, which was pooling on the floor and quickly drew the rune on the back of my hand.

"Those who touched my friends are going to die," I said. "I want to know who they were."

"Come on lads, don't be shy," someone shouted from the crowd.

A large man stepped forward. "How'd the punch taste, girl?" he asked Ellie. "I've got a lot more for you."

Ellie ignored him and continued to deal with a dying Mac, while I stood up. "And the one who stabbed Mac?"

Another man stepped toward me; one of his hands was covered in blood. "What are you going to do about it?"

Everyone laughed. Everyone except Helios.

"Why aren't you on the floor in pain anymore?" Helios demanded to know.

I ignored Helios, he would have his turn. Instead, I walked around Mac toward the knife wielder. No one moved, and no one spoke. I felt every eye on me as unknown to all, my magic coursed through my body once more. The venom all but forgotten, replaced by the rage that filled my body instead.

I stopped in front of the man who'd stabbed Mac and raised my hand, showing the newly created blade of fire. He went from transfixed to terrified in an instant as it dawned on him what was about to happen. I plunged the blade into his throat and twisted it. The heat from the blade cauterized the wound, and he fell to the ground beside me.

I turned back to the rest of the prisoners. My speech came out raw and full of rage, "Run."

Those closest to me very quickly realized that having a fully powered and exceptionally pissed off sorcerer standing next to them was a very good way to a short life expectancy. Unfortunately those who turned and ran did so right into the prisoners behind who were unaware that I'd just killed one of their comrades. The stampede was short and bloody, and it left several prisoners lying on the floor in pain as their allies used their bodies as a stepping board to safety.

Two prisoners thought they could try their luck, but blasts of hardened air to their legs very quickly ended that dream, along with any hopes that they'd be walking again soon.

"Alan, I need you over here," I shouted.

Alan rushed over, careful to avoid the prisoners who were just trying to get away. "What's up, boss man?"

"You're useless to me in here."

"Thanks for the pep talk."

"I need you to take over from Ellie. Keep pressure on the wound."

He did as was asked without complaint. "Holy shit, this guy is still alive. Can't you cauterize the wound?"

"If I use fire magic on him, it'll make things a lot worse. And I sort of need my magic to make sure we don't all die. Mac's harder to kill than me, so long as we get him to the ocean he'll be okay."

"What do I do?" Ellie asked.

"You still got your strength, yes?"

"Oh, yes."

"You see those assholes over the exit? One of whom was the guy who punched you."

A low growl escaped Ellie's throat.

"I need you to go show them that they need to move. If you happen to show the man who hit you why such acts are frowned upon, then no one will lose any sleep."

Ellie didn't need asking twice. She sprinted toward the group of seven inmates, slamming into the one who'd hit her and tackling him to the ground, before she sat on his chest and punched him in the face so hard that the sound of ruined bones made me wince.

I turned back to Helios, who was already two floors up and running as if he were on fire, which shockingly was what I had planned for him.

"Kill him," he shouted, pointing down at me.

A large man rushed me, taking a sweep with some sort of makeshift blade. I grabbed his wrist, wrapped his arm in a tendril of air and pushed. The bone broke like it was kindling, splitting through the skin. I wrapped air around my forehead and head-butted him. He didn't get back up.

A second inmate ran into me from behind, grabbing me around the waist. I set his arms on fire and he immediately let go, at which point I drove a blade of flame into his chest.

"Is that it, Helios? You can send them all after me; sooner or later, I'm going to get you."

"Nate, how long do we have before Mac dies?" Alan shouted.

"Not long, but Helios has the only working amplifier. I can't contact Anthony without it." I glanced up at the windowed box high above. "I can't risk him just waiting to look out. I won't be long."

I reached the first set of stairs, avoiding a punch, and rammed the head of my would-be attacker into the metal railing, knocking him silly. A blast of air sent him spiraling away.

I ran the next few sets of stairs, until I reached the fourth floor. "Helios," I screamed. "You can't run."

Helios stepped out of his cell several down from where I was standing. He had a long claw-like weapon in one hand. He dragged the blades across the concrete between the cells, and it tore through it like it was nothing.

"Not running," Helios said. "Getting ready to kill you."

The sounds of inmates banging something solid against the metal railing reverberated throughout the floor.

"My people like a good show."

"Let's have it then."

Helios charged at me, moving faster than I remembered when we'd last fought, dodging a blast of air, and tackling me, taking us both over the banister. We fell toward the ground, and I created a cushion of air beneath me. I hit the ground like a bomb, as the magic I used rushed out, cracking the concrete. My magic had softened the impact, but didn't completely remove it, and I was still in pain as I rolled to my feet.

Helios had hit the ground feet first, crushing the floor, but seemingly no worse for wear. He stepped out of the hole he'd created and walked toward me.

"I hope you're really good with that claw," I said.

"Let's see."

He darted forward, dragging the claw up toward my face. I moved in time to avoid being cut in two, but not quick enough to avoid the tips of the four claws as they sliced through my chest.

I struck him in the chest with a blast of air, which threw him back slightly, but didn't do enough to persuade him to stop. I had to be careful about Mac and Alan, who were close enough to us that Helios could use them to get to me at any time. And using too much powerful magic could leave them in a dangerous position. I needed to get Helios away from them.

Helios ran toward me once more, feinting with his claw and then punching me in the stomach as I avoided the blades. The blow was immense, and caused me to stagger back, trying to suck air back into my lungs. It was more powerful than I could have imagined. Helios had lost his ability to fly and use his fire, or change into his dragon-kin form, but not his ability to inflict pain.

"You had enough?" he asked, but didn't wait for an answer as he brought the claw down toward my head.

I caught his wrist, moving my head just in time. "No more," I told him and unleashed an electrical attack that ripped through his body, causing him to scream in pain. I released his arm and created a sphere in my hand, spinning it faster and faster as I poured electricity into it. I placed it against the skin on Helios's chest and released the magic. It poured all over Helios, tearing into him, burning him, and removing his ability to breathe. I'd used something similar on the troll I'd killed in Avalon, but the one I'd used on Helios wouldn't kill him. Selene, his sister—and someone I cared for very much—would never forgive me if I tore her brother in half.

I used air magic to keep him tethered in place while the rest of my magic did its job.

"Nate," Alan called out. "Anthony has opened the door. Remy came back with the lift. We need to go."

"Be right there," I told him without looking back.

I removed the magic and saw a bloody and battered Helios. I removed the remains of his claw and threw it aside. "How much do you think these people will follow you now that they've seen you be humiliated? You should have just let us be."

"Nate, we need to go," Alan called out.

"Are you working for the Reavers?" I asked.

He spat blood onto the floor. "Fuck no. I just wanted to kill you. If the Reavers are back, then your world is going to burn. And you along with it."

I punched him in the face. He fell back, but I caught hold of his prison fatigues and kept him upright as I drove my fist into his face over and over again, until someone grabbed me around the arm.

I spun to find Alan, standing before me, anger in his eyes. "Enough with this shit, we need to go or Mac will die."

I nodded and released Helios, pushing him down to the ground. "If I ever see you again, I'll kill you. Selene be damned, I will tear out your fucking heart."

I spun on my heel and left the broken prisoner, as hundreds of eyes watched their fallen leader, probably wondering how much they'd like to be in charge.

CHAPTER 

Remy's fur looked like he'd crawled through dirt for several miles, the normally red and white replaced with grays and blacks. "Is he going to be okay?" he asked as the lift ascended.

No one answered him. The stab wound in his back wasn't life-threatening at the moment, but having your throat cut when you're unable to access your abilities was a pretty good way of killing anyone, no matter the species.

The lift came to a stop and a medical team rushed in once the doors were open. They lifted Mac onto a gurney and wheeled him out, while the two injured guards were helped toward the medical facilities the prison had.

"He needs access to the ocean," I told them, and we all rushed down the corridor, toward the building's exit.

"If we tip him in there, he'll die from the fall," one of the medical staff said. "And we don't have time to winch him down to the ocean."

I paused. "Warden's office. The fish tank. Get him in the fish tank."

It was everyone else's turn to pause. The warden stood only a few feet away, when I suggested it. "Will it save him?" he asked me.

"I don't know. But it's better than letting him die."

Everyone pushed the gurney off toward the warden's office. "Just one of you," one of the medical guys said.

"I'm going," Ellie said, and they all rushed to try and save Mac's life.

"What the fuck was wrong with you down there?" Alan asked when we were alone.

"Don't know what you're talking about," I said and made my way to the exit.

Alan grabbed my arm and pulled me back. "You had your blinkers on. I get that the Reavers are a personal thing for you, but you ignored the fact that one of your friends is dying, just so you could continue to pound on Helios."

I opened my mouth to argue and closed it again. "You're right, sorry. I'm tired and frustrated and angry. Mac getting hurt, Helios trying to kill us, sort of made me lose my temper."

"Does anyone know where Livius ran off to?" Remy asked.

In the hurry of getting Mac medical treatment, I'd completely forgotten that Livius must be about somewhere.

"He's outside, talking to one of the pilots," a guard told us.

"He's responsible for this attack," I said, already running toward the exit. "Get a team to meet us at the helipad."

I burst through the front doors, and sprinted toward the helipad in the distance. The pilot who'd taken us to the island was prone on the ground as Livius forced the second pilot onto the helicopter. He saw us running and stopped, grabbing hold of the pilot by the throat, and dragging him out of the helicopter. Livius's arm was a mass of thick hair, and easily three times its normal size. He smiled and with one hand threw the pilot into the helicopter.

I stopped running and found that Alan and Remy were beside me. "You can't take us all on and win," I shouted to Livius, using my air magic to carry my words over the roar of the wind.

Livius continued to walk toward us as he changed, first his other arm, then his legs, the hairy muscles tearing through his trousers, finally his upper body and head, until Livius no longer looked even slightly human.

"Ogre," Remy whispered.

Livius the ogre stood nearly nine feet tall, and weighed probably as much as a small tank, if a tank had hands that could crush steel. Two huge tusks had formed from his teeth, curling up and out, and making sure he could no longer completely close his mouth. His dark green skin—where black hair wasn't covering it—was cracked and rough. He roared at us. It was easily heard over the din around us.

"Anyone got a really big gun?" Remy asked.

Ogres were slow, cumbersome creatures, but they were also hard to kill and healed almost instantly from any wound they received. They didn't need to be fast; they just needed to hit you once and that was it. Besides their strength, they just didn't stop. Ever. Once they were on the hunt, they kept coming, like some horror movie villain that just won't die.

Livius stepped over the remains of his clothes, the claws on the end of his toes digging into the tarmac surface.

"Over the edge," Alan said. "It's our only hope."

"That's your plan?" Remy said. "Get him three hundred feet away from where he stands. How are we meant to do that?"

The ogre began walking toward us, each step methodical and full of purpose. It was in no hurry; there was nowhere we could go that it couldn't follow.

"We split up and run," I said and turned to sprint off toward the edge of the island.

I glanced back a few seconds later and saw that the ogre had decided to come after me first. I made it to the edge of the island and searched for Remy and Alan, but found only Remy on the other side of the helicopter. Where the hell was Alan?

"Sorcerer first, then fox," Livius said with a growl. "Leave Alan 'til last. Want to enjoy it."

"You're going to work for your meal," I told him.

"Going to crunch your bones, little sorcerer. Going to suck the marrow from them." He stopped walking and something approximating a smile crossed its hideous face. "Fee-fi-fo-dead man."

"That's giants, you fucking idiot."

It charged and I dodged aside, rolled, and threw a blast of air at the ogre's legs. I might as well have been trying to blow down a tree with a feather. It changed direction and came at me once more, and I saw Remy run off to the building, hopefully to get me an armory. Or at least a lot of help.

There was ten feet, at most, between the ogre and me as I readied a sphere of lightning in my hand.

"Come see what this can do," I taunted him.

The ogre paused. They were hard to kill, but could still be hurt, and having a sphere of magic slammed into it was certainly going to do the latter. Unfortunately, its long arms meant that I couldn't get close enough to use it without risking losing one of my own.

A crash-like noise rang out all around us. I removed the sphere of lightning as it sounded again, like a massive force of waves slamming into an island. The ogre paused and turned around as a massive tentacle burst out of the water a hundred feet below us and wrapped itself around the ogre. The ogre tried to get away, but the tentacle was covered in suckers and spines, which tore apart the ogre's flesh as it attempted to escape.

Eventually the ogre vanished over the side of the cliff. I rushed over to look down and saw the giant eyes of an adult kraken staring up at me. It had used the massive rocks at the base of the cliff to drag itself free from the ocean and then reached up, taking the ogre as if it were nothing.

The kraken's normally red body pulsed green and purple as it opened its mouth, showing the razor sharp beak it used to tear its prey apart.

On another of its tentacles stood Alan, his translucent frame a sign that he was controlling the beast. Alan was a summoner, allied to the water element. He was capable of controlling the massive beasts that lived in the ocean of this world and of other realms. I never really knew how he managed to bring forth things like the kraken, which were extinct in our realm, and he was never all that forthcoming with information.

The kraken brought the no longer struggling ogre closer to Alan, until they were almost touching. Alan's body became solid once again and he glanced up at me. A moment later both tentacles were extended up toward me. I took an instinctive step back.

"Do you have questions for the ogre?" Alan asked, without emotion.

"Who do you work for?" I asked him.

The ogre glared at me and the kraken tightened its tentacle, causing it to cry out. I'd never heard an ogre even acknowledge that it felt pain before. The idea that Alan could control something so powerful was not a comfortable feeling.

"The Reavers," the ogre said with a gasp. When he finally spoke, his words tumbled from his mouth, "been here for years. Since just after Alan arrived. I needed to keep tabs on him until it was time to show the world we exist once more. We were under the impression that he knew where Felix was; Felix was always going to be a main target for us. We wanted to kill you, Nathan, but then after we hurt Fiona, Alan told me that it was you who knew of Felix's whereabouts. I was told to keep an eye on Alan anyway, just in case he was lying."

"Nate doesn't know shit," Alan admitted. "The second you people laid your filthy hands on my wife, I would have burned myself alive rather than tell you anything. I'm the only one who knows where Felix is. I'm going to help Nathan find him, and then we're going to destroy you Reavers as if you were nothing to us."

"You'll never destroy us all. Too powerful. We'll always be around."

Alan looked at me. "Any more questions?"

"Who was your contact? Who told you we were coming?"

"SOA agent. Don't know real name. Just know his voice. He told me that you'd be on your way. He said it didn't matter anymore. You could both die."

"Why? Why don't they need Alan or me to find Felix?"

"They found someone else."

"Who else knows, Alan?" I asked.

"Just me and . . . Fiona."

"You told her after all," I said.

"How can Fiona tell anyone though? Did she wake up?"

The ogre laughed. "I'm just told where I need to go. Doncaster, England. I'm sure there are already people there, searching the city for Felix."

Alan looked shocked, which quickly morphed to rage. "You still need him?" he asked me.

"No, go nuts."

"No, no, no," the ogre screamed over and over again as the tentacle holding him was lowered slowly toward the waiting maw of the kraken. I didn't need to look over the edge of the cliff to know what the screams signified, but Alan stood at the cliff edge, and didn't stop watching, not even as the crunching began.

The prison went into lock-down almost immediately after the death of the ogre. A squad of guards dressed in heavy armor and armed to the teeth were sent down to level ten. The first time in years, so we were told. The days of allowing the bottom three levels to do as they wished were apparently over.

Helios no longer had his kingdom to run. In fact, from what I was told after, Helios was in even worse shape than he'd been when I'd left him to bleed all over the prison floor. Apparently his old comrades had taken the opportunity to remove him from the hierarchy. He'd probably be back—looking for revenge on those who'd crossed him—once he'd healed up, but that would be a while.

Mac had survived, although he needed to be taken somewhere that was better equipped to deal with his requirements. The Avalon station in Wales, his normal home, would be able to do it. He forced the two medical personnel pushing his gurney toward the waiting helicopter to stop and waved me over.

"Not your fault," Mac said, his voice was hoarse and sounded exceptionally painful. "Find the Reavers. Stop them."

I promised him I would and turned back to Alan, Remy, and Ellie, none of whom looked all that happy with what had happened since arriving at the island.

"So, boss, what's next?" Remy asked. He'd been allowed a shower, getting rid of the grime and dirt that covered his fur.

"You going to help?" I asked Alan.

"They hurt my wife," he said softly, his anger still easy to hear. "I'm going to find the people who did it and feed them to the largest monster I can summon. We need to go to Doncaster. I can show you where once we get there."

"What happens if Felix tells us who's behind everything?" Ellie asked as we all made our way back into the prison building.

"We go find him and kill him," Alan said.

"And if Felix doesn't know?" Ellie asked.

"He knows something. We'll find out how much when we get there," I said. In truth, I hadn't considered that Felix wouldn't know something. The Reavers certainly believed he did, but even if he didn't, he might know the names of people who were involved in the older version of the group, maybe those would give us a clue where to go next.

The helicopter behind us took off as we reached the prison doors, where the warden was waiting for us.

"You've brought me a whole load of trouble," he said. "Avalon is going to be angry about what happened here. And *you*," he pointed a finger at me, "need to go. Alan killed a guard; whether it was in self-defense or not, that's going to take some explaining. You shouldn't have allowed him to do that."

"He didn't *allow* me to do anything," Alan retorted. "I didn't exactly give him a huge chance to argue with me. And your guard was a corrupt piece of shit."

The warden glared at Alan. "Not exactly the point, you're a prisoner and you killed a guard. Exactly what am I meant to do about that?" He took a deep breath. "Sorry, I'm just trying to figure out what I'm going to do."

"Tell people I killed the guard," I suggested. "Tell them he felt so guilty over what he'd done he killed himself, get Olivia to help you sell it. Alan's coming with me. I'll bring him back when we're done."

"We have another helicopter coming from the mainland. It'll be about twenty minutes. Then I want you all off my prison. Don't come back unless it's to drop off Alan. And Alan, get these bastards." He turned and walked off. I certainly didn't envy his position.

We each took a chair and I began to relax. Remy closed his eyes and was asleep a moment later.

"You know this is going to get worse," Alan said. "The second we find Felix, whatever Reavers they've sent there are going to tear through anything to come at us."

I nodded. "I know. But I can't go back to Avalon and wait for them to come to us."

"I just want you to know that this is nowhere near over." He sighed and rubbed his eyes. "You told me that Fiona was safe, that Lucie was looking over her. How did someone drag her memories out of her?" Alan had gotten angrier with every word, almost shouting the last sentence.

"I don't know," I told him, and then paused. "Kay and his Faceless were in the room with Fiona too."

"Kay?" Alan asked. "Why would Kay be in there?"

"I assume he wants to be there when Fiona wakes up so that he can get the names of those who attacked her."

"Covering him in even more glory when he single-handedly takes them down."

"Something along those lines, yes. And before you say anything, Kay doesn't have mind magic, so he's certainly not dragging anyone's mind."

"What about his Faceless?" Ellie asked with a yawn.

"If his Faceless was doing it, it would be on Kay's orders," I said. "I just can't see Kay betraying Avalon."

"Could the Faceless be controlling Kay?" Ellie asked.

I paused. It was theoretically possible, although I'd never heard of a Faceless betraying his master. Some of the Faceless were rune-scribed to ensure that their loyalty was total. "I don't know," was all I could answer. "He did say there'd be retribution for when I killed another Faceless. We need to see what Felix has. In the meantime, I'll get Lucie to keep an eye on Kay's Faceless." I walked over to the reception area as the doubt about the Faceless gnawed at me. He could very easily be involved, he could be going against Kay, although I'd never heard of a Faceless going against his master. There's always a first time for everything. I grabbed the phone, but the line was dead.

"Standard protocol to shut down all outside communications," Alan said. "I'd have called them myself otherwise."

I tore the phone free and threw it across the room. It hit a wall, leaving a big dent. "Fuck!"

"You okay?" Ellie asked.

"Tired," I said and rubbed my eyes. "Haven't slept for a while now."

"As soon as the helicopter lands, we'll use their radio to contact Avalon Island," Ellie said.

"There's a soldier there, Hendricks," I told him. "He'll get in contact with Lucie; let her know that someone went through Fiona's memories."

"You haven't told me I should never have mentioned Felix to Fiona," Alan said.

"No point really, what's done is done."

A helicopter—identical to the one we'd arrived in—landed on the helipad outside, and it wasn't long before we were in it, readying for takeoff. Remy immediately went back to sleep. Ellie asked the pilot if she could use their radio, so she sat up front to contact Hendricks. Alan remained awake; the intensity on his face made it clear he wasn't interested in talking.

"You know, it would be much easier if phone calls could be made directly through realm gates," Alan said.

"We'll get right on that," I told him and then closed my eyes to rest them.

"We really do have to stop meeting like this," a voice said.

I was sitting in some sort of deck chair in front of a serene lake. Birds fluttered over its still, dark surface. It was pleasantly warm, and a table sat beside me with a clear drink in a tall glass. I leaned forward and picked up the glass, smelling the liquid inside. Ice clinked together as the alcohol scent reached my nose.

"It's got vodka in it," my own voice said from behind me.

I turned and found myself walking toward me. Except it wasn't really me. Darkness spilled out from his eyes, covering most of his face.

"Erebus," I said. "It's been a while."

"No, it hasn't," he said and then paused. "Oh actually, I guess it has for you. We talk quite often when you're sleeping, but you don't remember it."

The news came as quite a shock. "How *often* are we talking about here?"

"Once a month. It's nice to touch base. I am, after all, you."

"You live in my subconscious, but you're not actually me, Erebus. You're just my magic given form. My n—"

"Don't call me a nightmare, it's really a terrible name." He removed the drink from my hand and sat opposite me. "Do you know why you're here?"

"I'm asleep, aren't I?" Panic sank in. "The venom in me will kill me?"

"Oh please, as if I'd let you die when I have a chance to stop it. I'm controlling your magic right now, and giving your conscious brain a little rest into the bargain. You know you've been using an awful lot of magic in the last few days."

"Are you telling me that because you want out?"

"Of course I want out, that's the entire reason for my existence. I get out and take control, giving you power beyond your dreams."

"Not interested."

"You will be one day. At least you will be one day when those damn marks on your chest go, and I can actually do more than take control for a few minutes." Erebus took another drink. "Anyway, that's not why you're here. At some point, your magic use is going to do one of two things, either you're going to have to let me out, or you're going to kill yourself."

I didn't have to let Erebus out to control me, no sorcerer *had* to let their nightmare out. They did because they wanted power, or because they were convinced to.

"I'm not going to kill myself," I explained.

"You're so stubborn. Sorcerers keep using magic and we pop up and give them the chance to use us to lessen the damage on their bodies. They say no, and keep using magic, guess what happens."

"I know what happens. We die, or you force your way out and take control."

"Can't do that. We have to be invited. Otherwise it doesn't work. If you keep using your magic to the extent you're currently using it, you can either let me out to relieve some of the pressure, or you'll die."

"And if I let you out, what guarantees do I have that you'll go back, or not kill anyone?"

"None. But then out of all the times you've let me out, have I ever stayed out longer than agreed, or killed people I shouldn't?"

I didn't trust Erebus, but I had to admit that he was telling the truth. He'd never outstayed his welcome, or killed those who weren't an immediate threat to me or people I was protecting.

"Did you bring me here just to tell me I've used too much magic?"

"Primarily, yes. At some point soon, you'll need my help and I will give it."

"You can tell the future now?" I asked with as much sarcasm as I could manage.

"No, I just know you. I know you're not going to slow down. You'll find Felix, the Reavers will find you, and you'll fight. It's what you do."

"Do you have any advice?"

Erebus nodded. "Don't die."

"That's not advice."

"It is. It's gloriously good advice too. I know what you know, Nathan. I can't tell you something you're not already aware of. Let me ask you a question that no one has bothered to ask yet. Answer honestly. Do you think Merlin is involved?"

"I don't know. No one wants to bring it up because, let's be honest, no one wants to suggest that he's even further gone than we'd expected. If Merlin had been involved, if he were trying to consolidate power or something, he'd have removed Elaine first. He hates how much power she has, but is unwilling to do anything to rectify it. All he does is spend time in his home. At least that's what I last heard. Maybe he's become more proactive, or insane, since I last spoke to him."

"Well, we're about to land, and you need to be awake. To be honest, you needed the sleep."

I swung my legs over the chair and stood up. "Thank you for that."

"Just be careful in Doncaster. The Reavers are probably waiting." He took a long drink. "Bye, Nate." And he clicked his fingers.

CHAPTER 23

I opened my eyes as the helicopter touched down. The bump woke the other passengers too, although Remy appeared to have been wide awake and was watching me with interest.

Once we were all out of the helicopter, Alan and Ellie walked off together, leaving Remy standing beside me. "You went to sleep," he said as the helicopter lifted off and began its ascent.

"So?"

"Your glyphs remained powered. How did you do that?"

"It's complicated."

Remy stared at me for a moment and then shrugged, walking off toward the waiting Alan and Ellie.

I caught them up a few seconds later. "So, where is he?" I asked Alan.

"He's near St. George's Minster."

"I'm sorry," I asked, unsure I heard him right. "Are you telling me that you put Felix near a church?"

"Seemed like the safest place at the time."

"How far is it from here?"

"Well, this is Robin Hood airport, so a half hour drive," Alan said. "If we had a car. Which, from the expression on your face, I'm going to take a guess and say we don't."

We left the airport using a private entrance staffed with Avalon employees, one of whom gave us a set of car keys to a baby blue Ford Kuga outside. We all climbed inside, with Ellie in the driver's seat, as I sat in the back with Remy.

"See you should have some faith," Ellie said dangling the keys in front of Alan.

"Faith in Avalon?" he mocked.

"Avalon does good too," Remy said.

That stopped the conversation dead.

"Hopefully, we can get Felix and arrange transport to Avalon Island before Lucie even needs to contact us," Remy continued.

I buckled my seatbelt. "Let's get going then."

I looked down at Remy "I think we may have to get you a disguise," I told him. "I think an upright walking fox might create a few questions."

Remy buckled his seatbelt. "I'll stay in the car in crowded places, these windows are tinted."

"We can't leave an animal in the car," I said. "Not even some-one who looks like an animal. If anyone spots you, they're liable to call the police, or smash a window to try and get you out."

I turned and moved the divider for the boot aside. It revealed some emergency supplies, such as lights, a first aid kit, and some blankets. "We can cover you."

Remy's eye's narrowed, but he nodded anyway. "I'll get on the floor behind the seats if it's really necessary. No one should be able to see me. But if there are no crowds, I'm not staying here. If we meet anyone, they can think I'm going to a costume party."

"As what?" Alan asked while Ellie navigated getting us out of the airport car park.

"Fantastic Mister Fox," Ellie said.

"There you go, problem solved."

"It's not really—" Alan started.

"I said, problem solved," Remy snapped.

Everyone was quiet for the rest of the twenty-five-minute journey, until we reached the Minster and pulled up outside it. While not a massive building, it's still a very impressive piece of architecture.

"Did you know this is the same spot as an old Roman fort?" Alan asked. "And at some point it was a Norman fort? Both well before the church was built, obviously."

I shook my head. "How do you know that?"

"I once used the place where I put Felix as a safe house of sorts. I did a lot of research on this whole area during one of my stays. This church was destroyed by fire one night, although that had nothing to do with me. I gave money to have it rebuilt. As did Queen Victoria for that matter."

The sun had set some time ago and the lights around the church—illuminating only parts of it from the darkness—gave it a more imposing appearance than it would have had during the daylight.

"So, how do we get to your hiding place?" Remy asked, as a few people walking by gave him an odd look, which he returned with a wave.

"Follow me."

We did as Alan asked and followed him around to the opposite side of the church, where several large trees stood. A little further on, and down a steep hill, was a small stone wall, which led to a drop of several more feet.

"Where are we?" I asked as we made our way around the wall to the pavement below.

"Well, all of this used to be woodland, so it was easier to keep the entrance hidden. But over time people cut down a lot of the trees and instead of being able to keep the entrance hidden from view with some simple tricks, I had to arrange for something more permanent."

We walked for a short time more until we reached Grey Friars' Road. A hundred meters up from there was a seven-foot-tall fence, with a metal gate painted blue with a 5mph sign on it. Oddly enough, the gate and fence only appeared to be protecting a small brick building with a metal door on one side. I couldn't have imagined that either the fence or the gate was much of a deterrent. There didn't appear to be a lock on the gate.

Alan touched his hand to the gate and the otherwise very large and permanent gate slowly swung open.

"Runes?" I asked

Alan nodded. "Better than a lock. I had an enchanter I know arrange them so only Felix or I can open the gate. It keeps people out."

The small brick building had a sign on the door that said *Do Not Enter. Danger of Death* written on it in big red letters.

"What is this?" Remy asked as he tapped the door with a nail, creating a hollow noise.

"This is the entrance to my little hideaway."

"Danger of Death?" I asked.

"A few kids have climbed the fence in the past. Some paint graffiti on the walls, but very few people want to open a door that says danger of death on it."

Alan touched the door and it began to vanish as if disintegrating before our eyes. "That's some expensive level rune spells," Remy said.

"I used to have enough money," Alan pointed out. "Then I met Nathan and that all went to shit."

I ignored Alan's taunt and looked inside the small brick hut. There was a ladder that led down into the darkness beyond, but that was it.

"Where does that go?" I asked Alan.

"There are catacombs under here. You pay enough public servants enough money over the years and they tend to lose the maps and original documents that prove it. They're older than even the Roman settlement that was here."

"How old?" I asked.

"You'll see," Alan said and began his descent down the ladder into the darkness.

I ignited my night vision and began climbing after Alan. I was about halfway down when light exploded all around me and I had to slam my eyes shut for a few seconds as I removed the night vision and stopped the brilliant white spots from being all I could see.

"Little warning next time," I said when I'd made it to the bottom of the ladder, which was easily fifty feet in length.

I looked around and found myself in a tunnel. Lights hung every dozen or so feet from wooden pillars that had been placed there. "What is this place?" I asked.

"It's perfectly safe. I think it was made by an earth elemental. I put the lights in about thirty years ago; I was fed up with carrying a torch everywhere."

We waited until Ellie and Remy had made the descent—the latter of whom did not stop complaining about it the entire way down—and then we followed Alan once again, as he led us down the tunnel that seemed to move deeper and deeper underground.

Eventually we all stopped again, this time at what appeared to be a dead end. Cold, wet stones were all around us, with no obvious exit in site, bar going back the way we'd come.

Alan placed his hand on the wall and, like the door above, the wall began to disintegrate before us. Beyond was a cavernous room that stretched maybe forty feet above us and a hundred feet in diameter. The room itself held a large pool of water in the center, but that was it. I walked over to the pool; the water was clear and inviting. I touched it and found it was cold enough to have just come straight from the fridge.

"What is this?" I asked.

"Like I said, this place is old," Alan said. "I'm guessing druids used it for something or other. That water, I have no idea where it comes from. Deep underground is the best guess, although there don't seem to be any noticeable holes to an underground reservoir. The water never goes down, no matter how much you use. There are runes carved into the rock inside it."

I glanced around at the five large exits from the cavern. "And those?"

"Bedroom, storage, food, whatever else you want them to be. This was someone's house."

"I've never heard of anything like this," Ellie said. "Have you, Nate?"

"Underground caverns and the like are fairly common. Magic keeps them safe from external damage, so they just sit there untouched for years. Or someone finds one and takes it for their own personal use. The water thing, that's new. I've never seen that before."

"So, Felix is down here?" Remy asked. "I smell . . . chickens."

"The tunnel there leads to a small farm. Chickens, vegetables, fruit, stuff like that. This place uses a similar method to get natural sunlight into here that The Hole uses. Only this place is several thousand years older."

"Where's Felix?" I asked, managing to pull myself away from the interesting sights of the cavern.

"He's probably waiting to see if the newcomers are a danger to him. Technically only him and me can come in here, but he's a paranoid bastard. He'll be out shortly."

I walked over to one of the tunnels. "What's down here?"

"Go look."

I did as suggested and soon found myself in a second, much smaller, cavern. It had artifacts covering the tables and cupboards that were scattered around the room. I walked over to a nearby chest and pulled it open. The gleaming white skull of a giant stared back at me, its massive head maybe five or six times the size of mine. I closed the lid and walked back to the rest of the group.

"See anything nice?" Alan asked with a smirk.

"Giant skull," I said.

Ellie and Remy shared a glance and then ran off in the direction I'd just come back from.

"You know how old that must be," Remy asked, when he returned, clearly astonished by what he'd found.

"The last giants in England were killed by Brutus over two thousand years ago. In fact, everything here looks new. Does Felix clean it all?"

Alan shook his head. "That enchanter friend of mine who performed miracles with the doors, yeah, well he told me that the amount of rune work and magic poured into this place was obscene. Everything was done to keep the contents pristine. He told me there wasn't enough money in the world for him to start meddling with the runes already here. The word dwarf was thrown about."

"How'd you find this place?"

"I was running from some rather nasty people with pitchforks and torches. You know the usual kind. I was heading toward the river Don, fell down here. Fifty feet straight into darkness. Thought I'd died. Managed to drag myself through the mud to this place. No one was here, so I claimed it as my own."

"You need to see some of the stuff in this place," Remy said as he returned. "You could live here for years and years based on the food here. And there are runes inscribed everywhere. I'm half terrified to touch anything." He said it with the kind of laugh that suggests he'd rather not take the chance though.

"There's enough weapons back there to start a small war," Ellie said. "How much of this stuff is stolen?"

"Most of it," Alan said. "I wasn't always a law-abiding citizen."

I coughed.

"Okay, I was never a law-abiding citizen. But I am trying to be."

"I know," I admitted. I really did believe that Alan—for all of his bluster and attitude—was trying to become a model citizen. He'd given himself over to prison in order to wipe his slate clean so that Fiona and he would have a future together. The man I'd known a few centuries ago wouldn't have even entertained the idea.

"So, where is Felix?" I asked.

"Maybe he hasn't heard us arrive," Alan said. "This way."

"Is he a prisoner here?" Ellie asked.

"He can come and go as he likes," Alan said. "But when he's down here, the runes shield him from tracking. He prefers to work down here in safety, only going up for short periods to buy anything he might need."

We walked after him down one of the tunnels. About half way down, the sound of music began to fill the immediate surroundings. The small cavern beyond contained a bed, a desk, and books. Lots and lots of books. Librarians would have glanced upon the sight and groaned with envy. There were more books there than any one person could possibly read in a lifetime. They had been put into the dozens of cupboards here, until they'd been full and then the books had been piled head high all around the floor. Littered among the space between the stacks of books were piles of paper.

The desk in the center of the room was occupied by a man with long gray hair, hunched over something. He was writing furiously. He stopped, appeared to think of something else, and then re-commenced writing.

"Did you hear the alarm to say someone had arrived?" Alan asked.

"Yeah, I heard. Knew it was you. It's always you."

"That's not exactly the point of a security system," Alan argued, but the man waved him away.

"Felix," I said.

Felix stopped writing and turned. "Nathan," he said and got up from the desk chair. He limped over and hugged me tightly. "Why are you here? It's dangerous. The Reavers, they're back."

"I know. They've killed people, hurt others. They're trying to kill you and me," I said.

"How do you know?" Remy asked Felix.

Felix tapped his head. "I might be down here, but I can still use my mind magic. It's how I've been able to collate all of this information. How I've been able to track them. I link with someone on the surface and use them to do some searching."

"You take over someone's mind without their permission?" Ellie asked. "Isn't that sort of . . . illegal?"

"I'm not taking it over," Felix snapped. "I'm just pushing them toward doing something I need them to do. Influencing them, if you wish. It lets me read their thoughts without them ever knowing I was there. I originally discovered the Reavers were back by accident. I've been monitoring them ever since. Been about twenty years now."

"Anything you can tell us?"

Felix nodded enthusiastically. "Lots. But I'm trying to get a pinpoint on whoever is in charge this time round. Until I do that, I can't give you anything."

"Why?"

"Because despite all of the names I've discovered, the dozens of them, I've never been able to track down those in charge. The leaders of this resurgence of Reavers elude me."

"My wife was looking into them too," Alan said. "It got her hospitalized."

"I heard. One of those whose mind I took knew about it. I'm very sorry, Alan. And while this may sound callous, is there any chance you have some of her research?"

I shook my head. "She's got it all booby-trapped. We can't get to it until she wakes up."

Felix looked deflated, but he placed his hand on Alan's shoulder. "She'll be okay. She's tougher than you."

Alan barely nodded.

"So why can't you find those in charge?" Remy asked.

"I don't know. No one knows who it is. And I mean no one. I haven't been able to risk taking anyone too high up in the organization, only lower or mid-level members. Nothing is shared about the hierarchy that happens outside of the individual groups of Reavers. It's very insular."

"But you think you have something?" Ellie asked.

Felix nodded enthusiastically. "I picked up some information about high-level members a few weeks ago from one of those I controlled. The same one who told me about Fiona's attack. They were worried she knew something she shouldn't. I couldn't get the names of those in charge, but I did get the names of some SOA agents who are helping."

"Any you feel like sharing?" I asked.

"One of them is Agent Kelly Jensen."

"Oh shit," I whispered.

"You know her?"

I nodded and explained how she was the one who got me to go to the hostage situation in West Quay. How she was the one in charge. "You sure?"

"A hundred percent. She works with a small team, including a griffin and a man by the name of Mortimer."

"Fucking hell, the whole lot of them were in it together." I very much wanted to punch something in the face. "How long do you need?"

"Twenty-four hours. I'm so close, Nathan, so very close. We can destroy them this time. Once and for all. Purge the stinking cancerous bastards from our midst."

"Okay," I agreed. "In twenty-four hours, whether you have those in charge or not, I'm going after Kelly Jensen. Just one more thing. Is Merlin involved?"

Felix shook his head, pushing his hair back over his shoulders before he spoke. "No, not this time. Elaine has him by the balls on this one. If Merlin does anything so brazen again, she can get him removed from his position. He won't risk that. No, this is someone else. This is *something* else too. The beginning of something bad, Nathan. Something evil." Felix paused and glanced up at me, a slight smile on his face. "I've been getting hints about things. About a change in the air. The ball has been rolling for years and now it's gathered enough speed to make it dangerous."

"How do we stop it?" Remy asked.

Felix's smile broadened. "Now that Nathan's here, we blow it into tiny little chunks."

"Yeah, I'll go get started, should I?" I said. "Look, you can't stay here. It's too dangerous. We'll all go to a hotel in Sheffield or Leeds, somewhere far enough away."

"I can't leave, Nate. I'm safe here. No one can get in except me or Alan."

"In that case, Alan and I will go see what we can find out around the town. If the Reavers are coming, I want to know who they're bringing and when they get here. They might know you're in Doncaster, but I doubt they know you're here. I want to be able to thin their ranks somewhat."

"I'm coming," Ellie said. "My nose is better than yours. And besides if I have to stay in here, I may just go crazy."

Everyone turned to look at Remy.

"He has live chickens and enough weapons for me to have tingly thoughts. I'm staying," he said, his voice suddenly serious. "Someone has to. Just in case those bastards do get through."

"We're going to make getting to you a death trap," I said. "By the time we're finished whoever the Reavers send are going to wish they hadn't bothered arriving in the city."

We said our goodbyes, and then Alan led us out of the cavern and up the ladder to the street outside. We all stood in the cool air as Alan replaced the door, which rematerialized just as miraculously as it had vanished originally.

I took a step and felt like I'd been punched in the chest. I stumbled back and looked down as blood spread out across my chest. I dropped to one knee, while my friends shouted and rushed to me.

"Nate, Nate, what happened?" Ellie asked, fear dripping from every word.

"I don't know," I admitted and touched my chest. The initial pain had vanished, replaced with numbness.

"There's some sort of weird residue on you," Alan said.

A growl sounded from Ellie's throat as several people walked through the open gate. Ellie and Alan sprang to action, but they were quickly subdued, each of them shot with some sort of dart.

Agent Kelly Jensen stood before me, with a smile on her face. The SOA agent I'd grabbed by the shirt was beside her, hatred burning in his eyes.

"Don't worry," she told me, crouching down to look in my eyes as she spoke. "Tranquilizers." She touched my shirt. "Had to use something a bit more impressive for you. An old friend wanted a shot." She moved my head and I saw Mortimer—the man who had murdered Liz and Edward Williams—a rifle over one shoulder, walking across the scrubland on the other side of the road from us.

"Not burning," I said.

"It's not silver. You're not allowed to die yet. You're to witness the death of everything you hold dear, that's your punishment for trying to destroy us all those years ago. That wasn't a normal bullet, though. You want to know what it is?"

I nodded, although it was difficult to raise my head afterwards.

Kelly placed her mouth next to my ear. "A manticore spine crafted into a bullet. You're going to be paralyzed in a few seconds. You won't die, but you're not going to be able to do anything to help your friends. I'm curious to see what happens to the venom already in your body."

"Don't kill them," I managed.

"Oh, no one here is going to die today. You've brought us to Felix. So they get to live for a while longer. At least until you wake up."

"How did you find me?" My eyelids felt heavy.

"I'm fae, and you lost blood at the hostage situation in West Quay. Which, by the way I was in charge of. When those idiots fucked up taking the Williamses and turned it into a clusterfuck, it was my idea to get you to go in. I figured maybe we could salvage something from the mess they'd created. Unfortunately, I couldn't kill you myself, not with so many non-Reaver witnesses. So you lost all that blood and I used it to track you. It takes ages to get going, but once it does, boom, nowhere you can run." She stood up and stretched, while a griffin landed beside her. "Don't kill him," she commanded.

The griffin walked toward me. "You should be grateful there's someone who wants you dead more than I do." He smashed the end of his spear into my head and the world went dark.

CHAPTER 

November 1888. London.

What the fuck does this mean?" I asked Fiona, waving the paper I'd found in her face.

She took it off me and read it through. "It says you went through the Harbinger trials at the age of thirteen. That Merlin and Felix were the ones responsible, and that Felix wasn't very happy with the idea."

"I know what it says," I snapped. "But I don't understand it. How is this even possible?"

"I . . . I don't know. I've never heard of such a thing. The minimum age for the Harbinger trials is a hundred. Putting a thirteen-year-old boy through that would be . . . insane. He'd be lucky to survive without permanent brain damage."

I glared at Fiona.

"Sorry, but I have no idea if this is even real."

"I don't know," I said. "Felix left a note saying sorry about everything. We've got to find him. The Reavers have him. We need to find him, I need to know if this is . . . is real." I felt light-headed, felt like someone had hit me in the head with a brick. I stepped back and sat down on the cold stone floor.

"Are you okay?" Fiona asked.

I shook my head. "If this is true, how many years of my life are a lie? A fabrication caused by Merlin and Felix for whatever reason they decided to fuck around with the head of a child . . . of me."

I wanted to storm off to find Merlin and force him to tell me the truth. But that wouldn't get me anywhere. And it would mean that Felix would still be missing, that Jack and his merry band of lunatics would still be free to kill. One job at a time.

There was a bang upstairs. Fiona and I froze.

"That was the front door," she whispered.

I closed the cabinets beside us and switched off the lamp. "Can you conceal us?" I asked Fiona.

"Of course," she said, and we backed up against the wall opposite the cabinets, beside the staircase a new arrival would have to descend. "If you move quickly this illusion will shatter though."

"That's fine, if I need to move quickly the illusion won't be needed anymore."

Illusions being created over a person by a conjurer feel tingly, as if your entire body is dying to be scratched. The sensation only lasts a few seconds, but a few seconds is still a long time when you have the notion that small insects are crawling all over your body. Standing in a basement full of various bugs didn't help matters.

"We'll just look like part of the wall, now," she said when finished. "You can talk, but only whisper. The illusion isn't calibrated for normal voice levels."

I glanced down and a large spider crawled over my shoe. I resisted the temptation to punt it across the room and it quickly crawled away when the door opened and light was cast down from the floor above.

"They could be hiding down there," one voice said. He had an accent that placed him from east London.

"Go fuckin' look then," the second man said. He was also English, but his accent was northern, possibly from up Newcastle way.

"We'll go together, there's two of them. I watched them come into the house."

"You don't think you can take two of them then? You can kill whores and people who don't fight back, but not some Avalon bitch and bastard?"

"You think you can take them both, be my fucking guest. Those drugs we got from Baker won't keep the trolls asleep for long. Do you wanna wake up with a bunch of trolls in a rage, because I know I don't. You down there," the man shouted.

"Are you fuckin' touched in the head?" the second man asked. "What fuckin' idiot is going to say, 'Yes, I'm right fuckin' here. Feel free to come down and stab me.'"

"Right, well we'll go together then."

Boots touched the top step, which creaked. There was a pause and then more steps, until they reached the bottom.

"There better be a light," the first man said.

"It's here," the second man told him and soon after the oil lamp was lit. "See there's fuck all here."

The second man was a good head taller than me, but slimmer. He had short hair that appeared to be balding at the front, and the appearance of someone who worked hard for a living. His chin jutted forward in an exaggerated way. He wore a long black coat that he had unbuttoned, and a curved dagger sat on his belt. The dagger was sheathed, but his left hand constantly hovered around the hilt of the weapon, waiting to use it. He played with a set of brass knuckles on his right hand, which was slightly red with blood. He'd used those knuckles recently.

The first man was barely five feet tall and stout, like a large barrel. He wore no coat, but was in a nice-looking gray suit. He removed a pocket watch from the breast pocket and flicked it open. "Got half hour," he told his comrade. He glanced around the cellar we were in and I noticed he had a waxed moustache. He appeared elegant and more refined than his friend, who had opened the cabinets with abandon.

"Fucking hell, look at all of this shit," he exclaimed and grabbed a handful of files. "Jack was right; this bastard had shit-loads on us all."

"Burn it. Felix won't be needing it again where he's going."

"We should leave it 'til last though, just in case we don't find those two." The second man glanced around the room. "I saw them come in. Where could they be hiding?" He drew his dagger and walked around the room, looking behind the cabinets and in any place that someone could possibly hide.

"They ain't here," the first man said. "This old place probably has secret tunnels and stuff. They could have left. They could be watching the house, waiting for *us* to leave."

"So that we lead them back to Jack? That's very clever. These two are devious little bastards."

"It's just a theory," the first man pointed out. "They could also be hiding under the beds upstairs."

The second man picked up some of the files from inside one of the cabinets and flicked through the paper, before throwing it up into the air. "Maybe we should bring Felix back here to watch his world burn before we kill him."

"That's up to Jack, not us."

"Yeah, well, maybe Jack should let us have a bit more freedom."

"And maybe Jack will cut your bollocks off if you ever let him hear you say that."

The second man mumbled something I couldn't hear, but he didn't sound too thrilled about being threatened. "We're all Reavers here. Jack's no better than anyone else."

"Except he is in every single way better than us. If you don't see that, your life is going to be a lot shorter than mine."

"He does let us cut up those women." The second man's smile could have been seen from the front door. "I enjoy that." He absentmindedly played with the blade on his knife. "When do you reckon he's going to let us get more? It's been a few weeks since the last one."

"You brought a lot of trouble our way with that last murder. Too messy."

"What about that bloke who's always with Jack? He sent a fuckin' kidney to the coppers. A kidney. Who does that? Who goes out of their way to piss off the fuckin' coppers? He's fuckin' nuts. Scares me more than Jack ever did."

"Well it's up to Jack who does what," the first man said, without looking up from the file he was reading.

"What's that?"

"It had a note on it for that Nathan bloke. Apparently they put him through the Harbinger trials."

"Like us?"

The first man nodded. "Looks that way."

"Did he fail too?"

"Doesn't say. He was thirteen years old though."

"Thirteen? And they say that we're monsters for killing folk. Putting a thirteen-year-old through those is . . . well, it's inhuman."

"I'm surprised you know what the word means."

"I'm surprised I haven't cut ya fuckin' throat."

The first man chuckled, although there wasn't any humor in it. "Just go search over there by the stairs, I'm reading."

The second man appeared irritated at being told what to do, but he did it anyway. He walked toward us, looking under the staircase. "There's no one here," he declared.

"I know, I just wanted your stink away from me," the first man said with a genuine laugh.

The second man stood still, glaring at his companion. "That wasn't funny."

He took a step back, ending only a few inches away from where Fiona and I hid. Fiona motioned with a slight move of her head, for me to glance down, where she held up three fingers. She dropped one finger, so only two remained, and I nodded for her to go ahead. She didn't bother dropping more fingers.

Fiona exploded from a standing position, launching herself up toward the man in front of us, who had no time to react before she'd rammed his head into the staircase. The first man turned at the noise and tried to run, but slipped on the papers at his feet, giving me ample time to throw a ball of air at him, which threw him back into the open cabinet behind.

He responded by grabbing several of the files, and throwing them at me, making it rain paper. He darted forward, the glint of a blade the first I knew of his plan before it swiped up at me through the paper haze.

I dodged aside, grabbed his wrist, and smashed my forearm onto his elbow. He shrieked out as the joint broke, but didn't drop the blade, so, keeping hold of his wrist, I stepped around him, kicking his legs out and putting all of my weight on the broken joint as he crashed to the floor.

He finally dropped the dagger after I broke his wrist, before a kick to the head sent him into the darkness that comes with being unconscious. I left one man and moved quickly to the other, who was straddling Fiona on the dirty floor, his dagger still in one hand, while he used the other to pin her arm to the floor. He noticed me, and for the briefest of seconds his concentration wavered. That was all Fiona needed. She grabbed the dagger from his hand, and plunged it into his thigh. He screamed out, and Fiona punched him in the jaw. I heard it break and he fell back to the floor.

Fiona stood and grabbed the dagger. "This is your femoral artery," she explained to him. "If I remove this dagger, it won't end well. It's silver, yes? I saw you at Mister Baker's place of business. I know that you're an alchemist. I know you're involved with the Jack the Ripper murders. I know that you're a Reaver. Are we clear on what I know?"

He mumbled something.

"Good, because I'm going to ask you some questions, and I want answers. I know your jaw is broken, but you can just answer with a yes or no, if you'd prefer."

I glanced over at the first man, who was groggily getting back to his feet. A blast of hardened air at his temple took him back to the ground with a crash. "I'm going to take him upstairs," I told Fiona. "You okay down here?"

Fiona grabbed the dagger hilt and twisted it slightly. The killer on the ground whimpered slightly. "I'm fine."

"Answer her questions and you may get out of this in one piece," I told him.

"No," Fiona told him, "you'll die here. The only question is how bad that death will be." She twisted the hilt again. "Shall we begin?"

I took the first man up to the same room that Felix had taken me to when I'd first arrived at the house with Alan and Diana, what felt like years previously, but had in reality only been a few days.

While the man was unconscious, I used the time to prepare for what I was going to need to do. When I was ready, I threw a pitcher of water in his face. He woke up with a start, and immediately struggled.

"I found some old chains when I was searching the house," I told him, pointing to the chains that ensnared him, tying him to a large metal ring that had been put into the floor. "They're pretty worn, but shouldn't be easy to break. You were out for a bit, so you can't be all that powerful."

"You have no idea what I am."

"You're fae," I said. "I noticed the wings when I carried you upstairs."

The façade evaporated from the man's face, replaced with a mouth full of razor-sharp teeth and larger than normal ears. Fae only changed their appearance when losing control, or hunting prey.

"What's your name?" I asked, ignoring the snapping of his jaws.

"I'm going to tear you—"

I punched him in the nose. "Shhh," I said softly. "Be nice, or I'm going to remove those teeth for you."

The façade slipped back over his face. "You're Nathan Garrett. You should be helping us, not fighting us."

"That's an interesting idea. Why should I be doing that?"

"We're doing this for Avalon, for all of us. We're doing this because of what we want Avalon to become."

"The only thing I want Avalon to become is devoid of deluded little animals like yourself."

The man tugged at the chains again. "What did you do to me?"

"Nothing," I admitted. "The chains though, well that's different. You see in one of these rooms, Felix has an arsenal. Seriously, dozens and dozens of weapons all lined up and on one side I found two ordinary looking chains. The links are a bit bigger than usual, but that's it. But then I discovered a link in the floor here to put chains. So, I said to myself, why would Felix want to hold people with chains?"

"Rune-marked chains, I'm glad he's under the watch of Jack. He deserves it."

"No runes. It wasn't until I picked them up that I realized what I was looking at. There's something about fae that not many people know. A dark fae and a light fae cancel one another out. If they come into contact, even from a few inches away, they nullify one another. Would you like to guess what's inside that chain?"

"A fae?" he said with a nervous laugh.

"Sort of. It's the hair of a light fae. I've seen these kinds of chains before; a blacksmith in Camelot makes them. One who several friends of mine spent a lot of time around as children. He once taught me about these. So, as long as that chain is near you, you're pretty much a human with some occasionally serious facial issues and wings. And I'm not sure if you've ever been told this, but translucent wings aren't scary."

"What do you want?"

"Where is Felix?"

"Whitechapel. You want the address?"

I didn't even bother to try and hide the shock.

"What? I give you the address, you rush over there and get yourself killed. Hopefully that gives me enough time to scarper, because I don't want to be the person Jack gets mad at. Jack killed a werelion because he fucked up. No magic, no powers, just knives. We weren't meant to let people know we aren't human, and the werelion bit some girl. So, yes, I'd really rather not be found having fucked up. Actually if you could kill my comrade, that would help. I could just tell Jack that he's the one who blabbed it all. Where is he anyway?"

"Indisposed. You're a Reaver?"

"Yes. I am a Reaver. Was BOA, took the Harbinger exam, and then wallop, no longer capable of becoming a Harbinger. Apparently it's my temperament. In my unconscious state I murdered a bunch of people. Shame it wasn't real."

"Must have been a real heartbreaker."

"You have no idea. I saw your name downstairs. Thirteen years old, eh? That's pretty evil. I assume it worked, because you're still with Avalon, and you're not dribbling every other word."

"What do you know about it?" I demanded.

"Nothing. I guess you want to find Felix and ask him. I guess, if you're nice and all, Jack might give you some time together. Probably not, though. *He's* not very nice."

"So, you and your partner downstairs, along with Jack and a fourth man, were Jack the Ripper?"

"There were five of us before the werelion was killed. But yes, we were Jack the Ripper. Well, him and about half a dozen other murderers. I guess you heard me downstairs. That buffoon I came in with started writing shit on walls, and hacking at the women. Two in one night, taking pieces of them, he wanted to make a name for himself."

"And this fourth man sent the kidney to the police?"

He nodded. "His name is Enfield. He's . . . he's a wrong 'en. I've met some seriously deranged individuals in my life—hell, one of them entered this house with me—but Enfield, he's a different level of twisted."

"Tell me about Jack."

"Jack's in charge. He's our captain . . . of sorts. The one with me tonight thought it funny to use Jack as the name of the murderer. Jack was livid, I thought he was going to kill the stupid bastard, but he didn't . . . obviously. He's not a man to cross."

"Who attacked me in the alley in Whitechapel? They wrote *From Hell* on my forehead. It would have been a few days ago, they killed two SOA agents."

"Oh shit, they killed Avalon agents? Wait a second, mate, that wasn't in the deal. That's why you're looking for us? I thought you were just mad because we left too many bodies around. Fuck. Fuck. Fuck. Fuck. Fuck."

"Who did it?"

"Enfield. He's the only one fucking crazy enough."

I'd known it couldn't have been either the man in the chair or the one Fiona was currently talking to, both were the wrong size and neither had the same resonance about them as the murderer in the alley. "What are Jack and Enfield?"

"Sorcerers, both of them. Never seen Enfield use anything but knives though. As for Jack, no idea what magic he can use apart from fire."

"How many did *you* kill?"

"What, this time? Four or five. Got some nice souls for Arthur to feed on. You do know we're giving these to Merlin, that he's approved this?"

I nodded.

"Made you sad to know that the big guy was allowing the murder of innocents? At first it was hard to get my head around too, but you soon get used to it. You're just cutting away the chaff so that the wheat can grow strong or something like that. Who gives a shit if a bunch of whores, homeless, and lowlifes vanish? That's why everyone was so angry with the idiot for drawing attention to things."

I grabbed a pen and paper from the table. "The address where Felix is."

He told me without needing to be asked again.

"If this is wrong—"

"You'll kill me?" he chuckled. "It's right, I swear. You're going to die a horrible death for getting involved."

"Who killed Baker?"

"Baker? Oh, that was all Enfield. He knew that Baker was going to get found out sooner or later. He decided to keep watch on things, just in case. We threatened Felix too, made him give you up. The second you all turned up, Baker was a dead man.

Enfield used you to deal with the troll. He's crazy as a box of cats, but he's not stupid."

"Doesn't matter how crazy or smart he is, he'll be dead soon enough."

"You think you're going to kill Enfield. Mate, unless you happen to have the Hellequin in your pocket, you've got no chance."

I smiled, and ignored his taunt. He had no way of knowing I used to go by that name. No one did. I had buried it long ago, but it still resurfaced every now and then, usually with some more fantastical tale attached to it. Hellequin was the boogeyman for the Avalon world. I was surprised people still remembered it, or that it had continued to grow in mythology.

"We'll see. What did you drug the trolls with?"

"Jorōgumo venom," he said. "Perfect venom for trolls. Give it to anyone else and it kills them slowly, give it to trolls and they fall asleep for a few hours. Felix betrayed you, you know that, yes? He betrayed you because we took the troll's kid. He agreed to help us if we brought the ugly little shit home. We had to drug the trolls to get close to them, but Jack didn't want to have a troll about the place, so we brought him home. We're nice like that."

"You kidnapped a child, threatened its life, and you also have a jorōgumo? Quite the list of accolades to add to the murder of innocent people."

He shrugged. "I don't know about us owning the spider thing. I've never seen one, which is a good thing; because they're nasty bastards I've heard."

He'd heard right.

Fiona appeared in the doorway covered in blood. "I got an address." She passed me a piece of paper; the address was the same as the man in the chair had offered.

"Well, it's nice to know you were telling the truth."

"Of course, like I said this is the quickest way for you to get dead."

Fiona walked around the back of the man. "And this is the quickest way for you." She rammed the blade into the top of the fae's skull. "Told your friend he was going to die. You die too."

When the fae was dead, Fiona went to the kitchen to wash her hands. I followed and stood a little away from her.

"You got a problem with what I did?" she asked.

I shook my head. "Just surprised."

"I'm undercover SOA; we have to do a lot of nasty things that surprise people."

"Did yours tell you about Jack and Enfield?"

Fiona scrubbed her hands and then set about drying them. "Yep. We're going to need Diana and Alan. Enfield sounds like a real problem."

"They're both problems."

Fiona threw the towel into the sink. "Let's go eliminate our problems, then. You can carry him; I just got my hands clean."

I carried the body of the fae down to the basement, laying it next to his murderous friend while Fiona threw file after file around the room, until the basement was awash with pieces of paper.

When she was done, Fiona passed me the file that contained my name. "You should keep this. Take it to Merlin. Maybe he can give you some answers."

"Are you sure about burning all this?" I asked.

"Felix has information on Avalon employees. If it ever got into anyone else's hands, there would be pandemonium. We can't risk it. Jack will have to give us the answers we need. He knows who was involved with these Reavers."

"I don't think Jack will be too forthcoming."

"Then Felix will have to be alive when we've finished dealing with Jack and Enfield." She removed several of the files from the remaining cabinet and passed them to me. "Hopefully something in there will help. It's just too dangerous to leave it as is. Too dangerous to leave this house here at all. Felix knows too much."

"You're not going to kill him," I said.

"My orders are to keep Avalon safe. Felix goes against those. You should have killed him when you were sent to."

I shrugged. "Maybe, but he's not going to die now either. I'm not going to help further the Reavers' aims by removing one of their obstacles."

Fiona's eyes never wavered from mine. "Fine, I didn't want to kill him anyway. I'm not in the habit of killing people who haven't deserved it. But we'll have to think of something else. He'll need to be hidden, and hidden very, very well. Also, these files still need to go."

I grabbed a few more of the files and carried them up toward the house. "I'll see you outside," I called back. I found a large box in Felix's study, and piled the files inside. The office, like most of the house, was devoid of anything that looked personal, but I managed to bust open Felix's safe and remove the money and other items from inside it. One of which was a drawing of Felix and a young child on some old paper. It had been framed some time ago.

Before I left, I also took the light fae chains from the floor. The blacksmith had long since died, and it felt unfair to destroy something so rare. By the time I was done, two large boxes were stashed by the front door, almost breaking from what they contained.

"Are you planning on moving house for him?" Fiona asked as she re-emerged from the basement and saw the boxes.

"Grab one," I said ignoring her comment. "We'll dump them on the coach."

"Felix can never come back here. Not now."

"I know, but I'm not going to punish him for going against Merlin."

Fiona picked up the box and dropped a few items from a nearby table into it. "I'm not without empathy for him."

We opened the door and found half a dozen wood trolls staring back at us.

"Where is Felix?" the largest troll asked, his massive head far too close to my own for me to be comfortable.

"People took him," I told them "Two of them are in the basement dead. The basement is on fire. We're going to go find Felix. But he can't come back here."

Another troll took the box from me, while a third did the same with the one that Fiona was carrying.

"We'll keep it all safe," the largest troll told us. He glanced behind me. "How long before the house burns down?"

"I don't know," Fiona admitted.

The large troll motioned for both of us to leave the house, which we did quickly. And then several of the trolls went into the house.

"We'll make sure Felix's things are safe. Come get them from us when you find him."

"And if they've killed him?" I asked.

"Are you going to try to save him?"

"Yes," I told him.

"Then we'll give them to you. I'm sorry about your coach driver, we got here too late." He turned and entered the house.

"I'm sorry your child was taken," I said. "Did they bring him back unharmed?"

The troll beside me pointed at a small wood troll sitting on the lap of a large female. "He is fine. Shaken, but okay."

"Good, I'm glad."

Fiona and I walked to the coach, and found the driver dead. His throat had been cut. Fiona helped bundle his body into the rear of the coach before she sat up front with me.

"Do you have a plan?" Fiona asked.

"We find Alan and Diana, and then we go get Felix back, killing anyone who gets in the way."

"Not before we've had some answers though."

"Oh, by the time we're done with them, they'll be falling over one another to give us whatever we want."

Fiona and I took the coach back to the safe house in Whitechapel, which turned out to be empty. Even though it was dark, there were still plenty of people out and about, so removing the body from the coach would have been a very public affair. Instead, we moved the coach to the patch of grass where Alan and I had been attacked only a few days earlier. This time there were no maniacs about, so we left the horses in peace and removed the body, dumping it in the carriage, where the darkness ensured it couldn't be seen even from a short distance away.

Returning to the house, we decided to wait for Alan and Diana to come back and went inside. Fiona went upstairs and changed her clothes, putting on a pair of dark trousers and white shirt. She tied her hair up into a bun and put a hat on it.

"Very fetching," I said with a smile, when she came downstairs.

"You going to change?"

I shook my head.

"I hope you two had a more productive time of it," Alan shouted from the hallway behind me.

I dried my hands and left the kitchen. "We know where they are," I told Alan and Diana.

"Where?" they both asked.

Fiona removed some paper from her pocket and passed it to Alan. "We got the address from the two members of the Reavers who took Felix."

"They have Felix?" Diana asked.

It took us a few minutes to explain everything to them, but they both remained quiet throughout.

"We're going to get him back, yes?" Alan asked.

I nodded and explained why Felix had betrayed us.

"So, what's the plan?" Diana asked. "I'd like to hurt the men who did this."

"We need to get Felix away from Jack and Enfield," I said. "Jack and Enfield . . . I don't care what happens to them. They have questions to answer, but once they've done so, they're going to be buried in unmarked graves somewhere. Then I'm going to see Merlin."

The atmosphere changed slightly at my last words.

"Merlin? Are you sure?" Alan asked.

"You can't accuse Merlin of knowing about this," Fiona said. "He'll deny it, and if he doesn't, he'll have you executed."

I'd wondered that very thing from the time I'd left Felix's house. "No, he'll tell me the truth and he won't have me executed. I hope not anyway. But it needs to be done. I need to know what Felix and Merlin did to me; I need to hear it from his own mouth. I need to know how many of my memories are lies."

"This address is a warehouse not far from here," Diana said. "It's still being built. You sure the person gave you the right address?"

"Yes," Fiona said. "It's definitely the right address."

"When do we go?" Alan asked.

"Now. We need to get this finished." I turned to Diana. "Your coach driver was murdered. I'm very sorry."

Diana looked toward the floor. "Just another reason for me to be involved. Have the murderers been punished?"

"Yes, they both died," Fiona said. "And not well."

Diana looked up at her. "Good. When this is done, I shall have his body returned to the ground. These Reavers have been nothing but a problem since they came to this city. I want to see that they are punished for this."

The word "returned" set off alarm bells. Who or what was her coachman, anyway? But this was hardly the time to ask. We told her where the body of her coachman could be found and then, when everyone was ready, we set off toward the warehouse ready to cause the Reavers some serious problems of their own.

CHAPTER 

November 1888. London.

The four of us crouched in the darkness outside the perimeter of the warehouse, near the district of Wapping. The building backed onto the river Thames, which was still and dark. As much as we were horrified by the crimes that had been discovered, I wondered how many were never uncovered after the *evidence* was disposed of in that river.

"They've got to know we're coming," Alan said.

"I imagine they do, yes," Fiona told him.

"I'm going to go in and scout the place," I told the three of them. "We have no idea if they have more help in there, and even less of one as to where Felix is being held. I'll look around and come back."

Diana and Fiona both looked ready to argue.

"How long do we give you?" Alan asked, looking at his pocket watch.

"Ten minutes. If I'm longer than that it's because they've grabbed me and then you'll probably hear the fight."

"Ten minutes, *exactly*," Diana said.

I nodded.

"You know, I'm a better hunter than you," she told me.

I nodded again. "Of course, but you'll also use that lovely bow to put one through their ears at the first opportunity. I'd rather they were alive to begin with."

Diana smiled. "Go, do your hunt."

I thanked her and climbed the fence, keeping behind various pieces of building apparatus as I ran the few hundred yards to the warehouse. I remained close to the warehouse wall as I made my way toward the rear of the building next to the river.

The warehouse windows at my eye level were blacked out, and I didn't fancy the idea of clambering up the side of the wall to see if the windows higher up gave me a better view of what was happening inside. I would have been too exposed for too long.

At the rear of the building there was a separate structure, which I assumed to be the offices for the management of the main warehouse. There was a staircase, which led up to the top floor. I ignored it and moved through the open rear doors of the warehouse and into the dark stillness beyond.

The warehouse floor, all several thousand square feet of it, was deathly quiet. I had no idea what the end function of the warehouse was, as all it contained were the tools and materials used to finish the building. The walls and roof were built, but the interior was still very much nowhere near completion.

Several small offices had been built in one corner, all of which turned out to be empty, and I'd soon made a complete lap of the interior of the warehouse. I glanced up at the walkways being added high above me. There was nowhere to hide up there. Wherever Jack and Enfield were, and wherever they'd hidden Felix, it wasn't inside the main warehouse building.

I left the warehouse and decided to search the lower level of the larger office building first. I made my way to the door, but found it locked. I readied a blade of fire and paused. Runes had been carved into the doorframe. The light from the fire showed them up. I had no idea what they did, but I guessed it wouldn't be good.

Instead of trying to find another way in, I doubled back and took the staircase up to the floor above. The door there was closed, but unlocked, and I was soon inside a long corridor that stretched the length of the building. Every few feet was another door, and after opening the third it was clear this was to be a series of offices. It probably allowed the management to overlook their workers, but not actually have to interact with them until they came and left the warehouse.

All of the rooms were empty, and by the time I'd reached the end of the corridor I was beginning to think that we'd been fed lies about the whereabouts of Felix and his captors. I glanced out of the window at the end of the corridor, and noticed the small dock that had been built below. A Thames sailing barge was bobbing gently beside it. At eighty feet long, it was a sizeable vessel, with more than enough room to stash Felix while Enfield and Jack hid.

"Ten minutes is up," Fiona said from behind me.

"You make an awful lot of noise for someone who's trying to sneak around," I pointed out. "I heard you walking up the stairs."

"Yet you didn't come to see who it was," she teased.

I ignored her taunt. "I'm more interested in that ship. Where are Alan and Diana?"

"They walked off toward the river; apparently Alan has a surprise he'd like to show her." She paused for a moment. "You do know that Alan Daly is a criminal against Avalon. He should be in irons, or at least in a sorcerer's band."

"I'm well aware of what Alan is," I replied, slightly terser than I'd intended. "He's also helping track down a group of murderers. He could have run a dozen times and hasn't."

"When this is over, he's going to have to be taken in for his crimes."

"When this is done, I'll make sure that happens. Until then he's working with us. If you have a problem with that, you're more than welcome to tell someone who cares later."

Fiona breathed out slowly. "You're not what I expected. I thought you'd be more of a stickler for the rules, more rigid. But you're letting a known criminal help you bring down people who are, to many, Avalon members."

"Avalon isn't a place of paragons and virtue, where all is good and the bad guys are easily spottable. Avalon's got just as much corruption as any other government."

"That's why I work for Elaine. Even so, it's strange that you've decided to work with him. I told Elaine about it. She says she trusts your judgment in most things. So I will too. I just wanted you to know that I find it strange, that it's not what I expected."

"Thank you for being honest. Alan will receive the punishment he deserves. But first, he agreed to help. Once that's done, he'll run as fast as he can."

"He's an interesting man too. A thief and scoundrel, who thinks only of himself, helping Nathan Garrett defend the defenseless. An odd set of circumstances."

"My whole life is an odd set of circumstances. You get used to it." I turned and pointed out of the window. "Right now, we need to get on that ship."

"Let's go then."

I followed Fiona back down the stairs, only stopping when we reached the end of the building. There was a good amount of space between us and the ship, and I doubted very much that running onto the pier was going to be the most silent of entries.

I thought I saw something and activated my night vision, spotting Diana, sans Alan, making her way under the pier, almost swimming in the horrid water that made up the river Thames. She stopped moving, and glanced over at us, raising her arm and pointing off to the side.

Following her directions showed Alan crouched down on the soft mud a hundred feet away.

"Is this part of a plan I was unaware of?" I asked.

"We decided to exclude you. It seemed easier," Fiona explained.

"Want to share what the plan is then?"

"Like I said, Alan has a surprise. We just have to wait for Diana's signal."

I had a really bad feeling about this. A feeling that was shockingly realized when Diana reached the ship and pulled herself up onto its deck. There was no one there to stop her as she crept across the ship and then vanished from view.

One minute felt like a hundred, but she eventually reappeared, moving slowly to the side of the ship, before dropping back into the river. A short time later, she rejoined us, bringing the smell of the water with her.

"What did you find?" I asked.

"Don't be annoyed, Nathan, you're a masterful hunter, but if you'd have come across Enfield or Jack, you'd have attacked them. You're not always the most patient of people."

I opened my mouth to argue that the point was the exact same one I'd used against her going off alone, and, probably wisely, thought better of it. "What did you see?"

"Felix is onboard, I can smell him. There are a few others there too. I couldn't go too far in, not without being spotted."

"Anything else?" Fiona asked.

"Blood. A lot of it too. People have been killed on that ship, and recently."

"What's the best way onto the ship?" I asked.

"We've got that covered," Diana said with a smile that made me very concerned. It was the kind of smile you'd see on a warrior before a battle, and you just know, with a hundred percent accuracy, that warrior was to be avoided at all costs.

Diana whistled, and I instinctively knew that it was a signal for Alan. I glanced over at him, but he'd already walked down to the water's edge, his body turning to translucent water as he moved. The moonlight seemed to bounce through him, until he vanished from sight.

It didn't take long for the water to become more violent, causing the ship to move erratically. The surface of the water broke and a large sea serpent crashed out of the river, bringing its long body down onto the ship's deck with an almighty roar of noise.

The serpent was maybe thirty feet long, with a massive, thick body. Its mouth was easily capable of biting a fully grown man in half. It used its two small but powerful arms, each tipped with claws to tear into the ship with aplomb.

The beast's head vanished below the deck, as the sounds of destruction rang through the night. The serpent's body shuddered suddenly and then went limp. A blood-covered man emerged from below the deck, a sabre in one hand.

Alan materialized on the riverbank, and collapsed to his knees. "Go to him," I told Fiona, as the bloody man spotted Alan and began to move toward him. "I'll get this guy. Diana, find Felix."

Fiona ran toward a motionless Alan, while the bloody man stepped onto the pier. He saw me running toward him and for a second I thought he smiled.

"Hello again," he said, with much enthusiasm as I reached the edge of the pier. "You come back to claim your friend?"

"We're going to get Felix and then I'm going to stop you and Jack. No more innocents are going to die because of you."

"You going to offer me the chance to surrender?"

I carried a belt of silver throwing knives at all times. There were six in total, and they'd gotten me out of a lot of trouble over the years. I removed two of the blades and motioned for the bloody man to come toward me.

"Brave little bastard. I recognize you from that alley. I'm glad I let you live, gives me a chance to correct that mistake properly."

"You're Enfield?"

Enfield bowed slightly, never taking his eyes from me. "Glad to hear my name has made its way to you. I'd hate for you to die at the hand of some anonymous lout. I assume the two we sent to Felix's house are dead? We told them to wait there and deal with anyone who arrived."

"Both dead," I admitted.

Enfield shrugged. "Shame, but their sort's two a penny, to be honest. Reaver raw recruits. So many people fail the Harbinger trials it's not difficult to grab a few who are disenchanted with how Avalon runs things. They always disapprove of the murders to begin with, and then they find out that Merlin ordered them.

That bit's a lie by the way, he didn't technically order them, he just doesn't care where the souls come from."

"Why are you telling me this?" I asked, and moved closer to him. My silver daggers were no match against a sabre, but I was sure my magic would even the odds.

"I like people to die knowing the truth. It brings me enormous satisfaction. People should know why they're dying. People shouldn't die with questions on their lips. Doesn't seem fair." He rubbed his chin with his free hand. "Well, some people anyway."

He moved forward as if he was made of water; his movements were smooth and fluid. He flicked the sabre up toward my neck, but I managed to deflect it with a combination of my knives and air magic. He quickly regrouped and a blade of ice formed on his free hand. He dropped the sabre to the floor.

"It's been a while since I fought a sorcerer. Wanna do this properly?" he asked with a smirk.

I blasted him in the chest with air magic, sending him sprawling to the ground several feet away. "I'd rather just kill you," I said and sprinted toward him. Enfield dropped to his knees and the water exploded up from beneath the dock, freezing in place, and creating a thick barrier between the two of us.

I threw fire magic at the ice, but whatever I melted just grew back again almost instantly. I took a few steps back and set the edges of the dock ablaze, controlling the fire until there was an inferno to either side of me. I pushed more and more fire from my hands as it moved toward the ice, attacking it from two sides.

The ice cracked and in a second exploded out toward me, becoming a hundred razor-sharp projectiles. A hastily created shield of air meant losing the fire, but it protected me enough to keep me alive. Some of the ice crept through, puncturing my arms and chest. I cried out in pain, and dropped to one knee as blood trickled down to my stomach and a still smiling Enfield appeared in place of his barrier of ice.

He raised his hand and all of the ice left my body, flying back toward him before turning to water and dropping to the smoldering dock.

"How are you feeling?" Enfield asked, removing a straight razor from his pocket and opening it to show me the blade. "I'm going to use this to cut your heart out. You hurt me with that little trick."

One of his hands was badly burned. I can't say I felt much sympathy for him.

He took a few more steps toward me and then stopped, concern on his face. "Why are you smiling?" he asked.

Black, blood magic glyphs crossed slowly over the back of my hands and up my arms. "Surprise." The blast of air that left my hands slammed into Enfield like a train, taking him off his feet and throwing him back several meters, until he collided with the remains of the sea serpent.

I got to my feet and walked toward him, increasing the pressure of the magic with every step, until I heard bones break and Enfield howled in pain. I released the air magic, and threw two of the silver blades at him, each one taking home in his thighs. I started to run. By the time I'd reached Enfield, the blade of flame that was in my hand was so bright Enfield couldn't look directly at it. I drove the blade into his chest, through his body and into the body of the serpent.

I removed the blade and took a step back, as Enfield crashed to his knees, blood pouring from the wound in his chest. Alan, who was himself being almost carried by Fiona, was helping Felix back toward the warehouse. I didn't see either Jack or Diana.

I turned back to Enfield, who was still trying to relearn how to breathe.

"You're going to answer some questions I have," I told him. "You faked being injured, didn't you?"

"Whatever I have to do. Now, these questions I have."

"You don't really think I'm going to tell you shit, do you? You can kill me, but there are plenty of Reavers out there waiting to take my place."

"That's why Felix is going to help us track you all down. All of you. We're going to give everyone a choice. Leave the Reavers or die. You're an antiquated idea that is as corrupt as anything I've ever seen. You're done."

"We're not done until someone a lot higher up than you says so."

"Who?"

"None of your concern," Enfield said dismissively. "Your win today is but a battle, you're never going to win the war." His tone suggested that I was an idiot for even considering a different outcome to what had happened.

His words didn't make me angry, they just made me more determined that I was going to win. There was no other outcome in my mind. "A war implies both sides are fighting. All the Reavers have done so far is bleed and die."

He waved the concern away. People like Enfield care little for anyone but themselves. "We'll see."

"Where are the souls of the people you killed?"

"Already sent back to Merlin."

"How many did you kill?"

"I forget," he said with a slight laugh. "Twenty, thirty? It was a good number. More importantly, it will keep Arthur alive for many years."

"What's in the rune-marked and locked factory building back there?"

"It's where we kept the souls. It's empty now, although you're welcome to have a look. Jack is the one who marked it. I'm sure once you've found him, he'll be only too happy to help."

"You're willing to sell out your boss awfully fast."

"You know nothing about anyone I serve. And you should pray you never do."

"I'm going to find them, then we'll see who'll be praying."

Enfield laughed, and then began coughing.

"You're deranged," I snapped. "If you make a move, I'll kill you." I watched as he got back to his feet.

He drove the silver dagger up under my ribs with incredible speed, twisting it before stabbing me again. I lashed out in shock and anger, blasting Enfield with powerful enough air magic that threw him to one side of the ship, where he impacted with a loud crack.

Blood poured from my side, and I looked up at Enfield, who smiled. Dozens of frozen spikes flew at me and I dove aside just in time to avoid them, causing myself even more pain. When I finally looked over at where Enfield had been, he was gone. I searched the river, hoping to see him swimming along the murky waters, but there was no sight of him.

The burning pain from the silver subsided as I pulled the dagger out, but I was still bleeding badly from the wound. I removed my shirt and used it as a bandage to try and stop the bleeding.

"Nathan," Diana called out from the riverbank beside me, dragging the unconscious body of a man from the water, and dropping him onto the mud. "Found Jack. He tried to swim away."

I raised my hand to wave and then decided that pain made that a bad idea. Diana was beside me moments later, helping me to stay upright.

"Where's Enfield?" she asked.

"He got away. We need to find him. What about Jack?"

"He'll live. Probably won't feel good about it though."

"I want to talk to him."

"It can wait until you're no longer bleeding all over the place. Let's go get you patched up."

I gave serious thought about arguing, but sometimes it's just easier to nod and let someone help make sure you don't die.

CHAPTER 

November 1888. London.

I was lying in front of the factory while Fiona looked at the wounds I'd received from being stabbed with one of my own silver blades. I can't say I was all that happy about it.

"You're a terrible patient," Fiona told me.

"Sorry. How's Alan?" I was lying on my side on a makeshift bed, which mostly consisted of pieces of timber Diana had found. It was neither comfortable nor warm.

"Resting, like I told him to. You on the other hand won't sit still for five minutes. I'm trying to stitch up this wound."

My magic would have healed the wound eventually, but healing from a silver blade takes time; hours or days. Neither of which I was in the mood to give it. I needed to talk to Jack, I needed answers and, damn it, he was going to give them if I had to crawl over to him and bounce his head off the floor.

"Your stitches will hold for now," Fiona said, slapping me gently on the leg. "Don't inflame the wound and you'll be fine. From the few days I've spent with you, I imagine exasperating is what you do best."

"It's a talent, that's true," I admitted and Fiona chuckled. "How's Felix?"

"You can see for yourself, he's in the factory."

I got down from the makeshift bed and glanced at my dirt- and blood-covered body. It had been a long few days. I needed a bath. But it would have to wait. I found Alan lying on some more timber as Felix stood next to Diana reading through various pieces of paper.

I cleared my throat.

Felix and Diana both turned to me.

"I'll leave you two alone," Diana said, and dragged Alan away as she walked past, until only Felix and I remained.

"You probably have a lot of questions," he said.

"I'm glad you're alive," I told him. "And yes, I do."

"Where would you like to start?"

"The truth. The Harbingers," I said with calm authority, although I certainly didn't feel calm.

"You were about thirteen when you first showed magical ability. Not an uncommon age, but your natural affinity toward using it was obvious. You learned quickly and soon outclassed anyone else your age. Not necessarily with power, you understand, but with a desire to be the best. You were willing to do more, to go further than the others, and you appeared to have an untapped potential that was worth exploring. Merlin was the one who decided you needed to go through the process of the Harbingers."

"Why?"

"I don't know. He just said it was necessary. I argued, of course, that no thirteen-year-old should ever be put through the strain, but he insisted, and eventually my choices were to be involved, or he'd find someone who would be. I couldn't risk that, couldn't risk someone who didn't know what they were doing performing the trials. So I stepped forward.

"Merlin told you that you were off to China for a decade. In reality, you were drugged and your body brought to an underground complex outside Camelot. There we trained you. During the day you'd live your life as if you really were in China. You felt loves and losses, you learned quicker than you ever could have in the real world. Within the first few weeks you'd mastered several languages, and were proficient in weaponry and hand-to-hand combat. The Harbingers are designed for the participants to learn a dozen times faster than in the real world."

"And at night, I didn't rest, I learned to fight." It wasn't a question.

"When your conscious mind was asleep, your subconscious took over, learning how to fight. Your body was put through its paces in real time. It has to be done that way, otherwise your mind will know how to do something, but your body won't be able to. For several years this took place. We allowed you to rest once every month for two days, letting your body and mind heal. And on more than one occasion I thought you might die, but you were strong. Terrifyingly strong."

"How many others went through what I did?"

"None. After it was done, Merlin decided to never put another person though the trials until they were of age. Mordred was meant to be after you, but it never happened."

That was a piece of news that truly surprised me. "Why not?"

"Merlin sent him on an errand instead, allowing him to grow in real time, not the one we created. I have no idea how it worked. Mordred returned when you were in China."

"Was I really in China that time?"

Felix nodded. "That was your first actual time in China. You probably wondered why you didn't know places you were meant to have visited. Merlin hadn't been to China for some time, so everything you were taught was based on old memories."

"Why keep this from me?"

"Because apart from Merlin and me, no one knows it happened. It breaks the very laws that Merlin set in place; tampering with a mind without consent. And on top of that, it was the mind of a child? He would have been investigated at the very least; no one in Camelot would have stood for that."

"So everything from thirteen to twenty-four is a lie. I loved people, I was in love. People I cared about died."

"It had to be real. It had to let us know how you'd deal with grief, with love and happiness. With anger and betrayal. We couldn't train you to become what you are and then discover that you were insane, someone who liked killing and did so without any thought for anything but their own gratification. I'm sorry that you had to go through all of that."

"Everything I knew was a lie." Anger bubbled up inside of me and I punched the ground, causing me to yell out as my wound hurt once again. "Did he ever put me through that again?"

Felix shook his head. "No. Once you've gone through the trials, you can't go through them again. Your mind immediately rejects it."

"Could *he* have had someone fuck with my memories since then?"

"You mean Merlin? The only way to do that now would be to use an immense level of blood magic. And it's not like the Harbinger trials. The trials are like the master hands of an expert pottery maker; we mold and craft things just right. Doing it with blood magic would be like hitting clay with a hammer. There's no telling just how many memories they'd alter or lose. If someone had done it, you'd either still be without memories, or you'd be a gibbering wreck."

That was at least some comfort. "Why did *you* keep this from me?"

"I was ashamed. Ashamed of what we'd done, ashamed of how we'd lied to you. We could have killed you, or mentally scarred you for life. The fact that you survived, and did so unscathed, shows just how much power you actually have."

"Did you put these marks on my chest?"

"The blood magic curse marks? No. I've never even seen them. Merlin told me about them, but blood magic isn't used during the trials. It's too unwieldy."

Neither of us said anything for some time, we just sat there in silence, while I tried to get my head around the idea that ten years of my life were not only a lie, but a lie perpetuated by people I'd trusted.

"You're going to run," I told Felix eventually. "You're going to run and hide. I don't blame you entirely for what happened, but I also don't ever want to see you again. You can live out your life in some remote spot somewhere and do whatever you like. We kept a lot of stuff from your house before it burned down."

"You burned my house down?"

I shot a glance at Felix full of barely contained anger.

"So, a new start, eh? Well, I suppose that's not too bad. When do I leave?"

"After I've spoken to Jack. In the meantime, I'd probably not want to be near me for a few hours."

I walked out of the warehouse, my anger bubbling softly inside me. "Where's Jack?" I asked Alan.

"Offices, up there," he said and pointed to the separate building. "Felix still alive?"

His smile dropped when I looked at him.

"Stay here," I told him, and I made my way up the stairs to the offices.

Diana stood outside the third door down. "I thought you'd want to talk to him. Let it be noted, I haven't threatened or touched him in any way."

I opened the door and found Jack, who was sitting on a chair beside a window that was too small for him to climb out of, although the fact that the window was smashed meant he'd probably tried at some point.

"Stand," I told him.

He sighed, but did as I asked, before straightening out his tie and smoothing down the suit jacket he wore. "Shall I dance now?"

I walked over to him and punched him in the stomach hard enough that he immediately dropped to his knees and began sucking in breath.

"You done?" he wheezed.

I wrapped air around my fist and hit him in the jaw, sending him to the carpeted floor. He spat blood and then sat back up, so I hit him again. This time, he stayed down longer.

"What do you want?" he asked as he pushed himself up to his knees. The second punch had split his lip pretty badly.

I hit him a third time, breaking his nose and sending blood across the carpet and up the wall beside him. He put his hand on the wall and I grabbed the scruff of his jacket and forced him to stand up.

"You have to tell me what you want," he demanded.

I punched him again and again, each time letting him drop to the ground before I dragged him back to a standing position.

Eventually he could only ask one question through his ruined mouth. "Why?"

I slammed him against the wall, and held him steady. "Why? Did you tell those people you murdered why you were killing them? Did they beg you to stop?"

I punched him in the stomach and let him fall to his knees.

"Don't you want answers?" he asked.

"Not really." I punched him again, knocking him back to the ground, where I started kicking him over and over in the ribs.

"You done?" Diana asked from the doorway, her voice completely calm.

I took a step back and looked down at the whimpering man. "Yeah, I'm done."

"Good, because I didn't want to have to stop you," she told me matter-of-factly. "I figured you'd want to actually ask him questions, not just kick his teeth down his throat."

"Jack the Ripper and his merry little band of murderers."

Jack shook his head. "Not my band."

"Are you saying you weren't killing those people?"

"I killed many over the years." He spat blood onto the floor. "I'm saying they weren't mine. I wasn't in charge."

"Enfield was, wasn't he?" I asked.

"He didn't want the others to know. He made them nervous. He made me agree to be the figurehead, but he was the one who made the decisions."

"Can you remove the runes from the door downstairs?"

Jack gave the barest of nods.

"Move. Now."

Diana and I followed Jack downstairs to the rune-marked door. Fiona and Alan joined us and we all stood back while Jack removed the runes, making it safe to open.

"It's done," he said after a short time.

"Diana, can you please keep Jack here company while we go take a look inside?" I asked.

Diana nodded and grabbed Jack by the arm, marching him away.

"If he tries anything, tear his arm off," I called after her.

From the look on Jack's face, she'd heard me and probably smiled at the suggestion.

I pushed the door open and stepped inside. It was one long room with dozens and dozens of pots and vases, all with opened tops. I picked up the first pot and flipped it over. Staring back at me was a dwarven rune.

"These were used to keep the souls of the victims fresh," I said, throwing the pot on the ground with a smash. I showed the mark to Alan and Fiona. "This rune allows them to do that."

"Same rune here," Fiona said, with a pot in each hand. She dropped them to the floor with results similar to mine.

"Me too," Alan confirmed.

"Can you destroy them all, and then gather them into a pile? Make sure that none of the runes can still be used. I'm going to finish my conversation with Jack."

"Hey, wait up," Alan said as I left the room.

I rubbed my eyes. "Whatever exceptionally witty remark you're about to make, please leave it for now."

"You're going to arrest me soon, I imagine. Fiona brought it up. She liked watching me as if I'm some sort of common criminal that might steal her purse."

"I'll ensure that all you've done goes toward lessening your sentence. But right now, I have other things to think about. When I head back to Avalon you can come with me. Until then, just don't run off. With the mood I'm in you wouldn't be happy when I caught you."

Alan nodded once. "I'm glad we got them. Jack the Ripper caught. We'll go down in history."

"No one is ever going to know about this. Jack is going to become a footnote in history." I turned to walk away and stopped. "Alan," I called back. Alan had just walked back into the building with the pots and his head appeared out of the doorway.

"How can I help?"

"Thank you," I said honestly meaning it.

"I might be crazy saying this, but it was my pleasure."

I left him to his pot destruction and found Jack and Diana. Jack was sitting on the floor, holding his hand to his eye.

"What happened?" I asked.

"Jack here thought that because I'm a woman, he could overpower me. Turns out, Jack isn't very good at actual fighting. He's more of a 'hide in the shadows like a coward and butcher helpless women' kind of killer."

I grabbed Jack's arm and stood him up. "We're going back to Avalon. You're going to tell the council everything that happened here."

"You don't actually think I'll do anything of the sort, do you?" he asked, with a slight laugh.

"You can do that, or I'll just bury you here."

"You may as well get a shovel then, because I'm not going to tell the Avalon council about the Reavers, or Merlin, or the murders of a bunch of whores. Not a chance."

I head butted him.

"That wasn't very mature," Diana said.

"It was that or kill him. Can you tie him up and get him on the coach, we've got a long journey and I don't trust myself not to just be rid of him."

Diana grabbed Jack by his hair and hoisted him upright. "My pleasure."

Jack opened his mouth to say something, but instead the explosion of a rifle sounded out around the warehouse. Jack stepped backward and collapsed to his knees, blood beginning to drench his shirt.

Diana and I dove into the warehouse as a second bullet tore into the side of Jack's head, snapping it aside with terrible force. I saw him topple forward, dead before he hit the ground.

Inside the warehouse Felix had crouched behind a stack of thick timber. "Who's shooting?"

I glanced out around the corner of my own stack of timbers and saw the rifleman walk off the dock toward us. Even with the considerable distance between us, I could tell it was Enfield from his clothes. He moved slower than he had before, his wounds from our earlier fight wouldn't have healed yet, but he didn't need to move fast when he was able to cover the distance much quicker with a bullet.

A round smashed into the timber not too far above my head, and I ducked back around the corner to relative safety.

"Can you see anything?" I shouted to Felix.

"Either Fiona or Alan has closed the door to the room, but he seems to be ignoring them. He's walking over to Jack. If you go now, you might be able to get the drop on him."

I moved quickly just as ice began to fill up the front of the warehouse at an incredible rate. I poured fire against it, but every time I did, the ice just returned. It soon became apparent that it was a waste of time.

"Nathan, are you in there?" Enfield asked from the warehouse entrance. "My job here is done. Jack is dead, we can't have him telling tales, now can we? I'll see you around. You too, Felix, you can't hide forever."

No one moved for several seconds, until the ice began exploding outward, impaling large shards all around the warehouse. One of which—a three-foot ice blade—tore through the wood only inches from my head.

No one spoke, until a few seconds later when Felix risked a glance. "He's off by the dock again."

I crept around the pile of timber and watched as Enfield stepped onto a small boat and eased off along the Thames. When he was out of sight, I risked a glance and then, with an air shield in place, stepped out of the warehouse. No one shot at me.

"What was the point of that then?" I asked Felix and Diana as they joined me outside of the warehouse.

"I'll go check on Fiona and Alan," Diana said and ran off toward the building they were in.

I made my way to Jack and looked down at the body, which was now on its front. A bullet hole sat in the back of his head, to go along with the one in the side of it and the one in his chest.

"That's overkill," I said. "He was already dead."

"Maybe Enfield just wanted to make sure," Felix suggested.

I wrapped air around Jack's remains and moved him slightly, just in case Enfield had left a nasty little surprise in the way of a mine under his body. Jack is moved, Jack gets to hurt anyone nearby. I'd seen it before, and Enfield was certainly devious enough to want to do it, but nothing happened.

Felix walked past me and looked behind several nearby stacks of wood and bricks. "Neither of us would have been able to see him here from inside the warehouse."

"So, what was he doing?"

Felix used his foot to move what looked like some rubbish and then turned, screaming at me to run. My body caught up to my brain an instant before the bomb exploded. The sound was instantly deafening, and I expanded the shield of air to include Felix, but it was too late, he'd thrown himself directly in between the explosion and me.

We were both knocked back, my head striking something hard that made my vision blur. I felt something trickle down my neck.

I wasn't sure if Fiona, Alan, and Diana were there a second or an hour later, but I hadn't moved and my ears hadn't stopped ringing. People shouted at me, and I nodded as my head cleared.

"Stay still," Fiona said as she crouched beside me. "Your stitches have re-opened, and you've cracked your skull something fierce."

"Felix?" I asked.

She shook her head. "I don't know. You're my main concern. Diana and Alan are dealing with Felix."

It didn't take long for Fiona to come to the conclusion that while I shouldn't be running around anytime soon, I wasn't in any immediate danger. My magic was already working hard to heal the silver wound, so adding a gash on my head hadn't helped matters, but I'd be okay, if a little groggy.

Fiona told me that Felix was being taken to the safe house and that Diana would wait with me until someone returned. I thanked her and closed my eyes, only opening them again when the rocking motion of the coach woke me.

"We're back," Diana told me as she opened the coach doors and slapped me on my leg.

I sat up and immediately wished I hadn't, as I fought the nausea that bubbled up. Diana helped me out of the coach and into the house, where I found a semi-conscious Felix lying on the kitchen table. A bowl of bloody water was on the table beside him. His shirt and trousers were missing.

"He okay?" I asked when I saw the mass of wounds dotted over his back and the backs of his legs.

"He'll live," Fiona told me. "It was a lot of silver though."

"Time bomb," Felix managed.

"Can you give us a second?" I asked everyone.

"Keep him calm," Fiona demanded. "Stress could kill him."

I waited for everyone to leave and then crouched beside Felix's head. One of his eyes was bloodshot, and his face was pale and sweaty.

"Thank you," I said.

"Had to make up for what we did. Didn't want to die for nothing in some hovel somewhere."

"You won't die for nothing. I'll make sure you're somewhere safe; somewhere you can do what you like. I hope you live a long, boring, and safe life, Felix."

Felix smiled and then passed out.

I left the kitchen and found everyone in the front room. Alan stood as I entered. "I guess you're taking me to Avalon now."

"Felix is unconscious," I told Fiona. "I need you to stay here until he's ready to be moved. Is that a problem?"

Fiona shook her head.

"Are you okay with that?" I asked Diana.

"I'll clear it with Brutus. Are you leaving?"

"Yes. Alan, you're staying here until Felix is mended. Then you're going to take him somewhere no one else knows about and ensure he's safe. That's your punishment."

"What?" Alan and Fiona asked at once.

"He's a criminal," Fiona explained.

"She's sort of got a point there," Alan surprisingly agreed.

"Don't care. He helped stop these murders, so I'm giving him a chance. Run, Alan, take Felix somewhere safe and then run, because the second I tell people that you're free someone is going to want to rectify that situation."

"You can't just let him go," Fiona snapped.

"I can do anything I damn well choose. Once Felix is well enough to leave, Alan takes him somewhere safe. You want to keep tabs on him, you can go with him. In fact that's not a bad idea. But I'm not taking him back to Avalon. As far as I'm concerned Alan's a lot better at making someone vanish than Avalon is. He's had more practice for a start."

"I'm going to be staying with him then," Fiona stated.

"Excellent," Alan declared. "How should I let you know where Felix is?"

"I don't want to know. No one but you should know. No one, are we clear?" I glanced to Fiona.

"In that case," Alan started. "Fiona. I will take Felix away alone, then in exactly one year, I shall return to this house. You can treat me how you see fit. Just give me one year. Preparations will need to be made for Felix."

Fiona glanced from me to Alan and then back. "I can't believe I'm trusting you, but deal. One year today. An hour later and I hunt you down and drag you back to Avalon myself. By your damned ears if necessary."

"Thank you, Nathan," Alan said. "And you too, Fiona."

"Don't fuck up," I said and left the room, fetching some clean clothes from my room.

Diana, Alan, and Fiona were all standing in front of the door as I made my way back downstairs.

"Be careful," Alan said. "Thanks for the chance."

"Try not to die," Fiona said. "I spent far too long patching you up."

I thanked them both and then turned to Diana.

"He won't be happy to see you," she said. "He will try to twist what he did. Don't let him."

"I don't plan on it."

She hugged me, which hurt more than a hug probably should. "Give him hell," she whispered.

Give Merlin hell, I thought. I hoped it wouldn't come to that. I hoped I could bring him back from his path, just as I'd told Elaine I wanted to. But I didn't believe a word of it. I was soon going to no longer be Merlin's employee. What that meant for me, I had no idea. All I could say for certain was that no matter what happened from the moment I arrived in Camelot, I wasn't going to be able to leave it and live the same life.

CHAPTER 27

Doncaster, England. Now.

Some people would probably be fine with waking up tied to something, unable to move. I'm not one of those people. My instinct is to kill everything within a few feet of me and then try to figure out who the bad guys are. Unfortunately, my current predicament made killing anything but time slightly more complicated. A pair of manacles on my wrists, connected to a large chain that shackled me to the ceiling, held me off the ground by at least a foot. Another pair—these attached to my feet, with a second chain leading to the floor—ensured the only place I was going was in tiny circular motions. I was not a happy person.

A lot of people would yell, they'd shout and scream. This usually ends up with someone getting hurt or dead. The best idea is to stay very quiet and figure out what's happening before you let people know you've woken up. It's almost a guarantee if they've gone to the trouble they had with me, that they're not your friends.

The memories of Kelly Jensen and her merry band of psychopaths popped into my head. The griffin was there too. I really wanted to kill that griffin.

I swallowed my anger and looked around the chamber we were in. It was obviously one of the rooms in Felix's hideaway, the walls told me that, although I certainly didn't remember anyone mentioning any rooms that contained manacles. Ellie was in a predicament similar to mine; blood had dried on her scalp. She'd probably woken up quicker than they'd been expecting and she'd given them some trouble. Her eyes were still closed, but she was breathing regularly.

Next to her was Alan. He appeared to have had the shit kicked out of him. His face was puffy and swollen. He breathed out and it rattled; something inside was broken, hopefully nothing too serious.

On the other side of me was Remy. Remy was wide awake, staring at me. "You took your fucking time," he whispered. He looked a bit worse for wear, but didn't seem to be in any discomfort.

"I'm sorry, was my being unconscious a big inconvenience?" I asked. "We're back in Felix's home, I assume." I just wanted to be sure.

"Your glyphs remained lit up even though you were unconscious. That's quite the trick."

Apparently Erebus was still ensuring that my magic remained active even if I wasn't consciously able to do it. I'd have to thank him for that next time we spoke. Although as my hands were shackled with silver I couldn't use my magic to get free, or attack someone. In fact, all I'd be able to do was use it to blast the ceiling apart, crushing everyone. Which, as far as escape attempts go, isn't the best idea.

Remy was the only one of the four of us not shackled both hands and feet. His hands were manacled to the shackles on the floor. He couldn't go anywhere, but at least he was on the ground. It was a start.

"What happened?" I asked.

"They shot you with a manticore spine. Who the fuck owns a manticore? Why would anyone actually decide they want to keep one of those ugly fuckers?"

"I feel we're getting off topic here," I reminded him. "What. Happened?"

"Right, well you went to sleep and they dragged us all down here, but Ellie here woke up. Tore some guy's arm off before they subdued her. By that point Alan and I had woken up, and they gave us all a kicking. Still, she tore some guy's arm off, which was pretty badass of her. If we find it, and then find him, can we beat him to death with it?"

I stared at my fox friend for a moment. "I'd rather use something more . . . stable for bludgeoning someone to death, but sure, why not? How long have you been down here?"

"Few hours maybe. Not entirely sure."

"Why are you awake and not them?"

"Oh, that's an easy one. They got hit more than I did."

That would do it. "Any idea how we're meant to get out of here in one piece?"

"Well, they've sort of left me alone. They didn't even bother to check if my manacles were the right size. They just figured, 'He's a fox, what the fuck is he going to do? Shed on us?' I tell you, people always underestimate the fox-human hybrids."

"You really need to put that in a newsletter. Send it around to everyone. Or you could get us the fuck out of here."

"I could but . . ." he stopped and sniffed the air. "Shut up." And he immediately pretended to be unconscious again.

"Oh, you're awake, that's pretty good news," a young man said as he entered the room. He was about six feet tall, and well built. His hair was shaved close to his head, leaving just a little stubble, and he wore jeans and a shirt that was splattered with blood.

"You're the SOA agent I grabbed by the scruff of his shirt outside the Williams house. I don't remember your name."

"My name is Richard."

"Can I call you Dick? You look like a Dick."

He punched me in the stomach. I coughed and spluttered.

"It's helpful that your stomach is right at punching level," he said.

"I got dick slapped," I said with a laugh.

He hit me again, and the air was driven from me.

"Please stop, I can't take being beaten up by someone called Dick."

He hit me for a third time.

"You seem to have some issues with people calling you Dick," I pointed out. "When you were younger, did you fall asleep and someone draw one on your face? Did they call you Dick Face? You can tell me, let the pain out."

A fourth punch and I spat blood over the floor.

"You might have noticed that I'm not taking you very seriously," I said. "I should point out that it's because I'm not. You fucking arrogant little twat."

"Maybe you'll take me seriously now."

My magic stopped and the pain of the venom coursing through my body caused me to cry out. It was nowhere near as painful as it had been, clearly my magic was doing its job, but I was still in agony.

"That's right, I'm a void," he told me.

"Did the Reavers put an advert in the paper for your kind?" I asked. Just as quickly as it had vanished, my magic returned.

"You murdered my brother back in an Avalon hospital. Do you remember him?"

"Was his name Dick too? I'm going to take a wild guess that your parents had a pair of dicks."

He punched me again. My stomach and ribs felt as if they were on fire.

"He won't get to live to see the Reavers' plan come to fruition, but then neither will you, if I get my say."

"What plan?" I asked. "So far your plan has been to try and find Felix and kill some people. That's not a plan, I'm pretty certain a plan is meant to have an end game."

"No one told you? We plan on taking over Avalon. How's that sound, tough guy?"

"Avalon?" I laughed and it hurt like hell, but it was totally worth it. "A friend of yours mentioned that before. I don't know what shit you're smoking, but how the hell are you going to do that?"

"We've got power, power you can't believe. We're going to find out exactly what Felix knows and then we're going to march to Camelot. Soon, Avalon Island will be under our control. Kelly has gone to see to it personally."

That was news I really hoped was more bluster than fact. "Why am I still alive then?"

"Because once we take Avalon, we're going to bring you there so you can watch as your friends are killed. All of them—Lucie, Olivia, Elaine, Tommy, every single one of these assholes here in this room. You die last, covered in their blood." He shouted the last sentence, sounding very pleased with himself. He certainly believed everything he was saying; the fanatical often do, even if their belief is so wrong no one else can understand it.

I stared at Dick for a moment. "Did you rehearse that little speech? It sounded rehearsed. The covered in their blood part especially, it's just so cliché. In fact killing me last is a terrible idea. You go to the trouble of keeping me alive just to watch me have my friends die? Is that meant to break me, am I meant to weep openly at the idea? Because if that's the case, you need to know who *I* am."

Dick laughed. "I know who you are. The mighty Hellequin. We've all been briefed on you. I have to say, so far I'm not that impressed."

"That makes me a little sad; I was hoping to impress you. I wanted you to be my groupie. Let me ask you something, how impressed are you at being able to breathe?"

"You're actually threatening me?"

"No, not me," I said dismissively. "But you really should have made sure that everyone was properly restrained. Just because someone is small, doesn't mean they're not dangerous."

"Hey, fucko," Remy said as he stood behind Dick.

Dick stammered and went for the gun on his belt, but he was far too slow. Remy was on him, jaws around his neck as Remy took the larger man to the floor.

Fox jaws aren't as strong as a wolf's, or even a domesticated dog's, but Remy wasn't exactly your normal fox, and like the rest of him, his jaws were much more powerful than they first appeared. A few seconds later and Dick stopped moving.

"I guess you're going to want me to let you down now," Remy said. "If you make a single joke about me playing with Dick, I will bite you."

"Give me credit, I'm a bit more subtle than that," I countered.

"Yeah, magic boy, real subtle." He searched Dick's body and sighed. "The key isn't here."

"So, where is it?" I asked.

"I don't know," he said looking all around him exaggerated fashion. "Allow me to use my amazing key finding ability and I'll get right back to you."

"Sarcasm isn't helping."

Remy shrugged. "Helps me."

"Just please go."

Remy walked off down the tunnel and I waited for him to return, hoping it would be sooner rather than later.

"Found them," he exclaimed and jangled the keys at me. A second later and he'd climbed up me, before proceeding to unlock the manacles around my wrists.

I fell to the floor with an unpleasant crash and a short time later, Remy had unlocked the shackles around my feet too.

We helped unlock and lower both Ellie and Alan to the ground, the former of whom stirred the second her manacles were removed, showing the silver necklace that had been wrapped around her hands.

I removed the chain and threw it aside, trying to ignore the burn marks around her wrists. "You okay?" I asked her.

Ellie nodded, and Alan began to stir beside me.

"They shot us both full of tranquilizer again," Ellie said. "I'm beginning to dislike that stuff."

"How you feeling, Alan?"

"Fucking peachy," he said. "That guy dead?"

"Yep," Remy told him.

"Good. So, what's the plan, fearless leader?"

"We get out of here, find Felix, get him away from these nutcases and then burn the fucking lot of them to the ground." I explained what Dick had said about Avalon Island.

"We'll need that helicopter again," Ellie said. "Felix first though."

"Any idea where he is?" I asked.

"No, he wasn't brought in here with us," Alan said. "We'll have to keep someone alive long enough to question them."

"You two up to this?" I asked Ellie and Alan.

Both replied with a nod.

We followed Remy out of the room and down the dark tunnel until we came to the massive open area with the pool in the middle. There were no guards about and Remy sniffed the air. "At least two guards in that direction," he said, pointing toward where we'd met Felix. He sniffed again. "More down those tunnels over there and there." He pointed to the tunnel where Ellie and Alan found weapons, and a third we hadn't been down.

"They come here, attack us, kidnap Felix, and now they're going to steal from me?" Alan said, his voice steady, but full of anger. "I'm off down there, who wants to join me?"

"Remy, go with Alan. If you can keep them alive, do so, otherwise, just be quick." I turned to Ellie. "You want to come hurt the people who attacked us?"

"Give me a moment."

There was a grunt, and then a tearing-like noise, immediately followed by an exhale of pain and something crunching. "All done," Ellie said, her voice now low and full of danger.

I turned back to her and found a six-and-a-bit-foot dark gray werewolf standing where Ellie once had. Ellie's clothes were torn apart, discarded on the floor.

"Be careful," I told Alan and Remy and then moved off toward our target.

It didn't take long to walk down the tunnel before the sounds of voices filled my ears.

"Have you found anything?" a woman asked.

"No, you?" a man replied, evidently annoyed at their lack of success.

"We need to find something, *he's* expecting something." Fear. Whoever the *he* was, he made them very scared.

I glanced over at Ellie. *He?* I mouthed.

"Maybe Felix didn't write anything down," she suggested. "I mean, maybe what they're doing to him will give them the answers they need."

"This isn't about answers; this is about removing any evidence for future allies of Felix to use. Whatever they discover up there isn't the point. We need to make sure there's nothing here that can link to those in power. Or would you like to go explain to Kelly why we found nothing?"

"But if there's nothing to find, then what's the point? Why not just burn it all?"

"Because they need to know all of the names on whatever list Felix kept of Reavers. It's called covering your ass. Now stop complaining and get on with it."

"I've been getting on with it for hours. There's nothing here we don't already know. We've found lists of Reaver names, but just rank and file. I don't even know how he managed to get all of the information he has."

"He must have had helpers."

"I'm sure we'll hear about that later; right now, we need to get on with this."

More paper was moved about and then the man said, "Richard has been in with those four for a long time. You think he's killed that sorcerer he wanted to give a kicking to?"

"No, he's not stupid. Some people with a lot more clout than us really want to do that themselves."

"Did you hear, he's meant to be Hellequin?"

"I doubt it. Hellequin could breathe fire and tear the souls from the wicked. This guy's a sorcerer who is about as weak as a kitten after being shot with that spine. He probably used the name to make himself feel big."

Ellie and I reached the mouth of the room, where both occupants had their backs to us. I motioned for her to move toward the woman, while I took the man, not out of any sense of chivalry but because the man was closer to me. I crept behind him and snapped up quickly, grabbing him around the neck and dragging him to the ground. I didn't see what Ellie did, but I heard the growl, the gasp, and then silence.

"Move and you die, painfully," I told him, and he went limp.

I released the Reaver and pulled him up, where he saw Ellie, who held his Reaver friend by the throat two feet off the floor.

"One of you will talk," I said. "The one who does first, lives. Where is Felix?"

"Doncaster Minster," the woman said immediately.

I drove a blade of air into the man's heart. I didn't know what he was, but I was pretty certain that it wasn't going to be fun for him. He leaned forward and then pitched to the floor.

"Why are you all so easy to overcome?" I asked. "I thought Reavers were the elite who couldn't be Harbingers; so far none of you have really been too much bother."

"Harbingers? We never went to being Harbingers, we're just people who believe that Avalon should be under new management. We're a group who believed in the Reavers' ideals of power and the destruction of our enemies."

Ellie let the woman drop to the ground. "Who *are* your enemies?" she asked.

"Whoever we're told they are. Traitors, those who would defile Avalon with their lies and false promises. Those who make Avalon weak."

"And I'm on that list?" I asked. "As is Felix?"

"Felix betrayed us, and together you were responsible for the destruction of the Reavers as they were. As they still should be."

"And what did you do for Avalon before you decided to join the Reavers?"

"SOA," she said proudly.

"Same as your friend there?" Ellie asked.

The woman nodded. "You know you'll never be able to stop the Reavers, not truly. Doesn't matter how much you attack us, there will always be those who are unhappy with Avalon, unhappy at the people in power and how they squander it, running a once great organization into the ground. We will not go away quietly."

"We found the others," Remy said as he entered the room. "None of them would talk to us though, so we had to dispose of them. If all Reavers are like this, we shouldn't be too worried, they couldn't conquer an anthill."

"These are just the dregs," I said turning back to the woman. "What's your name?"

"Sophie."

"How old are you, Sophie?"

"Seventy-eight. I'm a sorcerer."

"Not even old enough to have your second element. Whoever is in charge is taking those who are easy to influence and getting them to do the shit jobs, like guard this place and search through paper. They told you that you'd have a place in this new world, didn't they?"

"Power," she said, a twinkle in her eyes.

"Power," I repeated. "You were never going to get power. You were going to be sacrificed as soon as possible. They only left you down here because they assumed you could keep us all locked up without much hassle, but you couldn't even do that. The truly powerful ones have gone to Avalon, haven't they?"

She didn't move, until Ellie grabbed her throat once more. Then she couldn't nod enough. "The griffin is dealing with Felix."

"Should we get rid of her?" Remy asked.

"No, she's going to come with us. She's going to watch her great and powerful Reavers torn asunder."

"Felix will already be dead," Sophie declared. "They took him to the Minster to torture him."

"For what? And why a church?"

Sophie shrugged. "No one was in, so they thought it would make a fitting final resting place for Felix. And he knows things."

"Names, is that it? Felix knows the names of the people who are running the show. But why would they care if you're going to go to Avalon and show the world who you are anyway?"

I could tell from her expression that Sophie had no idea.

"You find any useful weapons in your travels?" I asked Alan and Remy.

They both smiled. "You're going to want to see this."

When we'd first arrived at the cavern and Ellie had told me she'd found enough weapons to start a small war, I assumed she was exaggerating. She wasn't. If anything she undersold it. Weapons adorned every wall: swords, glaives, shields, guns, and even a bazooka in one corner.

I didn't fancy blowing up a large part of the city, so I settled for a nagamaki, a Japanese sword with a two-foot-long blade attached to a handle of about the same length. It was a bit like a katana, but with an extra-long handle, or tsuka.

The tsuka on the nagamaki was wrapped in red and black silk, and as I picked it up, I knew that whoever had made it had done so with utmost care and devotion.

"Never seen one of those before," Ellie said as she stood beside me.

"They were used to fight people on horses," I told her. "I once fought a general who used one."

Ellie placed a finger against the flat of the blade, and quickly withdrew it. "Silver."

I nodded. "I thought as much. Don't need silver to kill a griffin, but it can't hurt." I picked up the sheath and placed the blade inside. "Everyone ready?"

Remy had found his sabre, which he was cleaning in the corner, occasionally mumbling that whoever had touched her last had to be removed from her. Yeah, some people talk to their weapons. Yes, it's weird, but that doesn't mean I don't understand it.

Alan had chosen a pair of M1911 pistols, and was busy loading the magazines. The nickel shone as if new, and I wondered if Alan had stolen all of the things in this cavern.

"I'm done," Ellie said.

"Not taking anything?"

She raised the deadly claws on her hands. "Don't need anything else."

I turned to Sophie. "There's going to be a lot of killing soon. While I'm not above killing people because they're in the way, or because they could cause me problems in the long run, I'd rather leave someone alive for Elaine to talk to. That person is going to be you."

"I'd rather you killed me," she said, a newly ignited fire in her eyes.

"I know, but Elaine will have questions. So your options are to be handcuffed in the room with all the food, or the one with the dead body of your friend, Dick.

"Dick?" she questioned.

"Oh, Richard, I called him Dick."

"Richard is dead? He was in charge of those of us who were placed down here. He was a favorite of Kelly's. You'd best hope to whatever god you believe in that *she* doesn't find you once she discovers what you've done. She'll tear you apart."

"Good to know," I explained. "Now choose."

"The food."

Alan tossed me a sorcerer's band that he picked up from a box beside him, along with a pair of extra-long chain handcuffs. I took Sophie through to the food storage and handcuffed her to some piping that led down from the sink. She had enough room to move about and eat as she needed.

She didn't fight as I applied the sorcerer's band. "Someone will come for you soon. But you have enough food and water here for months, so don't worry."

"You took away my magic."

"I'm not in the habit of leaving captured sorcerers to their own devices when they want nothing more than to see me dead. You'll do without your magic for a while."

"I hope they kill you."

"You'd best not, otherwise you're probably not going to be happy to see them when they realized we let you live."

"You can't destroy an idea," she shouted at me as I walked away.

"Watch me."

CHAPTER 

The four of us left the cavern and made our way back up the ladder to the outside. I'd expected to have to fight, or at least dispose of people placed to watch the exit, but there was no one there. Either the Reavers were so overconfident that they didn't think we'd be a threat once we were in manacles, or they were incompetent. Either way, they were going to pay for it.

It was a good thing it was nighttime, as I imagined that a humanoid fox with a sabre almost the size of himself, a werewolf, and someone carrying a giant sword might have had an adverse reaction. In fact out of the four of us, Alan was the least likely to cause a commotion, which was concerning in and of itself.

We hurried back toward Doncaster Minster, thankfully avoiding anyone on the journey, and quickly scaled the stone wall, using the trees and shadows to stay hidden a few hundred feet from the church.

"You smell anything?" I asked Remy and Ellie.

Both took a big sniff and paused. "Blood," they said together.

"Where from?"

"Inside the Minster," Ellie said.

"I need you three to scout the outside. I'm going in to find Felix."

"I'm coming with you," Alan said. "Not a request, Nate."

"Okay, but getting Felix out is part 'A' of this plan. Killing the bastards who took him can wait."

"Agreed."

Alan didn't wait, and took off toward the Minster at a steady run. I cursed under my breath and caught him up as we reached the building itself.

"There are two entrances," he explained. "One on the opposite side of the building to here, and one around the corner; we need to go through the one closest as it's not used. It should be locked up."

"How do you know this?"

"I've spent a lot of time in the city. I like it here. Everyone is nice, people don't know who I am, and it's easy enough to get away from here quickly if I need to. Besides, I like architecture. And this is a beautiful building, so if we can get Felix back without destroying it, I'd be grateful. I had to pay to get it fixed once; I don't feel like doing it again."

"I promise I won't break the church. For a moment there, I thought you cared more about Felix than money." I turned away.

Alan grabbed my arm. "Apart from Fiona, there are very few people I care about more than money. Felix is one of them. You asked me to keep him safe, and I did. And I grew to like the old bastard. Even helped him with his research."

"How?"

Alan had the appearance of someone who had said something he wished he hadn't. "Later," he said quickly, walking past me and around the corner to the large double doors.

I tried the metal handle; it was locked, just as Alan had said. I could have cut through, or around, the lock with fire magic, but anyone inside who wasn't Felix was certainly going to hear it. Instead I placed my hand against the lock and concentrated, allowing my air magic to flow into the lock.

Using magic to unlock a door is hard work. It basically means I have to use my magic to figure out where all of the notches on the key would be, and then use the exact amount of pressure to turn them all at once. Fortunately, the lock on the door was old and within a minute it was open. It would have been quicker, but Alan wouldn't stop asking me if I was done.

I stood and slowly pushed open the door, which thankfully didn't creak too loudly. Alan and I stepped into the church and I closed the door. Alan held one of the guns in his hand. A sorcerer was difficult to kill, and without a body of water nearby Alan couldn't turn into his water form even to escape, let alone to summon anything.

We moved under an arch and behind some nearby pews. Glancing over the top of them gave us a great view all the way from where we were to the far end of the Minster. Beautiful stained glass adorned every window, with one large piece at the far end of the Minster just behind a sizeable organ, which was opposite an ornate pulpit. A bell tower that sat above the front of the church had scaffolding under it.

"Can you see Felix anywhere?" I asked.

Alan shook his head. "There's a room up behind the pulpit. Unless they've put him under the floor, he'll probably be in there."

"Under the floor?"

"It's how the place was heated. These floorboards come up—" he stopped. "You're not interested in this are you?"

"Not right now," I admitted through gritted teeth.

We crept along the outside of the pews, pausing after each of the four massive marble columns that sat between every few rows, until we reached the door behind the pulpit.

I placed my hand against the door and allowed air magic to flow into the room beyond. The magic would flow back out, giving me a signal whenever it found something alive. I've used it several times in the past, but only in small confined spaces; it's not strong enough to use for an entire church, which is why I didn't use it before I picked the lock outside.

I got one ping. I grabbed the door handle and turned it, pushing the door open to reveal a tied and battered Felix sitting in a chair in front of a desk. His face was a mask of dried blood, and his head hung loosely.

For a moment I feared the worst, and then he groaned and opened his eyes. "Nate?" he said, his voice weak.

His hands had been tied behind him with cable ties, and someone had put a sorcerer's band on him. The ties had bitten into the skin around his wrists, and blood had begun to pool on the floor behind the chair. Other than a lot of bruising and cuts, the only serious thing was a knife wound to his ribs.

"Silver blade," he told me.

"We're going to get you out of here," Alan said as I cut through the bonds and Felix sagged forward onto him.

"They're going to come back. You need to go."

"Not leaving without you," Alan assured him.

We each put one of his arms over our shoulders and we walked Felix to the door.

"Stop," he said. "I need to tell you something first."

"We'll discuss it when we're free," I told him.

"No," Felix snapped, with as much force as he could manage. "Now."

Alan and I shared a glance and then lowered Felix into the chair near the door.

"Okay, you don't have long," Alan said.

"I'm dying, lads," Felix said softly. "The knife would have been okay if I didn't have this thing on me." He raised his arm to show us the sorcerer's band. "But the blade was coated with that damn spider venom. I can feel it tearing me up inside. In a few hours I'll be gone."

"We'll get that fucking band off, and you'll be fine," I assured him, glancing down at my own illuminated glyphs.

"You know I won't be," he said. "I've been in here for several hours already with this wound."

"We should have gotten here sooner," Alan said.

"And then you'd be dead too," Felix snapped. "Damn it, Alan, I've taught you better than to do self-blaming nonsense."

"What do you want to tell us?" I asked.

"We don't have time for this," Alan said.

"I made contact with . . . mostly criminals," he winced in pain and took a few seconds to control his breathing. "They infiltrated the Reavers, feeding me details about what they were doing. They tricked a high-ranking member of my location. I took control of his mind and used him as a way to ferret out more members."

"How did you manage that?" I asked.

"Ah, I broke his mind and made him believe that one of my allies was his trusted lieutenant and that all information should be shared with him. Took me a long time, and took a lot out of me, but he was invaluable in getting me information on the higher ranks, people like Kelly Jensen."

What he'd just described went against Avalon's laws. He'd destroyed a mind, and if anyone discovered that, he'd be executed for it. Fortunately for him, I had no intention of telling anyone.

"Okay, the rest can wait," Alan said.

"Just listen," Felix said, his tone hard. "This is important, if I don't make it, you need to know. Liz Williams was one such ally. As was her husband, and a man she helped before he was murdered. Fiona was another. Alan here another. They all searched into Reaver activity and got information back to me.

"But someone began removing them from circulation, one at a time. They've killed the Reaver I'd taken control of, along with anyone who worked for him. After that they started going after my allies. They had prepared to attack Avalon, but the discovery that one of them was feeding me information made them wait. They needed to check that I hadn't taken anyone else. It's why I only took low-level members after that."

"How'd they discover that you'd done this?" I asked.

"I've been wondering that myself. Not until now. Not until they tried to kill you too, Nathan."

"Did someone betray you?"

"No. I was stupid. They discovered that the Reaver I was using was betraying them, and they used someone with mind magic to tear the information free from his head. It led them to my involvement, and the start of this whole thing. I set this off, Nate. I'm so sorry." His words appeared to have taken even more out of him and he slumped forward.

"I know of a rune that might bypass the sorcerer's band, it could allow you to use your magic to keep yourself alive."

"Then do it," Alan snapped. "And let's fucking leave."

"Or it could backfire and kill him in an even worse manner than the venom."

"No," Felix declared. He sounded exhausted and in pain, but even so, he put a lot of force behind that one word. "You're talking about a dwarven rune. How do you know it?"

"Long story."

"I'm too weak. Let's just get to my home, I don't want to die out here."

"You're not dying anywhere," Alan told him. "You're too damn stubborn."

Alan and I helped Felix stand and opened the door only to find a group of people waiting for us, standing around the pews. There were ten in all, including Mortimer, the man who'd killed the Williamses. The griffin who'd infected me with the jorōgumo venom was sitting on the edge of one of the pews, his massive wings folded behind him. I felt a sudden urge to cut the bastard in half.

"I see you found the old fucker," the griffin said with a laugh. He slammed the butt of his spear into the wooden floor, which cracked from the impact. "I was surprised you all got free from the group we'd left down below for you. You were meant to wait for people to come and kill you."

"I'm not very patient," I said. "I figured I'd find those responsible rather than wait for them to come to me."

"Are you going to give us the option to surrender or die?" the griffin asked with a chuckle.

I shook my head. "Nope. You're just all going to die. Painfully for the most part."

I couldn't risk a fight. There was no telling what would happen with Felix so close. It would have been too easy for him to get hurt.

The griffin snapped his fingers, the double doors opened, and Sophie walked inside, followed by two large men. She had the smile of someone who'd suddenly decided they were in control of a situation.

"My dearest Sophie," the griffin said. "I'm glad you weren't killed."

"Oh for fuck's sake. How'd she get free?" I whispered to Alan.

Alan shrugged. "I may have forgotten to put the runes back when we left the cavern."

"Not a great time to be forgetful," I seethed.

"Because one more bad guy is going to make all the difference."

"What if they've destroyed Felix's notes?"

"We have Felix. I'm sure he can tell us."

"Are you two done?" the griffin asked. "I'm not interrupting am I?"

"I just realized, I don't know your name," I said to him.

"Corath," he said with pride. "I'm happy you'll know the name of your killer. Could you please call your werewolf and fox friend in?"

"I don't see why I should," I said.

"Because if you don't, those two men who came here with Sophie will go out into the city. You don't want to know what their idea of a good time is."

"It's okay, Nate," Remy said as he stepped through the open door with Ellie behind him. "We've been listening in."

"Excellent. Everyone is here," Corath said. "It's so much better than random bloodshed. We're not monsters, after all. We want what's best for Avalon, and therefore best for all of us."

"You want what's best for you," Remy countered as he walked over to stand beside me. Even though he had to walk past the Reavers, no one tried to stop him; clearly they were very confident in their position and didn't see him as a threat. More fool them. "Avalon doesn't factor into it."

"Believe what you like, rodent."

"Rodent?" Remy snapped. "Fuck you, Tweety."

Corath's wings flickered briefly, as he snarled.

"So, now that we're all here," Ellie interrupted, "what are you going to do? This is a pretty small enclosure. Killing us in here will result in a long fight first."

"We're all going to go down to the cavern again. And then you're all going to die."

"I thought I had to be kept alive," I pointed out.

"You're too much trouble alive. You can die now, I'm sure I'll be forgiven when I give your head to those in charge. Speaking of which, I have a gift for you." He snapped his fingers at one of the two men who'd come in with Sophie, and he darted from the building.

His glee at those words turned my stomach. I knew something bad was about to happen.

The man returned a few moments later with two men and a woman in tow. The woman and one of the men were in their late forties, while the second man was considerably older. They all appeared scared and confused.

"This is the Father who works here," Corath explained, "along with his wife and an unfortunate member of his congregation.

Sophie, please escort the human filth into the room behind Nathan and his companions."

Sophie did as she was told, gaining a growl from Ellie that made her jump as she walked past us.

The man who'd brought them in handed Corath a leather sack. "One last thing. Nathan, are you aware that we tracked you? That Kelly used your blood to discover where you were?"

I nodded. "She said something about it just before you hit me with your spear."

Corath's forehead wrinkled in a look of amusement. "We were told to kill you at first, Nathan, something public. But then as it became apparent that we were unsure if you or Alan was the key to finding Felix, it was decided to follow you. Turned out we didn't need Alan either, Fiona's mind was cracked. And now you all get to die.

"But before all of that, I decided to go pay a visit to a friend of yours. I wanted to make sure that you understood how angry you'd made me." He threw the bag up, and I immediately knew whose head had left its confines, before it struck the floor a foot away from me and rolled to a stop.

Lir's blank expression stared up at me.

"He was a very stubborn man for a drugged-up drunk. I was surprised he put up much of a fight at all, but eventually he was overcome. Refused to tell us anything, although by the time we'd been working on him for a few hours, it was evident that he knew nothing of note. Still, some people are so worthless that they deserve to die. I thought you'd like to see him again before you died. You were friends, yes?"

I ignored him and took a step back, closer to my comrades. There were too many enemies, too many ways in which people could get hurt. The humans, Felix, all of them needed to be away from here. I couldn't ensure their safety.

"You can't hide in the shadows," Corath said.

"Alan, I want you to take Felix into the room behind us," I whispered, using my air magic to carry my words to them. "Remy and Ellie, go with them. Keep the humans safe, get them away from here. Kill anyone who tries to stop you."

"You can't seriously think you can take on a dozen people alone," Alan said.

He was right; I had exactly zero chance of surviving such an encounter. "Let me worry about that. Get those people to safety, and then get back here to help. I'm going to keep the Reavers busy."

"By dying?" Ellie asked. "It's a suicide run, Nate. You're tired, and beaten. You need time to heal, you can't do this."

I shook my head. "I'll be fine. Just please . . . when I tell you to go, go. Don't argue."

Remy placed his paw in my hand and squeezed slightly. "Give them hell."

"I'm not going to be able to keep my promise, Alan," I said, and without waiting for a reply, I told them all to run. The four of them moved as quickly as possible into the room behind me. There was a scream, a thud, and then silence. I guessed Sophie was no longer an issue.

"Have you lost your mind?" Corath asked me. "Your only allies have run away. We'll just kill you and then kill everyone in there too. If they've escaped that makes the hunt much more fun. Either way they'll be dead."

I remained silent, standing in the shadows that concealed my face, and tried something I'd never attempted before. I internally contacted my nightmare. *Erebus, can you hear me?*

"*Yes, Nathan.*" The voice inside my head said. "*Your use of magic has placed me closer to the surface of your consciousness than would normally be possible. I told you, if you kept using magic, that either I would need to come out, or you would pass out from exhaustion. In your current condition, this would probably result in your death.*"

There was a pause between us, while Corath continued talking, although I wasn't paying much attention to his words.

"*You're still concerned that I will try to take control of your body. You know I cannot do that. Those blood curse marks stop it from happening. I am not the monster you believe. I've helped you before. I've kept you alive. That is my only desire; to keep you alive.*"

Then I willingly free you to do what I cannot.

"*This will render you unconscious afterwards, maybe for several hours. I can keep your body alive with magic, but it will be weak. You may not feel all that well upon waking.*"

It was a risk I had to take. We had to get to Avalon, had to warn Elaine about what was happening. I couldn't risk dying; I couldn't risk my friends dying. I had to do what needed to be done to ensure we all survived. *Do it.*

"*It will be my pleasure.*"

If I'd been able to see Erebus I was certain he'd have been smiling, and a shiver went through me.

CHAPTER 

Having a nightmare take control of your body is an odd experience. I still maintained a conscious awareness of what was happening, but it was as if I were looking through eyes that were no longer my own.

"I'm sorry, did you say something?" Erebus asked.

The last time the nightmare had taken control of my body was over a century earlier. His voice had sounded almost alien back then, but now just sounded like a lower version of my own. It was still uncomfortable to listen to though.

"I said, it's time to give up," Corath said, glancing to the men who were moving slowly toward me.

"I'd tell them to stop, if I were you," Erebus said.

"You don't sound like Nathan," Corath said, and motioned for the men to stop.

"Nathan can't be here right now. He would very much like to be, but he's trusted me to finish the job. He's quite angry that you killed Lir. He liked him. You should be grateful that you'll be dead before Mac gets hold of you. I don't think you'd enjoy that meeting very much."

"And who are you?" Corath asked.

Erebus stepped forward, showing the darkness that now covered my face.

"A nightmare," one of the men gasped, immediately stepping back, fear on his face.

"My name is Erebus," he said. "You should not have killed Lir. You should not have attacked Felix. You should not be here."

Corath pointed to the Reavers close to the Minster doors. "You four go after the others," Corath told them before leveling the tip of his spear at Erebus. "The rest of you. Kill him."

Only the four Reavers moved as they ran from the building.

"If it helps facilitate matters, I'm not a full . . . *nightmare*," Erebus said, almost sighing the final word. "I probably will be easier to kill than someone who had complete control over their host."

Violence sounded from outside of the church. But inside, no one moved.

"Cowards," Erebus sighed and flung a whip of flame at the nearest man; it wrapped around his head as the victim struggled, burning himself every time he tried to grab hold of the fiery whip. Erebus yanked the man forward with all of his strength, pulling the Reaver from his feet and straight into a flaming blade that cut his head from his shoulders in one movement.

The next few seconds were a whirlwind of brutal efficiency. Nightmares showed sorcerers just what they could do, the very best they could be. It was why nightmares were so seductive; the power they held up for you to see was an addictive substance. Combine that with an ability to heal that even a werewolf would be impressed with, and immense strength, and you have a being that is lethally dangerous.

Erebus caught one Reaver—one of the men who'd arrived with Sophie—in the chest with a blade of air, which quickly changed to engulf and crush the man. His broken body dropped to the floor alongside the corpse of his brethren.

Erebus turned and blasted a third Reaver through the double doors, destroying them, along with a large portion of the pews that sat in front of them. Three Reavers down in less than two minutes, and Corath hadn't even moved.

"It's true, these new Reavers are nothing more than useless muscle," Erebus said. "These are not people who took the Harbinger trials. These are not warriors. They're thugs." He pointed at Corath. "And you are their leader."

"Kill him," Corath screamed.

Earth exploded from beneath Erebus's feet, throwing him back toward the pulpit, but he used air magic to land upright.

"You have an earth elemental," Erebus said, almost absentmindedly.

The earth elemental tore chunks free from the Minster wall and threw them at Erebus as if it were nothing. He dodged them, but was forced into the reach of a werewolf, who hit Erebus in the side of the head before grabbing him and throwing him across the room, where he slammed into the wall.

Pain rocketed through his mind, although Erebus gave no outward sign of feeling anything as he crashed back to the floor. Before he could move, a fourth man sprinted toward him, enveloping him in massive arms, and running through the stone wall without even stopping.

The man was a siphon, and from the agony that raged through Erebus's mind, it was draining his power at an alarming rate.

The siphon stopped running and released his grip on Erebus, who took a step back, removing the blade of lightning from the siphon's chest. The siphon crashed to his knees and with one sweep of the nagamaki, Erebus severed his head from his shoulders.

The remaining Reavers piled out of the church into the cool nighttime air of Doncaster. It was fortunate that the field they stood on was both badly lit and far enough away from any populated areas that no one noticed, otherwise having the police turn up could have turned a difficult fight into an impossible one.

Erebus didn't pause; he sprinted right at the Reavers, throwing balls of flame at them to force them apart. The earth elemental created a shield of rock, but a sphere of air magic in Erebus's hand destroyed it and a moment later the earth elemental was dead as a second sphere, this one of lightning, tore into his chest. The release of magic threw him back into the church as the magic ripped him apart. Erebus didn't wait to see if it worked, he already knew it would. These people weren't soldiers, hardened by years of battle; they were idiots who believed that their power meant they were better than others.

A werewolf charged toward Erebus. It barreled into him, tackling him to the ground and tearing into his chest with razor sharp claws. Erebus reached up and grabbed the werewolf under the neck, letting loose with a blast of fire magic that tore out the throat of the werewolf. He pushed the screaming wolf off him and paused, breathing heavily, as his wounds healed. He looked around to find dead Reavers all around the church; Remy, Alan, or Ellie had killed some as they'd taken Felix and the humans to safety. Mortimer and Corath were all that remained. Mortimer drew two blades and walked toward Erebus, while Corath hovered just behind.

Erebus feinted attacking Mortimer—who dodged aside—and then threw the nagamaki at Corath. The blade pierced one of the griffin's wings, tearing part of it, and he crashed back to the ground with a blood-curdling scream. Erebus's attention was still on the writhing griffin when Mortimer darted forward and slashed one of his blades up toward Erebus's face. The nightmare moved quickly, avoiding being blinded, but Mortimer's second blade whipped around quicker, catching Erebus across the chest.

Mortimer stepped back and smiled. "You got the upper hand last time, but jumping out of that window had taken a lot out of me. I won't make that mistake again."

He dashed toward Erebus, his knives a blur of motion. One cut across Erebus's arm, and a blast of magic sent Mortimer spinning away from him. More pain went through Erebus's head; the knives were silver.

Erebus threw a plume of flame at Mortimer, who didn't move until the last second and then darkness appeared in front of him and the flame just vanished. For a second Mortimer looked weaker, but his wicked smile soon returned.

"Fae," Erebus rumbled.

Mortimer tore his shirt off, casting it aside. "I was a Harbinger," he said. "I was one of the elite warriors of Avalon. Until I was on a mission and someone tore my wings off."

He moved back and to the side, so that Erebus could see the horrific wounds on his back. Parts of the wings remained, but they were far too small to allow him to fly.

"Do you know what happened when I returned to Avalon?" Mortimer screamed. "Those in charge cast me out of the Harbingers. They said I was 'too damaged,' that I was no longer able to function at such a high level. And then Kelly came to me, told me I could help Avalon still, that I could join the Reavers.

And I jumped at the chance. I'm going to take this all the way to Elaine, and then I'm going to skewer her and ask her how well I'm *functioning*."

Erebus remained passive.

"And you," Mortimer continued. "You were given everything by Avalon, and you threw it away. You are everything I should have been. Given every opportunity to change things in Avalon, given every advantage, and you squandered it all because your ethics got in the way."

"You can't use your full fae abilities without your wings," Erebus said. "That's a shame."

Mortimer's anger appeared to bubble over and he charged Erebus, who threw a ball of flame at him, which after a foot just hovered in the air between them. Mortimer dodged to one side, trying to come around the ball just as it exploded, throwing out flame for several feet on either side. I'd never even considered using my fire magic in such a way; the possibility of being able to wield the power that Erebus used was intoxicating. I had to remind myself that Erebus would take control of my body if given the chance.

Mortimer threw himself under the explosion, putting him directly in line with Erebus, who kicked out at his ribs, lifting him from the ground and dumping him several feet back. Mortimer was quickly on his feet, his knives slashing out at Erebus, who dodged and weaved, using air magic to push Mortimer's arms aside. But even so, Mortimer managed to get in a few good cuts with his silver knives, leaving Erebus bleeding from the arms and chest.

Another ball of fire thrown by Erebus was swallowed by more darkness. Erebus struck out with a blade of lightning, but Mortimer dodged it, swiping under the blade, and cutting through Erebus's side. No matter what Erebus did, Mortimer was too fast to catch, and any magic that got close was absorbed by the darkness that Mortimer could control. I could sense Erebus's frustration at the matter, as he sought a way to stop Mortimer, while Corath was still unable to fly.

At the thought of Corath's name, Erebus glanced over at the griffin. He was on his knees, trying to stop the massive amount of blood that was pouring from his ruined wing. He wasn't going anywhere anytime soon.

The memory of fighting Mortimer outside of the Williamses' home flashed to the front of my mind. He'd been considerably weaker then, unable to use his fae powers, nor fast enough to stop mine.

"That does not help me, Nathan," Erebus said aloud, and then smiled slightly. He moved back toward the ruined church wall, and sent out six tendrils of air, each one invisible to Mortimer as they snaked along the wall. When they were in the correct place, Erebus sent out another plume of flame, which Mortimer easily avoided on his way to another attack.

Erebus snapped the tendrils tight, hardening the air as they wrapped around large chunks of stone that were hurled toward Mortimer at high speed. He dodged the first three skull-sized stones, but the fourth hit him on his knee, dropping him to the ground, where another slammed into the side of his skull.

Erebus glanced up as Remy sprinted across the open ground to where Corath was getting back to his feet. The griffin never saw the smaller man until Remy was too close for him to do anything. Remy's sabre struck the griffin and they went down fighting.

"Your skull is probably fractured," Erebus told Mortimer. "You certainly won't be moving quickly for a while. But just to make sure." Erebus used air magic to lift another of the stones and bring it down on Mortimer's knee with a loud crack.

Mortimer screamed in pain, as Erebus did the same with the other knee.

"I only do this to ensure that Nathan is safe. Your continued movements do not permit that."

Erebus looked over at the fight between Remy and Corath to discover that Ellie was also helping. Corath was missing a wing and was on his knees as Remy stabbed his sabre into his head.

"I guess I'm done here," Erebus told Mortimer. "Please do tell Nathan's friends that you're to be kept alive. I believe he'd like to talk to you." Erebus brought the stone down on Mortimer's head once more, knocking him out, before he sat down on the wet grass and allowed me control once again. I was conscious for a moment and then passed out.

CHAPTER 30

I woke up in bed in the cavern where we'd met Felix. Ellie was on a chair next to me, dozing quietly, her feet propped on the end of the bed.

"Morning," I said with a smile.

Ellie lazily opened her eyes and gave me a brief smile before looking at her watch. "Two hours," she said. "I was expecting you to be out for longer."

"Did I miss anything?"

"Felix is in his room, Alan hasn't left him. Mortimer is in our old torture room, enjoying the delights of having Remy never shut up."

"Corath is dead, I assume?"

"The griffin? Yep, very dead. I ended up using your sword to take its head off. The rest of the Reavers are in the same state, although most of those kept their heads. We managed to get hold of Hendricks on Avalon Island and arranged for a helicopter landing. Alan told him about Kelly and her group who are on their way. Alan said he knows Hendricks and vouched for him."

"What did Hendricks say?"

"Kelly's group isn't there yet, but he'll be on the lookout. He's not sure who is and who isn't a Reaver. Apparently Olivia and her people found the rest of the people on the list that Reaver gave you. All dead. They found Fiona's supervisor too. Looks like he's been dead for a while. Lucie thinks the Reavers killed him before attacking Fiona. Hendricks is going to stop people going through the realm gate, he feels that there's a sudden need for the realm gate to undergo maintenance. It won't be operational for a few hours yet. Probably start working the second we arrive. It means Hendricks won't be able to get through to Avalon though; he can't risk activating the gate and then having Kelly and her people see it working. Getting to Lucie and Elaine is going to be up to us when we arrive."

"Mac is going to want to know about his father. They killed Lir to get to me. I don't think the fact that we've killed Lir's killers is going to be much solace to Mac. How long before the helicopter can be ready?"

"It should be an hour at the most; we've arranged for it to land on the field opposite this place up above."

I swung my legs out of the bed and grabbed a clean T-shirt from the floor. I didn't know where it had come from, and I didn't really care, I was just glad to be wearing something not covered in dirt or blood.

"Felix or Mortimer first?" I asked.

"Felix. I don't know how long he has left."

I made my way through the cavern and found Felix lying on a bed with Alan beside him. "How's he doing?" I asked.

Alan didn't look away from Felix when he spoke, "Not good, Nate." His voice contained none of its normal light tone.

"How about you?"

"Not even a little bit okay."

I placed my hand on his shoulder. "I'm sorry, Alan, I really am."

"He taught me that there was a better way than how I'd been living. He was the one person who'd gotten through to me. Without him, I would still be running around trying to avoid being killed. He taught me how to be a better person. And that person managed to bag himself a wife like Fiona. Now she's in a hospital bed in Avalon, and I'm here with Felix. He's going to die. And I've wanted to stay busy since I found out about Fiona, but I'm so terrified that I'll get back to Avalon and she'll be dead too. I don't want to think of her in a hospital bed, dying."

There was nothing I could say to make him feel better. No words would have offered comfort, but I had to try anyway, "Fiona will be okay."

"You don't know that, Nate. But let's say she is, let's say I get to Avalon and Fiona's okay. That she's healed. I wasn't there to help her. I wasn't there to stop her being attacked. I agreed to go to jail in return for a full pardon of past crimes. And when this is over, I'll be going back."

"No, you won't," I told him.

He turned to me, surprise on his face.

"We'll arrange for you to go free. I'll call in some favors. You're helping Avalon, it's the least they can do."

"And if that doesn't work?"

"I hadn't considered it."

Alan laughed. "And people say I'm cocky."

"I'll come back in a bit, when Felix has woken up."

"He's going to die soon," Alan said, his demeanor flicking back to somber.

"I know," I agreed, and wished I could be wrong.

"We can't get that damn sorcerers band off. If we could, he'd have a chance, but the venom . . . the venom is too much. I'm surprised he's not in agony."

"He's strong, and he's a fighter. The venom will soon begin to destroy him at a faster rate."

Alan was silent for a moment. "Use the rune."

"It might not work. It will almost certainly drain him of whatever energy remains."

"At least he will die with his magic in use."

"If this triggers the band, we're about to learn how magical napalm feels."

I created a shield of air between Felix and us, and Alan passed me a pen, which I used to draw the rune on Felix's arm. The effect of the completed rune was immediate; Felix's eyes shot open as blue glyphs shone across his arms. Water exploded from his palm, drenching the floor and wall opposite the bed. The glyphs quickly dimmed, and the magic stopped as Felix sat up.

"What the hell have you done?" he asked me, when he caught a look at his arm. He created a ball of water in his palm and was slowly rotating it. "I have to keep using this magic now, just long enough to keep the venom at bay. Is that how it works?"

I nodded.

"I had him put the rune on," Alan said. "It's better than dying in agony."

"I'm still going to die in agony, you fool," Felix chastised. "I can almost feel the rune feeding on my energy. Do you use this often?"

"No, only when necessary."

"You're more powerful than I'd imagined, Nate." He closed his eyes and breathed slowly for a few seconds. "Nate, can you leave me and Alan alone to talk?"

I nodded. "I'll come back in a little while."

"Thank you," Felix said.

I left him and Alan alone, setting set off toward Remy and Mortimer, an easy thing to do considering I could hear Remy talking about the time he first watched a television.

I entered the chamber and found Mortimer manacled to the floor. Whoever had put the manacles on had used the same ones that had held Remy. He was covered in bruises and cuts, but otherwise appeared to be okay.

"Ummm . . . Remy, why are you telling him about your TV watching?" I asked as he sat a few feet away from our prisoner.

"I was told not to hurt him physically. Figured I'd try boring him. I've so far discussed broccoli, the use of corpses in siege weapons, how to shoe a horse, and now my first experience with television."

"Make him stop," Mortimer pleaded. "He just won't stop."

"I'm quite parched," Remy admitted. "I guess I should go get a drink." He stood and stretched. "I assume we'll be going soon."

"Soon," I told him. "Dealing with Mortimer and Felix first. Be ready to go in about forty-five minutes."

"I'll keep myself busy 'til then."

When Mortimer and I were alone, I sat beside him. "You know I'm going to kill you in here?"

"I figured as much. You're mad about the Williamses."

"About a lot of things. That's just one of them. You shouldn't have killed them."

"They betrayed the Reavers. They were always going to die. Liz's refusal to give you up just sped up the timeline a little."

"Oh, I understand why you killed them. But you shouldn't have. Shouldn't have involved me either. The second you came after me, I was going to destroy you."

"It was a risk that Kelly decided to take. In hindsight, maybe we should have sent more experienced people after you. Kelly wasn't exactly swimming with first-class killers."

"Cannon fodder."

"That's pretty much it, yes. Only a handful of us ever went through the Harbinger trials. The griffin hadn't either. He just really didn't like you."

"Why?"

"He hated Hades, and his control over Tartarus. He was never going to get to Hades or his kin, so you were the next best thing."

"Who is in charge?"

"I don't know." He quickly raised his hands. "No need to torture me, I can't tell you what I don't know."

"I know you all work in small sects, I want information about them."

"There are a few dozen of them. Most consisting of a few actual Reavers bulked up with raw recruits. Each only knows the hierarchy for their sect. Only Kelly knows who she answers to. The rest of us answer to her."

"And you don't know who Kelly answers to?"

"Someone big," he told me. "Someone very high up the food chain. But she's not going to say more. And I certainly don't know."

"Why are you being so cooperative?"

"Why not? You caught me. I either talk or I get tortured and then talk. Besides, even if you bring down Kelly, there's still plenty more Reavers out there. Plenty more killing our enemies, while we wait for the chance to take back Avalon."

"Killing Elaine is the main aim then."

"Elaine, and those who support her."

"Merlin?"

"Merlin doesn't support Elaine; Merlin can barely stand to be in the same city with her."

"Is he involved in this?"

"I don't know, I don't answer to Merlin."

"So, that's it? That's all you know."

"I'm a soldier. And apparently not a very good one, since you captured me. What more do you actually want to know? Because I've now told you everything. Anything else I say will just be a rehash of what has already been said. Kelly is in charge, she's going to kill you. If she doesn't, there are plenty of people still out there who will. How's that for a summary?"

"You didn't need to kill Lir." I stood and stretched.

"*I* didn't, the griffin did."

"You didn't try to stop him though."

"No, I wasn't going to fight a griffin over some drunken stoner."

"Anything else?"

"For months we tried to break Alan. We had that guard threaten him, his wife, people he loved. Then his wife began investigating, and she wouldn't stop. We had to punish her, but it was difficult to do. She's very powerful and has powerful allies; it had to be done just right. We also needed to send Alan a message to tell us what we wanted to know. Unfortunately that sort of backfired."

"Do you know who attacked Fiona?"

"Nope. My guess is someone important. They wouldn't have sent low-powered people after her. She'd have turned them to pulp. Now are you going to kill me or not? Because I have nothing more to say."

I sighed and plunged a blade of lightning into Mortimer's head. He died silently and quickly, and with less suffering than he probably deserved.

"So, none of them knew anything," Remy said.

"How long have you been there?"

"Long enough, I'm pretty good at staying hidden. Even if we destroy this group, there are others out there."

"One thing at a time. First I'm going to see Felix. Then we'll go back to Avalon and deal with Kelly and any remaining Reavers."

"I want the ones who attacked Fiona. That's all I ask. I want to make sure the rest of these bastards know who they're dealing with. I want to make sure no more of these Reavers think to come after any of us."

Felix was sitting up in his bed when I returned. Alan was nowhere to be seen, and I wondered what had happened between the two of them.

"You came back. Good," Felix said, his voice raw. He looked even worse than when I'd last seen him. "Your little rune is killing me. I might have been able to keep it going if I hadn't already been injured, but in the state you found me, I've no chance. I'm not complaining, I'd rather die this way than crippled with pain while I vomit up my own lungs."

I wished there could have been another way. "I'm sorry about the Reavers. They managed to get hold of you twice. I shouldn't have let that happen."

"Oh shut up, you sound like Alan. You weren't around the first time, and you were unconscious the second. I have some things to tell you, so no interruptions. Firstly, you need to see Merlin." He held up his hands. "Don't complain, you need his help. There are a large enough number of Reavers out there that if something isn't done about them they'll become a serious threat. Avalon will need to deal with them. Elaine will need backing to do this. Merlin is the only person who can ensure that she has enough backing. Without him, it'll always be Elaine trying to push through an act that arrests Avalon people. With Merlin, it's an act of defense. You need him on your side, Nathan."

"Why me though? Why do I have to be the one who talks to him?"

"Because if you go, it won't be seen as pressuring. You go to him, you apologize for whatever happened between you, and you get his help. And yes, I said apologize. I know he did wrong, but this is the bigger picture."

I seethed internally, but accepted his point. "I can't guarantee he'll even see me."

"Oh he'll see you. Any time someone comes to apologize, he'll always see them. He's far too eager to be told how he was right all along.

"Now, this next thing is important. While that griffin and his friends were taking turns giving me a kicking, he let slip something. I know who's in charge of this sect, and at least another two. Enfield."

I sat down on the nearest chair I could find. "Enfield? Well that can't possibly be good."

Guilt settled inside of me. I should have gone after Enfield. I should have stopped him there and then. But I didn't, I was so busy dealing with my own shit that I cast him aside, and now innocent people were dead. That was at least partially on me. "Looks like he's finally surfaced. It's been long enough that I thought, sorry, hoped, that the bastard might have died. But this time, once we get the answers we need, I'm going to make sure he can't hurt anyone else ever again."

I took a deep breath and a thought hit me. "Wait. Mortimer said that Kelly was getting her orders from someone high up. That's Enfield. So we find Enfield and we can hopefully find the people who are responsible for all of this. Any ideas where he is?"

Felix shook his head and winced. "Damn it," he snapped and then took a deep breath. "No."

"We'll find him."

"I know you will. I now need to ask you a favor."

"Anything. Well, anything so long as I can keep my clothes on."

Felix laughed, which turned into a cough. "Damn it, boy, don't do that." Felix reached for a glass of water and took a long drink. "Keep Alan safe."

"I think Alan knows how to stay safe."

"Alan knew how to run. He ran from everything, even you. When I first met him in London, all those years ago, it was the first time he'd actually chosen to stick around and help, not because he was paid, or because he had no choice. He's a different man to the one back then."

"I know," I agreed. "He's done a lot to change his life. Due in no small part to you and Fiona."

"And now I'm going to be dead, and Fiona is hurt. I don't want Alan to run away from anything. I don't want him to revert back to type. Be there for him. He likes you, he always has. I think he respects you more than he wants to let on. These last few decades—before he went to The Hole—were special to me. It was like I had a son. I want him to do great things, I know he can. He just needs to believe in himself, and have people who believe in him. Some people in Avalon would be a little too quick to write him off again if he ever stepped out of line."

"What am I meant to do with him?"

"Give him a purpose."

"A job? You want me to employ Alan? To do what, exactly?"

"Not you personally, but you could arrange something. We both know you have contacts in and outside of Avalon. Please do it."

"I will," I promised. I meant it too. Alan had come a long way, and it would be a shame to see him revert back to the thieving little bastard who'd caused trouble wherever he went, leaving others to clean up his mess.

Felix looked visibly relieved. "When I took you through the Harbinger trials, I was amazed at your tenacity. At the time you didn't seem to have the most power, you weren't the smartest, or the fastest, or the strongest, but you did whatever it took to get things done. And now you have a level of power to go alongside it. I heard over the years that you managed to learn necromancy. That true?"

I nodded.

"And you let your nightmare out. Don't deny it, I saw what you did."

"Didn't have a choice."

"You're playing a dangerous game, Nathan. You can't trust them, they'll tell you such sweet things, and promise you they're only doing what's best. But that magic wants control of you, make no mistake about it. If you let it, it will consume you. Becoming a nightmare is a pretty good way to get yourself killed."

I didn't see a need to bring up the curse marks, or how my nightmare had taken a different name. "I know what I'm doing."

"Every sorcerer says that. But as it's you, I'll take your word for it." Felix smiled. "Have you ever considered teaching others to do what you do? Not just the fighting, or being badass, I mean training someone to be another Hellequin."

"The world doesn't need another Hellequin. And I'm not mad keen on the idea of training someone up to kill people. I do enough of that already."

"How about defend themselves, their loved ones? You could do that, you could teach people how to be better at who they are. I think you'd be good at it."

"I think I would create a monster."

"No you wouldn't, you're just scared that you'd be unable to separate the defense from the killing. Killing is the end result, but your training goes further than that. Besides, who in our world isn't a killer?"

"That's not a reason to personally add to the total."

"Maybe not. But instead of being all high and mighty, ask yourself this: if you could teach someone you care about what you do, what you're capable of, and it saved their life, and the lives of people they loved, would it be worth it?"

I opened my mouth to speak, but found no words wanted to come out.

"Can you fetch Alan for me?" Felix said before I was able to sort through the words in my head. "I want to talk to you both."

I went off to find Alan, and discovered him sitting by the pool of water. He was flicking the cool contents across the pool.

"Felix wants you," I told him.

He stopped what he was doing. "Yeah, I guess he's going to die now." Alan went back to flicking the water.

"What is wrong with you?"

"I'm angry, angry that out of everyone he has to die. I finally found people I give two shits about and they're all getting hurt or dying. If this is the life you lead when you have friends, then you can fucking well take it back."

"It doesn't work like that, mate," I said and sat beside him.

"I had a family once. A long time ago. A village on the border of Scotland. I was only about fifteen and was still unsure exactly what I was. My parents, being as great as they were, pretty much abandoned me to whichever holy man they could find."

"I ended up in another village, working for a priest there. I grew up with those people, I finally felt like I belonged somewhere. One day a group of Vikings came to our village. They killed everyone, burned the place to the ground and stole whatever they wanted. I was out at sea when it happened, reveling in my powers. Everyone I cared about died in one afternoon of blood and fire."

"I'm sorry."

"Fuck being sorry. It was a long time ago. It took me ten years to track down the people who did it. I destroyed their village, and everyone in it. And I do mean everyone. Right then I pledged to never give a shit about anyone but me. I wasn't going to go through that again. And for hundreds of years it worked just fine. And now I care about people and look where it gets me."

"Don't be an ass," I said. "You love people, you lose people. It's part of life. But when you lose someone you care about, you don't let go of all that they meant to you. You never truly lose the people who mattered the most in life."

Alan glanced up from the pool. "Did you get that line from a Disney film?"

"Probably a fortune cookie, I forget. The point is, you're going to lose people who matter, we all do. Felix says you've changed, that you're a better man than you were. Prove him right."

Alan stood up. "This whole acting like a grownup thing sucks. And I'm nearly a millennium old."

"Enfield is behind all of this." I'd considered not telling Alan until later, but I wanted him to know what was going to happen.

"We going to hunt him down?"

"God, yes."

"Good, let's go see the old man then."

We found Felix slumped over in bed. Alan rushed to his side, pushing him back as a ragged breath left Felix's mouth. "You two took your time," he said.

"I don't want you to die," Alan said. "There are still things I want to learn. Still things I need you for."

"You spent hundreds of years being an asshole," Felix said with a smile. "Now, a little later than most, you've grown up. Good things are worth the wait. I'm proud of you, boy . . . Alan."

Alan rubbed his eyes and I felt like leaving them alone.

"Don't you fucking go anywhere, you're next," Felix said, making me smile.

"And what do you want me to do?"

"Take my soul when I'm gone. Use it. And when you find Enfield, kill him. Can you do that?"

"I don't know if I can. I can only take the souls of people who died fighting."

"What the fuck do you think I've been doing?" He raised the rune on his hand toward me. "You painted this on me so I could keep fighting. I'm not lying down and waiting for death."

I thought about his words. It was worth a try. "If I can take it, I will, I promise."

"And you kill Enfield."

"He's not going to be long for the world once we find him," I promised.

Felix reached under the bed and produced a bottle of whiskey. "Grab some glasses from the food cavern. Bring the fox and wolf back here too."

I did as asked and was soon standing in front of Felix with Ellie and Remy on one side and Alan still sitting beside him. We each had a glass of whiskey in hand.

Felix raised his glass. "To friends, to those you love, may you always hold them close. And to your enemies, may you always make them burn."

We all raised our glasses and then knocked back the strong liquid.

Felix began to close his eyes. I reached out with my necromancy to touch his soul. He didn't have long, seconds rather than minutes. "Say your final words," I told everyone.

"Good-bye, Felix," Remy said. "It was a pleasure."

"Give the afterlife hell," Ellie told him.

I reached over and grabbed his hand, squeezing it slightly. He squeezed it back, the barest amount of power in use. "Be at peace. I'm honored to have known you."

Alan stood and lent forward, kissing Felix on the forehead. "You're the closet thing I ever had to a father, and the one man I'd be proud to call my dad."

Felix turned slightly toward Alan and a smiled flickered across his face, and then he passed.

CHAPTER 

January 1889. Camelot.

By the time I'd reached the realm gate on Avalon Island and passed through into the realm of Albion, my anger at what Merlin had done was still burning brightly inside me. When I was only thirteen years old, he'd had Felix take me through the Harbinger trials. Merlin had lied to me, and I wanted answers.

Merlin's home was just outside of the city of Camelot, and I took a carriage from the realm gate intending to go all the way to his property. I wasn't even halfway there when the tightness in my gut got worse and worse with every passing moment.

When the carriage stopped suddenly, I was at first confused. It was still some distance to Merlin and for a moment I wondered if there'd been an accident up ahead. I put my head out of the carriage window and was met by Elaine.

"Care for some company?" she asked.

"Not really," I told her.

She pushed me back inside and climbed into the carriage, dismissing her guard, who didn't appear to be too impressed with the notion of leaving her alone.

"You can follow, if you must," she eventually agreed.

"You want to tell me why you decided to come see me?" I asked.

"You're off to see Merlin, yes?" She was concerned, whether it was about what I'd do to Merlin, or what he'd do to me, I didn't know.

I wasn't surprised. Elaine had a knack for knowing things she probably shouldn't. "How'd you know?"

"Educated guess. How is Felix?"

"No idea. Hopefully hidden by now."

"You know Merlin won't like that."

"Merlin is about to learn a few things he might not like," I said, angry that Elaine was telling me something I already knew. "He can add it to the list."

Elaine placed a hand on my shoulder and squeezed slightly. "Look, I know that you're angry with Merlin. He used the souls taken by the Reavers to feed Arthur, but getting into a confrontation with him won't help."

I told her about the Harbinger trials.

Elaine sat back and placed a finger over her lips and appeared to ponder the correct response. "You have evidence?"

I removed a piece of paper from my coat pocket and passed it over to her. It was the same paper I'd found in Felix's basement.

"I'd heard rumors about you being taken to the trials as a young boy."

"You knew?" I snapped.

"Not with certainty."

"You should have told me."

"With no evidence? You'd have gone to Merlin, who would have denied everything, and probably gotten Felix killed centuries ago. You still have no concrete proof about what you were involved in."

I couldn't believe what I was hearing. "Felix himself told me about his part in what happened. I'm going to see what Merlin has to say about it."

"You're going to get yourself killed then."

"I'm not planning on dying, Elaine. I plan on getting out of him whatever he did. I plan on stopping his lies. I plan on getting him to stop using the Reavers. By the way, Fiona will be back soon with a list of Reaver names. The Reavers need to be no more."

"Once I've seen the evidence, the Reavers will be dealt with, I can promise you that. With evidence, Avalon won't be able to stop their destruction." Elaine paused for a moment. "What are you going to do if he won't back down?"

"I don't know. I don't even know what I'm going to say. But I need to confront him. I need to hear it from his own lips. Then I'll decide."

"Don't do anything rash, Nathan. You've not seen him in person for many years. He might not be the man you once knew and looked up to."

The carriage stopped and I opened the door. "Then that makes two of us." I stepped out into the cold night. "You can wait if you wish."

"I do."

"You understand why I have to do this."

"I do. That does not mean I have to like it. The repercussions could be immense."

"I know," I agreed. "But I can't pretend anymore. There need to be answers, and I will get them."

"Do not push him too far. He is a man to fear."

"Yes, well in the mood I'm in, he should be afraid of me."

Elaine suddenly appeared even more melancholy. "That's the problem, Nathan, he always has been."

Merlin's home was a massive castle, with five floors—as well as an underground complex—and dozens of staff. When your house has an east and west wing, you know it can comfortably be described as too big for one person.

It hadn't changed much since I'd last been here; there were still guards to let me into the property, and more guards inside who watched me as I walked through the drafty hallway to the rear of the building, the main entrance to the complex below. There were half a dozen secret passageways—that I knew of—which were dotted around the castle, although I doubted that even Merlin was able to keep track of them all.

Several members of staff said hello, but most saw my arrival and went back to whatever they were doing. In addition to enough guards to defend a small country, Merlin's paladins also lived in the castle. And there wasn't a single one of those I wanted to bump into. They were fanatical in their commitment to Merlin, and more than a little difficult to be around because of it.

I turned a corner and complained inwardly. A paladin stood in front of the entrance to Merlin's complex.

"Stop," the paladin said, raising his hand as if that was all that could possibly be needed. You could have scraped the arrogance off him, it shone even brighter than his mirror-like armor.

"I'm here to see Merlin," I told him.

"Identify yourself."

I took a breath, reminding myself that they were only doing a job. "Nathan Garrett."

The paladin didn't even seem to register that I'd said anything.

"You're not wearing a helm, and your hair is short, so maybe you're just deaf and there's nothing in your ears. My name is Nathan Garrett, please let me through."

"I don't think I shall be doing that. You should leave."

"Can you move out of the way?"

His hand dropped to the hilt of his broadsword, which sat on his hip. "Do not make me ask again."

"If you draw that sword, I'm going to make you eat it," I said, my anger creeping up. "I need to see Merlin."

"And I told you no. Merlin is not accepting visitors. You may leave."

I took a step toward him, and he removed part of the blade from its scabbard.

"Enough," a man shouted as he walked toward us.

The paladin dropped to one knee as if on command. "My Lord Gawain, Merlin has forbid anyone from entry."

"Do you really think that includes his right-hand man?" Gawain asked. "Move aside and open the door, or I shall move you."

The paladin slinked aside and Gawain opened the door for me, motioning for me to enter. I did so without glancing at the paladin, there was no point in rubbing in his defeat.

"Thank you," I said as we descended the long, winding staircase, my words echoing all around us.

"I could hardly allow you to fight one of my paladins. What's so important anyway? It's been a very long time since your last visit, I was beginning to think you'd forgotten about us."

Gawain was an honest man, someone who always tried to do the right thing, no matter the consequences. The only problem was his unwavering loyalty to Merlin. If I'd told him what had happened, he would have said I was mistaken, or lied, or anything so his precious bubble of a life wasn't disturbed. Lancelot, one of his closest friends, had betrayed Arthur, and by extension Merlin and Avalon, and then Mordred, his own brother, had done the exact same thing, but on an even worse scale. Since then, Gawain was about as loyal to Merlin and Avalon as any one man could possibly be. He'd been given command of the paladins and while he pretended he was still the fun-loving man I'd known centuries ago, he had no sense of humor when it came to Arthur or Merlin.

"Not quite, old friend," I said with as much cheer as I could manage. "What is Merlin doing that's so important?"

"Reading, I imagine. He spends most of his time involved in books these days, trying to undo my brother's curse." Anger radiated from him. Gawain wasn't fond of talking about his brother. An understandable consequence of being related to Mordred.

We reached the bottom of the stairs and I walked through the torch-lit cavern that led to Merlin's chambers. There were three main rooms, two of which belonged to Merlin as his living space, although as we walked past them—both with their doors open—there appeared to be more paper, books, and various writing implements than actual living space.

We reached the double doors that signified the final room, and Gawain pushed them open. Inside was a big enough space to have contained four houses. It was a massive structure with a walkway high above me where half a dozen paladins stood, all watching the floor below. I knew from experience that there were doors up there that led to chambers for the paladins to rest and make their way back to the main house above.

As one the paladins all turned toward Gawain and me. I could feel their eyes boring into me as we walked across the marble floor. I took two steps and stopped. In the center of the room was something that resembled a gigantic aquarium; it was ten feet long and completely cylindrical in shape. Various tubes and devices were attached to the outside of the tank, which was also littered with runes that glowed a deep red. The water-like substance inside was crystal clear, allowing me to see the occupant. Arthur.

I walked over to the aquarium, ignoring the gazes from above and placed my hand against its cool glass. Arthur floated in the water-like substance that was inside it. I'd never discovered what exactly it was; Merlin wouldn't reveal his method of creating it. My best guess was that it was normal water modified by the use of runes. It was slightly denser than normal water, although it still behaved in the same way.

Arthur was still clean-shaven, and his hair was exactly the same shoulder-length chestnut color it had been when he'd been lowered into the tank. The substance kept him in a sort of suspended state. He looked dead. The wound to his chest where Mordred had plunged the cursed blade of his sword was still raw and discolored. Now Arthur was barely alive. Using the souls of innocent people to feed on.

"I wondered if you'd ever come back," Merlin said from behind me.

"Get everyone out of here," I said, barely keeping my anger in check. "We need to talk."

"Do you forget who you're talking to?" His voice contained more amusement than anger, but a moment later I heard Gawain ask if everything was okay and then footsteps above as the paladins returned to their quarters.

"Now, why don't you turn around and talk to me like a man?"

I did as was asked and saw Merlin in the flesh for the first time in countless years. The old stories were just that. They painted Merlin as an elderly man with flowing white hair, carrying a big staff that doubled as a wand. Merlin did not look elderly, he appeared to be in his mid to late forties, but was actually about five thousand years older than that. He did have long white hair, that much was true, although his hair had always been that color as long as I could remember. He'd grown a beard since I'd last seen him, which was short and neat. Merlin was a few inches taller than me, and considerably less bulky, but I knew the strength that lay under his expensive suit. He was not a man to be taken lightly.

"You're feeding Arthur the souls of the murdered," I said, keeping my rage in check. Getting angry would achieve nothing.

"Don't be overly dramatic. Arthur is fed the souls of those we vanquish. It keeps him alive much better than magic."

"You don't know, do you? You sit in here and give orders, but never actually bother to learn what happens when those orders are carried out. You told the Reavers to collect souls for Arthur? Well, they've been doing that, they've been murdering people, innocent people, in London."

"No one in London is innocent, it's a cesspool of corruption and vice."

I snapped. "Fuck you, Merlin. I've just spent the last few days hunting down Reavers for butchering men and women and taking their souls. Human souls at that. They told me that you allowed this to happen."

"I don't have the luxury of asking questions. They bring the souls, I keep Arthur alive. And if you swear at me again, I shall make you regret it, Nathaniel."

"They're murdering people, don't you care?"

"Not really. Humans don't live long enough to bother me one way or another. A few less in London is hardly a cause for concern."

"They were responsible for the Jack the Ripper murders. Their leader is a man by the name of Enfield."

"Enfield? A valuable member of my staff."

"He's a murderer."

"So are you."

"I don't kill for pleasure. I don't kill for fun and games. I certainly don't kill random innocent people."

Merlin walked toward me. "What do you want me to do?"

"Stop the Reavers. Cease all of their operations. We need to stop them from murdering people to bring you souls."

"Do you know how long a soul allows Arthur to live for?" Merlin placed his hand on the glass of the tank, as if stroking Arthur's hair. "Decades. Depending on the soul. Only human souls will do for some reason, possibly a final joke by Mordred. He would never expect us to kill humans so that Arthur could live. But I will do whatever I must."

"You allow them to kill humans?"

"Allow? I don't allow them to do anything. I leave it in their capable hands and they bring me what I want. I don't care where they get them from, so long as they do."

"This will be your last shipment, I've destroyed every vessel I could find."

Merlin rounded on me with rage in his eyes. "You utter fucking idiot. Do you understand what you've done? You've condemned Arthur to die."

"He's already dead, or he may as well be," I shouted, slamming my hand on the tank. "Look at him, he's not spoken or moved in over a millennium."

The blast of water hit me in the chest, lifted me from my feet, and dumped me several feet away. "Don't ever touch this tank again. It is the only thing keeping *your king* alive. Do you understand me?"

I got back to my feet. "You're allowing the murder of innocent humans to keep a dead man alive. You have to stop."

"Have to? Do you hear yourself? I don't have to do anything. I'm keeping Arthur alive, and that's all there is to it. If I have to harvest the souls of every single human in England, I will. As for the Reavers taking the lives of the innocent, and killing for pleasure. You killed the men responsible for your wife's murder, you took pleasure in it. You murdered countless hundreds over the years in the name of Avalon, and some just because they were in your way. Do you think none of those I sent you after were innocent?"

The memory of finding my wife's body flashed to the front of my mind, bringing with it a cool rage. "What?" I said through gritted teeth, unwilling to trust myself to say more.

"Do you really believe that I only sent you after the wicked, the evil? I sent you to kill those who needed killing. If they didn't have an evil life story, I made one up. Told you what you needed to hear."

I was dumbfounded. "You've lied to me my whole life," I said eventually. "You put me through the Harbinger trials at thirteen, and now you tell me that you had me kill innocent people for you?"

"Only a few times. You were always fine with taking the lives of those who deserved it, but I have other . . . tools that will kill without their conscience getting in the way. Eventually I just had you do whatever you pleased. It was easier that way, and it kept you away from me and my plans. Yes, I lied to you, yes I put you through the Harbinger trials, but those trials made you a better person, a more capable person. And those lies were so you'd do what you needed to. So what's your point? Would you like to sit there and cry about it?

"You come here, with your anger and your self-righteousness. Where was that self-righteousness when you went to America and slaughtered people? Where was it when you tortured people for information, when you threatened and killed?"

I got back to my feet, rage almost burning through me.

"I do what needs to be done. As do you. But I don't have the luxury of crying over it. I always thought you were able to put aside your emotions to do what was necessary, apparently I'm wrong. You were Merlin's assassin, killing people who needed to be killed, and then you took the Hellequin name, and you were feared. People fell into line without you having to do anything. All of that was possible because of who you are, because of what I made you. And those Harbinger trials did that. And if you think I'm going to stop having the Reavers kill whomever they choose in my quest to heal your king, you're out of your damn mind."

I punched him. It contained my rage and anger, my hurt at being lied to, and my frustration at how far Merlin had slipped. It was powerful enough to knock Merlin onto his ass, and for a second I thought, this is it, this is where he tries to kill me.

"Stop," Gawain shouted as he sprinted in between us. "Just stop, before this goes further."

"What are you thinking?" Gawain asked me, and then turned to Merlin. "And is what he said true? Are we killing innocents to keep Arthur alive?"

Merlin got to his feet, ignoring Gawain and stepping up toward me. "That's the one and only shot you get. Now go do your job. Leave, and don't come back for a few more centuries."

"No," I said softly. "I'm done with you, Merlin. I'm finished. I don't want to work with you, or for you, or even know that what I'm doing is helping you. I'm no longer in your employ."

"You can't just quit."

"I can. And you can't stop me. Not unless you're going to kill me. Are you going to kill me?"

Merlin stared a hole through me, and then turned to Gawain. "Get this . . . gentleman out of my sight." He turned back to me. "You will never sully my home with your presence again."

"What about the souls?" Gawain asked.

"What about them?" Merlin snapped. "This man won't accept what we need to do to keep Arthur alive. Once you've removed him from this place, return to me and I'll explain it to you. Goodbye, Nathaniel Garrett."

"Go fuck yourself, Merlin."

I turned and walked away, fully aware that Merlin wanted to carry out his threat after I swore at him the first time. Gawain was behind me in an instant, a shield between Merlin and me.

We walked in silence until we reached the front door.

"Don't come back, Nathaniel," Gawain said. "Not for a very long time."

"He's not the man I thought he was. He's twisted, and on a dark and dangerous path."

"Then we will have to continue to shine brighter than ever so he can find his way. It's a shame you don't understand that. Good-bye."

He closed the door and I made my way back to the coach and Elaine. I knew that Gawain would go back to Merlin, who would twist his actions to make it look like he was a hero, doing what was needed. And Gawain would accept it. He couldn't bear to think that Merlin might be wrong. It would be his downfall one day.

"So how did that go?" Elaine asked as I climbed back in.

"I'm done here."

"You finally left Merlin's employ? I guess we'll need to find you something else to do."

"No, not with Merlin, I'm done with Avalon. I'm finished with this whole place."

"Nathan, you can't . . ."

"I can, and I will. You need to track down these Reavers and stop them. They're going to keep killing, and Merlin isn't bothered about where the souls come from, so long as they keep coming."

"I'll do all I can. Is there anything you need?"

"Only one thing, to get out of this realm as quickly as this carriage will take me."

CHAPTER 32

Avalon Island, England. Now.

The helicopter landed a few hours after we'd left the body of Felix in his cavern. Alan had arranged for people to collect both Felix and the dead Reavers, the latter of whom would be disposed of by the various creatures who live in every city and feast on the dead. Felix would be sent wherever he wanted to be buried. The journey had been done in silence. Once Felix had died, I'd taken his soul, and with it his knowledge of the Reavers. I knew names and the occasional face of everyone that Felix had discovered. But the one I wanted to find above all others was Enfield, the man in charge of Kelly Jensen and her band of psychopaths.

Hendricks, the guard on the island, met us at the landing pad. He looked like he hadn't slept in a while.

"Anything to tell us?" I asked when we were far enough away from the noise of the rotors.

"There's been no one coming through here. Trust me; they couldn't arrive without us knowing it."

"Thanks for that," I told him and shook his hand.

"Do you think any of my people are Reavers?"

"You got a list of names?"

Hendricks nodded and passed me a notebook. "I figured it wouldn't hurt for you to look them over, just in case."

I flicked through the pages. "None," I told him eventually. "You're clean."

"Excellent. I assume you're going to want to go straight through the realm gate."

"Please. Have you spoken to anyone in Camelot?"

"I spoke to Lucie yesterday. Fiona was doing okay."

Alan looked visibly relieved. "Thank you," he said.

Hendricks took us all to the realm gate, and wished us luck as we walked through into Albion.

"I'm going to go see Fiona," Alan told us. "What about you?"

"I'd come with you," I said, "But I need to get changed and have a shower. I can't turn up to the hospital with bloody clothes. And I imagine the paladins are already going to be on edge when they see me. I'd rather my wardrobe not be a reason for my death."

"Go to my place, there's bound to be something there you can wear." Alan thought about it. "Shit, I don't have a key."

"I'll take him," Remy said. "I live opposite anyway, so it'll be nice to wash."

"What about you, Ellie?" I asked.

"I'm going to see Olivia and Tommy," she told us. "I want to know what's happening with the naming ceremony, and let Olivia know about what happened."

"Come find me when you're done," I said. "Maybe ask Olivia and all of the LOA to come with her. I think I might need back-up."

"You think Merlin is going to handle your meeting badly?" Remy asked.

"The last time I saw him, I told him to fuck off and punched him in the jaw. I don't think it'll go well, no."

"You punched Merlin?" Alan asked. "And I thought I had authority problems."

"Yeah, well, I can't imagine a century is enough that it's going to make him want to see me. It might be worth getting Elaine to come with me too. Although that might make matters even worse. Basically I'm screwed no matter what I do."

"You think Felix was right?" Ellie asked. "That you need to see Merlin?"

"Unfortunately, yeah. Elaine pushed through the destruction of the Reavers last time by telling people they were killing innocent humans. She'd never get away with it again. Too many people would see it as her not doing her job right the first time. She needs Merlin's backing."

"Do you think he'll give it?"

"I have no idea. A century is a long time for him to hate Elaine and me."

"What happens if he says no?" Remy asked.

"That's a bloody good question, and I have no idea."

"That's reassuring," Alan said. "Now I'm going to see my wife."

We all went our separate ways, with only Remy staying with me as we caught one of the cars to the district where he and Fiona and Alan lived. It was considerably colder in the city than it had been when I was last here only a few days earlier. Storms were probably due. It was certainly the time of year for them. Winter in Camelot was a cold, miserable time if you didn't like snow, or if you were, like Remy, under five feet tall.

We both stood outside Fiona and Alan's house and stared at the door. "I know I was only here a few days ago, but it feels like a lifetime."

"I know what you mean. I want to go see Fiona, I'm almost itching to. I'd best get washed, and I'll meet you out here in half an hour. Let's go get you a key first."

We crossed the road and Remy placed his paw against the palm reader next to his front door. The door clicked and I glanced over to my left, where I saw Kelly Jensen.

There was no time to say anything. I threw up a shield of dense air in between Remy and the front door as an explosion rocked the house. The door was torn apart and thrown at us in a million pieces. I managed to deflect the majority of the blast, but the shockwave hit Remy and me, and flung us back onto the pavement with a heavy thud.

A bullet struck the side of the pavement about an inch from my head as Kelly Jensen ran toward us. I got back to my feet throwing up another shield to deflect the bullets, until she was out of them. And then she dropped the gun and used her light magic to blind me, before tackling me to the ground.

Punch after punch landed on my face as I raised my arms to protect myself as best I could. All of a sudden her weight was lifted from my chest accompanied by a grunt of pain from her and a low growl from Remy. My eyes began to readjust and I saw Remy punching Kelly in the back of the head with one hand, while he used his claws to dig into her shoulder and hold on. She scrambled back to her feet and twisted herself, blasting Remy in the chest with her light magic, the smell of burning fur and his scream of pain filling all around me.

"You've ruined everything. But you're going to die for it," Kelly said as she took Remy's sabre and walked over to me, blood trickling down the front of her face from a cut on her forehead.

I rolled to my feet and lashed out with a plume of flame, which forced Kelly to dodge back, putting distance between us. She launched a blast of light, but I turned away as it lit up the street. When I turned back, I saw her running toward me, the sabre out in front like a lance. I readied a sphere of lightning, but Kelly jumped aside and her wings unfurled from her back, tearing through her blouse. She batted them once and she lifted into the sky. I removed the sphere of lightning from my hand; I couldn't throw it at people and even if I could have, if I'd missed and hit one of the houses in the street, I'd have done considerable damage to it and maybe anyone inside.

"We're at a sort of stalemate here," I shouted.

Kelly was ten feet off the ground, still clutching the sabre and still looking mightily pissed off. She threw the sabre at me, which was easily avoided, and then light leapt from her fingertips. The ground burned everywhere the light touched, and my hastily created shield of air did very little to stop the sudden barrage. I was soon tearing off my T-shirt to stop it from burning me when it caught fire.

"I thought light fae were meant to be nice," I shouted. "I guess that's been proven as a myth."

"Nice?" Kelly shrieked. "Fuck your nice." Light began to fill the space in front of her, a huge amount of power that was going to do a lot of damage to whatever it hit.

"You shouldn't have involved me," I told her as a tendril of air magic left my hand and snaked toward the sabre that still lay on the road a few feet from me.

"I'm going to see you burn."

Kelly was so bright that she was hard to look at. Remy moved slightly and Kelly's head snapped toward him. I took the chance and used the air to whip the sabre up to Kelly. She didn't notice it until the final moment, just before it pierced her ribs, going up toward her heart.

Kelly's energy exploded, bathing everything with intense light, which I had to shield my eyes from. A thud soon after signified Kelly dropping to the ground, and when I turned back to her, she was writhing on the floor, cursing the name of pretty much everyone she could think of.

Remy limped over to her side and grabbed the sabre, pulling it free, and making Kelly shout out. "Silver blade," he said. "Won't kill her, will hurt like fuck."

"How did you get in here?" I asked Kelly. "You didn't go through the main realm gate. Hendricks didn't lie about that." It dawned on me almost immediately. "There's a second realm gate in Albion, isn't there?"

Kelly smiled, although the pain remained in her eyes.

"Where is Enfield?"

"Who?" she asked with mock innocence.

An explosion from behind made me turn around to see Remy's house as part of the front wall collapsed.

"Sorry, Remy."

He turned back to Kelly and advanced on her, his claws out. "Where is Enfield?"

"Probably killing your friends by now," Kelly said, and had to stop herself from laughing.

"The hospital," I cursed. "He's there isn't he?"

Kelly nodded slowly.

I passed Remy his sabre. "Stay here; get Elaine or someone to come help sort her out. If she fucks around, kill her."

"I think I can take a fox," Kelly said. "Enfield is going to kill you, sorcerer."

I smashed a ball of hardened air into the side of her head, which knocked her cold. "Shut up," I snapped.

The street was beginning to fill with people leaving their houses. It hadn't been long since the first explosion, and I noticed that several of those standing around were armed. I didn't want anyone trying to stop Remy.

"My name is Nathan Garrett," I shouted. "You can call me Hellequin."

There were murmurs, which I waited to finish.

"This woman here is Agent Kelly Jensen of the SOA. She's tried to kill my companion, Remy Roux, another SOA agent, and me. She is a traitor to Avalon and its way of life. If anyone wants to contact Elaine and get her here, that would be very useful. This whole area is about to be crawling with various Avalon officials, but if you want to help before they get here, make sure she doesn't escape. And make sure no one tries to kill her. If any of you are considering helping *her*, know this. Once I'm done with her boss, I will come for you. It will not be a nice conversation."

People looked from me to the still prone Kelly, who now had the tip of Remy's sabre at her throat. Several members of the crowd removed phones and began dialing, while others showed their credentials as an agent for one of Avalon's agencies.

"You going to be okay?" I shouted to Remy, who gave me the thumbs up. I spoke to several members of the crowd, one of whom passed me his phone so I could talk to one of Elaine's guards, a man I trusted. They assured me that they would be there within minutes, so I set off toward the hospital hoping for the best. Hoping that Kelly had been lying, but knowing in my heart that I wasn't going to be that lucky.

I managed to get one of the cars to take me to the hospital, which was certainly faster than running would have been, although the fact that the car couldn't speed was more than a little infuriating.

I almost tore the door off as I left the car, immediately sprinting toward the hospital front entrance, which I barreled through and continued until I'd reached the lifts. The wait for one to arrive and then to take me up to the right floor was agonizing. I considered using my air magic to propel me up the stairwell, but I had no idea what I'd be facing up above. Even so, I felt considerable relief when the doors opened and I stepped out and saw that the guards were still at their station.

"Has Alan been this way?" I asked.

"About twenty minutes ago," he told me.

I breathed a sigh of relief and thanked the guard before setting off toward Fiona's room. Each of the three checkpoints was manned, and there didn't appear to be anything untoward happening as I reached the high-security area.

My confidence fell apart as I moved around the corner to where Fiona's room was. The half dozen SOA agents outside the room were prone across the floor. I didn't need to move to each of them to tell that they'd been killed. Blood soaked the hallway floor, with more splatter along the walls. The first agent had stab wounds along with signs that fire magic had been used on him.

I moved to Fiona's door and readied a ball of fire as I kicked the door open and stepped inside. Fiona was sitting on the floor beside her bed, her eyes were open, although they looked glassed over, and she was still out of it.

Alan was being held by the throat up against the far wall, his feet dangling helplessly off the ground. The Faceless who held him in place didn't even turn to look at me until I'd taken a step toward him.

"I will kill him if you come any closer," the Faceless said without emotion.

"I will kill you if you hurt him," I said. "Enfield."

A chuckle escaped the Faceless's lips and he dropped Alan to the floor, before removing his mask—the same mask that Kay's faceless wore—and tossing it aside. "How'd you know?"

"Kelly said you'd be here."

"Is she dead?"

"She wasn't when I left."

"I do hate to waste talented individuals. So, how are things? You look well."

"You've been Kay's Faceless all this time?"

"Everyone needs a job."

"Does Kay know who you are?"

"Of course, I do," Kay said from behind me.

I spun to face him and blocked a punch to my jaw, countering with a kick that hit Kay in the chest and sent him back out of the room. I tried to take a step forward, but couldn't. Kay walked off down the hallway as my body felt heavy, slow. I dropped to my knees as Enfield came into view, red glyphs adorning his arms.

"I couldn't do this back in the nineteenth century, but do you remember when I did this to you back in Tartarus. Knocked you silly and you didn't even know who I was."

My eyes felt heavy, but just before I could pitch forward, Alan tackled Enfield out of the room. The fight was brutal and quick, as Enfield gained the upper hand, before breaking Alan's arm and smashing his head into the wall. He followed up with a kick to Alan's head before a blast of air from my hands separated them, and I had to listen as Enfield's footsteps faded as he ran off, presumably with Kay in tow.

I got back to my feet, feeling groggy but otherwise uninjured. "You okay, Alan?" I shouted.

"Fucking dandy," he said. "You going after them, or what?"

"Just getting my bearings again."

Alan winced as he cradled his arm. "Check on Fiona for me."

I knelt beside her and lifted her chin.

"Nate," she whispered. She sounded weak and exhausted. "Kay is behind it all. That's why he attacked me."

"He attacked you?"

"Him and some woman. Don't know her though."

"Was it Kelly Jensen?"

Fiona shook her head and then slumped forward. I caught her and put her back on the bed.

"You need to stop Kay and his Faceless," she said weakly. "They're going to try and kill Elaine."

"I promise I'll stop them."

"Is my husband all right?"

I glanced behind me as Alan got back to his feet, which involved a lot of swearing. "He'll be fine. Are you okay?"

Fiona nodded. "Just go get them."

I turned and ran out of the room, reaching the end of the corridor when Alan shouted me back.

"What's wrong?" I asked him.

"Nate, Enfield used his magic to tear into Fiona's mind while she was dying."

"I'll get him, don't worry." I turned and continued running through the hospital, finding each of the security checkpoints empty. It wasn't until I reached the lobby that I discovered why, when a squad of heavily armed men were all waiting for me as the lift doors opened.

I was wrestled to the ground and pinned there, while guns were pointed at my head. There was no point in arguing, it would have just made it worse. I only hoped I could sort it out before Kay and Enfield tried to kill Elaine, resulting in even more deaths.

CHAPTER 

Does someone want to let him go?" Lucie asked as she entered the hospital reception.

"We've been given orders by Kay, ma'am," one of the SOA agents who'd tackled me to the ground said. "He said this man here tried to attack him."

"This man here is Hellequin. Now let him go or I'll make your life a lot less pleasant in future years." Lucie's tone practically begged anyone to piss her off more than she already was.

The agent removed the bonds from my hands.

"Fiona is awake," I told Lucie. "Kay and his Faceless attacked both her and Alan. Oh, and his Faceless is Enfield."

"The guy who led a group of Reavers who were Jack the Ripper?"

"The very same asshole. As I tried to explain to these gentlemen several times, they're going to try and kill Elaine. You need to get people over there."

"Already done. Alan grabbed one of the emergency phones upstairs and used it to contact me. I always knew that Kay was crooked, but to go against Avalon." She paused. "That's unexpected."

"You okay?" I asked.

"No. I'm angry. Really, really angry. I've locked down the entire realm, no one is getting in or out. We're going to find these sons of bitches, and then I'm going to take great pleasure in kicking them both in their ballsack." She rubbed her forehead. "But anger later, first let's find them both."

"His Faceless . . . sorry, Enfield, told me that he was the sorcerer who attacked me at Hades's compound last year. Kay was involved in breaking out Cronus if that's the case. He was working with the Vanguard."

"The Vanguard and Reavers working together. That can't possibly be good news. But what's his end game? Hera was the one who wanted Cronus free, it was her plan. Is Kay working for her? Or are they both working for someone else?"

"Questions for later, maybe. First thing is to find Kay and Enfield."

"I can have people looking into it."

"Good, I'm going to have a look around his office in the SOA building. If he's into something stupid, he'll have left evidence there."

"You can't possibly think going alone is a good idea."

"If you have a better one, I'm all ears."

"I've got one," Tommy said from behind me.

I turned around as my friend strolled into the hospital. A lot of the SOA agents nodded their greetings. Tommy was a bit of a legend among the SOA; the fact that he'd quit when Kay took control didn't appear to have diminished people's opinion of him.

"I'm coming with you," he said. "Can't let you get killed just before you're meant to be at Kasey's naming ceremony."

"You don't have to do that," I protested.

"Yeah, I do. Kay was the reason I quit working here. He's a nasty little shit and if I can help bring him down, I'm all for it. Besides, you need the help. And I can track them to where they went, saves wandering the city looking for them."

"Thanks."

"We'll keep an eye on Fiona and Alan," Lucie told us. "But I can't put a citywide announcement out for Kay's arrest. If he has SOA people under his control, it could turn into a war out there. The LOA have taken charge of the investigation, and apart from those in the SOA I know are loyal to me, I'm not taking any chances. The rest of the SOA are still under lockdown. No matter what Kay's plan is, I'd rather you managed to get him before other options need to be discussed."

In other words, we were on our own for now.

"Kelly knows of a second realm gate in Albion," I told her. "I don't know where it is though."

"A second gate?" Lucie asked, surprised. "Shit. We'll get her to talk, don't worry."

We told Lucie we'd be in touch and Tommy and I left the building, where he immediately took a deep breath. "They went this way."

"How do you know that's Kay's smell?" I asked as we walked through the hospital grounds to the nearby car park.

"He smells like blood," he said. "Always has."

"Like blood?"

"When a sorcerer uses magic they smell different, it's like they smell of power, or death, depending on the person. But very few smell of blood." He paused and glanced back at me. "You know what that means don't you?"

Kay always did like to use his blood magic to hurt people. Blood magic is addictive and scary stuff, but is usually only used by sorcerers for healing or increasing the power of their spells. I'd lost my ability to use it when my necromancy activated, but I'd used blood magic just as much as anyone else when it was available. For a sorcerer to smell of blood, that would indicate that Kay was using blood magic a lot . . . that he was possibly a blood leech. And that would be very, very bad, because that means he could be involved with blood curses and sacrifices. Basically all the bad stuff that blood magic allows.

"Shit," I whispered.

"That about sums it up," Tommy agreed and continued walking, before stopping once again in front of an empty parking space. "They got into a car."

"Well, they could be anywhere then."

"Car fifteen," he said, pointing to the number plate on the car beside it. "The cars all park themselves in numerical order. So car fifteen is the one they took."

"How does that help?"

"Get in," he told me and opened the front door of car sixteen.

I opened what would have been the passenger-side door—if the car had been fitted with a steering wheel—and waited for Tommy to explain what he was going to do.

One of his fingers grew long, the nail forming a claw. "You see the road out there?" he said while he prized off the center console of the car, just above the destination indicator, and flung it onto the back seats. "Well those little sensors take a sort of fingerprint for every single car that goes along the road, feeding all of that data into a central processor in a building about a mile away."

"Why can't we just contact that building and have them tell us where car fifteen went?"

"Because in the century since you were last here, the ability to gain information has gotten slower, not quicker. By the time we've contacted them, and they've contacted their higher-ups to see if they can share that information, Kay would have enough time to get a nap in before his murderous plan."

"Okay, so what are you doing?"

"Like I said, each of these cars leaves a fingerprint when they go over the surface." He held down one of the buttons beneath the screen until it turned completely blank. "It's a little-known trick, but you can program any of these cars to think that they're another car. They all store the last half a dozen routes in their memory. You just need to find the one you want."

The screen came back to life and a few taps later, the car's engine started. "Now it thinks we're car fifteen," Tommy said with just the right amount of smugness.

"How do you know about this?" I asked.

"Some of Olivia's people were the ones involved in the creation of this system. They told her, she told me."

The car began moving off as Tommy reaffixed the center console to appear that nothing had happened.

It didn't take long before we knew the car was headed to the city limits. A few minutes later it stopped behind car fifteen, which had been abandoned.

I glanced across the open fields that sat between us and a massive home in the distance.

"Kay's mansion," I said as I climbed out of the car.

"We'd best hurry then," Tommy said and we both set off at a jog, although mine was considerably wearier than his. There was nowhere an ambush could logistically be arranged, the entire area was one flat plain, but a forest began directly behind Kay's home, with thick trees stretching up as high as any redwood could manage. It was a good spot for a sniper, but we made it to the imposing front gate of the property without incident.

The gate opened with no more than a slight push, and Tommy and I walked through the immaculate garden to the front door, which was ajar.

"This feel weird to you?" I asked.

"More than a little," he agreed and took a big sniff. "Kay was here, and recently too."

"What about Enfield?"

"The Faceless? I can't get anyone else's scent, just Kay's. You think he's waiting for us?"

"I assume so, yes. Can't imagine why though."

I moved slowly into the mansion, with Tommy right behind me. The foyer was both gigantic and full of light, which came in from the floor-to-ceiling windows along the front of the building. The room was full of artwork and artifacts like vases. It was the kind of room someone would have if they wanted everyone to know how cultured and important they were.

We moved through the house, using Tommy's nose to distinguish between old scents and new ones, until we came to the rear of the building. The doors that led to the woodland behind the house were open.

"He's out there," Tommy said with a low growl. "This feels like a trap."

"Yes, yes it does." I stepped outside and scanned the tree line. "Any chance you can smell anyone other than Kay?"

"No, not from here."

We crossed the open land between the trees and the house, and stopped a few hundred feet short when Kay stepped out of the shadows. "Welcome to my humble abode," he said, with a wave of his hands.

"You're going to come with us, Kay," I told him. "You and Enfield."

"Ah, but Enfield isn't here. I'm sorry about that, but he's gone off to do his job. And I'm about leave this little realm and relocate somewhere else until Elaine's successor can be chosen; hopefully they'll be a little more open to doing things the proper way."

"You mean by making people fear you?" Tommy said, his words dripping contempt.

"Is there a better way to get what you want?" It wasn't just a flippant mark, Kay genuinely believed that fear was the best way to get results.

"Kay, you come with us, or we're going to take you," I told him. "You don't really want to fight me, do you?"

Kay stared at me for what felt like a long time. "No, I can't say I do, Nathan. You were always more than you appeared. The revelation that you are Hellequin was a shock, I won't lie. I heard you killed Mordred too. That was an even bigger shock.

"But I can't stand here all day, I have important work to do. I need to prepare for what's coming. So, no, I don't think I want to fight you, but I'm not going to go with you either."

I took a step toward Kay and readied my magic. "Then we're going to take you."

Kay stepped back into the shadows of the trees. "Then come get me."

By the time we'd reached the trees, Kay had vanished into the darkness beyond. Tommy took a step forward and then stopped as if frozen in place. "Death," he whispered. "So much death. Nate, something is wrong here. Something I can't quite put my finger on. But I've smelled it before."

I created a blade of flame in my hand and overtook Tommy as I entered the woods.

There were grunts of pain from behind me as Tommy shifted into his wolfbeast form.

"Definitely something I've smelled before," he said, his voice now deeper and more menacing. "Something very bad."

"Can you smell Kay?" I asked.

"He went that way," he told me, bounding off in front. His wolfbeast form wasn't as fast or agile as his pure wolf, but it was stronger. A lot stronger.

A few hundred meters into the woods they opened out a bit, allowing more room to move. Another hundred and the trees stopped when we arrived at a clearing. There were half a dozen dead Avalon guards all around the entrance to a cave.

"Second realm gate," I said. "It's got to be down there."

"So is Kay," Tommy said with a sniff. "And something else is watching us from the trees above."

It wasn't often that Tommy sounded genuinely concerned, and his tone made me search the treetops for some evidence of his worry. "There's nothing there," I told him.

"There is, trust me on this."

I used my magic to change my vision, allowing me to see in thermal vision, or as close as magic could get to it. I couldn't see anything for a while, and then something scurried around the trunk of a massive tree. I switched off the thermal vision just as strands of web hit me in the wrist. I used my free hand to cut through the web with my blade of fire, but more strands shot out toward Tommy and me. We dodged them all, diving behind nearby trees.

"What is it?" Tommy shouted.

"Jorōgumo," I said, and noticed that my hand was cut where the web had hit me. I raised my hand to Tommy, showing him the wounds. "Although her web couldn't do that the last time I encountered one."

"Hello, Nathaniel. Although I guess you go by Nate now," a woman said, accompanied by the rustle of leaves as she made her way through the bushes. "It's been a long time."

Tommy risked a glance around the tree trunk. "It's a giant fucking spider woman thing. Wait, is that the female we let live back when we were trying to find Mordred before he killed those two princes?"

"I assume so, yes," I told him.

"Oh shit."

"I've waited centuries, Natha . . . Nate," the jorōgumo said. "You let me live, and after I dragged my useless husband back into the forest, I mated and then ate him. It was only then I learned the true horror of what you'd done to me. I can't have children anymore. All of my babies that you killed that day, they were my last."

"You killed her babies?" Tommy questioned.

"Hundreds of venomous spiders," I corrected.

"Good."

"How'd you end up here?" I shouted.

"Kay found me. Brought me here and gave me prey in exchange for my venom. When he told me that you were chasing him, I offered to stay and remove you. And I get your wolf friend into the bargain."

"Ummm . . . hate to break this to you, lady," Tommy said. "But there's no hope in hell you can take me and Nate all by yourself."

"Oh, I never said I was alone."

There was a low roar that came from above, before a crash signified that whatever it was had landed beside the jorōgumo. I glanced around the tree and really wished I hadn't.

"You look pale, what is it?" Tommy asked.

"Manticore." A manticore is a large red lion, with bat wings and a large scorpion-like tail, which it uses to shoot venomous spines that, as I knew far too well, can quickly paralyze and render its victim unconscious. Its mouth is like that of a shark, with several rows of razor-sharp teeth. It eats every part of its prey, including bones and clothes.

"Are you fucking kidding me?" Tommy glanced around his tree, and narrowly missed having several venomous spines hit his face. "Okay, our odds of survival just took a drastic spin down the shitter."

"You want the manticore or the spider-beast?" I asked.

"I want to have never decided to come with you. I'll take the big, ugly lion."

"I'm going to enjoy feasting on you, wolf," the manticore said, its voice sounding almost musical.

"They can talk?" Tommy said.

"This your first one?" I asked.

He nodded. "You?"

"Third."

"How'd you kill the others?"

"Luck. Just avoid the tail and claws and mouth, and you'll be fine."

"That's the shittiest pep-talk anyone has ever given. I'm regretting my choice in becoming your best friend."

"Too late now," I said with a smile. I spun to the side of the tree and threw a ball of fire at the pair of monsters. They both easily moved aside, but it gave Tommy the opening he needed to sprint around the tree and barrel into the manticore's ribs at full speed, taking it off its feet and smashing it into the nearest tree trunk. The manticore screamed in pain, and Tommy narrowly avoided becoming skewered by its tail.

"You have more important things than your friend," the jorōgumo told me. "I'm glad to see you remembered me."

Jorōgumo are half spider, half human. The woman was naked from stomach to neck. Her face had two dark mandibles that had torn through the skin around her jaw, one on either side, and two long fangs protruded from the top of her mouth. Her dark abdomen was now that of a spider, with six dark legs, each one tipped with a sharp claw. Her belly was almost touching the ground, she was getting ready to attack.

"Can't really forget," I said. "Although I wish I hadn't shown you mercy and let you live."

"Mercy?" she screamed. "You murdered my family, you tore me apart."

"You were trying to eat me," I pointed out. "And what in the world makes you think you can win this time?"

"Experience," she said and spat at me.

I dodged the venom, which bubbled and sizzled as it hit the tree trunk behind me. I blasted her legs with air magic. She staggered to one side and spat again, this time turning at the last second to send out a stream of her web, which caught me in the leg, tearing at my jeans and stopping my momentum solid.

She dragged the web back, dumping me on the wet woodland floor. I swiped at the web with another fire blade, cutting through it, but two more strands hit my arm, pinning me once again.

"I know all about your fire and air magic, Nate. You almost burned me to death once, remember?" More web wrapped around my hand. She pulled it tight and I felt the web slice into my flesh.

I spun on the ground, cutting through the webbing once again and scrambled back to my feet. I burned the web off, noticing the tiny hooks that covered it.

"Took me a long time to perfect that," she said. "Webbing that cuts people who try to escape. The more you struggle, the more it bleeds you." She smiled as the manticore charged at me.

I dodged aside, my hand only just evading the deadly jaws of the animal, and rolled along the ground, throwing a torrent of air at it and driving it back toward the jorōgumo, who jumped up into the trees above.

"You okay?" Tommy asked. He was bleeding from a cut on his chest, but appeared to be otherwise unhurt.

"Grand, thanks. You?"

"Bastard will not go down. It's like punching a wall. I tear chunks out of it and it just wants to keep fighting."

As if on cue the manticore shook its massive head and roared, fixing his glare back on Tommy and me. "Get ready," I whispered.

"For what?" Tommy asked.

"You'll see." I gathered my magic inside of me, the glyphs on my arms brightening as a sphere of fire magic began to rotate in my palm. It moved faster and faster until it was a blur. "Come get some," I told the manticore, who roared again and charged us.

I stood my ground, feeding more and more power into the sphere. The manticore threw spines and charged at me. It was the opening I was waiting for. Just before the monster was almost on top of me I plunged the sphere into its head. And released the magic. The flames all but consumed the beast, tearing into the flesh and muscle that surrounded its skull.

"Now," I shouted.

Tommy ran past me at the manticore, tearing out its throat a second later as the beast struggled to cope with the flames that were both blinding it and causing it considerable pain.

A web struck my back and I was pulled from my feet, back to the ground. Tommy was winning against the manticore, and had only attention for the fight in front of him as the jorōgumo landed on top of me, her massive leg pinning my arms to the ground. She let her venom drip onto the ground next to my arm. "What can you do now, Nate? There's nothing you can do that I won't come back from. I will feast on your dying body, and I will do it slowly so that you can understand the pain I went through."

Web began to cover my legs and in moments it had reached my knees. I created a blade of fire on my hand.

"Go ahead," she teased. "See what happens when you cut into my flesh now. The venom is all through my body. Cutting me will just spill it across you. It'll kill you even quicker."

I removed the blade and merged the fire and air glyphs. The sky grew immediately darker, and the sound of thunder exploded in the skies above us.

"Even the heavens want you dead," she said with a chuckle.

I concentrated on my breathing and moved my hands so that one was pointed toward the jorōgumo and the other straight up.

"Any final comments?"

"This is going to hurt like crazy."

She opened her mouth. "Yes, yes it is."

The lightning exploded high above us, giant red and purple streaks across the sky. One of them shot down toward my outstretched hand, and in an instant it traveled down through my body, where it mixed with my magic, and then out through my other hand. Right into the jorōgumo.

I hadn't used this type of attack since I'd fought Cronus, and only used it now in a desperate act. Cronus had survived that attack. The jorōgumo wouldn't. The force of the blast flung her against a nearby tree, which vaporized when the magic hit it, along with several feet of the land that surrounded it. Earth was flung up all around, and by the time the deafening noise of the thunder above had died down there was nothing but a smoldering crater where the jorōgumo had once been. Pain exploded through my body. The lightning in Albion was considerably more potent, and I hadn't been ready to absorb it. The fingers on my hand where the lightning had entered were broken and deformed, the skin cracked open, the wounds cauterized.

Tommy was by me in an instant. He looked at my hand. "Shit, Nate."

"Ouch, pain, ouch," I said with a forced smile. "Manticore dead?"

"Tearing its head off kills it, yes?"

I nodded.

"Very dead. How about the spider queen?"

"Over there."

Tommy walked over and dropped down several feet to the bottom of the crater. "Shit, Nate," he repeated when he reappeared. "There's not really a body to find. Lots of bits, though. We need to get you to a hospital." He winced.

"What's wrong?" I asked the pain in my hand forgotten.

"My back is cut up pretty good. That thing had some damn sharp claws. Also it bit me on the leg. I don't think I'll be doing much fighting against Kay, sorry."

"We need to stop him."

"In your current predicament, do you think you can use magic to do it?"

I tried to move my fingers and roared in pain. "No. Not so much. I don't need my hands to use magic, but without one of them, I'd be pretty hampered. Not sure how long I could keep it up."

"Then we're both hurt and need help." Tommy glanced down the nearby cave entrance. "Let's get you looked at."

"If there's a realm gate down there, Kay could already be gone."

"Then we're not in any hurry. Besides, Enfield is still out there. Elaine is in danger, and you need to heal. Both of those things need to be dealt with more urgently than Kay."

"And you're hurt."

"Yeah, but I'm more capable of dealing with pain than you are."

I raised an eyebrow. "Yes, that must be it." I lay back on the dirt. "We need to find that son-of-a-bitch."

"We'll find Kay, and he'll get his, just not right now. Now let's go tell everyone how I saved your life and fought both the manticore and jorōgumo single-handed, while you cried like a baby. They'll knight me for this."

I laughed, which caused my hand to hurt, which in turn caused me to swear at Tommy. "Brave Tommy of Kissmyass."

"That's Sir Tommy, knave."

I laughed again. It hurt again. I hate my best friend.

CHAPTER 

Tommy and I managed to find a car that we could pile into, and took a moment to breathe while it ferried us to the palace. Tommy's clothes were ruined, so he was still in werebeast form when the car stopped and I opened the door.

There were dozens of people littered around the palace; most appeared to belong to the palace guard, although there were a lot of agents from all three branches of Avalon agencies that were creating a cordon to stop people from gaining entry to the building. Me in my blood-stained, torn clothing and Tommy with his . . . less than timid appearance gained the attention of the heavily armed men and women very quickly.

When people with guns and swords—not to mention the obvious growls and crackles of energy from those who didn't need guns and swords—sounded out, we did as we were told and lay down flat on the ground with our hands behind our backs. It was easier for us to do as we were told and explain later than to get into a fight and piss everyone off. Considering my substantial talent for the latter, sometimes I have to fight my overwhelming urge to not do as I'm told.

Once they realized who we were, and decided we weren't a threat—a difficult thing to accomplish when one of you is just a mass of teeth, claws, and muscle—we were allowed into the palace, where some spare clothing was given to Tommy. He wandered off to speak to some people, while I jogged through to the main chamber, where Elaine sat at her place within the council, her elbows on her desk and the palms of her hands over her eyes. Several people bustled around her.

"How's it going?" I shouted over the din of a dozen people all talking at once.

The room fell silent and Elaine glanced up at me. She looked tired, but still managed to smile. "I hear Kay is behind this."

"Looks that way."

There were several hushed whispers throughout the chamber.

"I'd like a moment alone with Nathan," Elaine said without it ever sounding like it was a request.

Once we were alone she descended the stairs and hugged me. "I'm glad you're safe."

"Me too. Kay escaped. Enfield is his Faceless, he's coming for you."

"Why would Kay do this? Why would he try to kill me?"

"He wants you out of the picture, to make Avalon feared throughout all the realms. He thinks that's best for when his brother awakens. Personally, I think someone he works for has fed him a bunch of shit. Kay was never the type to have enough patience for the long game. I'm surprised you gave him the job you did."

"I didn't. Merlin put him forward and the council voted for him. Barely. I'd rather have had Vlad the Impaler as head of the organization. It's why I agreed with Hades to allow Lucie to take the job as assistant director."

My pause was enough for her to realize she'd mentioned something she shouldn't have. "Ah, I assumed you knew that.

Hades and Lucie came to me just after the Second World War. They wanted Kay kept an eye on. Hades had his doubts about the man, and Lucie was looking for a job within Avalon. It worked well, she's excellent. She's also on her way here with Olivia. I want to talk to them about their plan to capture this Enfield. And yes, I said capture. We have questions for him."

"I can't see him being the answering type."

"Do you believe he can get to me?"

"Anyone can get to anyone with enough patience, talent, and luck. He's got the first two. He worked as a Faceless for Kay for over a century, he must have patience in abundance."

"I'll have to have it petitioned for Kay to be excommunicated from Avalon. I can't have him running around out there arranging plans to try and kill me, or anyone else for that matter."

"We'll find him."

"Yes, we will," Olivia said as she walked over to where Elaine and I stood. Lucie and Tommy flanked her, along with several guards, who stood back and kept their distance. Fiona, using a walking stick, and Alan took the rear.

I walked over to Fiona and hugged her. "I'm glad you're okay," I whispered. "You had a lot of people worried."

"I'm fine," she said. "Well, I'm on the mend, which is pretty much the same thing."

"I'm good too, thanks," Alan interrupted, holding up the cast on his broken arm for emphasis. "Got beat up by a psychopath, and I've got to wear this for a few days but other than that, just dandy." He looked serious, but kept glancing at Fiona, his hand locked tightly in hers.

Fiona rolled her eyes. "He's milking it."

"Do you have a plan?" Elaine asked, interrupting us.

"We're going to use you as bait," Lucie told her. She unrolled a map, spreading it over the circular table that Elaine and I had been standing in front of. "We want to take you to the east of here, as if leaving the city."

"That's by that woodland where we were attacked when I first arrived," I said.

"Those woods are perfect cover for someone to hide. We've put enough people in them to make it look like we're taking it seriously, but leaving enough gaps for someone with Enfield's talents to exploit the weaknesses we've created."

"Why would Enfield go there?" Elaine asked.

Fiona stepped forward.

"It's good to see you up and about," Elaine said with genuine warmth.

"Thank you, ma'am. Kay and that spider woman were the ones who attacked me in my home. But Enfield was the one who searched through my head for information on Felix. It took him a while, but he found it. The funny thing about mind magic is that if you remain locked to another person as you search through their memories for a great length of time, the route goes both ways. I saw Enfield and Kay discussing your murder; I saw that he planned to do it away from the palace. He knew that if word ever got out that you'd be inundated with security. He also knows your escape plan. Go east, out of Camelot to the secure compound next to the river."

Elaine was shocked. "No one is meant to know that. Only my security and guards know it."

"My guess is, you have a leak in your guards," Alan said. "A pretty big one."

We all looked to Elaine and waited for her to speak, but she remained quiet for several seconds, as her expression hardened. She didn't like to lose her temper in front of so many people, but she was pretty close to doing so. If she found Kay before her people did, I didn't pity what she'd do to him.

"Let's say that Enfield takes the bait," Elaine theorized, her voice steady and soft. "What's to say that someone else isn't going to pull the trigger, what if Enfield is what we're meant to be looking at while someone else slips a dagger in my ribs?"

"Nothing," Olivia said, inspiring zero amounts of confidence. "Although the fact that we'll have people with you at all times, people we trust, including us, should go some way to ease those concerns."

"I want Nate there too," Elaine said.

"Like you could keep me away," I said and flexed my almost healed fingers. I'd used a portion of Felix's soul to heal myself. My hand was going to be sore for a while, but at least the broken bones had set.

"How long before we're ready to go?" Elaine asked.

"Our people are working on it," Lucie told everyone. "We need to ensure that Enfield has enough time to get there. It's close to residential homes and hotels, we don't want any engagement to spill over." She looked at me. "No big magical bursts. I don't want any innocent people to get hurt."

"And what about whoever else is working for Enfield and Kay?" I asked. "What if they start opening fire on whoever is nearby?"

"Do you have a way to find out who is loyal and who isn't?" Olivia asked. "A quick way, I mean."

"Give me a list of names," I told everyone. "I have Felix's memories in my head. Most are jumbled up still, but I recognize names of Reavers. That should narrow it down."

"The SOA are still stood down," Lucie said. "Several members are unaccounted for, they appear to have vanished into the realm, or left it altogether."

"Hendricks said that everyone on the list Bushy gave is dead."

Lucie nodded. "Someone killed them all. There were another four not on the list there too. It looks like they weren't expecting an attack. It was at an outpost about twenty miles north of the city."

"Enfield?"

"I don't know, but when we find him, I plan on asking." Lucie's words were said with absolute certainty. There was no doubt in her mind that she'd be having that conversation with Enfield. She left the chambers, returning a few minutes later with a memory stick and a laptop, while everyone was in the middle of discussing how Enfield was going to be subdued.

"Kill him," Alan said.

"I've explained," Elaine said, rather tersely. "We need him alive."

"Maim him then. He hurt Fiona; I want him to feel some pain for that."

"Oh, he'll feel pain," Elaine assured him. "But we can't kill him. We need him in one piece."

Lucie placed the laptop in front of me and opened the lid. "There are a lot of names here, a thousand throughout all of Avalon. I've narrowed it down to just those SOA agents working within Camelot itself, and exported the data to a spreadsheet. Are you sure that no one outside of the SOA is involved?"

I searched through Felix's memories. "Only the SOA was corrupted. And only those who worked within branches that Kay created."

Lucie changed a few things in the spreadsheet. "That narrows it down to a few hundred."

"Give me a few minutes then." I took the laptop and walked off to Elaine's chair before taking a seat and reading through the list of names. I highlighted each one when I recognized it. Out of the three hundred and nineteen names on the list, seventy-six were Reavers.

"Out of every chair here, you pick mine," Elaine said with a chuckle. "If Merlin saw you there, he'd have had an aneurism."

I told them all how many names were in my head.

"That's less than I was expecting," Lucie said.

"Are there names in your head that aren't on the list?" Olivia asked.

"I wrote them all down in the next tab. There's another fourteen."

Olivia and Lucie scanned the names before passing the laptop to Fiona and Elaine.

"I know some of these people," Fiona said. "I'm friends with some of them. Are you sure?"

"Some people might have the same name, so they need to be gone through and eliminated, but everyone on that list is a name that Felix discovered were working with the Reavers."

"I want everyone on this list arrested and taken in for questioning," Elaine told Olivia. "You okay to oversee that?"

"The SOA won't like LOA agents arresting people," Alan said, verbalizing what everyone else was probably thinking.

"Don't care. Olivia, I know you're in charge of the investigation into what happened, but as of right now, you're also on point for the arrest and interrogation of these people. This will be a permanent rank increase, although your new job title can wait. Assemble people you trust and hunt them down. I'll have your new rank cleared with the council . . . somehow, but I'm enacting emergency rules to have you outrank every member of the SOA, including the director." She turned to Lucie. "Kay did us a favor by being a traitor, it means that there's a job opening that needs to be filled. You are, as of now, the director of the SOA. You will give Olivia every single assistance in rooting out the corruption that Kay started. Officially, Olivia will answer to me and the council members I select to oversee this operation. Unofficially, I trust you both will work well together."

"Yes, Elaine," Olivia said with a bow. "I'll get to work on it."

"Of course," Lucie said with a smile. I got the feeling that anyone trying to put one over on the Lucie and Olivia team was going to have a very bad time of things.

"Good. Lucie, let's get this plan for me to be a giant bullseye in motion. Nate, you're with me, mostly so I can keep an eye on you. Alan and Fiona, please accept my apologies that I'm leaving. When I return, I'd like to talk to you both about how you're doing."

As we were leaving, Alan grabbed my arm. "When you get him, give the bastard a kick from me."

"I think he's going to be getting a lot of those in the coming weeks."

"And he will deserve all of them."

I glanced over at Fiona, who was reading the list of names on the laptop. "Is she okay?"

"I think so. She's exhausted, but refused to stay in bed. And she's jumpy. She didn't expect Kay to attack her in her . . . *in our home*. I'm full of barely controlled rage, the only reason I'm not out there hunting this cunt down is because she needs me more."

"She'll be okay," I said. "And once this is over, she'll never have to worry about Kay or the Reavers again."

"We said that before, remember?" Alan said. "When we took the Reavers to pieces? When Elaine had them hunted down and arrested or executed. You remember that, yes? What's so different?"

"We didn't have Lucie and Olivia doing it. I don't think they're going to be so lax."

"You have a lot of faith in your friends."

I glanced at Alan and then back to Fiona. "That's because my friends are worth having faith in."

"Where's Remy?" I asked Lucie as we left the palace.

"Hospital. He took a bit of a whack from that explosion, so we're keeping an eye on him. He should be fine though."

"And Kelly."

"Interrogation."

I left the conversation there as we were joined outside by Tommy and about a dozen agents, none of whom I'd met before. But I was pretty confident that if Olivia or Lucie had allowed them to take part in the mission they'd been thoroughly vetted. Both of them had been betrayed by people they trusted: Olivia by Reid a few years ago, and Lucie by Kay and a large number of SOA agents.

"Nate, you got a second?" Fiona called from behind me.

I nodded and walked over. "What's up?"

Fiona looked weak, and tired. But determined too. "When this is all over," she said with a pause. I could hear the pain in her voice as she spoke, "you and I need to talk. I was looking into someone before I got attacked. Nothing to do with the Reavers . . . well I hope not, but it is something you have to know about. I can't tell you now, too much going on, but before you leave Albion, promise you'll come see me."

"Of course," I said, somewhat taken aback by the concern in Fiona's voice. "Everything good?"

She forced a smile. "Sure, it's just something you need to see. Good luck."

I watched her walk away and then turned back to the motorcade that had been arranged, pushing the thoughts of Fiona's words aside as I had another job to do. There were four black SUV-looking cars parked up outside the rear of the palace, each with thin red lights that went along the side of the bodywork. The lights pulsed slowly. I climbed into the car second from front, with Elaine right beside me. Lucie took the front car, with Tommy who'd decided to tag along.

"These are a bit different to the ones I normally see in Camelot," I told Elaine as I sat down on the comfortable leather seats.

"They're not on pre-set destinations. And they're only used by dignitaries. I've been told they're pretty much unstoppable short of an attack by a tank."

We were soon off, and I sat back watching out of the tinted window as the weather outside turned to heavy rain. Rain would make things more difficult for those tracking Enfield, but it might make it more difficult for him to launch an attack.

After a few minutes of driving, Elaine caught my attention. "Do you think he'll take the bait?"

"I hope so. He's too dangerous to just leave out there."

"I heard that he threatened you in front of the palace when you last saw me."

"Yeah, he wasn't too thrilled that I'd killed another Faceless." I still didn't have a clue who Reid's master was. Which meant I had more enemies out there. That in itself was hardly a new position to be in, but not knowing their identities gave me an uncomfortable itch between my shoulder blades. It was not a fun feeling.

"Maybe the Faceless need to change. Too many are loyal to bad people."

"Best of luck with that. I know people like yourself and Hades don't like them, but far too many do. They won't give them up willingly. Avalon was born out of an ideal, but over time that ideal has been corrupted and twisted so that those in power maintain their status quo, and to hell with anyone else. The few who do good, yourself included, are swamped by the shit from everyone else, creating a system that can work, but doesn't always do what's best for everyone. Avalon is too entrenched in its own self-absorbed existence to be able to change now. Not without massive, sweeping reforms, the kind that Merlin and his friends will never allow, let alone those who have a vested interest in keeping everything as it currently is."

"That's a very depressing view of our system."

"It probably is," I agreed. "But it's about as honest a one as I can give." I knew there was still good in Avalon. I knew there were still people who wanted what was best for people, but even so I still believed it was more corrupt than it had ever been in the past. I still wanted nothing to do with it. That sort of corruption spreads and you need a special sort of person to touch it and not be tainted. I wasn't convinced I was one of those people.

"I still believe that we can do a lot of good."

"I know. That's why I admire what you do. But as I've told you before, there are not enough people who believe as you do. Too many want to use Avalon for their own aims."

"You've become cynical in your old age."

I laughed. "Possibly. Or more of a realist. Either way it's a pretty depressing outlook."

"We're reaching the woods," one of the other agents in the car told everyone. "Be ready."

The cars continued to roll past the wood and the park where I'd fought a group of Reavers alongside my friends only a few days ago. A few minutes later we passed the field without incident.

"I guess Enfield decided not to risk it," Elaine said. "Well, we'll get to the safe house and then I'll make sure he's tracked down."

"How long is it from here to there?" I asked.

"About half hour until we're outside Camelot, another fifteen until the safe house," one of the agents said. "Sit back and relax. It's all open country from here on. He'd be insane to attack now."

I did wonder whether I should point out that I didn't think sanity was something that Enfield had in abundance, but decided not to break the slight relief that there hadn't been an attack.

We left the city without incident, and large buildings populated by pieces of greenery changed to expansive plains and woodland, with the occasional outpost dotting the landscape.

"We're just coming up to the compound," another agent said and ten seconds later all hell broke loose.

Explosions sounded from under the car in front of us, and I saw it stagger to a halt. The same happened to us, and as I turned to look out of the rear window, I saw the same thing happening there too. It took all of five seconds for the entire motorcade to cease moving and create five very large targets.

There was a lot of shouting soon after, as agents exited the vehicles, demanding that Elaine stay inside as it was far too dangerous for her to be out and about. I wondered if telling them that Elaine was an accomplished sorcerer who would give Merlin a run for his money would change their minds, but it's best not to interrupt agents when they're doing their job.

I pushed open the door beside me.

"Nate, get back in the car," Lucie shouted from outside.

I promptly ignored her and closed the door before getting on my knees and glancing under the car. The tires had all been blown out, along with a lot of electrical equipment that was usually attached to the underside of the car. The metal had been peeled back by one explosion and then a second had destroyed the car's organs. Small craters marked the earth.

I stood back up and brushed myself down. "Mines," I said to no one in particular.

I glanced around and couldn't see anything that would trigger concern. The sturdy front gate of the safe house was a thirty-second walk from the motorcade. There was no way Enfield could get to Elaine once she was in there. Runes adorned pretty much every surface, and I was certain that Kay wouldn't order Enfield to use a nuclear weapon to get inside. Not much point in a murderous takeover if you've turned the place into a radioactive wasteland.

The agents appeared to be as confused as I was. Lucie walked over to me. "As you're not doing as you're told, do you at least see something helpful?"

"I don't get this as a plan. Stop the cars just outside of one of the safest places in Albion. Doesn't make much sense."

We turned toward the sound of the gate's motors groaning to life, and watched as the massive black structure slowly moved aside, giving free access to the courtyard just beyond. Enfield stepped around the corner, and every single agent and guard was suddenly very ready for a fight. Weapons, both magical and otherwise, were trained at Enfield as he stepped out of the compound and raised his hands.

"Don't you fucking move," Lucie shouted, her sidearm quickly out of its holster as she walked toward him.

Enfield raised his hands. "I'm not moving anywhere. But I'd stay where you are, if I were you."

Lucie stopped walking.

"Smart girl," Enfield said, managing to use as much of a patronizing tone as he could probably manage. He shrugged out of his coat, letting it fall to the ground before opening one of his hands to show a phone in his hand. "Those mines that stopped your cars, they aren't really the biggest problem you have."

Panic flashed in the eyes of some of the agents.

"Don't worry," Enfield said; clearly he'd noticed it too. "You're all safe. But you see, this phone here, it links to a massive number of bombs I've planted all around the hospital."

He let everyone have a moment to take that in.

"I know what you're thinking," he said finally. "Shoot me in the arm, and disarm the bomb." He used his free hand to pull back the sleeve of his jumper. There were runes carved into his flesh, the blood still looked fresh.

"Blood magic," I said.

"Give that man a cookie," Enfield said with a chuckle. "The phone number is already programmed; these runes are all that's stopping this technology from sending that call. If anything happens to them, the phone transmits. And then you have a lot more bodies to deal with."

"What do you want?" Lucie asked.

"To talk to Elaine."

"So you can kill her? I don't think so."

"I don't want her dead," Enfield said. "That was Kay's plan."

"You're his Faceless," I pointed out.

"Not even a little bit. Oh, I see where the confusion came from, what with me dressing like it. Well, that was just for show. You see a certain Nate Garrett killed Kay's last Faceless. You remember Reid, yes?"

I nodded. "He worked for Kay? What about the person I spoke to on the phone when Reid was dying, was that you?"

"No, just an SOA agent who wanted very badly to impress Kay. He was dead about ten seconds after the call was ended. I buried him not too far from here, actually. I've had a key to this place for years. It helps that Kay was one of the people who helped design it. I used to use this place as a dumping ground for those who annoyed me. There are a few bodies around here."

"So, what do you want then?" Lucie asked, ignoring his boast. There would be a time for questions later. Hopefully.

"I've already told you. I want to talk to Elaine. So, if you could run along, I'll give you a few seconds to get it sorted."

Lucie walked past me and opened the door to Elaine's car. I didn't hear the conversation that followed, but Elaine was soon beside me, radiating anger.

"What do you want?" she asked.

"Kay wants you dead," Enfield told her. "You probably know this. I really don't care one way or another about the status of your breathing. I don't work for Kay; if anything he works for me. I let him run with this stupid notion of using a bunch of untrained idiots to re-create the Reavers, but it was always doomed to fail. No, you see, you being alive is neither here nor there. The people I work for don't consider you a threat; if they did they'd have executed you years ago. But I knew that if I just came to you in Camelot then some idiot who supported Kay would assume I was being a traitor and try to kill me. I can't really have that."

Elaine looked surprised. "And you think I won't kill you?"

"Oh you will, but not until you've questioned me."

"Do you work for Merlin?" I asked.

"Good question, Mister Garrett. No, I do not. Never have. Of course I worked with the Reavers, but that was more to extend other people's plans rather than to help Merlin. I don't want him dead or anything, but I'm not going to be jumping in front of a bullet for him either."

"So whom do you work for?"

"My liege." He smiled.

Lucie and I shared a look of concern. "That's what the Vanguard who attacked Hades's compound said last year," she said. "They said they were doing it for their liege."

"Lots of dots connecting are there?" Enfield asked. "I can't actually tell you about any of the people I work for. Physically can't. But they're coming. And the person who leads that group has been waiting for such a long time for their revenge. They're going to change the world."

"So you can't tell us anything, you can't give us a single shred of information? What use are you?" I asked.

"Oh, I'm sorry, I'm not going to give you a choice. You're going to keep me alive and take me back with you to Camelot."

"Why are we going to do that?" Elaine asked. "Because of the bombs?"

"Nope. They were just to get your attention. Just to make sure you play by the rules."

"What rules?" Elaine snapped, her temper beginning to show.

Enfield dropped to his knees. "I invoke the Accords."

CHAPTER 35

The hours that followed Enfield's surrender were somewhat surreal. He gave the location of every single one of the dozen bombs he'd planted in the hospital, although no one trusted him, and a telepath was brought in to see if he was lying. Unfortunately, the telepath also tried to gain information about whom Enfield worked for and the backlash knocked him out for several hours.

I decided to leave everyone to it and go for a walk around the gardens that sat at the rear of the palace. I found an empty bench beside a large pond and sat down, watching the fish come to the surface as if they expected me to throw them some food.

"I wondered where you'd gotten to," Tommy said as he sat beside me. "Elaine wants to talk to you."

"About Enfield, I assume."

"That's my guess. She told Olivia to find you, Olivia found me first. I know nothing more than that."

"This trip didn't exactly turn out how you'd expect, eh?"

"No, I can't lie; this wasn't what I had in mind."

"Any thoughts about postponing the naming ceremony? There are still people out there we haven't found."

Tommy's response was immediate. "Not a chance. Not only would Kasey tear a chunk out of anyone who suggested it. Neither

Olivia nor Elaine will allow anyone to stop a naming ceremony because of outside threats. It's going to be the single best-guarded ceremony in history."

That was good to know. "How is Kasey doing, anyway? I hope all of this hasn't put too much of a downer on her time here."

"She's more interested in her naming ceremony than the Reavers. Ellie is keeping her occupied. I'm due back there once I fetch you. We've scheduled it for tomorrow, by the way. It'll be here, at the palace. Noon. Don't be late."

"I'll be there," I promised. "Best not keep Elaine waiting; I'm sure she has bad news for me."

"You think Enfield wants to fight you, don't you?"

"I imagine so."

The Accords were designed centuries ago to stop wars between disputing groups. Instead of armies killing one another, the Accords provide for one-on-one fights where the person invoking the Accords gets to pick their opponent, while the opponent gets to pick the stipulations, such as weapons allowed, or when the fight will stop. The only thing that's constant is that there's no magic or special abilities allowed, and if anyone interferes then the group cheating is immediately declared the loser and the winning group gets to decide their fate.

Once declared, the Accords have to be seen through to the end. The last person who had used them against me had died from a gunshot wound to the throat a few seconds later. I don't think I'd be able to get away with such an act in Camelot though. Not without forfeiting my own life in the process.

"I don't understand why he would want to use the Accords anyway," Tommy said as we walked toward the palace entrance. "I mean, I know whoever uses it has to have a trial by combat and everything, but what does he think is going to happen if he wins? They're not just going to let him go. He's playing a game here."

"Of course he is, but I'm not sure they have a choice. I guess we'll find out."

We found Elaine inside the chambers sitting alone at her desk. "Tommy, can you leave Nate and me alone?" she asked.

Tommy patted me on the shoulder. "Best of luck."

"I don't think he completely trusts me," Elaine said when we were alone.

"He worked for Avalon for a long time. I think he's just cautious about you. It took a long time for you to get to the position you're in, a long time when Merlin wasn't exactly running things to any great degree. I think he hopes you don't go the same way."

"And he doesn't know why I asked for you. His loyalty is obvious."

"It goes both ways," I assured her.

"You inspire loyalty in a lot of people. Lucie, Olivia, Alan, Tommy, all of them would fight for you if need be, not to mention Hades and several members of his family."

"I *am* a wonderful person."

Elaine laughed. "Do you know why you're here?"

"Enfield wants to fight me as part of the Accords?"

Elaine walked toward me. "Nope. Not you."

That was a bit of a surprise. "Who then?"

"Fiona."

That was an even bigger surprise. "What? That's insane. For a start she's injured. She can't do anything until she's healed. That could take days or weeks."

"Enfield has said he'll wait until she's recovered."

"I know Fiona can take care of herself, but even if she were fully fit, Enfield *will* kill her. No matter the stipulations for winning, he'll make sure she dies. When I fought him in 1888, he was formidable. Fiona stands no chance of defeating him."

"We've agreed that it will be until someone submits or is rendered unconscious, but I don't think Enfield will let her quit easily. In fact, that's exactly what Alan and Fiona said. She also couldn't come up with a way to avoid it. If Fiona forfeits the fight, then Enfield is automatically declared the winner."

"What does he want for winning?"

"You."

"Well, that's shit. Surely there's something in the Accords that means Enfield can't ask for the death of his enemy as a reward?"

"And that's very true. But he doesn't want your death, he wants you to be the one to walk him through Camelot to the realm gate and then take him to a place of his choosing. A place he won't reveal until he's out of this realm."

"So it's a trap. This whole thing is a trap so he can get me somewhere of his choosing and kill me?"

"That's my summation, yes. He, at best, badly hurts Fiona, devastating Alan, her friends, and hurting Avalon. After that, he gets you, one of Fiona's friends, to put aside your anger and march him out of the realm. And you can't kill him until you've reached your destination. By which point, I assume there will be an army waiting for you."

"So, how do we stop this from happening? Any chance we can just kill him?"

"No, if we go around killing people who cite the Accords that's going to lead to a dangerous precedent. If Enfield had given a substitute for him to fight, then we could have substituted anyone else, but the fact that he chose Fiona doesn't give us a lot of leeway."

I wracked my brain for an answer, and then I had that tiny sliver of an idea, the kind that pops into your head and then vanishes just as you begin to grasp it, but you know it was there.

"How much do you trust me?" I asked Elaine.

"Like you were my own son," she told me without pausing.

"Can you get Fiona and Lucie in here? Probably Alan too since I doubt he'll be leaving her side anytime soon."

"You've got a plan?"

"Yeah, but I don't think anyone is going to like it."

"Does anyone die? And are the rules of Avalon broken?"

"Maybe and I don't think so, in that order."

Elaine raised an eyebrow in question, but left the chambers to fetch the people I'd asked to see. They all returned, with Olivia and Tommy in tow, a few minutes later.

"So what's your plan?" Alan asked.

"Fiona. You can't take Enfield. He will kill you," I said. "You're injured and only came out of a coma a few hours ago. Frankly, I'm amazed you're walking at all. I have two plans. The first is . . . Fiona, can you cast an illusion that will make me look like you?"

"No, that's not possible. Certainly not well enough to keep you looking like me for an entire fight."

"Right, plan two. I need you to forfeit." And then I told everyone my plan.

Everyone shouted at once, mostly at me, mostly with swearing and calling into question my mental acuities. I believe the words dumbass and fuckwit were used on more than one occasion.

"I'm not planning on getting killed," I assured everyone. "But this is the only way to keep me and Fiona alive."

"Does it go against the Accords?" I asked.

Lucie, Olivia, and Elaine walked off to speak to one another. They weren't gone long. "No," Olivia said. "It's a hell of a gray area though. You can't just spring this on him once he's accepted Fiona's forfeit. You'll need to be out of the arena, but somewhere open with few chances for his escape."

I thought about the best location. "The field we drove past, the one where we were attacked. Have your people in the woods. I'll tell Enfield there. He might try to run. I guess we'll see."

"You sure you want to do this?" Elaine asked. "He won't take it well."

"I'm not going to let him get away with killing Fiona, or anyone else. This is going to end in Camelot, today."

"We'll make the preparations," Elaine said. "I suggest you do the same."

The place where all Accord disputes are settled is called the arena. Not the most original of names, I'll grant you, but it does exactly what it says on the arch leading to it. The arena is a large, oval pit, which is covered half in grass and half wooden floor. Seats are all around the arena much like a Roman amphitheater, although on a much smaller scale. The arena seats about five hundred people, although as I walked under the arch and down to the front row, I noticed it was full of members of the council, including a few very powerful figures within Avalon's world. Whether they were supporting Fiona or Enfield, it was hard to tell.

Elaine stood in the middle of the oval and raised her hands for silence. Runes had been carved into the wooden floor of the structure so that those in the back of the arena could hear without problems.

"Tonight a dispute will be settled," Elaine started. "Enfield has requested Fiona as his opponent."

Both contestants were already in the oval. They looked at one another and then nodded to Elaine.

"Before we start, you will both tell us what you wish to have as your prize if you win." She pointed to Enfield first.

"Nathan Garrett will escort me from this city, out of the realm, to a place of my choosing."

"And Fiona."

"You tell us where Kay is."

Enfield smiled. "Deal."

"This fight will be until one can no longer compete through being rendered unconscious or submits. Do either of you have anything else to say?"

Fiona nodded. "I forfeit."

The crowd exploded with noise; most appeared to be unimpressed with the verdict. Enfield smiled; in fact he beamed, before looking at me and winking.

I made my way to the oval and the crowd grew quiet again.

"It is Fiona's right to forfeit," Elaine said.

"You did the right thing," Enfield said. "I really didn't bear you any ill will." He turned toward me. "I guess you're mine now."

"That's what people tell me," I said.

"We're leaving," he said to Elaine.

Elaine stood between him and me.

"Move aside, Lady Elaine. You're impeding Avalon's own law."

She stepped aside and Enfield completed his journey toward me, stopping a foot away. "I know you want to kill me, Nathan. I get that. But you can't, not without going against Avalon law."

I was aware that his words had traveled to everyone in the arena.

"We should leave," I said softly. "Now."

"Don't want me to revel in my victory?" Enfield laughed, and I had to remember not to attack him.

"I'll be coming with you," Elaine said, and the faintest flicker of anger shone on Enfield's face. "It'll be easier for me to explain to Avalon agents what you're doing. It will ensure no one tries to stop you."

"You can't actually pull anything, so that's fine with me," he told her, his tone full of snide. "Can't possibly go against Avalon law, now can we?"

It wasn't long until we set off out of the Arena, with Elaine walking a few meters in front of us, telling guards and anyone else who tried to interfere that it was fine. By the time we went back to the palace—nothing more than a five-minute walk—we'd been stopped half a dozen times.

"We'd be best walking around to the east and then double back when we're closer," I said. "Otherwise we're going to be stopped every few seconds."

"And that bothers you?" Enfield asked.

"If you die, it falls to Elaine and her people. I couldn't give two shits what happens to you, but I care about her."

Enfield sighed. "Fine, we'll do it your way. No matter to me."

As we reached the park, a fairly large crowd had decided to join us, mostly consisting of those who had been deprived of a real contest at the arena, along with guards, agents, and a general mix of people who simply wondered what the hell was going on.

"You know, I've got some stories to tell you," Enfield said. "Would you like to hear them?"

"Do I have a choice?"

"Do you remember Montana? The first time you met Sky?"

"Of course."

"You weren't meant to meet her. I jumped her before she could get to that ranch. You were meant to be long gone before she arrived, but obviously you found that body and the rest is history."

I stopped walking. "Are you telling me you were involved in Montana, with the lich?" The lich in question had taken over a small town; its inhabitants believed that it was there to help make them rich and powerful. He'd lied to them all. And I'd made sure they'd all been punished for their crimes.

"Someone got that book to the man who would use it to become the lich; that someone was me."

The book was a step-by-step guide for a sorcerer to turn themselves into one of the most terrifying monsters I'd ever encountered. One that had left me for dead.

"People died," I said, keeping my anger in check.

"My masters wanted it done, so I did it. I believe it was a test to see how liches perform. Unfortunately, after that disaster and then the death of another lich only a few years ago, one you personally killed, it was decided the experiment was over. Shame really."

I didn't bother telling him that it was Olivia who'd killed the lich in the end. "Anything else?"

"Oh, Simon Olson in Maine. Remember him? Do you remember that he had visitors? That someone was checking up on his progress to find some people we needed? Guess who?"

"You were there too?" I kept the shock out of my voice, not wanting to give him the satisfaction of seeing me even slightly flustered.

"I've been lots of places. Simon was meant to find someone who could create his own guardians. We could have marched into any realm we felt like with guardians we could create ourselves. You managed to fuck all of that up too. Do you see why my masters don't like you? You're always in the wrong place at the wrong time. It's infuriating."

I walked off to a nearby steep bank and glanced down at the stream below.

Enfield turned to me. "You really want to show all of these people that you won't follow through with the law?"

"Oh, I'm following the law," I explained.

"This isn't taking me out of the realm."

"No, I'm not going to be doing that."

"He dares to defy your laws." He proclaimed at the top of his voice.

"Explain, Nate," Elaine demanded. She had to be seen as having no part in all of this.

"I don't want to take him to the realm gate; in fact I refuse to do so."

"Do you have any reason why this is the case?" she asked.

"Because this piece of shit tried to have me killed, tried to have my friends killed, and I don't see why I should have to help him anymore."

"I demand retribution," Enfield said. "Someone bring me a blade and I'll take his head here and now."

Elaine removed a blade from the scabbard of a nearby Avalon guard, and passed it reluctantly to Enfield.

"On your knees," he said to me, pointing the tip of the sword to my heart.

I did as I was told.

"Do you have any final words, before I run you through?" he asked.

"Nate, just take him to the gate," Elaine pleaded.

"Fuck you, Enfield," I said.

"No, I don't think so."

"I invoke the Accords," I shouted. "And I challenge Enfield to fight."

CHAPTER 36

To say that Enfield was unhappy would downplay his complete tantrum that followed my invocation of the Accords. He had to be wrestled to the ground and his sword removed, while I sat there looking as smug as I possibly could.

"You can't do this," Enfield said for the hundredth time.

"Actually, that was my concern too," I told him. We were sitting opposite one another in the park, while the various Avalon representatives who'd followed us now argued amongst themselves about whatever politicians argue about. Everything, and nothing, I assumed.

"You see, I too was worried that it went against Accord law, but it doesn't."

"Of course it does, you smug prick," Enfield snapped. "You can't use the Accords on me when I just used them."

"Actually, turns out I can. You see you challenged a member of Avalon, and specifically a member of the SOA. So your problem was with them. I'm not a member of any Avalon agency, and I don't work for Avalon in any capacity. I'm outside of that remit. So I could challenge you, because the original challenge couldn't be given to me to perform."

Enfield's face dropped.

"You thought you were so clever," I continued. "Turns out you shouldn't have picked a fight with an agent of Avalon. Maybe you should have picked Tommy, or even Alan, neither of those work for Avalon. But you didn't. And you're a stupid idiot for it."

"You're not going to get away with this."

"I already have. People like you think they know the law, but they don't really. You throw about the general idea because you think that'll scare people off, but you don't know shit. The Accords were only meant to be used in times of possible war. They weren't created for a criminal to use to get out of being arrested. I can't think of many criminals who'd want to do it. But because you picked Fiona, singled her out, you forced yourself to take the part of one organization fighting another. In this case, you picked a fight with Avalon. So, now I am picking a fight with you and your entire organization.

"The organization of people against you and your masters. It's not a catchy name, I'll admit."

"How many members do you have in this group?" he demanded. "Otherwise it's just you and then your declaration of the Accords is still illegal."

I stood up, and thankfully everyone fell silent. "How many people here want to join my organization against assholes like Enfield here?"

Alan, Tommy, and Fiona were the first three who took a step forward, followed by Lucie and Olivia.

"Ta very much," I said and sat back down. "Enough people for you?"

"I won't tell you anything," he declared.

"We already know you can't tell us anything of use. I don't care about that." I leaned forward and whispered, "I'm betting enough of these people work for the same group as you though. And I'd like to send them a message. So, congrats, you get to deliver it. Well, when I say deliver it, I mean I kick the shit out of you."

"You think you can take me?"

I smiled. "With a song and dance in my heart."

Enfield was mercifully quiet after that, until Elaine bid everyone for quiet. "The declaration of the Accords is legal. Nate will fight Enfield. However, Enfield gets to pick the stipulations."

"No magic," he said immediately.

"That is standard for all fights," Elaine pointed out.

"Yes, but I want us both wearing sorcerer's bands to ensure it."

There were murmurs of approval in the crowd, and Enfield couldn't have looked more pleased with himself if he'd discovered that he could, in fact, lick his own scrotum. "Let's see how you cope now, you piece of a shit."

I remained quiet, but was a little concerned to the point that I missed the rest of what Elaine was talking about.

"Do you agree?" she asked me.

"Eh?" I managed.

"Enfield has requested that the fight be here, now, and that there be no weapons allowed, save for what you can pick up during the fight. It's also to the death, Nate." She leaned over and whispered to me, "A number of those here are quite keen on that idea."

"Sounds good to me," I said loud enough for everyone to hear.

One of the guards—a young woman with a round face—brought over three sorcerer's bands and attached the first one to Enfield's wrist, with an audible click. He shivered for a moment and then smiled. The guard placed the band on my wrist and paused. "I'm sorry, I have to do this," she said softly, without meeting my gaze. And then attached a second just above the first. "That's for your necromancy."

"Don't be sorry," I told her.

She looked up at me and nodded once, before clicking the band shut. The effect was immediate, as the glyphs that had been in regular use on my arms for several days vanished at once. I dropped to one knee, while Enfield laughed across from me. His laughter stopped when I glanced up at him and winked. I got back to my feet and brushed my knees down.

"The venom left my body a few hours ago," I told him.

The crowd had grown even larger since we'd arrived at the park, now consisting of a massive group of over a thousand people, who encircled us. I spotted Tommy and Olivia. Tommy gave me the thumbs up, but I noticed that Olivia's and his hands were squeezed tight against one another.

"I hope you can do this," Elaine said as she walked past me.

Me too, I thought.

"When you're ready," Elaine shouted and then stepped back.

Enfield sprinted toward me, and when I moved aside, kicked out toward me. I blocked the kick, but he followed it up with a second and a third, each one coming quicker than the last. Even without his magic, Enfield was a formidable opponent. He kicked out at my lower leg, which I blocked, and he lashed out with a fist. I moved aside and snapped a punch of my own at his jaw, but he grabbed my arm, bending it back and locking the joint, before turning and throwing me over his shoulder to the ground. I narrowly missed a stomp to the head as I rolled away, but couldn't avoid the kick to my chest as I got back to my feet.

I landed on the ground, the air having left me before I ever reached it. I expected to have Enfield try to follow up immediately and when that didn't happen, I got back to my feet to discover he was standing there waiting for me.

"Didn't think it would be that easy, did you?" I asked.

I walked over to him and threw a quick jab at his jaw, which he easily avoided, but he walked right into the kick to his knee, which took him down to a kneeling position, before I caught him in the chest with a powerful enough punch that he fell to the dirt. I took a step back and motioned for him to stand.

He did so, using the back of his hand to wipe the blood that was trickling from his mouth. Without warning he dashed toward me, with more punches and kicks, each one avoided or blocked and returned with more of my own. By the time we were done, we both had split lips and dirt-covered clothes, and I noticed that he changed his fighting stance to protect sore and vulnerable ribs.

Enfield moved in with a vicious kick to my ribs, but I'd already seen it coming and kicked up at his calf muscle, defusing it of any power and causing him to limp back. Instead of allowing him a moment to breathe, I piled on the pressure, catching his injured calf with my knee, and then smashed my elbow into his exposed ribs. Enfield tried to push me back, and I grabbed his wrist, twisting it and swiping out at his feet, dumping him on the ground headfirst. I kept hold of the wrist and stepped over his arm, locking the elbow in place and then wrenched the limb back as hard as I could. The shoulder popped and Enfield screamed in pain, but I hadn't expected him to ignore it and roll to the side, dragging me over and forcing me to release my grip.

I rolled back to my feet and found Enfield already on his. His left arm hung uselessly, so he used his legs and feet to keep me at a distance while he moved around the clearing. I grabbed an errant kick, but he launched up with the other foot, twisting as he did. I released his foot, but the kick still connected with my jaw, staggering me just enough to put some distance between us. I rubbed the side of my face and prepared for another round, but Enfield had walked to a nearby tree, smashing his elbow into the trunk. He roared out in pain, but unfortunately for me, his arm was no longer dislocated.

"Everything you do, I can counter," he said rotating his arm. "I am better than you."

I said nothing, which only seemed to increase his anger. He ran toward me, tackling me to the ground, where he threw a punch at my head. I caught it, locking my arms around the limb and then lifted my legs so that I had him in a triangle chokehold. Enfield didn't have a lot of options, and even as he punched me again and again in my ribs, I refused to let go. It was only when he picked me up and dumped me on my head that my hands began to loosen their grip. On the third time, he swung me at the tree and I released my grip, falling to the ground, but kicked out, catching him in the nose, which crunched from the blow.

He staggered back, and I tackled him to the ground, pummeling his chest and head. Enfield caught my wrist and punched me in the ribs, one of which I felt pop. I lost concentration for a second, and he pushed me off, catching me again in the ribs. The air in my lungs left my body, and I deliberately put some distance between us so that I could breathe through the pain.

Enfield slowly got back to his feet, his eyes never leaving mine. We were both in pain, both using trees to keep ourselves upright.

I pushed myself away from the tree and moved toward Enfield, keeping my hands up in a fighting stance. He kept his hands down until the last second and then launched at me, his fingers trying to gain purchase in my flesh, all pretense of form having vanished. I smashed my forearm into his nose, which crunched again and began streaming blood. He caught me in the groin with a knee that made my eyes water, so I head-butted him and pushed him face first into the tree beside us. A blow to his ribs made him gasp with pain; I brought my knee up into his gut and cracked his temple with my elbow, sending him sprawling on the leaf-covered ground.

He grabbed my leg, trying to unbalance me, so I drove my knee into his jaw, snapping his head aside. I grabbed his hair and dragged him upright before head-butting him again. He stumbled back, and I spun around, catching him in the chest with a kick that floored him. He scrambled away, getting back to his feet just in time to receive another kick to the chest that sent him tumbling down the steep bank behind.

I reached the edge of the bank and watched Enfield get back on his feet. He waved me to come join him. I moved down the bank carefully until I was standing in six inches of rapidly flowing, freezing cold fresh water. There'd be no more running, no more distance. There was simply nowhere to go that didn't involve scrambling back up the bank. Large rocks littered the stream, and I had to watch where I put my feet on the riverbed.

Enfield threw the first punch, which I blocked, striking out at his injured ribs. He grabbed my arm and dragged me over him into the freezing water, which took my breath away. He forced my head under the water, pushing it down into the soil. The cold startled me and I punched out with everything I had. The blow landed right on Enfield's temple, knocking him aside, allowing me to sit up and cough up the water that had been forced down my throat. I turned back to my foe, but he hit me in the side of my head with a rock. I fell back into the water and tried to fight back as more blows fell onto me. My vision began to go dark and I knew that he was going to kill me. The grip of his hands as it forced my head under the water seemed limitless, as if he couldn't possibly be any stronger, while my own strength was slipping away on the current of the stream.

I began to sag as death closed in. Dying in a fucking stream at the hands of an asshole like Enfield made me angry. Very, very angry. I opened my eyes, and hadn't realized that I'd even closed them. I felt new strength inside of me and I struggled at Enfield's iron grip, grasping at anything around me in an attempt to fight back. I took hold of something and smashed it with everything I had against Enfield's head. The tension stopped and I did it again, and again. He tried fighting my hand off, but I hit him in his broken rib and he fell off me into the stream. I immediately rolled to the side, my head finally leaving the water, and threw up the liquid inside me. My vision was shaky and as I coughed and spluttered, I knew that I'd been close to death.

I got back to my feet, and although I was wobbly, and my chest and throat felt as if they were on fire, I was not going to let Enfield win. I took the few steps toward him as he was getting upright and drove my fist into the side of his head. He crashed back down to his knees and I linked my fingers around the back of his head and drove my own knee into his face, again and again. Then I released him and grabbed his ears, pulling his head toward my knee with terrifying force. His face was a ruined mess after the second blow, but he threw a fist of stream soil at my face and I had to move to avoid it, giving him time to get away.

I stalked him, and threw the object I had in my hand at him, which turned out to be his ear. It made a splash as it hit his chest and flopped into the water. He punched out at me, but I grabbed the arm, wrapped my arms around his, and wrenched his elbow to one side, which snapped it like kindling. I released his arm and dragged him out of the water, pushing him up against the bank. I threw punch after punch at him, snapping ribs and causing unknown internal damage to his organs. Every time he toppled to one side, I pushed him upright once more and continued with the punishment until my hands were raw and swollen.

"You're done here," I told him.

He pushed me with his good arm, so I broke it for him, his ruined mouth was no longer capable of crying out, but he made a gargled noise and dropped to his knees.

"Is this enough?" I shouted to the spectators above us. It had begun to rain again and I was grateful for it as it washed Enfield's blood from my hands. "I have no desire to murder people while others watch."

"He wanted it to the death, Nate," Elaine said, and it took me a moment to figure out where she was.

"Have I won?" I asked everyone, ignoring Elaine as I dragged Enfield out of the water.

"Yes," several people, including Elaine said.

I raised my wrist. "Then get these fucking things off me."

There was talking above me, but the guard who'd placed the sorcerer's bands on my wrist slid down the bank and used her key to remove them. Magic flowed back into me, and it was beautiful.

"His too," I told her, before adding, "Please."

She did as she was asked and I thanked her, and it didn't take long for the noises in Enfield's chest to begin to sound normal again.

"Enfield, you wished death here," I said loud enough for everyone to hear. "But I want you to die a sorcerer, not as someone missing his magic. I want your allies up there to know that it doesn't matter how powerful you are, if you fuck with me and mine, I will destroy you. A friend of mine asked, as he died, if I could do him a favor. So consider this the last request of Felix Novius." I accessed Felix's soul, and a battle-axe, one of my two soul weapons—a physical manifestation of my power of necromancy, which destroys the soul, not the physical body—appeared in my hand. "I think he'd approve of my final words to you. Eat shit and die you fucking cockwomble." And I drove the blade of the axe into Enfield's skull.

Enfield twitched once and then pitched forward into the stream. I'd struck someone in the head with the axe before and they'd lived, but with Enfield, I knew he was dead. I glanced up at the crowd once more, and then crashed to my knees.

"What the hell is going on here?" a voice demanded from above me. I glanced up and saw Merlin, his expression moving from annoyed to murderous the second he laid eyes on me.

CHAPTER 37

To be fair to Merlin, he didn't try to kill me there and then, while I was standing in a stream. I dragged myself up and onto the park, while everyone who didn't want to be part of Merlin's annoyance made themselves scarce. Even so, a committed group of people hung around the edges of the park, presumably to figure out if Merlin was going to kill me or not. Merlin had wandered off with Elaine, and the heat of their conversation was obvious considering their body language. I sat next to the same tree that Enfield had used to fix his arm and tried to convince myself that telling Merlin to fuck off was a good idea.

Tommy and Lucie had decided to sit beside me, and Olivia and half a dozen guards had joined them soon after Merlin's arrival.

"So, this must be awkward for you," Tommy said.

"Yes, that's certainly one way of putting it," I suggested.

"I think you might have made a few more enemies today. Your little speech before you killed Enfield will quickly spread," Lucie told me.

"I never was very good at keeping my mouth closed."

"Nate didn't do anything wrong," Tommy said. "Merlin can't do anything."

"Never stopped him before," I pointed out and then got to my feet. The fight between Elaine and Merlin appeared to be over, although whether that was because they'd come to an agreement or because several paladins had arrived remained to be seen.

"Is that Gawain?" Tommy asked.

"Yep," I said.

"His armor sure is shiny. I'm assuming he doesn't get out much."

"Rumor has it he's changed a lot since you left," Olivia said. "He's more withdrawn, more intent on keeping Merlin and Arthur safe. Anything for Avalon and all that."

"The paladins have always been fanatical," Lucie said. "He's just even more fanatical than most."

Elaine beckoned for me to join her, so I walked across the field feeling like I was about to be scolded for misbehaving in class. It was a fairly ridiculous thought that a sixteen-hundred-year-old sorcerer could be worried he was about to be told off, but Merlin's appearance was always akin to that of a teacher.

"He's angry you're here," Elaine said. "Angry you've caused disruption. He wants an explanation from you."

"Excellent," I said and before Elaine could stop me I walked over to Merlin. He looked almost exactly the same as when I'd last seen him, although he'd decided to wear long black robes for some reason.

Gawain stepped in between us. "If you place one hand on Merlin, I will cut you down."

I stared at the man who at one point I'd have considered a friend. "Don't threaten me, Gawain. We both know it's the move of someone who doesn't actually have the ability to back up his words."

"Have you come to apologize?" Merlin asked me, pushing an angry Gawain aside.

"For what?"

"Striking me, or stopping me from keeping Arthur alive, or maybe disrupting my realm? Pick which one you think is best."

"No to all three. I'm about as likely to grow wings and fly as I am to say sorry."

"Still the same Nathan. Let me guess. All of this death and destruction, it was all to help people you care about? I wish you'd felt that way about Arthur."

"I helped protect Arthur for hundreds of years," I said through gritted teeth. "He was my friend, and my king. These people, including Kay, had conspired to kill Elaine and remove anyone whom they deemed unworthy of their time."

"And that's my concern, why? If Elaine was murdered, heaven forbid by the way, but if she was, then someone else would take her role. She does not run Camelot."

"Who does then?"

"I do," he snapped.

"Then maybe you should actually do it. Maybe you should stop spending all of your time with a dead man and take your head out of your ass long enough to see that people here are unhappy. That all you've managed to do is foster a division that threatened to break apart everything you say you care about. You've put every single person in this realm, and countless millions outside of it, in jeopardy because you can't bear to let someone else take away a piece of your grand plan. Avalon needs Elaine, it doesn't need you anymore."

The earth beneath my feet began to shake slightly, and I knew it was Merlin's power.

"You dare?" he spat. "You dare suggest that I'm not doing the best for this realm? For these people?"

"You're doing what you always did. What's best for Merlin. Fuck everyone else."

A mass of rock burst free from the ground and slammed into my chest, driving me back with immense force. Water covered my arms and turned to ice, freezing me in place.

"You think you can come back here and tell me how to run things?" he demanded. "You're nothing, no one, a pathetic shell of someone I used to think could do some good in this world. I'm sure, if your parents were alive to see you today, they would be ashamed to know you. It's a good thing no one knows who they are, it saves them the bother of their dishonor."

Orange glyphs flared over my arms and the ice melted, allowing me to sit up.

"Go on, use your magic against me," Merlin demanded. "Show the people who you are."

"Have you lost your mind?" Elaine exploded at Merlin. "You attacked first, you came here full of anger and demanding answers. I don't answer to you. And neither does Nate, not anymore."

"Everyone in Avalon answers to me," Merlin snapped.

"Not anymore they don't," I said when I was back to my feet. "People want someone to lead them who isn't a self-absorbed asshole. Someone who will keep them safe from threats like the Reavers. You clearly can't or won't. You're as ineffectual at governing this realm as you are at bringing Arthur back to life."

I knew it was a mistake the second I said the words. A darkness spread over Merlin's face and he lashed out, smashing ice into my body, and lifting me ten feet above the ground.

"If anyone interferes, kill them," he said to Gawain, who drew his sword.

"Nate?" Tommy called out.

"I'm okay," I told him.

"I should have left you to die on that road as a child," Merlin said as he walked toward me.

I used my fire magic to melt the ice, but the second any of it trickled away, it was replaced by even more, which got tighter and tighter across my arms and chest.

"I'm going to show you what I do to traitors," he said and huge shards of ice formed in front of him.

I concentrated with everything I had until thunder could be heard above me. Then the ice vanished and I dropped to the ground. I was unable to stand, my entire body felt like it had been in a vice. All the same, my glyphs still shone as brightly as they ever had. I was not going to go down without a fight. Merlin would kill me, there was no other option, but he'd know he'd been in a contest.

Merlin stood only a few inches away, and glanced down at me. "Lightning, eh? You going to use that on me, boy?"

"Fuck you," I said, although my words were a stutter. "You knew about the second realm gate, didn't you? Did you know that Kay would betray everyone? Did you know that the Reavers were back?"

"Of course I knew about the gate. How do you think I have people come and go without Elaine and her people hearing about it? How did you think the Reavers came and went before you had them destroyed? Kay was going to do it sooner or later, I guess he got a better offer. And as for the Reavers returning, of course I'd heard. I hear everything. I just don't bother with petty squabbles among people who are unimportant."

"People died, you asshole. What happened to you? I don't believe you were always this cold . . . this cruel."

"Wasn't I? Or did you just want a daddy figure in your life so badly that you ignored those things?"

I wanted to wipe the sneer off of his face, but I kept my peace as he continued. "I always taught you that to win you do whatever it takes. It appears that lesson was lost on you."

The thunder rumbled above us again.

Merlin glanced up at the sky. "You want to fight me? You'll die, your friends soon after. You know they'll get involved, you know I won't let that lie."

The clouds above dissipated and my glyphs vanished.

"Good choice. It's a shame it ended up this way, you could have been something great, but you've chosen your path and will have to live with the consequences." He walked back to Elaine. "You deal with this. But I want him punished for his attitude toward me."

"He doesn't work for you," Elaine pointed out again.

"Then banish him from Avalon, I never wish to see him again. He is no longer welcome within this realm."

Elaine kept Merlin's gaze without blinking. "You don't have the authority to do that. It would have to go to a vote. A vote, I will assure, you won't win."

For a moment I thought Merlin was going to snap. "You're right," Merlin said with glee. "Nathan no longer works for me. You know what, Nathan? I think that it's about time we made that official, don't you?"

"What are you talking about?" I asked.

"Did you think when you walked out that no one wanted to come after you for your betrayal? No, I put word out that you were off limits. You were to be left alone, until I deemed otherwise. I think you've outstayed my patience. As of now, if any of my paladins decide to hunt you down to put you in your place, I'll let them." He looked at his watch. "Let's say one week. In one week, if you ever return to Camelot my paladins have my permission to find and punish you."

"Are you telling me that you're going to order Nate's death?" Elaine asked shocked.

"Oh no, not death. Punishment. If one of them happens to go overboard, that's a shame. Can't be helped. You'll do well to remember that this is *my* realm, I made those laws, and I gave you a seat on the council in the first place. What I do is no consequence to you or anyone else who lives here, because I allow them the very privilege of living here. I'm done allowing Nathan that same privilege." Merlin turned to me. "The next time I see you will be because you came back and my paladins had you brought before me bloody and broken. Leave this place and never come back."

And with that Merlin turned and walked away.

"One week," Gawain said. "I got him to agree to that. I know that you've got your friend's naming ceremony tomorrow, and I know these people are important to you. I'd advise you to keep your head down and stay out of his notice until you leave. Get your stuff done and then don't ever come back."

"How many of your paladins will track me down outside of this realm?"

"I won't send any of them after you. But I can't stop them if you come back." Gawain nodded toward Elaine and then walked off, a dozen paladins in tow.

"Wow, you stood up to the old bastard," Tommy said. "A lot of people here saw that."

"Yeah, for all the good it did me. I guess I'm here for a week and then I'll leave. I'm going to wring out every single second I can before I leave this realm though, I'm not letting Merlin think he's won easily."

I wondered if the paladins would really come after me. Probably. And I doubted I'd survive too many of their attacks. They were trained to kill people who crossed Merlin.

"So, is this all done?" Tommy asked.

Elaine turned and watched as Merlin and his paladins left. "Merlin has done something far worse today than just ignoring the people of this realm. He came out here and practically declared that his paladins will deal with anyone who dares disagree with him. He's turned them into his own personal shocktroops. I won't have that. And neither will most of the council. Something will have to be done, and soon."

"Any idea what?"

Elaine shook her head sadly. "For now, I'd take him at his word, Nate. You have a week to leave. But I won't have Merlin declaring himself a tyrant in all but name. The SOA will also have to be completely rebuilt. With what's happened with Kay and now Merlin's outburst, a lot of people are going to be worried in the coming months; it's my job to ensure they don't do anything stupid, and that they're safe."

"You still need to track down the rest of the Reavers," Tommy said. "That might not be a small job."

"I got one of my necromancers to take Enfield's soul," Elaine said. "We'll find out whatever he knew."

"Good, because I didn't want to have those memories in my head," I told her. I got back to my feet. "Now I want a shower, a change of clothing, and maybe a drink. Actually scrap that, I want a drink first."

"Now that's the best idea anyone has had today," Olivia said as she rejoined us. "That was some fight, Nate."

"He was an evil sack of shit, but a tough one," I agreed. "Now you guys get to do the clean-up, because apparently I'm done here."

"Remember what I said, Nate. I won't have his people try to kill you," Elaine promised. "But I'd stay away for a while. They won't come after you outside of Avalon."

"Don't worry, I don't plan on returning anytime soon. Merlin's paladins will try to kill me no matter what you say, and I will have to kill some of them, or they'll kill me. Either way it's more dead in Avalon. I think you've had enough of that recently." My body lurched forward as the crushing tiredness of the last few days hit me.

Tommy caught me. "Come on, Nate, let's get you somewhere you can rest."

"Good plan." He helped me walk a few steps before I stopped him and turned back to Elaine, Olivia, and Lucie. "It's good to see Avalon is in excellent care. I hope you all get it to become the place you deserve it to be."

CHAPTER 

I don't remember getting to my hotel room, or getting in bed. In fact I don't really remember much about the remainder of the day. I know that when I woke up the clock said I'd been asleep for twelve hours, and I felt refreshed. Maybe Erebus was responsible for that, or maybe I was giving him too much credit. Either way, I felt better than I'd felt in days.

I wasn't even out of the bed when someone began pounding on the door. I padded over, only just realizing I was in my boxer shorts before I opened it. I quickly grabbed a bathrobe from the back of a nearby chair before returning to the door. Kasey stood in the hallway outside tapping her foot on the ground. She wore a Spider-Man T-shirt and a pair of jeans.

"Is that what you're wearing?" I asked. "If the ceremony's casual wear, I'll be much happier."

"It's not, I'm just here to make sure you're awake. Looks like I got here just in time. Are you okay? You looked like roadkill when they brought you in."

"Thanks for that. Means a lot."

"Hey, I was worried."

"Apparently, not worried enough not to mock me for it though."

Kasey laughed. "What can I say? I'm my father's daughter." Her face turned serious. "You sure you're okay now?"

"Sore, but manageable."

Kasey reached over to something in the corridor and produced a suit bag. "In that case, this is for you. Apparently it will fit you."

"Who checked?"

"My mum says she knows your size by looking at you. Also, they burned your clothes, they did not look good."

"Probably for the best," I agreed.

"My dad will fetch you in two hours." She turned and walked off before stopping and looking back at me. "Thank you for this. Seriously, having you there is something I cherish. It wouldn't be the same otherwise."

"It's my pleasure."

"Have you decided what you're going to say?"

"I have not. I figured I'd tell everyone it would be my job to make you awesome."

Kasey laughed. "That would probably be the first time anyone said that in a naming ceremony."

"I'll think of something, I promise. Thanks for the suit."

"See you in a few hours."

I closed the door and took my suit to the bed, spreading the bag over the ruffled duvet and unzipping it. The suit jacket was gray with matching trousers and waistcoat. There was also a light gray shirt and dark blue tie. I'd just finished looking through it all when there was another knock at the door. I opened it and Olivia stood there holding a pair of walnut-colored shoes. She was also only wearing jeans and a T-shirt.

"Everything okay?" she asked, passing me the shoes.

I nodded.

"Cufflinks are in the shoe. Don't forget."

"I won't."

"How are you feeling?"

"Good. Kase seems calm."

"Externally yes, internally she's somewhat nervous. And she's her father's daughter in her temper."

"Oh, so you're having a barrel of fun."

"I'm going to throttle Tommy and Kasey and go to the pub. If you don't see us, you know why."

I laughed. "I'll make sure I'm on time and dressed then."

"You'd best, or she'll hunt you down."

I laughed again.

"Not a joke." And with that she walked off.

I had less than two hours to get ready and get to the palace. Not a problem, so I put my clothes on the back of a chair and sat on the bed to watch Avalon TV for a half hour. Avalon TV was basically a selection of shows and movies that people had recorded in the Earth realm and then brought through to Albion. There were twenty channels and not one of them showed twenty-four-hour news, something I was genuinely happy about. Thirty minutes turned into forty-five when I finally got back off the bed and walked to the shower. The bathroom was well stocked with more types of aftershave, body lotion, and various smelling shower washes than any one person could possibly want. I grabbed the shower gel that smelled the nicest and had the hottest shower I could possibly bear. The hot water felt lovely, although the fact that the water turned pink was a tangible reminder of what I'd done only a few hours earlier.

It took me half an hour to get dried and dressed, mostly because I took my time and watched some TV in the middle of it. When the door knocked again, I was dressed and had used some of the aftershave I'd found in the bathroom. I thought about having a shave, but I've always hated doing it with hotel razors, so the stubbled, rugged look would have to do. I opened the door to find Tommy in the hallway. He wore a black suit with pinstripes, a purple tie, and a fedora.

"You ready?" he asked.

I nodded. "Whose idea was the cufflinks, by the way?" I showed him the little silver swords that adorned my shirtsleeves.

"Olivia picked your clothes. You can thank her."

We walked out of the hotel and got into a car outside.

"Nervous?" I asked when Tommy mispronounced palace about three times before getting it right.

"Yes, although for Kasey more than me." Tommy paused and took a deep breath. "You figure out what you're going to say?"

"Why does everyone keep asking me that?"

Tommy's smile was full of warmth. "Because winging it probably isn't the best idea."

"I'll come up with something by the time we get to the palace. What's Ellie saying?"

"She'll talk about her wolf side, leaves a lot of scope for you."

"Tommy," I said patiently. "My skills aren't exactly something a fifteen-year-old needs to be taught."

"You don't have to train her to be a killer, Nate. I trust you'll figure out something."

We sat in silence for the remainder of the journey while I tried to figure out what I was going to say. When we reached the palace there was a congregation outside.

Olivia walked over to me and hugged me. "You look great," she whispered.

"Thanks, you too," I said, meaning it. She looked amazing in her blue satin dress, with matching shawl and high heels.

"Even Alan made an effort," she said pointing over at the clearly uncomfortable man in the blue suit. "Fiona had been invited already, but it's nice to have her husband here with her."

"It's weird seeing everyone dressed up," I said.

Remy walked up between us. He wore a suit I was certain had to have been made especially for him. "I heard what happened with Enfield and Merlin. It's sort of the talk of the town. Nathan Garrett, Hellequin, killer of bad guys and the person who stood up to Merlin."

"Today is about Kasey," I said. "Everyone else can have their glances and whispers. I'll give a shit tomorrow."

Tommy patted me on the back. "You ready?"

I nodded. "I know what I'm going to say."

"Fancy sharing?" Olivia asked and then raised a hand to stop me. "I think I'd rather be surprised."

We all walked into the palace, and I had to admit that I noticed the glances and people looking away when I returned them. I pushed it aside, and we reached the main chambers.

"You know almost the entire council came in for this?" Lucie told me. "Apparently they wanted to see what would happen."

"Well, won't this be fun then?"

The guards opened the double doors and the roar of noise inside washed over me. We all walked into the din, which quieted when Elaine stood. She wore a simple black jumpsuit and stood next to Kasey, who looked as nervous as any one person possibly could. Kasey looked incredibly grown up in her blue dress, and I noticed the look of utmost pride on Tommy's and

Olivia's faces as Kasey made her way toward the center of the chambers.

"Kasey Elizabeth Carpenter," Elaine said, quieting everyone else in the room.

"Yes, ma'am," Kasey said.

"We don't normally have these kinds of numbers for a naming ceremony here. In fact this might be the most people we've had turn up in some time. Because of the turnout, I'll be conducting this ceremony myself."

I recognized several people in the chamber, not all of them friends. Many of them appeared to be the same group who'd watched me kill Enfield and stand up to Merlin.

"You're aware that a naming ceremony is a great milestone in a person's life," Elaine continued. "When Avalon recognizes them as having come into their abilities, and when they begin their journey to become a fully fledged member with the rights of all members. You are no longer a child, and I can see from the looks on the faces of your family and people around this chamber who know them, that they are very proud to have such a young adult as you. You do them a great honor by being the smart, capable person you have turned into."

Kasey nodded slightly and wiped at her eyes.

"Will the first sentinel step forward."

Ellie stood beside Kasey and took hold of her hand.

"State your name and position within Avalon," Elaine ordered.

"Ellie O'Neil," she said. "I'm the female alpha in the South of England werewolf pack."

"And, Ellie, what will you bring to Kasey's life?"

"I will teach Kasey how to be the best wolf she can possibly be. I will be there for her when she needs me, and will help her in any way I can as she grows into the amazing woman I know she'll become. I will be a rock for her."

Kasey hugged Ellie.

"Thank you, Ellie. And now for the second sentinel. Please make your way to the center of the chamber."

"You got this," Tommy whispered as I walked past and stood next to Kasey, who smiled at me.

"And your name?" Elaine asked with a slight smile.

"Nathaniel Garrett," I told her. "I don't really have a rank within Avalon. You can use vagabond or ronin if you like."

Elaine stifled a smile and someone behind me chuckled.

"That's quite all right. And what will you bring to Kasey's life."

"I'll protect her in every way I . . ." I paused. "No, I won't do that."

There was a general murmuring all around me.

"I'll always be honest with her, always be there when she needs me. These are promises I've already made. This needs to be something more. I always said I would never pass on the lessons I've learned," I continued, creating silence once again. "I always said I should keep that knowledge to myself, that it was too dangerous to pass on. But I was wrong. I won't protect Kasey, because I won't need to. I'll teach her how to protect herself. I'll teach her how to be the person I wish I could be. A better person. She will learn what I know and use it as a force of good. That's my promise right here."

Elaine's jaw dropped open, and the silence in the chambers could have been cut with a very blunt knife.

Kasey was staring at me. "Seriously? You're going to teach me how to be Hellequin?" she asked.

I shook my head. "I'll teach you to be better. I'll teach you how to protect yourself and the people you love."

Elaine cleared her throat and everyone was quiet again. "With those words I announce Kasey Elizabeth Carpenter a member of Avalon. You have so been named, may your time here be one of joy."

Kasey hugged Ellie and me and then ran over to her parents.

"That was not what I expected," Ellie said.

"Nor me," I said with a smile and made my way to Elaine who was walking down to meet us.

"Kasey is going to be taught how to protect herself by a man a lot of people fear," Elaine said. "You know that in itself will protect her?"

"That's the plan," I said. "This isn't about Hellequin protecting her, this is about her protecting herself. I want to train her to be the best she can be."

"What changed your mind about training people?" she asked.

"She's my best friend's daughter. I will do everything in my power to keep her safe. And this is within my power." I watched as Kasey made her way around the people who wanted to congratulate her.

"Are you serious?" Olivia asked, joining us.

I nodded. "I'm not going to teach her about being the boogeyman, or making people fear her. But training her how to protect herself, about what types of things she can expect in the world when she leaves school? Hell, yes, I can do that."

Tommy walked over and hugged me. "Thanks, Nate. Knowing it's you training her is good. As much as I'd love to do it myself, we both know it would only result in arguments. Thank you for that."

"A friend gave me the idea. Apparently my previous viewpoint was high and mighty."

"I'm sorry about Felix," Tommy said. "He was an asshole, but I liked the guy."

"That appeared to be the consensus," I said.

I turned to Elaine. "Have you got a minute? I need a favor. A big one."

"Of course."

"I'll see you all later," I told my friends and followed Elaine up the stairs to her private room behind the chambers.

"And what favor might this be?" she asked the second we stepped inside and I closed the door.

The room was sparsely decorated, with a table, chair, and several rows of full bookcases. There were no paintings, or pictures, nothing of hers apart from the books.

"It's not officially my office yet," she said. "Not until Merlin steps down for good. And that's very much depending on what the council decides. As you know, change isn't fast around here. There's going to be plenty of political horse-fuckery before we actually get a plan for what happens next."

"Horse-fuckery?" I asked with a laugh.

Elaine tried very hard not to smile. "I stick by my choice of phrase."

"I need you to pardon Alan," I said, suddenly serious.

"He willingly went to jail to expunge his record. He has several weeks left. He also killed a guard, although from the way I hear it, the guard was corrupt and Warden Phillips has officially said that it was you who killed him."

"I think he's earned his release. I wouldn't be here today without him. Release him and find him a job. A good job too, something he won't get bored with. Hell, let him go after Kay, he'll like that."

"I'll talk to the LOA director, who I might add I've already pissed off by promoting Olivia from regional director to Special Operations director, as she deals with all of the Reaver fallout."

"Tell him I'll owe him a favor."

"That might actually work. As for the task force that's trying to find Kay, I'm sure I can speak to Lucie and Olivia and figure something out. You do know the 'Nate is Hellequin' information is now well and truly out of the bottle?"

"Took long enough."

"Yes, well, I wouldn't be too thrilled. People are going to come after you. Nate Garrett wasn't always liked by everyone, but Hellequin was feared by people who weren't used to feeling that emotion."

"Hopefully most of them will think twice after what happened yesterday."

"Ah, yes, Enfield. We have the names of everyone Kay worked with. It's a sizeable list, but we'll get through it. We've raided Kay's home too. He was the most arrogant man I've ever met. He had notebooks of details on the plan. He really never thought he'd be caught before he was done. We'll track him. We're also setting up a guard post at the second realm gate, which is about half a mile underground, by the way. Hopefully once we know where he's gone, we'll be able to capture him."

"No you won't, he's gone. He won't be back until he's ready. Where does the gate take you to?"

"It comes out just outside of Edinburgh."

"Are you sure there are only two realm gates?"

"We're searching for more, just in case. Also, I need to thank you for bringing his plot to my attention." She smiled. "Thank you, Nathan."

"You're welcome."

"It's now my turn to ask you for a favor."

"Go on."

"As you know, Remy's house was blown up. He's an excellent agent, but he doesn't always play well with others. I want you to take him with you back to Earth realm. He has a new job, and he can't do it here."

"And this new job is? I think a walking, talking fox is going to be a bit of a giveaway in even the most liberal areas of the UK."

"He's going to live in Tintagel and work with those who man the ferries. That's his official job. Unofficially, he's your liaison with me."

"Okay, I can do that. What's happening with Lir's body?"

"His son, Mac, has been notified. He's justifiably angry and will be helping us track down the rest of the Reavers. In fact he's already left for Europe to look into a group of them. I almost pity their fates when he finds them. He did have a message for you though." She opened a drawer on the desk and passed me a sealed envelope. "Read it when you leave."

"Thanks."

"It was good to see you again, even under such shitty circumstances." She embraced me and we just stood there for a moment hugging one another. "Please keep safe," she said as we pulled apart.

"You too. Whoever Enfield and Kay worked for, they're not going to stop."

"Can I give you some advice?"

"Of course."

"Don't stop with just Kasey. Train others like her."

"One thing at a time, first I'll train Kasey, and then I'll make my own army."

"I'm not kidding. People will follow you, and that's a powerful trait to have. The more people you can train to be safe, the harder it'll be for people to go through them to get to you. And, in the long run, the harder it'll be for whomever Kay and Enfield take their orders from to gain a foothold here. I'd rather have people turn up asking for work who have been trained by you than by someone at their school."

"We'll see where it goes."

"The last few years have seen a lot of things happen that suggest something is coming. You've been involved in some, and we've stopped a few others, but they keep coming. At some point the people behind them are going to show themselves. Just be careful, okay? I've lost plenty of people I care about over the years, I don't want to lose anyone else."

"If you ever need me, you contact me and I'll come running."

"And what about Merlin and his threat? He will carry that out, you know. I can disapprove, but I can't stop him, not without council approval. And like I said a few minutes ago, that's going to be slow. Could take months, could take years. Are you prepared to risk that?"

"It doesn't matter now. At some point me and Merlin are going to have to finally have it out."

"He'll kill you if that happens."

I left Elaine in her office and walked back out into the now empty chambers. I had no idea when I'd be back in Camelot after my remaining six days were up, but I would be back. And when I did come back, neither Merlin nor his paladins were going to stand in my way.

EPILOGUE

Six days after the naming ceremony I found myself sitting in the park that had been the center of so much conflict during my time in Avalon, when Remy sat beside me. "You need to go see Fiona."

"I know. I thought you'd already gone through the gate."

"Not just yet. Been waiting for you. Your friends left a few days ago, even that incredibly attractive werewolf, Ellie. Ah, if only she were a fox and that wasn't the creepiest thing I've ever said."

"Yes, thanks for the mental image."

"Sorry about that. It's been an eventful few days though. A lot has changed here, people are talking about Hellequin and how he stood up to Merlin and his cronies, how he killed an evil madman. They'll have you being the romantic hero soon, the one who swoops in to rescue damsels from dragons."

"I don't know many damsels," I said. "Or dragons for that matter."

"You really planning on dragging out this whole *six days* thing, then?"

"Yep. Have you seen the paladin who's following me around?"

"The guy in the oh so inconspicuous black suit? Apparently they didn't explain the idea of plain clothes very well."

"I spent four hours sitting here the other day while it pissed it down. I know it was childish, but it was funny to see him just sit there and not move."

"Nice you had some fun with it."

I stood and stretched. "You coming with me to Fiona's?"

Remy nodded.

The walk wasn't very long, and my paladin shadow was there every step of the way. I could have lost him, but what would be the point, he was clearly no threat to me. Besides, I didn't care what he told Merlin.

We reached Fiona's house and knocked as Remy looked longingly at the burned-out husk that used to be his home. "My guitar was in there," he said wistfully.

"Guitar?"

"I was learning how to play. I was getting pretty good. You haven't seen a guitar being played until you've seen 'Stairway to Heaven' played by a fox."

I stared at him for a moment. "That's . . . I'd like to see that."

"See, everyone always does. You heard from Mac?"

"He left me a letter."

"Really? What did it say, or is that some kind of secret?"

I thought back to the short letter: *Nate. I'm going to find any remaining Reavers. I'm going to kill them all until their rot is gone from this planet. Thank you for the justice of ending my father's murderer. Thank you for saving my life. I should have treated you more like the friend you were. I'm sorry for that.*

"He's going to deal with some issues," I paraphrased.

Alan opened the door and beckoned us both inside.

"How's everything going?" I asked him.

"Good. Elaine tells me I'm to be part of the task force to track down Kay, and that my prison term has been finished. Know anything about those?"

"Nope, not a damn thing. Good news though."

"Of course you don't. Well, thank you all the same. Fiona's in the study, down the hall."

I followed Alan's directions and found Fiona sitting behind her desk reading something on a computer screen. She saw me come in and stood up. Her injuries had been fully healed for a few days now.

"I'm glad you came," she said.

"You told me it was important. I turn up. What's going on?"

Fiona walked over to a bare patch of wall and brushed an illusion aside, revealing a safe. She entered a code and opened it before removing a blue file. "Before you see this, you need to know something. I've known about these for a few months, but didn't tell you simply because I assumed they were fake. I've had them tested by everything and everyone I know who might be able to figure out the answer to that question. They've all told me they're real. You're going to want to sit down."

I did as Fiona asked, and she passed me the file. I opened it and was very grateful to her for the idea of sitting.

"These can't be real," I said immediately.

"They are, I promise," she assured me.

There were half a dozen black and white photos, all from what appeared to be inside a bank of some kind. "Where were these taken?"

"A bank in New York, a year ago. He entered it at night, robbed the place, and these were the photos that the CCTV installed there captured."

In each photo a man stood looking up at the camera. Each camera was different, it was as if the man had walked up to it and dared it to take a photo of him. The man was my height, with short dark hair. He had a patch over one eye, and the skin tone on one of his hands was different to his bare arms.

"Mordred," I whispered. "He's dead."

No one said anything.

"I killed this man myself," I said, louder. "Mordred is dead."

"He's alive, Nate," Fiona told me. "He was alive as of a year ago, at any rate."

"I saw his body, he had a sniper round go through his eye."

"I'm sorry."

For several years I'd believed I'd finally rid the world of the curse that is Mordred. To see him come back to life and be so brazen as he robbed a bank was almost as if he were taunting me. I threw the pictures across the room.

"Nate?" Fiona said.

"Do you have any idea where he is now?"

"No, there's been no sighting of him since this robbery. He's vanished."

The anger subsided. "He'll pop back up again at some point, and then I guess I'll just have to kill him a second time. Hell, I'll kill him a hundred times if it means he'll eventually stay dead."

"I'll keep monitoring my contacts for information on him, but I wanted you to know."

"Thanks." I sat there, my mind racing. Mordred was alive. I'm sure he was aware that I was the one who'd sent him to his grave, or at least tried to, and if that was the case, I didn't have to track Mordred down. He'd come to me. And then I'd have the chance to make sure he stayed dead.

ACKNOWLEDGMENTS

No matter how many books I write, and how many acknowledgments go inside them, my wife Vanessa will always be the first person I thank. Her patience and support is unwavering, and I couldn't be doing this job without it.

My three beautiful children, who are one of the reasons I write. The fact that they appear to think that their dad being an author is equal parts cool and embarrassing will always bring me no end of happiness.

To my parents who appear to show no slowing down in their support of my work. Thank you for always sounding interested when you ask what I'm working on, even if it really isn't that interesting.

Thank you to my agent, Paul Lucas, and all of the hard work he has put into helping my books and career. I'm very much appreciative of it. Also, he plays Dungeons and Dragons, which makes him both geekier and cooler than me.

To Jenni Gaynor, my all-around brilliantly smart editor. My books are better because you worked on them. Thank you.

D. B. Reynolds and Michelle Muto are not only my beta readers; they're also two of the most talented writers I know, and more importantly, my good friends. Thank you for always taking the time to answer any questions or doubts I have about my work.

I wouldn't be writing this acknowledgment today without all of your help over the years.

To Emilie, Sana, and the rest of the 47North UK team. You're always available to answer questions, and it's been a pleasure to work with you. A special thank you goes out to Neil Hart. The fact that Neil traveled from London to spend several hours with me at my Waterstones book launch is something I will always be grateful for.

To my friends and family who have supported me over the years: Thank you. Without that support I never would have gotten published in the first place.

To the other 47North authors: Our little secret group has always been a place of information, laughter, and incredibly inappropriate jokes. And I couldn't imagine a world where that doesn't happen.

A very special thanks goes out to the UK Police Force. One officer in particular, who would like to remain unnamed, helped me with any questions regarding hostage situations and how they're dealt with. Thank you very much for all of your time and help. Any errors in the book are mine and mine alone, and I apologise for them.

Last, but by no means least, thank you to everyone who has read and enjoyed my books over the years. Here's to many more.

ABOUT THE AUTHOR

Photo © 2013 Sally Beard

Steve McHugh is the author of the popular Hellequin Chronicles. He lives in Southampton on the south coast of England with his wife and three young daughters. When not writing or spending time with his kids, he enjoys watching movies, reading books and comics, and playing video games.